SHADOWS IN THE ATTIC READER

Foundational Classic Horror

Edited By

JACOB HADDON

Published by Apokrupha Books
Cover by Lynne Hansen

apokrupha.com

Table of Contents

Introduction

In short, reprint anthologies were the textbooks for my education in the field.

—*J.F. Gonzalez*

"Anthologist" has an air about it. And yet, as I was assembling this book, I felt the role of an anthologist more than ever.

There are over 500 works mentioned by J. F. Gonzalez in his *Shadows in the Attic* series. They stretch in time from Gilgamesh to *The Twilight Zone*. The *Reader* is intended to be a companion book to *Shadows in the Attic*. I joked that *Shadows* is the lecture, and *Reader* is the homework.

To say choosing the stories that would fill these pages was difficult is an understatement. As an editor of *LampLight* magazine I was putting together a collection of stories for an issue that fit the tone and mood of *LampLight*. Stories were chosen based on both merit, and the timing of which they were submitted.

But with *Reader*, the job was a little different. The original short ("short") list for the anthology put the page count upwards of 1,200. Was this to be a tome? A text book? Or a survey to compliment?

As I trimmed, hard decisions had to be made to create space. And space is what is needed here, a survey, as I said, of works that give the reader a taste of each of the sections in

J. F. Gonzalez's *Shadows in the Attic* rather than, as the first table of contents was doing—overflowing, overwhelming.

It did mean some of my personal favorites did not make it. Works such as "An Occurrence at Owl Creek Bridge" and "The Monkey's Paw," both influential and important works, were left out to make space for "Unseen—Unfeared" and "August Heat"—works that in their own way were as important, but slowly being forgotten.

Because this is not a 'greatest hits' collection of horror shorts. This was instead a trip through the memory, a guided tour through the past, a reprint anthology to add to the textbooks of the genre.

The work would have been easier with Jesus's consult. Working on *Reader* and *Shadows* always has an emotional toll as the one person I long to talk to about these books I cannot.

I consulted the best resource I had, the text of *Shadows* for each of these. The truth is that had I gone with the 1,200 page anthology it would have still been too short. There are too many stories to celebrate. Too many tales lost in the crooks of the attic.

But don't worry, reader. There will be more homework assignments in your future.

For now, let us head to the third floor, and dig through the boxes and trunks stored in the attic and see what darkness we can find.

– Jacob Haddon, 2023

SHADOWS
IN THE ... ATTIC
READER

Foundational
Classic Horror

People of the Pit (1918)

A. Merritt

North of us a shaft of light shot half way to the zenith. It came from behind the five peaks. The beam drove up through a column of blue haze whose edges were marked as sharply as the rain that streams from the edges of a thunder cloud. It was like the flash of a searchlight through an azure mist. It cast no shadows.

As it struck upward the summits were outlined hard and black and I saw that the whole mountain was shaped like a hand. As the light silhouetted it, the gigantic fingers stretched, the hand seemed to thrust itself forward. It was exactly as though it moved to push something back. The shining beam held steady for a moment; then broke into myriads of little luminous globes that swung to and fro and dropped gently. They seemed to be searching.

The forest had become very still. Every wood noise held its breath. I felt the dogs pressing against my legs. They too were silent; but every muscle in their bodies trembled, their hair was stiff along their backs and their eyes, fixed on the falling lights, were filmed with the terror glaze.

I looked at Anderson. He was staring at the North where once more the beam had pulsed upward.

"It can't be the aurora," I spoke without moving my lips. My mouth was as dry as though Lao T'zai had poured his fear dust down my throat.

"If it is I never saw one like it," he answered in the same tone. "Besides who ever heard of an aurora at this time of the year?"

He voiced the thought that was in my own mind.

"It makes me think something is being hunted up there," he said, "an unholy sort of hunt—it's well for us to be out of range."

"The mountain seems to move each time the shaft shoots up," I said. "What's it keeping back, Starr? It makes me think of the frozen hand of cloud that Shan Nadour set before the Gate of Ghouls to keep them in the lairs that Eblis cut for them."

He raised a hand—listening.

From the North and high overhead there came a whispering. It was not the rustling of the aurora, that rushing, crackling sound like the ghosts of winds that blew at Creation racing through the skeleton leaves of ancient trees that sheltered Lilith. It was a whispering that held in it a demand. It was eager. It called us to come up where the beam was flashing. It drew. There was in it a note of inexorable insistence. It touched my heart with a thousand tiny fear-tipped fingers and it filled me with a vast longing to race on and merge myself in the light. It must have been so that Ulysses felt when he strained at the mast and strove to obey the crystal sweet singing of the Sirens.

The whispering grew louder.

"What the hell's the matter with those dogs?" cried Anderson savagely. "Look at them!"

The malemutes, whining, were racing away toward the light. We saw them disappear among the trees. There came back to us a mournful howling. Then that too died away and left nothing but the insistent murmuring overhead.

The glade we had camped in looked straight to the North. We had reached I suppose three hundred mile above the first great bend of the Koskokwim toward the Yukon. Certainly we were in an untrodden part of the wilderness. We had pushed through from Dawson at the breaking of the Spring, on a fair lead to the lost five peaks between which, so the Athabascan medicine man had told us, the gold streams out like putty from a clenched fist. Not an Indian were we able to get to go with us. The land of the Hand Mountain was accursed they said. We had sighted the peaks the night before, their tops faintly outlined against a pulsing glow. And now we saw the light that had led us to them.

Anderson stiffened. Through the whispering had broken a curious pad-pad and a rustling. It sounded as though a small bear were moving towards us. I threw a pile of wood on the fire and, as it blazed up, saw something break through the bushes. It walked on all fours, but it did not walk like a bear. All at once it flashed upon me—it was like a baby crawling upstairs. The forepaws lifted themselves in grotesquely infantile fashion. It was grotesque but it was—terrible. It grew closer. We reached for our guns—and dropped them. Suddenly we knew that this crawling thing was a man!

It was a man. Still with the high climbing pad-pad he swayed to the fire. He stopped.

"Safe," whispered the crawling man, in a voice that was an echo of the murmur overhead. "Quite safe here. They can't get out of the blue, you know. They can't get you—unless you go to them—"

He fell over on his side. We ran to him. Anderson knelt.

"God's love!" he said. "Frank, look at this!" He pointed to the hands. The wrists were covered with torn rags of a heavy shirt. The hands themselves were stumps! The fingers had been bent into the palms and the flesh had been worn to the bone. They looked like the feet of a little black elephant! My eyes traveled down the body. Around the waist was a heavy band of yellow metal. From it fell a ring and a dozen links of shining white chain!

"What is he? Where did he come from?" said Anderson. "Look, he's fast asleep—yet even in his sleep his arms try to climb and his feet draw themselves up one after the other! And his knees—how in God's name was he ever able to move on them?"

It was even as he said. In the deep sleep that had come upon the crawler arms and legs kept raising in a deliberate, dreadful climbing motion. It was as though they had a life of their own—they kept their movement independently of the motionless body. They were semaphoric motions. If you have ever stood at the back of a train and had watched the semaphores rise and fall you will know exactly what I mean.

Abruptly the overhead whispering ceased. The shaft of light dropped and did not rise again. The crawling man became still. A gentle glow began to grow around us. It was dawn, and the short Alaskan summer night was over. Anderson rubbed his eyes and turned to me a haggard face.

"Man!" he exclaimed. "You look as though you have been through a spell of sickness!"

"No more than you, Starr," I said. "What do you make of it all?"

"I'm thinking our only answer lies there," he answered, pointing to the figure that lay so motionless under the blankets we had thrown over him. "Whatever it was—that's what it was after. There was no aurora about that light, Frank. It was like the flaring up of some queer hell the preacher folk never frightened us with."

"We'll go no further today," I said. "I wouldn't wake him for all the gold that runs between the fingers of the five peaks—nor for all the devils that may be behind them."

The crawling man lay in a sleep as deep as the Styx. We bathed and bandaged the pads that had been his hands. Arms and legs were as rigid as though they were crutches. He did not move while we worked over him. He lay as he had fallen, the arms a trifle raised, the knees bent.

"Why did he crawl?" whispered Anderson. "Why didn't he walk?"

I was filing the band about the waist. It was gold, but it was like no gold I had ever handled. Pure gold is soft. This was soft, but it had an unclean, viscid life of its own. It clung to the file. I gashed through it, bent it away from the body and hurled it far off. It was— loathsome!

All that day he slept. Darkness came and still he slept That night there was no shaft of light, no questing globe, no whispering. Some spell of horror seemed lifted from the land. It was noon when the crawling man awoke. I jumped as the pleasant drawling voice sounded.

"How long have I slept?" he asked. His pale blue eyes grew quizzical as I stared at him. "A night—and almost two days,"

I said. "Was there any light up there last night?" He nodded to the North eagerly. "Any whispering?"

"Neither," I answered. His head fell back and he stared up at the sky.

"They've given it up, then?" he said at last.

"Who have given it up?" asked Anderson.

"Why, the people of the pit," replied the crawling man quietly.

We stared at him. "The people of the pit," he said. "Things that the Devil made before the Flood and that somehow have escaped God's vengeance. You weren't in any danger from them—unless you had followed their call. They can't get any further than the blue haze. I was their prisoner," he added simply. "They were trying to whisper me back to them!"

Anderson and I looked at each other, the same thought in both our minds.

"You're wrong," said the crawling man. "I'm not insane. Give me a very little to drink. I'm going to die soon, but I want you to take me as far South as you can before I die, and afterwards I want you to build a big fire and burn me. I want to be in such shape that no infernal spell of theirs can drag my body back to them. You'll do it too, when I've told you about them—" he hesitated. "I think their chain is off me?" he said.

"I cut it off," I answered shortly.

"Thank God for that too," whispered the crawling man.

He drank the brandy and water we lifted to his lips.

"Arms and legs quite dead," he said. "Dead as I'll be soon. Well, they did well for me. Now I'll tell you what's up there behind that hand. Hell!"

"Now listen. My name is Stanton—Sinclair Stanton. Class 1900, Yale. Explorer. I started away from Dawson last year to hunt for five peaks that rise like a hand in a haunted country and run pure gold between them. Same thing you were after? I thought so. Late last fall my comrade sickened. Sent him back with some Indians. Little later all my Indians ran away from me. I decided I'd stick, built a cabin, stocked myself with food and lay down to winter it. In the Spring I started off again. Little less than two weeks ago I sighted the five peaks. Not from this side though—the other. Give me some more brandy.

"I'd made too wide a detour," he went on. "I'd gotten too far North. I beat back. From this side you see nothing but forest straight up to the base of the Hand Mountain. Over on the other side—"

He was silent for a moment.

"Over there is forest too. But it doesn't reach so far. No! I came out of it. Stretching miles in front of me was a level plain. It was as worn and ancient looking as the desert around the ruins of Babylon. At its end rose the peaks. Between me and them—far off—was what looked like a low dike of rocks. Then—I ran across the road!

"The road!" cried Anderson incredulously.

"The road," said the crawling man. "A fine smooth Stone road. It ran straight on to the mountain. Oh, it was road all right—and worn as though millions and millions of feet had passed over it for thousands of years. On each side of it were sand and heaps of stones. After while I began to notice these stones. They were cut, and the shape of the heaps somehow gave me the idea that a hundred thousand years ago they might have been houses. I sensed man about them and at the same time they smelled of immemorial antiquity. Well—

"The peaks grew closer. The heaps of ruins thicker. Something inexpressibly desolate hovered over them; something reached from them that struck my heart like the touch of ghosts so old that they could be only the ghosts of ghosts. I went on.

"And now I saw that what I had thought to be the low rock range at the base of the peaks was a thicker litter of ruins. The Hand Mountain was really much farther off. The road passed between two high rocks that raised themselves like a gateway."

The crawling man paused.

"They were a gateway," he said. "I reached them. I went between them. And then I sprawled and clutched the earth in sheer awe! I was on a broad stone platform. Before me was—sheer space! Imagine the Grand Canyon five times as wide and with the bottom dropped out. That is what I was looking into. It was like peeping over the edge of a cleft world down into the infinity where the planets roll! On the far side stood the five peaks. They looked like a gigantic warning hand stretched up to the sky. The lip of the abyss curved away on each side of me.

"I could see down perhaps a thousand feet. Then a thick blue haze shut out the eye. It was like the blue you see gather on the high hills at dusk. And the pit—it was awesome; awesome as the Maori Gulf of Ranalak, that sinks between the living and the dead and that only the freshly released soul has strength to leap—but never strength to cross again.

"I crept back from the verge and stood up, weak. My hand rested against one of the pillars of the gateway. There was

8

carving upon it. It bore in still sharp outlines the heroic figure of a man. His back was turned. His arms were outstretched. There was an odd peaked headdress upon him. I looked at the opposite pillar. It bore a figure exactly similar. The pillars were triangular and the carvings were on the side away from the pit. The figures seemed to be holding something back. I looked closer. Behind the outstretched hands I seemed to see other shapes.

"I traced them out vaguely. Suddenly I felt unaccountably sick. There had come to me an impression of enormous upright slugs. Their swollen bodies were faintly cut—all except the heads which were well marked globes. They were—unutterably loathsome. I turned from the gates back to the void. I stretched myself upon the slab and looked over the edge.

"A stairway led down into the pit!"

"A stairway!" we cried.

"A stairway," repeated the crawling man as patiently as before, "It seemed not so much carved out of the rock as built into it. The slabs were about six feet long and three feet wide. It ran down from the platform and vanished into the blue haze."

"But who could build such a stairway as that?" I said. "A stairway built into the wall of a precipice and leading down into a bottomless pit!"

"Not bottomless," said the crawling man quietly. "There was a bottom. I reached it!"

"Reached it?" we repeated.

"Yes, by the stairway," answered the crawling man. "You see—I went down it!

"Yes," he said. "I went down the stairway. But not that day. I made my camp back of the gates. At dawn I filled my knapsack with food, my two canteens with water from a spring that wells up there by the gateway, walked between the carved monoliths and stepped over the edge of the pit.

"The steps ran along the side of the rock at a forty degree pitch. As I went down and down I studied them. They were of a greenish rock quite different from the granitic porphyry that formed the wall of the precipice. At first I thought that the builders had taken advantage of an outcropping stratum, and had carved from it their gigantic flight. But the regularity of the angle at which it fell made me doubtful of this theory.

"After I had gone perhaps half a mile I stepped out upon a landing. From this landing the stairs made a V shaped turn and ran on downward, clinging to the cliff at the same angle as the first flight; it was a zig-zag, and after I had made three of these turns I knew that the steps dropped straight down in a succession of such angles. No strata could be so regular as that. No, the stairway was built by hands! But whose? The answer is in those ruins around the edge, I think—never to be read.

"By noon I had lost sight of the five peaks and the lip of the abyss. Above me, below me, was nothing but the blue haze. Beside me, too, was nothingness, for the further breast of rock had long since vanished. I felt no dizziness, and any trace of fear was swallowed in a vast curiosity. What was I to discover? Some ancient and wonderful civilization that had ruled when the Poles were tropical gardens? Nothing living, I felt sure—all was too old for life. Still, a stairway so wonderful must lead to something quite as wonderful I knew. What was it? I went on.

"At regular intervals I had passed the mouths of small caves. There would be two thousand steps and then an opening, two thousand more steps and an opening—and so on and on. Late that afternoon I stopped before one of these clefts. I suppose I had gone then three miles down the pit, although the angles were such that I had walked in all fully ten miles. I examined the entrance. On each side were carved the figures of the great portal above, only now they were standing face forward, the arms outstretched as though to hold something back from the outer depths. Their faces were covered with veils. There were no hideous shapes behind them. I went inside. The fissure ran back for twenty yards like a burrow. It was dry and perfectly light. Outside I could see the blue haze rising upward like a column, its edges clearly marked. I felt an extraordinary sense of security, although I had not been conscious of any fear. I felt that the figures at the entrance were guardians—but against what?

"The blue haze thickened and grew faintly luminescent. I fancied that it was dusk above. I ate and drank a little and slept. When I awoke the blue had lightened again, and I fancied it was dawn above. I went on. I forgot the gulf yawning at my side. I felt no fatigue and little hunger or thirst, although I had drunk and eaten sparingly. That night I spent within another of the caves, and at dawn I descended again.

"It was late that day when I first saw the city—."

He was silent for a time.

"The city," he said at last, "there is a city you know. But not such a city as you have ever seen—nor any other man who has lived to tell of it. The pit, I think, is shaped like a bottle; the opening before the five peaks is the neck. But how wide the bottom is I do not know—thousands of miles maybe. I had begun to catch little glints of light far down in the blue. Then I saw the tops of—trees, I suppose they are. But not our kind of trees—unpleasant, snaky kind of trees. They reared themselves on high thin trunks and their tops were nests of thick tendrils with ugly little leaves like arrow heads. The trees were red, a vivid angry red. Here and there I glimpsed spots of shining yellow. I knew these were water because I could see things breaking through their surface—or at least I could see the splash and ripple, but what it was that disturbed them I never saw.

"Straight beneath me was the—city. I looked down upon mile after mile of closely packed cylinders. They lay upon their sides in pyramids of three, of five—of dozens—piled upon each other. It is hard to make you see what that city is like—look, suppose you have water pipes of a certain length and first you lay three of them side by side and on top of them you place two and on these two one; or suppose you take five for a foundation and place on these four and then three, then two and then one. Do you see? That was the way they looked. But they were topped by towers, by minarets, by flares, by fans, and twisted monstrosities. They gleamed as though coated with pale rose flame. Beside them the venomous red trees raised themselves like the heads of hydras guarding nests of gigantic, jeweled and sleeping worms!

"A few feet beneath me the stairway jutted out into a Titanic arch, unearthly as the span that bridges Hell and leads to Asgard. It curved out and down straight through the top of the highest pile of carven cylinders and then it vanished through it. It was appalling—it was demonic—"

The crawling man stopped. His eyes rolled up into his head. He trembled and his arms and legs began their horrible crawling movement. From his lips came a whispering. It was an echo of the high murmuring we had heard the night he came to us. I put my hands over his eyes. He quieted.

"The Things Accursed!" he said. "The People of the Pit! Did I whisper. Yes —but they can't get me now—they can't!"

After a time he began as quietly as before.

"I crossed the span. I went down through the top of that— building. Blue darkness shrouded me for a moment and I felt the steps twist into a spiral. I wound down and then—I was standing high up in—I can't tell you in what, I'll have to call it a room. We have no images for what is in the pit. A hundred feet below me was the floor. The walls sloped down and out from where I stood in a series of widening crescents. The place was colossal—and it was filled with a curious mottled red light. It was like the light inside a green and gold flecked fire opal. I went down to the last step. Far in front of me rose a high, columned altar. Its pillars were carved in monstrous scrolls—like mad octopuses with a thousand drunken tentacles; they rested on the backs of shapeless monstrosities carved in crimson stone. The altar front was a gigantic slab of purple covered with carvings.

"I can't describe these carvings! No human being could— the human eye cannot grasp them any more than it can grasp the shapes that haunt the fourth dimension. Only a subtle sense in the back of the brain sensed them vaguely. They were formless things that gave no conscious image, yet pressed into the mind like small hot seals—ideas of hate—of combats between unthinkable monstrous things—victories in a nebulous hell of steaming, obscene jungles—aspirations and ideals immeasurably loathsome—

"And as I stood I grew aware of something that lay behind the lip of the altar fifty feet above me. I knew it was there—I felt it with every hair and every tiny bit of my skin. Something infinitely malignant, infinitely horrible, infinitely ancient. It lurked, it brooded, it threatened and it—was invisible!

"Behind me was a circle of blue light. I ran for it. Something urged me to turn back, to climb the stairs and make away. It was impossible. Repulsion for that unseen Thing raced me onward as though a current had my feet. I passed through the circle. I was out on a street that stretched on into dim distance between rows of the carven cylinders.

"Here and there the red trees arose. Between them rolled the stone burrows. And now I could take in the amazing ornamentation that clothed them. They were like the trunks of smooth skinned trees that had fallen and had been clothed with high reaching noxious orchids. Yes—those cylinders were like that—and more. They should have gone out with the dinosaurs. They were—monstrous. They struck the eyes like a blow and they passed across the nerves like a rasp. And nowhere was there sight or sound of living thing.

"There were circular openings in the cylinders like the circle in the Temple of the Stairway. I passed through one of them. I was in a long, bare vaulted room whose curving sides half closed twenty feet over my head, leaving a wide slit that opened into another vaulted chamber above. There was absolutely nothing in the room save the same mottled reddish light that I had seen in the Temple. I stumbled. I still could see nothing, but there was something on the floor over which I had tripped. I reached down—and my hand touched a thing cold and smooth—that moved under it—I turned and ran out of that place—I was filled with a loathing that had in it something of madness—I ran on and on blindly— wringing my hands—weeping with horror—

"When I came to myself I was still among the stone cylinders and red trees. I tried to retrace my steps; to find the Temple. I was more than afraid. I was like a new loosed soul panic-stricken with the first terrors of hell. I could not find the Temple! Then the haze began to thicken and glow; the cylinders to shine more brightly. I knew that it was dusk in the world above and I felt that with dusk my time of peril had come; that the thickening of the haze was the signal for the awakening of whatever things lived in this pit.

"I scrambled up the sides of one of the burrows. I hid behind a twisted nightmare of stone. Perhaps, I thought, there was a chance of remaining hidden until the blue lightened and the peril passed. There began to grow around me a murmur. It was everywhere—and it grew and grew into a great whispering. I peeped from the side of the stone down into the street. I saw lights passing and repassing. More and more lights—they swam out of the circular doorways and they thronged the street. The highest were eight feet above the pave; the lowest perhaps two. They hurried, they sauntered, they bowed, they stopped and whispered—and there was nothing under them!"

"Nothing under them!" breathed Anderson.

"No," he went on, "that was the terrible part of it—there was nothing under them. Yet certainly the lights were living things. They had consciousness, volition, thought—what else I did not know. They were nearly two feet across—the largest. Their center was a bright nucleus —red, blue, green. This nucleus faded off, gradually, into a misty glow that did not end abruptly. It too seemed to fade off into nothingness —but a nothingness that had under it a somethingness. I strained my eyes trying to grasp this body into which the lights merged and which one could only feel was there, but could not see.

"And all at once I grew rigid. Something cold, and thin like a whip, had touched my face. I turned my head. Close behind were three of the lights. They were a pale blue. They looked at me—if you can imagine lights that are eyes. Another whiplash gripped my shoulder. Under the closest light came a shrill whispering. I shrieked. Abruptly the murmuring in the street ceased. I dragged my eyes from the pale blue globe that held them and looked out—the lights in the streets were rising by myriads to the level of where I stood! There they stopped and peered at me. They crowded and jostled as though they were a crowd of curious people— on Broadway. I felt a score of the lashes touch me—

"When I came to myself I was again in the great Place of the Stairway, lying at the foot of the altar. All was silent. There were no lights— only the mottled red glow. I jumped to my feet and ran toward the steps. Something jerked me back to my knees. And then I saw that around my waist had been fastened a yellow ring of metal. From it hung a chain and this chain passed up over the lip of the high ledge. I was chained to the altar!

"I reached into my pockets for my knife to cut through the ring. It was not there! I had been stripped of everything except one of the canteens that I had hung around my neck and which I suppose They had thought was— part of me. I tried to break the ring. It seemed alive. It writhed in my hands and it drew itself closer around me! I pulled at the chain. It was immovable. There came to me the consciousness of the unseen Thing above the altar. I groveled at the foot of the slab and wept. Think—alone in that place of strange light with the brooding ancient Horror above me— a monstrous Thing, a Thing unthinkable—an unseen Thing that poured forth horror—

"After awhile I gripped myself. Then I saw beside one of the pillars a yellow bowl filled with a thick white liquid. I drank it. If it killed I did not care. But its taste was pleasant and as I drank my strength came back to me with a rush. Clearly I was not to be starved. The lights, whatever they were, had a conception of human needs.

"And now the reddish mottled gleam began to deepen. Outside arose the humming and through the circle that was the entrance came streaming the globes, They ranged themselves in ranks until they filled the Temple. Their whispering grew into a chant, a cadenced whispering chant that rose and fell, rose and fell, while to its rhythm the globes lifted and sank, lifted and sank.

"All that night the lights came and went—and all that night the chant sounded as they rose and fell. At the last I felt myself only an atom of consciousness in a sea of cadenced whispering; an atom that rose and fell with the bowing globes. I tell you that even my heart pulsed in unison with them! The red glow faded, the lights streamed out; the whispering died. I was again alone and I knew that once again day had broken in my own world."

"I slept. When I awoke I found beside the pillar more of the white liquid. I scrutinized the chain that held me to the altar. I began to rub two of the links together. I did this for hours. When the red began to thicken there was a ridge worn in the links. Hope rushed up within me. There was, then, a chance to escape."

"With the thickening the lights came again. All through that night the whispering chant sounded, and the globes rose and fell. The chant seized me. It pulsed through me until every nerve and muscle quivered to it. My lips began to quiver. They strove like a man trying to cry out on a nightmare. And at last they too were whispering the chant of the people of the pit. My body bowed in unison with the lights—I was, in movement and sound, one with the nameless things while my soul sank back sick with horror and powerless. While I whispered I—saw Them!"

"Saw the lights?" I asked stupidly.

"Saw the Things under the lights," he answered. "Great transparent snail- like bodies—dozens of waving tentacles stretching from them— round gaping mouths under the luminous seeing globes. They were like the ghosts of inconceivably monstrous slugs! I could see through them. And as I stared, still bowing and whispering, the dawn came and they streamed to and through the entrance. They did not crawl or walk—they floated! They floated and were—gone!

"I did not sleep. I worked all that day at my chain. By the thickening of the red I had worn it a sixth through. And all that night I whispered and bowed with the pit people, joining in their chant to the Thing that brooded above me!

"Twice again the red thickened and the chant held me— then on the morning of the fifth day I broke through the worn links of the chain. I was free! I drank from the bowl of white liquid and poured what was left in my flask. I ran to the Stairway. I rushed up and past that unseen Horror behind the altar ledge and was out upon the Bridge. I raced across the span and up the Stairway.

"Can you think what it is to climb straight up the verge of a cleft world —with hell behind you? Hell was behind me and terror rode me. The city had long been lost in the blue haze before I knew that I could climb no more. My heart beat upon my ears like a sledge. I fell before one of the little caves feeling that here at last was sanctuary. I crept far back within it and waited for the haze to thicken. Almost at once it did so. From far below me came a vast and angry murmur. At the mouth of the rift I saw a light pulse up through the blue; die down and as it dimmed I saw myriads of the globes that are the eyes of the pit people swing downward into the abyss. Again and again the light pulsed and the globes fell. They were hunting me. The whispering grew louder, more insistent.

"There grew in me the dreadful desire to join in the whispering as I had done in the Temple. I bit my lips through and through to still them. All that night the beam shot up through the abyss, the globes swung and the whispering sounded—and now I knew the purpose of the caves and of the sculptured figures that still had power to guard them. But what were the people who had carved them? Why had they built their city around the verge and why had they set that Stairway in the pit? What had they been to those Things that dwelt at the bottom and what use had the Things been to them that they should live beside their dwelling place? That there had been some purpose was certain. No work so prodigious as the Stairway would have been undertaken otherwise. But what was the purpose? And why was it that those who had dwelt about the abyss had passed away ages gone, and the dwellers in the abyss still lived? I could find no answer—nor can I find any now. I have not the shred of a theory.

"Dawn came as I wondered and with it silence. I drank what was left of the liquid in my canteen, crept from the cave and began to climb again. That afternoon my legs gave out. I tore off my shirt, made from it pads for my knees and coverings for my hands. I crawled upward. I crawled up and up. And again I crept into one of the caves and waited until again the blue thickened, the shaft of light shot through it and the whispering came.

"But now there was a new note in the whispering. It was no longer threatening. It called and coaxed. It drew."

A new terror gripped me. There had come upon me a mighty desire to leave the cave and go out where the lights swung; to let them do with me as they pleased, carry me where they wished. The desire grew. It gained fresh impulse with every rise of the beam until at last I vibrated with the desire as I had vibrated to the chant in the Temple. My body was a pendulum. Up would go the beam and I would swing toward it! Only my soul kept steady. It held me fast to the floor of the cave; And all that night it fought with my body against the spell of the pit people.

"Dawn came. Again I crept from the cave and faced the Stairway. I could not rise. My hands were torn and bleeding; my knees an agony. I forced myself upward step by step. After a while my hands became numb, the pain left my knees. They deadened. Step by step my will drove my body upward upon them."

"And then—a nightmare of crawling up infinite stretches of steps —memories of dull horror while hidden within caves with the lights pulsing without and whisperings that called and called me—memory of a time when I awoke to find that my body was obeying the call and had carried me half way out between the guardians of the portals while thousands of gleaming globes rested in the blue haze and watched me."

Glimpses of bitter fights against sleep and always, always—a climb up and up along infinite distances of steps that led from Abaddon to a Paradise of blue sky and open world!

"At last a consciousness of the clear sky close above me, the lip of the pit before me—memory of passing between the great portals of the pit and of steady withdrawal from it— dreams of giant men with strange peaked crowns and veiled faces who pushed me onward and onward and held back Roman Candle globules of light that sought to draw me back to a gulf wherein planets swam between the branches of red trees that had snakes for crowns."

"And then a long, long sleep—how long God alone knows—in a cleft of rocks; an awakening to see far in the North the beam still rising and falling, the lights still hunting, the whispering high above me calling."

"Again crawling on dead arms and legs that moved—that moved —like the Ancient Mariner's ship—without volition of mine, but that carried me from a haunted place. And then—your fire—and this—safety!"

The crawling man smiled at us for a moment. Then swiftly life faded from his face. He slept.

That afternoon we struck camp and carrying the crawling man started back South. For three days we carried him and still he slept. And on the third day, still sleeping, he died. We built a great pile of wood and we burned his body as he had asked. We scattered his ashes about the forest with the ashes of the trees that had consumed him. It must be a great magic indeed that could disentangle those ashes and draw him back in a rushing cloud to the pit he called Accursed. I do not think that even the People of the Pit have such a spell. No.

But we did not return to the five peaks to see.

Unseen—Unfeared
(1919)

Francis Stevens

I.

I had been dining with my ever-interesting friend, Mark Jenkins, at a little Italian restaurant near South Street. It was a chance meeting. Jenkins is too busy, usually, to make dinner engagements. Over our highly seasoned food and sour, thin, red wine, he spoke of little odd incidents and adventures of his profession. Nothing very vital or important, of course. Jenkins is not the sort of detective who first detects and then pours the egotistical and revealing details of achievement in the ears of every acquaintance, however appreciative.

But when I spoke of something I had seen in the morning papers, he laughed. "Poor old 'Doc' Holt! Fascinating old codger, to anyone who really knows him. I've had his friendship for years—since I was first on the city force and saved a young assistant of his from jail on a false charge. And they had to drag him into the poisoning of this young sport, Ralph Peeler!"

"Why are you so sure he couldn't have been implicated?" I asked.

But Jenkins only shook his head, with a quiet smile. "I have reasons for believing otherwise," was all I could get out of him on that score, "But," he added, "the only reason he was suspected at all is the superstitious dread of these ignorant people around him. Can't see why he lives in such a place. I know for a fact he doesn't have to. Doc's got money of his own. He's an amateur chemist and dabbler in different sorts of research work, and I suspect he's been guilty of 'showing off.' Result, they all swear he has the evil eye and holds forbidden communion with invisible powers. Smoke?"

Jenkins offered me one of his invariably good cigars, which I accepted, saying thoughtfully: "A man has no right to trifle with the superstitions of ignorant people. Sooner or later, it spells trouble."

"Did in his case. They swore up and down that he sold love charms openly and poisons secretly, and that, together with his living so near to—somebody else—got him temporarily suspected. But my tongue's running away with me, as usual!"

"As usual," I retorted impatiently.

He beamed upon me engagingly and rose from the table, with a glance at his watch. "Sorry to leave you, Blaisdell, but I have to meet Jimmy Brennan in ten minutes."

He so clearly did not invite my further company that I remained seated for a little while after his departure; then took my own way homeward. Those streets always held for me a certain fascination, particularly at night. They are so unlike the rest of the city, so foreign in appearance, with their little shabby stores, always open until late evening, their unbelievably cheap goods, displayed as much outside the shops as in them, hung on the fronts and laid out on tables by the curb and in the street itself. Tonight, however, neither people nor stores in any sense appealed to me. The mixture of people, mostly bareheaded, unkempt and generally unhygienic in appearance, struck me as merely revolting. They were all humans, and I, too, was human. Some way I did not like the idea.

Puzzled a trifle, for I am more inclined to sympathize with poverty than accuse it, I watched the faces that I passed. Never before had I observed how bestial, how brutal were the countenances of the dwellers in this region. I actually shuddered when an old-clothes man, a gray-bearded Hebrew, brushed me as he toiled past with his barrow.

There was a sense of evil in the air, a warning of things which it is wise for a clean man to shun and keep clear of. The impression became so strong that before I had walked two squares I began to feel physically ill. Then it occurred to me that the one glass of cheap Chianti I had drunk might have something to do with the feeling. Who knew how that stuff had been manufactured, or whether the juice of the grape entered at all into its ill-flavored composition? Yet I doubted if that were the real cause of my discomfort.

By nature I am rather a sensitive, impressionable sort of chap. In some way tonight this neighborhood, with its sordid sights and smells, had struck me wrong.

My sense of impending evil was merging into actual fear. This would never do. There is only one way to deal with an imaginative temperament like mine—conquer its vagaries. If I left South Street with this nameless dread upon me, I could never pass down it again without a recurrence of the feeling.

I should simply have to stay here until I got the better of it—that was all.

I paused on a corner before a shabby but brightly lighted little drug store. Its gleaming windows and the luminous green of its conventional glass show jars made the brightest spot on the block. I realized that I was tired, but hardly wanted to go in there and rest. I knew what the company would be like at its shabby, sticky soda fountain. As I stood there, my eyes fell on a long white canvas sign across from me, and its black-and-red lettering caught my attention.

SEE THE GREAT UNSEEN!

Come in! This Means You!

FREE TO ALL!

A museum of fakes, I thought, but also reflected that if it were a show of some kind I could sit down for a while, rest, and fight off this increasing obsession of nonexistent evil. That side of the street was almost deserted, and the place itself might well be nearly empty.

II.

I walked over, but with every step my sense of dread increased. Dread of I knew not what. Bodiless, inexplicable horror had me as in a net, whose strands, being intangible, without reason for existence, I could by no means throw off. It was not the people now. None of them were about me. There, in the open, lighted street, with no sight nor sound of terror to assail me, I was the shivering victim of such fear as I had never known was possible. Yet still I would not yield.

Setting my teeth, and fighting with myself as with some pet animal gone mad, I forced my steps to slowness and walked along the sidewalk, seeking entrance. Just here there were no shops, but several doors reached in each case by means of a few iron-railed stone steps. I chose the one in the middle beneath the sign. In that neighborhood there are museums, shops and other commercial enterprises conducted in many shabby old residences, such as were these. Behind the glazing of the door I had chosen I could see a dim, pinkish light, but on either side the windows were quite dark.

Trying the door, I found it unlocked. As I opened it a party of Italians passed on the pavement below and I looked back at them over my shoulder. They were gayly dressed, men, women and children, laughing and chattering to one another; probably on their way to some wedding or other festivity.

In passing, one of the men glanced up at me and involuntarily I shuddered back against the door. He was a young man, handsome after the swarthy manner of his race, but never in my life had I see a face so expressive of pure, malicious cruelty, naked and unashamed. Our eyes met and his seemed to light up with a vile gleaming, as if all the wickedness of his nature had come to a focus in the look of concentrated hate he gave me.

They went by, but for some distance I could see him watching me, chin on shoulder, till he and his party were swallowed up in the crowd of marketers farther down the street.

Sick and trembling from that encounter, merely of eyes though it had been, I threw aside my partly smoked cigar and entered. Within there was a small vestibule, whose ancient tesselated floor was grimy with the passing of many feet. I could feel the grit of dirt under my shoes, and it rasped on my rawly quivering nerves. The inner door stood partly open, and going on I found myself in a bare, dirty hallway, and was greeted by the sour, musty, poverty-stricken smell common to dwellings of the very ill-to-do. Beyond there was a stairway, carpeted with ragged grass matting. A gas jet, turned low inside a very dusty pink globe, was the light I had seen from without.

Listening, the house seemed entirely silent. Surely, this was no place of public amusement of any kind whatever. More likely it was a rooming house, and I had, after all, mistaken the entrance.

To my intense relief, since coming inside, the worst agony of my unreasonable terror had passed away. If I could only get in some place where I could sit down and be quiet, probably I should be rid of it for good. Determining to try another entrance, I was about to leave the bare hallway when one of several doors along the side of it suddenly opened and a man stepped out into the hall.

"Well?" he said, looking at me keenly, but with not the least show of surprise at my presence.

"I beg your pardon," I replied. "The door was unlocked and I came in here, thinking it was the entrance to the exhibit—what do they call it? the 'Great Unseen.' The one that is mentioned on that long white sign. Can you tell me which door is the right one?"

"I can."

With that brief answer he stopped and stared at me again. He was a tall, lean man, somewhat stooped, but possessing considerable dignity of bearing. For that neighborhood, he appeared uncommonly well dressed, and his long, smooth-shaven face was noticeable because, while his complexion was dark and his eyes coal-black, above them the heavy brows and his hair were almost silvery-white. His age might have been anything over the threescore mark.

I grew tired of being stared at. "If you can and—won't, then never mind," I observed a trifle irritably, and turned to go. But his sharp exclamation halted me.

"No!" he said. "No—no! Forgive me for pausing—it was not hesitation, I assure you. To think that one—one, even, has come! All day they pass my sign up there—pass and fear to enter. But you are different. You are not of these timorous, ignorant foreign peasants. You ask me to tell you the right door? Here it is! Here!"

And he struck the panel of the door, which he had closed behind him, so that the sharp yet hollow sound of it echoed up through the silent house.

Now it may be thought that after all my senseless terror in the open street, so strange a welcome from so odd a show-man would have brought the feeling back, full force. But there is an emotion stronger, to a certain point, than fear. This queer old fellow aroused my curiosity. What kind of museum could it be that he accused the passing public of fearing to enter? Nothing really terrible, surely, or it would have been closed by the police. And normally I am not an unduly timorous person. "So it's in there, is it?" I asked, coming toward him. "And I'm to be sole audience? Come, that will be an interesting experience." I was half laughing now.

"The most interesting in the world," said the old man, with a solemnity which rebuked my lightness.

With that he opened the door, passed inward and closed it again—in my very face. I stood staring at it blankly. The panels, I remember, had been originally painted white, but now the paint was flaked and blistered, gray with dirt and dirty finger marks. Suddenly it occurred to me that I had no wish to enter there. Whatever was behind it could be scarcely worth seeing, or he would not choose such a place for its exhibition. With the old man's vanishing my curiosity had cooled, but just as I again turned to leave, the door opened and this singular showman stuck his white-eye-browed face through the aperture. He was frowning impatiently. "Come in—come in!" he snapped, and promptly withdrawing his head, once more closed the door.

"He has something there he doesn't want should get out," was the very natural conclusion which I drew. "Well, since it can hardly be anything dangerous, and he's so anxious I should see it—here goes!"

With that I turned the soiled white porcelain handle, and entered.

The room I came into was neither very large nor very brightly lighted. In no way did it resemble a museum or lecture room. On the contrary, it seemed to have been fitted up as a quite well-appointed laboratory. The floor was linoleum-covered, there were glass cases along the walls whose shelves were filled with bottles, specimen jars, graduates, and the like. A large table in one corner bore what looked like some odd sort of camera, and a larger one in the middle of the room was fitted with a long rack filled with bottles and test tubes, and was besides littered with papers, glass slides, and various paraphernalia which my ignorance failed to identify. There were several cases of books, a few plain wooden chairs, and in the corner a large iron sink with running water.

My host of the white hair and black eyes was awaiting me, standing near the larger table. He indicated one of the wooden chairs with a thin forefinger that shook a little, either from age or eagerness. "Sit down—sit down! Have no fear but that you will be interested, my friend. Have no fear at all—of anything!"

As he said it he fixed his dark eyes upon me and stared harder than ever. But the effect of his words was the opposite of their meaning. I did sit down, because my knees gave under me, but if in the outer hall I had lost my terror, it now returned twofold upon me. Out there the light had been faint, dingily roseate, indefinite. By it I had not perceived how this old man's face was a mask of living malice—of cruelty, hate and a certain masterful contempt. Now I knew the meaning of my fear, whose warning I would not heed. Now I knew that I had walked into the very trap from which my abnormal sensitiveness had striven in vain to save me.

III.

Again I struggled within me, bit at my lip till I tasted blood, and presently the blind paroxysm passed. It must have been longer in going than I thought, and the old man must have all that time been speaking, for when I could once more control my attention, hear and see him, he had taken up a position near the sink, about ten feet away, and was addressing me with a sort of "platform" manner, as if I had been the large audience whose absence he had deplored.

"And so," he was saying, "I was forced to make these plates very carefully, to truly represent the characteristic hues of each separate organism. Now, in color work of every kind the film is necessarily extremely sensitive. Doubtless you are familiar in a general way with the exquisite transparencies produced by color photography of the single-plate type."

He paused, and trying to act like a normal human being, I observed: "I saw some nice landscapes done in that way—last week at an illustrated lecture in Franklin Hall."

He scowled, and made an impatient gesture at me with his hand. "I can proceed better without interruptions," he said. "My pause was purely oratorical."

I meekly subsided, and he went on in his original loud, clear voice. He would have made an excellent lecturer before a much larger audience—if only his voice could have lost that eerie, ringing note. Thinking of that I must have missed some more, and when I caught it again he was saying:

"As I have indicated, the original plate is the final picture. Now, many of these organisms are extremely hard to photograph, and microphotography in color is particularly difficult. In consequence, to spoil a plate tries the patience of the photographer. They are so sensitive that the ordinary dark-room ruby lamp would instantly ruin them, and they must therefore be developed either in darkness or by a special light produced by interposing thin sheets of tissue of a particular shade of green and of yellow between lamp and plate, and even that will often cause ruinous fog. Now I, finding it hard to handle them so, made numerous experiments with a view of discovering some glass or fabric of a color which should add to the safety of the green, without robbing it of all efficiency. All proved equally useless, but intermittently I persevered—until last week."

His voice dropped to an almost confidential tone, and he leaned slightly toward me. I was cold from my neck to my feet, though my head was burning, but I tried to force an appreciative smile.

"Last week," he continued impressively, "I had a prescription filled at the corner drug store. The bottle was sent home to me wrapped in a piece of what I first took to be whitish, slightly opalescent paper. Later I decided that it was some kind of membrane. When I questioned the druggist, seeking its source, he said it was a sheet of 'paper' that was around a bundle of herbs from South America. That he had no more, and doubted if I could trace it. He had wrapped my bottle so, because he was in haste and the sheet was handy.

"I can hardly tell you what first inspired me to try that membrane in my photographic work. It was merely dull white with a faint hint of opalescence, except when held against the light. Then it became quite translucent and quite brightly prismatic. For some reason it occurred to me that this refractive effect might help in breaking up the actinic rays—the rays which affect the sensitive emulsion. So that night I inserted it behind the sheets of green and yellow tissue, next the lamp prepared my trays and chemicals laid my plate holders to hand, turned off the white light and—turned on the green!"

There was nothing in his words to inspire fear. It was a wearisomely detailed account of his struggles with photography. Yet, as he again paused impressively, I wished that he might never speak again. I was desperately, contemptibly in dread of the thing he might say next.

Suddenly, he drew himself erect, the stoop went out of his shoulders, he threw back his head and laughed. It was a hollow sound, as if he laughed into a trumpet. "I won't tell you what I saw! Why should I? Your own eyes shall bear witness. But this much I'll say, so that you may better understand—later. When our poor, faultily sensitive vision can perceive a thing, we say that it is visible. When the nerves of touch can feel it, we say that it is tangible. Yet I tell you there are beings intangible to our physical sense, yet whose presence is felt by the spirit, and invisible to our eyes merely because those organs are not attuned to the light as reflected from their bodies. But light passed through the screen, which we are about to use has a wave length novel to the scientific world, and by it you shall see with the eyes of the flesh that which has been invisible since life began. Have no fear!"

He stopped to laugh again, and his mirth was yellow-toothed—menacing.

"Have no fear!" he reiterated, and with that stretched his hand toward the wall, there came a click and we were in black, impenetrable darkness. I wanted to spring up, to seek the door by which I had entered and rush out of it, but the paralysis of unreasoning terror held me fast.

I could hear him moving about in the darkness, and a moment later a faint green glimmer sprang up in the room. Its source was over the large sink, where I suppose he developed his precious "color plates."

Every instant, as my eyes became accustomed to the dimness, I could see more clearly. Green light is peculiar. It may be far fainter than red, and at the same time far more illuminating. The old man was standing beneath it, and his face by that ghastly radiance had the exact look of a dead man's. Besides this, however, I could observe nothing appalling.

"That," continued the man, "is the simple developing light of which I have spoken—now watch, for what you are about to behold no mortal man but myself has ever seen before." For a moment he fussed with the green lamp over the sink. It was so constructed that all the direct rays struck downward. He opened a flap at the side, for a moment there was a streak of comforting white luminance from within, then he inserted something, slid it slowly in—and closed the flap.

The thing he put in—that South American "membrane" it must have been—instead of decreasing the light increased it—amazingly. The hue was changed from green to greenish-gray, and the whole room sprang into view, a livid, ghastly chamber, filled with—overcrawled by—what?

My eyes fixed themselves, fascinated, on something that moved by the old man's feet. It writhed there on the floor like a huge, repulsive starfish, an immense, armed, legged thing, that twisted convulsively. It was smooth, as if made of rubber, was whitish-green in color; and presently raised its great round blob of a body on tottering tentacles, crept toward my host and writhed upward—yes, climbed up his legs, his body. And he stood there, erect, arms folded, and stared sternly down at the thing which climbed.

But the room—the whole room was alive with other creatures than that. Everywhere I looked they were—centipedish things, with yard-long bodies, detestable, furry spiders that lurked in shadows, and sausage-shaped translucent horrors that moved—and floated through the air. They dived—here and there between me and the light, and I could see its bright greenness through their greenish bodies.

Worse, though; far worse than these were the things with human faces. Mask-like, monstrous, huge gaping mouths and slitlike eyes—I find I cannot write of them. There was that about them which makes their memory even now intolerable.

The old man was speaking again, and every word echoed in my brain like the ringing of a gong. "Fear nothing! Among such as these do you move every hour of the day and night. Only you and I have seen, for God is merciful and has spared our race from sight. But I am not merciful! I loathe the race which gave these creatures birth—the race which might be so surrounded by invisible, unguessed but blessed beings—and chooses these for its companions! All the world shall see and know. One by one shall they come here, learn the truth, and perish. For who can survive the ultimate of terror? Then I, too, shall find peace, and leave the earth to its heritage of man-created horrors. Do you know what these are—whence they come?"

This voice boomed now like a cathedral bell. I could not answer, him, but he waited for no reply. "Out of the ether—out of the omnipresent ether from whose intangible substance the mind of God made the planets, all living things, and man—man has made these! By his evil thoughts, by his selfish panics, by his lusts and his interminable, never-ending hate he has made them, and they are everywhere! Fear nothing—but see where there comes to you, its creator, the shape and the body of your FEAR!"

And as he said it I perceived a great Thing coming toward me—a Thing—but consciousness could endure no more.

The ringing, threatening voice merged in a roar within my ears, there came a merciful dimming of the terrible, lurid vision, and blank nothingness succeeded upon horror too great for bearing.

IV.

There was a dull, heavy pain above my eyes. I knew that they were closed, that I was dreaming, and that the rack full of colored bottles which I seemed to see so clearly was no more than a part of the dream. There was some vague but imperative reason why I should rouse myself. I wanted to awaken, and thought that by staring very hard indeed I could dissolve this foolish vision of blue and yellow-brown bottles. But instead of dissolving they grew clearer, more solid and substantial of appearance, until suddenly the rest of my senses rushed to the support of sight, and I became aware that my eyes were open, the bottles were quite real, and that I was sitting in a chair, fallen sideways so that my cheek rested most uncomfortably on the table which held the rack.

I straightened up slowly and with difficulty, groping in my dulled brain for some clue to my presence in this unfamiliar place, this laboratory that was lighted only by the rays of an arc light in the street outside its three large windows. Here I sat, alone, and if the aching of cramped limbs meant anything, here I had sat for more than a little time.

Then, with the painful shock which accompanies awakening to the knowledge of some great catastrophe, came memory. It was this very room, shown by the street lamp's rays to be empty of life, which I had seen thronged with creatures too loathsome for description. I staggered to my feet, staring fearfully about. There were the glass-floored cases, the bookshelves, the two tables with their burdens, and the long iron sink above which, now only a dark blotch of shadow, hung the lamp from which had emanated that livid, terrifically revealing illumination. Then the experience had been no dream, but a frightful reality. I was alone here now. With callous indifference my strange host had allowed me to remain for hours unconscious, with not the least effort to aid or revive me. Perhaps, hating me so, he had hoped that I would die there.

At first I made no effort to leave the place. Its appearance filled me with reminiscent loathing. I longed to go, but as yet felt too weak and ill for the effort. Both mentally and physically my condition was deplorable, and for the first time I realized that a shock to the mind may react upon the body as vilely as any debauch of self-indulgence.

Quivering in every nerve and muscle, dizzy with headache and nausea, I dropped back into the chair, hoping that before the old man returned I might recover sufficient self-control to escape him. I knew that he hated me, and why. As I waited, sick, miserable, I understood the man. Shuddering, I recalled the loathsome horrors he had shown me. If the mere desires and emotions of mankind were daily carnified in such forms as those, no wonder that he viewed his fellow beings with detestation and longed only to destroy them.

I thought, too, of the cruel, sensuous faces I had seen in the streets outside—seen for the first time, as if a veil had been withdrawn from eyes hitherto blinded by self-delusion. Fatuously trustful as a month-old puppy, I had lived in a grim, evil world, where goodness is a word and crude selfishness the only actuality. Drearily my thoughts drifted back through my own life, its futile purposes, mistakes and activities. All of evil that I knew returned to overwhelm me. Our gropings toward divinity were a sham, a writhing sunward of slime-covered beasts who claimed sunlight as their heritage, but in their hearts preferred the foul and easy depths.

Even now, though I could neither see nor feel them, this room, the entire world, was acrawl with the beings created by our real natures. I recalled the cringing, contemptible fear to which my spirit had so readily yielded, and the faceless Thing to which the emotion had given birth.

Then abruptly, shockingly, I remembered that every moment I was adding to the horde. Since my mind could conceive only repulsive incubi, and since while I lived I must think, feel, and so continue to shape them, was there no way to check so abominable a succession? My eyes fell on the long shelves with their many-colored bottles. In the chemistry of photography there are deadly poisons—I knew that. Now was the time to end it—now! Let him return and find his desire accomplished. One good thing I could do, if one only. I could abolish my monster-creating self.

V.

My friend Mark Jenkins is an intelligent and usually a very careful man. When he took from "Smiler" Callahan a cigar which had every appearance of being excellent, innocent Havana, the act denoted both intelligence and caution. By very clever work he had traced the poisoning of young Ralph Peeler to Mr. Callahan's door, and he believed this particular cigar to be the mate of one smoked by Peeler just previous to his demise. And if, upon arresting Callahan, he had not confiscated this bit of evidence, it would have doubtless been destroyed by its regrettably unconscientious owner.

But when Jenkins shortly afterward gave me that cigar, as one of his own, he committed one of those almost inconceivable blunders which, I think, are occasionally forced upon clever men to keep them from overweening vanity. Discovering his slight mistake, my detective friend spent the night searching for his unintended victim, myself; and that his search was successful was due to Pietro Marini, a young Italian of Jenkins' acquaintance, whom he met about the hour of 2:00 A.M. returning from a dance.

Now, Marini had seen me standing on the steps of the house where Doctor Frederick Holt had his laboratory and living rooms, and he had stared at me, not with any ill intent, but because he thought I was the sickest-looking, most ghastly specimen of humanity that he had ever beheld. And, sharing the superstition of his South Street neighbors, he wondered if the worthy doctor had poisoned me as well as Peeler. This suspicion he imparted to Jenkins, who, however, had the best of reasons for believing otherwise. Moreover, as he informed Marini, Holt was dead, having drowned himself late the previous afternoon. An hour or so after our talk in the restaurant, news of his suicide reached Jenkins.

It seemed wise to search any place where a very sick-looking young man had been seen to enter, so Jenkins came straight to the laboratory. Across the fronts of those houses was the long sign with its mysterious inscription, "See the

Great Unseen," not at all mysterious to the detective. He knew that next door to Doctor Holt's the second floor had been thrown together into a lecture room, where at certain hours a young man employed by settlement workers displayed upon a screen stereopticon views of various deadly bacilli, the germs of diseases appropriate to dirt and indifference. He knew, too, that Doctor Holt himself had helped the educational effort along by providing some really wonderful lantern slides, done by micro-color photography.

On the pavement outside, Jenkins found the two-thirds remnant of a cigar, which he gathered in and came up the steps, a very miserable and self-reproachful detective. Neither outer nor inner door was locked, and in the laboratory he found me, alive, but on the verge of death by another means that he had feared.

In the extreme physical depression following my awakening from drugged sleep, and knowing nothing of its cause, I believed my adventure fact in its entirety. My mentality was at too low an ebb to resist its dreadful suggestion. I was searching among Holt's various bottles when Jenkins burst in. At first I was merely annoyed at the interruption of my purpose, but before the anticlimax of his explanation the mists of obsession drifted away and left me still sick in body, but in spirit happy as any man may well be who has suffered a delusion that the world is wholly bad—and learned that its badness springs from his own poisoned brain.

The malice which I had observed in every face, including young Marini's, existed only in my drug-affected vision. Last week's "popular-science" lecture had been recalled to my subconscious mind—the mind that rules dreams and delirium—by the photographic apparatus in Holt's workroom.

"See the Great Unseen" assisted materially, and even the corner drug store before which I had paused, with its green-lit show vases, had doubtless played a part. But presently, following something Jenkins told me, I was driven to one protest. "If Holt was not here," I demanded, "if Holt is dead, as you say, how do you account for the fact that I, who have never seen the man, was able to give you an accurate description which you admit to be that of Doctor Frederick Holt?"

He pointed across the room. "See that?" It was a life-size bust portrait, in crayons, the picture of a white-haired man with bushy eyebrows and the most piercing black eyes I had ever seen—until the previous evening. It hung facing the door and near the windows, and the features stood out with a strangely lifelike appearance in the white rays of the arc lamp just outside. "Upon entering," continued Jenkins, "the first thing you saw was that portrait, and from it your delirium built a living, speaking man. So, there are your white-haired showman, your unnatural fear, your color photography and your pretty green golliwogs all nicely explained for you, Blaisdell, and thank God you're alive to hear the explanation. If you had smoked the whole of that cigar—well, never mind. You didn't. And now, my very dear friend, I think it's high time that you interviewed a real, flesh-and-blood doctor. I'll phone for a taxi."

"Don't," I said. "A walk in the fresh air will do me more good than fifty doctors."

"Fresh air! There's no fresh air on South Street in July," complained Jenkins, but reluctantly yielded.

I had a reason for my preference. I wished to see people, to meet face to face even such stray prowlers as might be about at this hour, nearer sunrise than midnight, and rejoice in the goodness and kindliness of the human countenance—particularly as found in the lower classes.

But even as we were leaving there occurred to me a curious inconsistency.

"Jenkins," I said, "you claim that the reason Holt, when I first met him in the hall, appeared to twice close the door in my face, was because the door never opened until I myself unlatched it."

"Yes," confirmed Jenkins, but he frowned, foreseeing my next question.

"Then why, if it was from that picture that I built so solid, so convincing a vision of the man, did I see Holt in the hall before the door was open?"

"You confuse your memories," retorted Jenkins rather shortly.

"Do I? Holt was dead at that hour, but—I tell you I saw Holt outside the door! And what was his reason for committing suicide?"

Before my friend could reply I was across the room, fumbling in the dusk there at the electric lamp above the sink. I got the tin flap open and pulled out the sliding screen, which consisted of two sheets of glass with fabric between, dark on one side, yellow on the other. With it came the very thing I dreaded—a sheet of whitish, parchmentlike, slightly opalescent stuff.

Jenkins was beside me as I held it at arm's length toward the windows. Through it the light of the arc lamp fell—divided into the most astonishingly brilliant rainbow hues. And instead of diminishing the light, it was perceptibly increased in the oddest way. Almost one thought that the sheet itself was luminous, and yet when held in shadow it gave off no light at all.

"Shall we—put it in the lamp again—and try it?" asked Jenkins slowly, and in his voice there was no hint of mockery.

I looked him straight in the eyes. "No," I said, "we won't. I was drugged. Perhaps in that condition I received a merciless revelation of the discovery that caused Holt's suicide, but I don't believe it. Ghost or no ghost, I refuse to ever again believe in the depravity of the human race. If the air and the earth are teeming with invisible horrors, they are not of our making, and—the study of demonology is better let alone. Shall we burn this thing, or tear it up?"

"We have no right to do either," returned Jenkins thoughtfully, "but you know, Blaisdell, there's a little too darn much realism about some parts of your 'dream.' I haven't been smoking any doped cigars; but when you held that up to the light, I'll swear I saw—well, never mind. Burn it—send it back to the place it came from."

"South America?" said I.

"A hotter place than that. Burn it."

So he struck a match and we did. It was gone in one great white flash.

A large place was given by morning papers to the suicide of Doctor Frederick Holt, caused, it was surmised, by mental derangement brought about by his unjust implication in the Peeler murder. It seemed an inadequate reason, since he had never been arrested, but no other was ever discovered.

Of course, our action in destroying that "membrane" was illegal and rather precipitate, but, though he won't talk about it, I know that Jenkins agrees with me—doubt is sometimes better than certainty, and there are marvels better left unproved. Those, for instance, which concern the Powers of Evil.

Lukundoo (1927)

Edward Lucas White

"It stands to reason," said Twombly, "that a man must accept of his own eyes, and when eyes and ears agree, there can be no doubt. He has to believe what he has both seen and heard."

"Not always," put in Singleton, softly.

Every man turned toward Singleton. Twombly was standing on hearthrug, his back to the grate, his legs spread out, with his habitual air of dominating the room. Singleton, as usual, was as much as possible effaced in a corner. But when Singleton spoke he said something. We faced him in that flattering spontaneity of expectant silence which invites utterance.

"I was thinking," he said, after an interval, "of something I both saw and heard in Africa."

Now, if there was one thing we had found impossible, it had been to elicit from Singleton anything definite about his African experiences. As with the Alpinist in the story, who could tell only that he went up and came down, the sum of Singleton's revelations had been that he went there and came away. His words now riveted our attention at once. Twombly faded from the hearthrug, but not one of us could ever recall having seen him go. The room readjusted itself, focused on Singleton, and there was some hasty and furtive lighting of fresh cigars. Singleton lit one also, but it went out immediately, and he never relit it.

Chapter I

We were in the Great Forest, exploring for pigmies. Van Rieten had a theory that the dwarfs found by Stanley and others were a mere cross-breed between ordinary negroes and the real pigmies. He hoped to discover a race of men three feet tall at most, or shorter. We had found no trace of any such beings.

Natives were few, game scarce; food, except game, there was none; and the deepest, dankest, drippingest forest all about. We were the only novelty in the country, no native we met had ever seen a white man before, most had never heard of white men. All of a sudden, late one afternoon, there came into our camp an Englishman, and pretty well used up he was, too. We had heard no rumor of him; he had not only heard of us but had made an amazing five-day march to reach us. His guide and two bearers were nearly as done up as he. Even though he was in tatters and had five days' beard on, you could see he was naturally dapper and neat and the sort of man to shave daily. He was small, but wiry. His face was the sort of British face from which emotion has been so carefully banished that a foreigner is apt to think the wearer of the face incapable of any sort of feeling; the kind of face which, if it has any expression at all, expresses principally the resolution to go through the world decorously, without intruding upon or annoying anyone.

His name was Etcham. He introduced himself modestly, and ate with us so deliberately that we should never have suspected, if our bearers had not had it from his bearers, that he had had but three meals in the five days, and those small. After we had lit up he told us why he had come.

"My chief is ve'y seedy," he said between puffs. "He is bound to go out if he keeps this way. I thought perhaps..."

He spoke quietly in a soft, even tone, but I could see little beads of sweat oozing out on his upper lip under his stubby mustache, and there was a tingle of repressed emotion in his tone, a veiled eagerness in his eye, a palpitating inward solicitude in his demeanor that moved me at once. Van Rieten had no sentiment in him; if he was moved he did not show it. But he listened. I was surprised at that. He was just the man to refuse at once. But he listened to Etcham's halting, difficult hints. He even asked questions.

"Who is your chief?"

"Stone," Etcham lisped.

That electrified both of us.

"Ralph Stone?" we ejaculated together. Etcham nodded.

For some minutes Van Rieten and I were silent. Van Rieten had never seen him, but I had been a classmate of Stone's, and Van Rieten and I had discussed him over many a campfire. We had heard of him two years before, south of Luebo in the Balunda country, which had been ringing with his theatrical strife against a Balunda witch-doctor, ending in the sorcerer's complete discomfiture and the abasement of his tribe before Stone. They had even broken the fetish-man's whistle and given Stone the pieces. It had been like the triumph of Elijah over the prophets of Baal, only more real to the Balunda.

We had thought of Stone as far off, if still in Africa at all, and here he turned up ahead of us and probably forestalling our quest.

Chapter II

Etcham's naming of Stone brought back to us all his tantalizing story, his fascinating parents, their tragic death; the brilliance of his college days; the dazzle of his millions; the promise of his young manhood; his wide notoriety, so nearly real fame; his romantic elopement with the meteoric authoress whose sudden cascade of fiction had made her so great a name so young, whose beauty and charm were so much heralded; the frightful scandal of the breach-of-promise suit that followed; his bride's devotion through it all; their sudden quarrel after it was all over; their divorce; the too much advertised announcement of his approaching marriage to the plaintiff in the breach-of-promise suit; his precipitate remarriage to his divorced bride; their second quarrel and second divorce; his departure from his native land; his advent in the dark continent. The sense of all this rushed over me and I believe Van Rieten felt it, too, as he sat silent.

Then he asked:

"Where is Werner?"

"Dead," said Etcham. "He died before I joined Stone."

"You were not with Stone above Luebo?"

"No," said Etcham, "I joined him at Stanley Falls."

"Who is with him?" Van Rieten asked.

"Only his Zanzibar servants and the bearers," Etcham replied. "What sort of bearers?" Van Rieten demanded.

"Mang-Battu men," Etcham responded simply.

Now that impressed both Van Rieten and myself greatly. It bore out Stone's reputation as a notable leader of men. For up to that time no one had been able to use Mang-Battu as bearers outside of their own country, or to hold them for long or difficult expeditions.

"Were you long among the Mang-Battu?" was Van Rieten's next question.

"Some weeks," said Etcham. "Stone was interested in them and made up a fair-sized vocabulary of their words and phrases. He had a theory that they are an offshoot of the Balunda and he found much confirmation in their customs."

"What do you live on?" Van Rieten enquired.

"Game, mostly," Etcham lisped.

"How long has Stone been laid up?" Van Rieten next asked.

"More than a month," Etcham answered.

"And you have been hunting for the camp?" Van Rieten exclaimed. Etcham's face, burnt and flayed as it was, showed a flush.

"I missed some easy shots," he admitted ruefully. "I've not felt ve'y fit myself."

"What's the matter with your chief?" Van Rieten enquired.

"Something like carbuncles," Etcham replied.

"He ought to get over a carbuncle or two," Van Rieten declared.

"They are not carbuncles," Etcham explained. "Nor one or two. He has had dozens, sometimes five at once. If they had been carbuncles he would have been dead long ago. But in some ways they are not so bad, though in others they are worse."

"How do you mean?" Van Rieten queried.

"Well," Etcham hesitated, "they do not seem to inflame so deep nor so wide as carbuncles, nor to be so painful, nor to cause so much fever. But then they seem to be part of a disease that affects his mind. He let me help him dress the first, but the others he has hidden most carefully, from me and from the men. He keeps his tent when they puff up, and will not let me change the dressings or be with him at all."

"Have you plenty of dressings?" Van Rieten asked.

"We have some," said Etcham doubtfully. "But he won't use them; he washes out the dressings and uses them over and over."

"How is he treating the swellings?" Van Rieten enquired.

"He slices them off clean down to flesh level, with his razor."

"What?" Van Rieten shouted.

Etcham made no answer but looked him steadily in the eyes.

"I beg pardon," Van Rieten hastened to say. "You startled me. They can't be carbuncles. He'd have been dead long ago."

"I thought I had said they are not carbuncles," Etcham lisped. "But the man must be crazy!" Van Rieten exclaimed.

"Just so," said Etcham. "He is beyond my advice or control." "How many has he treated that way?" Van Rieten demanded. "Two, to my knowledge," Etcham said.

"Two?" Van Rieten queried. Etcham flushed again.

"I saw him," he confessed, "through a crack in the hut. I felt impelled to keep a watch on him, as if he was not responsible."

"I should think not," Van Rieten agreed. "And you saw him do that twice?" "I conjecture," said Etcham, "that he did the like with all the rest."

"How many has he had?" Van Rieten asked.

"Dozens," Etcham lisped.

"Does he eat?" Van Rieten enquired.

"Like a wolf," said Etcham. "More than any two bearers."

"Can he walk?" Van Rieten asked.

"He crawls a bit, groaning," said Etcham simply.

"Little fever, you say," Van Rieten ruminated.

"Enough and too much," Etcham declared.

"Has he been delirious?" Van Rieten asked.

"Only twice," Etcham replied; "once when the first swelling broke, and once later. He would not let anyone come near him then. But we could hear him talking, talking steadily, and it scared the natives.

"Was he talking their patter in delirium?" Van Rieten demanded.

"No," said Etcham, "but he was talking some similar lingo. Hamed Burghash said he was talking Balunda. I know too little Balunda. I do not learn languages readily. Stone learned more Mang-Battu in a week than I could have learned in a year. But I seemed to hear words like Mang-Battu words. Anyhow, the Mang-Battu bearers scared."

"Scared?" Van Rieten repeated, questioningly.

"So were the Zanzibar men, even Hamed Burghash, and so was I," said Etcham, "only for a different reason. He talked in two voices."

"In two voices," Van Rieten reflected.

"Yes," said Etcham, more excitedly than he had yet spoken. "In two voices, like a conversation. One was his own, one a small, thin, bleaty voice like nothing I ever heard. I seemed to make out, among the sounds the deep voice made, something like Mang-Battu words I knew, as nedru, metababa, and nedo, their terms for 'head,' 'shoulder,' 'thigh,' and perhaps kudra and nekere ('speak' and 'whistle'); and among the noises of the shrill voice matomipa, angunzi, and kamo-mami ('kill,' 'death,' and 'hate'). Hamed Burghash said he also heard those words. He knew Mang-Battu far better than I."

"What did the bearers say?" Van Rieten asked.

"They said, ', Lukundoo!'" Etcham replied. "I did not know the word; Hamed Burghash said it was Mang-Battu for 'leopard.'"

"It's Mang-Battu for 'witchcraft,'" said Van Rieten.

"I don't wonder they thought so," said Etcham. "It was enough to make one believe in sorcery to listen to those two voices."

"One voice answering the other?" Van Rieten asked perfunctorily. Etcham's face went gray under his tan.

"Sometimes both at once," he answered huskily.

"Both at once!" Van Rieten ejaculated.

"It sounded that way to the men, too," said Etcham. "And that was not all." He stopped and looked helplessly at us for a moment.

"Could a man talk and whistle at the same time?" he asked.

"How do you mean?" Van Rieten queried.

"We could hear Stone talking away, his big, deep-cheated baritone rumbling along, and through it all we could hear a high, shrill whistle, the oddest, wheezy sound. You know, no matter how shrilly a grown man may whistle, the note has a different quality from the whistle of a boy or a woman or a little girl. They sound more treble, somehow. Well, if you can imagine the smallest girl who could whistle keeping it up tunelessly right along, that whistle was like that, only even more piercing, and it sounded right through Stone's bass tones."

"And you didn't go to him?" Van Rieten cried.

"He is not given to threats," Etcham disclaimed. "But he had threatened, not volubly, nor like a sick man, but quietly and firmly, that if any man of us (he lumped me in with the men) came near him while he was in his trouble, that man should die. And it was not so much his words as his manner. It was like a monarch commanding respected privacy for a deathbed. One simply could not transgress."

"I see," said Van Rieten shortly.

"He's ve'y seedy," Etcham repeated helplessly. "I thought perhaps...."

His absorbing affection for Stone, his real love for him, shone out through his envelope of conventional training. Worship of Stone was plainly his master passion.

Like many competent men, Van Rieten had a streak of hard selfishness in him. It came to the surface then. He said we carried our lives in our hands from day to day just as genuinely as Stone; that he did not forget the ties of blood and calling between any two explorers, but that there was no sense in imperiling one party for a very problematical benefit to a man probably beyond any help; that it was enough of a task to hunt for one party; that if two were united, providing food would be more than doubly difficult; that the risk of starvation was too great. Deflecting our march seven full days' journey (he complimented Etcham on his marching powers) might ruin our expedition entirely.

Chapter III

Van Rieten had logic on his side and he had a way with him. Etcham sat there apologetic and deferential, like a fourth-form schoolboy before a head master. Van Rieten wound up.

"I am after pigmies, at the risk of my life. After pigmies I go." "Perhaps, then, these will interest you," said Etcham, very quietly.

He took two objects out of the sidepocket of his blouse, and handed them to Van Rieten. They were round, bigger than big plums, and smaller than small peaches, about the right size to enclose in an average hand. They were black, and at first I did not see what they were.

"Pigmies!" Van Rieten exclaimed. "Pigmies, indeed! Why, they wouldn't be two feet high! Do you mean to claim that these are adult heads?"

"I claim nothing," Etcham answered evenly. "You can see for yourself."

Van Rieten passed one of the heads to me. The sun was just setting and I examined it closely. A dried head it was, perfectly preserved, and the flesh as hard as Argentine jerked beef. A bit of a vertebra stuck out where the muscles of the vanished neck had shriveled into folds. The puny chin was sharp on a projecting jaw, the minute teeth white and even between the retracted lips, the tiny nose was flat, the little forehead retreating, there were inconsiderable clumps of stunted wool on the Lilliputian cranium. There was nothing babyish, childish or youthful about the head; rather it was mature to senility.

"Where did these come from?" Van Rieten enquired.

"I do not know," Etcham replied precisely. "I found them among Stone's effects while rummaging for medicines or drugs or anything that could help me to help him. I do not know where he got them. But I'll swear he did not have them when we entered this district."

"Are you sure?" Van Rieten queried, his eyes big and fixed on Etcham's.

"Ve'y sure," lisped Etcham.

"But how could he have come by them without your knowledge?" Van Rieten demurred.

"Sometimes we were apart ten days at a time hunting," said Etcham. "Stone is not a talking man. He gave me no account of his doings, and Hamed Burghash keeps a still tongue and a tight hold on the men."

"You have examined these heads?" Van Rieten asked. "Minutely," said Etcham.

Van Rieten took out his notebook. He was a methodical chap. He tore out a leaf, folded it and divided it equally into three pieces. He gave one to me and one to Etcham.

"Just for a test of my impressions," he said, "I want each of us to write separately just what he is most reminded of by these heads. Then I want to compare the writings."

I handed Etcham a pencil and he wrote. Then he handed the pencil back to me and I wrote.

Chapter IV

"Read the three," said Van Rieten, handing me his piece. Van Rieten had written:"An old Balunda witch-doctor."

Etcham had written:

"An old Mang-Battu fetish-man."

I had written:

"An old Katongo magician."

"There!" Van Rieten exclaimed. "Look at that! There is nothing Wagabi or Batwa or Wambuttu or Wabotu about these heads. Nor anything pigmy either."

"I thought as much," said Etcham.

"And you say he did not have them before?"

"To a certainty he did not," Etcham asserted.

"It is worth following up," said Van Rieten. "I'll go with you. And first of all, I'll do my best to save Stone." He put out his hand and Etcham clasped it silently. He was grateful all over.

Chapter V

Nothing but Etcham's fever of solicitude could have taken him in five days over the track. It took him eight days to retrace with full knowledge of it and our party to help. We could not have done it in seven, and Etcham urged us on, in a repressed fury of anxiety, no mere fever of duty to his chief, but a real ardor of devotion, a glow of personal adoration for Stone which blazed under his dry conventional exterior and showed in spite of him.

We found Stone well cared for. Etcham had seen to a good, high thorn zareeba round the camp, the huts were well built, and thatched and Stone's was as good as their resources would permit. Hamed Burghash was not named after two Seyyids for nothing. He had in him the making of a sultan. He had kept the Mang-Battu together, not a man had slipped off, and he had kept them in order. Also he was a deft nurse and a faithful servant.

The two other Zanzibaris had done some creditable hunting. Though all were hungry, the camp was far from starvation.

Stone was on a canvas cot and there was a sort of collapsible camp-stool-table, like a Turkish tabouret, by the cot. It had a water-bottle and some vials on it and Stone's watch, also his razor in its case.

Stone was clean and not emaciated, but he was far gone; not unconscious, but in a daze; past commanding or resisting anyone. He did not seem to see us enter or to know we were there. I should have recognized him anywhere. His boyish dash and grace had vanished utterly, of course. But his head was even more leonine; his hair was still abundant, yellow and wavy; the close, crisped blond beard he had grown during his illness did not alter him. He was big and big-cheated yet. His eyes were dull and he mumbled and babbled mere meaningless syllables, not words.

Etcham helped Van Rieten to uncover him and look him over. He was in good muscle for a man so long bedridden. There were no scars on him except about his knees, shoulders and chest. On each knee and above it he had a full score of roundish cicatrices, and a dozen or more on each shoulder, all in front. Two or three were open wounds and four or five barely healed. He had no fresh swellings, except two, one on each side, on his pectoral muscles, the one on the left being higher up and farther out than the other. They did not look like boils or carbuncles, but as if something blunt and hard were being pushed up through the fairly healthy flesh and skin, not much inflamed.

"I should not lance those," said Van Rieten, and Etcham assented.

They made Stone as comfortable as they could, and just before sunset we looked in at him again. He was lying on his back, and his chest showed big and massive yet, but he lay as if in a stupor. We left Etcham with him and went into the next hut, which Etcham had resigned to us. The jungle noises were no different than anywhere else for months past, and I was soon fast asleep.

Chapter VI

Sometime in the pitch dark I found myself awake and listening. I could hear two voices, one Stone's, the other sibilant and wheezy. I knew Stone's voice after all the years that had passed since I heard it last. The other was like nothing I remembered. It had less volume than the wail of a new-born baby, yet there was an insistent carrying power to it, like the shrilling of an insect. As I listened I heard Van Rieten breathing near me in the dark; then he heard me and realized that I was listening, too. Like Etcham I knew little Balunda, but I could make out a word or two. The voices alternated, with intervals of silence between.

Then suddenly both sounded at once and fast. Stone's baritone basso, full as if he were in perfect health, and that incredibly stridulous falsetto, both jabbering at once like the voices of two people quarreling and trying to talk each other down.

"I can't stand this," said Van Rieten. "Let's have a look at him."

He had one of those cylindrical electric night-candles. He fumbled about for it, touched the button and beckoned me to come with him. Outside the hut he motioned me to stand still, and instinctively turned off the light, as if seeing made listening difficult.

Except for a faint glow from the embers of the bearers' fire we were in complete darkness, little starlight struggled through the trees, the river made but a faint murmur. We could hear the two voices together and then suddenly the creaking voice changed into a razor-edged, slicing whistle, indescribably cutting, continuing right through Stone's grumbling torrent of croaking words.

"Good God!" exclaimed Van Rieten. Abruptly he turned on the light.

We found Etcham utterly asleep, exhausted by his long anxiety and the exertions of his phenomenal march, and relaxed completely now that the load was in a sense shifted from his shoulders to Van Rieten's. Even the light on his face did not wake him.

The whistle had ceased and the two voices now sounded together. Both came from Stone's cot, where the concentrated white ray showed him lying just as we had left him, except that he had tossed his arms above his head and had torn the coverings and bandages from his chest.

The swelling on his right breast had broken. Van Rieten aimed the center line of the light at it and we saw it plainly. From his flesh, grown out of it, there protruded a head, such a head as the dried specimens Etcham had shown us, as if it were a miniature of the head of a Balunda fetish-man. It was black, shining black as the blackest African skin; it rolled the whites of its wicked, wee eyes and showed its microscopic teeth between lips repulsively negroid in their red fullness, even in so diminutive a face. It had crisp, fuzzy wool on its minikin skull, it turned malignantly from side to side and chittered incessantly in that inconceivable falsetto. Stone babbled brokenly against its patter.

Van Rieten turned from Stone and waked Etcham, with some difficulty. When he was awake and saw it all, Etcham stared and said not one word.

"You saw him slice off two swellings?" Van Rieten asked. Etcham nodded, chokingly."Did he bleed much?" Van Rieten demanded.

"Ve'y little," Etcham replied.

"You hold his arms," said Van Rieten to Etcham.

He took up Stone's razor and handed me the light. Stone showed no sign of seeing the light or of knowing we were there. But the little head mewled and screeched at us.

Van Rieten's hand was steady, and the sweep of the razor even and true. Stone bled amazingly little and Van Rieten dressed the wound as if it had been a bruise or scrape.

Stone had stopped talking the instant the excrescent head was severed. Van Rieten did all that could be done for Stone and then fairly grabbed the light from me. Snatching up a gun he scanned the ground by the cot and brought the butt down once and twice, viciously.

We went back to our hut, but I doubt if I slept.

Chapter VII

Next day, near noon, in broad daylight, we heard the two voices from Stone's hut. We found Etcham dropped asleep by his charge. The swelling on the left had broken, and just such another head was there miauling and spluttering. Etcham woke up and the three of us stood there and glared. Stone interjected hoarse vocables into the tinkling gurgle of the portent's utterance.

Van Rieten stepped forward, took up Stone's razor and knelt down by the cot. The atomy of a head squealed a wheezy snarl at him.

Then suddenly Stone spoke English.

"Who are you with my razor?"

Van Rieten started back and stood up.

Stone's eyes were clear now and bright, they roved about the hut.

"The end," he said; "I recognize the end. I seem to see Etcham, as if in life. But Singleton! Ah, Singleton! Ghosts of my boyhood come to watch me pass! And you, strange specter with the black beard and my razor! Aroint ye all!"

"I'm no ghost, Stone," I managed to say. "I'm alive. So are Etcham and Van Rieten. We are here to help you." "Van Rieten!" he exclaimed. "My work passes on to a better man. Luck go with you, Van Rieten."

Van Rieten went nearer to him.

"Just hold still a moment, old man," he said soothingly. "It will be only one twinge."

"I've held still for many such twinges," Stone answered quite distinctly. "Let me be. Let me die in my own way. The hydra was nothing to this. You can cut off ten, a hundred, a thousand heads, but the curse you can not cut off, or take off. What's soaked into the bone won't come out of the flesh, any more than what's bred there. Don't hack me any more. Promise!"

His voice had all the old commanding tone of his boyhood and it swayed Van Rieten as it always had swayed everybody.

"I promise," said Van Rieten.

Almost as he said the word Stone's eyes filmed again.

Then we three sat about Stone and watched that hideous, gibbering prodigy grow up out of Stone's flesh, till two horrid, spindling little black arms disengaged themselves. The infinitesimal nails were perfect to the barely perceptible moon at the quick, the pink spot on the palm was horridly natural. These arms gesticulated and the right plucked toward Stone's blond beard.

"I can't stand this," Van Rieten exclaimed and took up the razor again. Instantly Stone's eyes opened, hard and glittering.

"Van Rieten break his word?" he enunciated slowly. "Never!"

"But we must help you," Van Rieten gasped.

"I am past all help and all hurting," said Stone. "This is my hour. This curse is not put on me; it grew out of me, like this horror here. Even now I go."

His eyes closed and we stood helpless, the adherent figure spouting shrill sentences. In a moment Stone spoke again.

"You speak all tongues?" he asked quickly.

And the mergent minikin replied in sudden English:

"Yea, verily, all that you speak," putting out its microscopic tongue, writhing its lips and wagging its head from side to side. We could see the thready ribs on its exiguous flanks heave as if the thing breathed.

"Has she forgiven me?" Stone asked in a muffled strangle.

"Not while the moss hangs from the cypresses," the head squeaked. "Not while the stars shine on Lake Pontchartrain will she forgive."

And then Stone, all with one motion, wrenched himself over on his side. The next instant he was dead.

When Singleton's voice ceased the room was hushed for a space. We could hear each other breathing. Twombly, the tactless, broke the silence.

"I presume," he said, "you cut off the little minikin and brought it home in alcohol." Singleton turned on him a stern countenance.

"We buried Stone," he said, "unmutilated as he died."

"But," said the unconscionable Twombly, "the whole thing is incredible."

Singleton stiffened.

"I did not expect you to believe it," he said; "I began by saying that although I heard and saw it, when I look back on it I cannot credit it myself."

The Ghost in All the Rooms (1727)

Daniel Defoe

A certain person of quality, being with his family at his country seat for the summer season, according to his ordinary custom, was obliged, upon a particular occasion of health, to leave his said seat and go to Aix-la-Chapelle, to use the baths there. This was, it seems, in the month of August, being two months sooner than the usual time of his returning to court for the winter.

Upon thus removing sooner than ordinary he did not then disfurnish the house, as was the ordinary usage of the family, or carry away his plate and other valuable goods, but left his steward and three servants to look after the house. And the padre or parish priest was desired to keep his eye upon them too and to succor them from the village adjoining, if there was occasion.

The steward had no public notice of any harm approaching, but for three or four days successfully he had secret strange impulses of dread and terror upon his mind that the house was beset, and was to be assaulted by a troop of banditti, or as we call them here housebreakers, who would murder them all, and after they had robbed the house would set it on fire. And this followed him so fast and made such an impression upon his mind that he could think of nothing else.

Upon this, the third day he went to the padre or parish priest and made his complaint. Upon which the priest and the steward had the following discourse, the steward beginning thus:

"Father," said he, "you know what a charge I have in my custody and how my lord has entrusted me with the whole house, and all the rich furniture is standing. I am in great perplexity about it and come to you for your advice."

Priest: Why, what's the matter? You have not heard of any mischief threatened, have you?

Steward: No, I have heard nothing. But I have such apprehensions and it has made such impression upon me for these three days that—

Here he told him the particulars of the uneasiness he had been in and added, besides what is said above, that one of the servants had the same and had told him of it, though he had communicated nothing to that servant in the least.

Priest: It may be you dreamed of these things?

Steward: No, indeed, padre! I am sure I could not dream of them, for I could never sleep.

Priest: What can I do for you? What would you have me do?

Steward: I would have you first of all tell me what you think of these things, and whether there is any notice to be taken of them.

Here the padre examined him more strictly about the particulars, and sent for the servant and examined him apart and being a very judicious honest man, he answered him thus:

Priest: Look you, Mr. Steward, I do not lay a very great stress upon such things, but yet I don't think they are to be wholly slighted. And therefore I would have you be upon your guard, and if you have the least alarm, let me know.

Steward: That is poor satisfaction to me to be upon my guard, if I am overpowered. I suppose if any villains have a design to attack me the know my strength.

Priest: Shall I reinforce your garrison?

Steward: I wish you would.

Priest: Well, I'll send you some men with firearms to lie there this night.

Accordingly the priest sent him five stout fellows with fusees, and a dozen of hand grenadoes with them, and while they continued in the house nothing appeared. But the padre, finding nothing come of it and being loath to put his patron to so continued a charge, sent for the steward and in a chiding angry tone told him his mind.

Priest: I know not how you will answer it to my lord, bu you have put him to a prodigious expense here, in keeping a garrison in the house all this while.

Steward: I am sorry for it, padre, but what can I do?

Priest: Do! Why, compose your mind, and keep up your heart, and don't let my lord spend two or three hundred livres here to cure you of the vapours.

Steward: Why, you said yourself, padre, that it was not to be wholly slighted.

Priest: That's true; but I said also I would not lay too great a stress upon it.

Steward: What must I do then?

Priest: Do? Why, dismiss the men again and take what care you can. And if you have any notice of mischief that may be depended upon, let me have notice too, and I will assist you.

Steward: Well, then, the good angel must protect my lord's house, I see, for nobody else will.

"Amen," says the padre, "I trust the good spirits will keep you all." So he blessed the steward (in his way) and the steward went away grumbling very much that he took away his garrison and left him to the good spirits.

It seems, for all this, that the steward's notices, however secret and from he knew not who, were not of so light an import as the padre thought they were. For as he had this impulse upon his mind that such mischief was brewing, so it really was, as you will see presently.

A set of robbers, who had intelligence that the nobleman with his family was gone to Aix-la-Chapelle, but that the house was left furnished and all the plate and the things of value were left in it, had formed a design to plunder the house and afterwards to burn it, just as the steward had said.

The were two and twenty strong, in the whole, and thoroughly armed for mischief. Yet while the additional force which the padre had placed to reinforce the steward were in the house, of whom, including the other four, three sat up every night, they did not attempt it.

But as soon as they heard that the guard was dismissed, they formed their design anew, and to make the story short they attacked the house about midnight. Having, I suppose, proper instruments about them, they soon broke open a window and twelve of them got into the house, the rest standing sentinel at such places they though proper, to prevent any succours from the town.

The poor steward and his three men were in distress. They were indeed above stairs, and had barricaded the staircases as well as they could, hearing the fellows were breaking in. But when they found they were got in, they expected nothing but to be kept above stairs till the house was plundered, and then to be burnt alive.

But it seems the good spirits the priest spoke of, or somebody else, made better provision for them, as you will see presently.

When the first of the fellows got into the house, and had opened the door and let in as meany of their gang as they thought fit, which as above, was twelve in number, they shut the door again and shut themselves in; leaving two without the door, who had a watchword, to go and call more help if they wanted it.

The twelve ranging over the great hall found little there to gratify their greedy hopes. But breaking next into a fine well furnished parlour where the family usually sat, behold! in a great easy chair sat a grave ancient man with a long full-bottomed black wig, a rich brocaded gown, and a lawyer's laced band, but looking as if in great surprise, seems to make signs to them for mercy; but said not a word, no they much to him, except that one of them, starting, cried, "Ha! Who's here?"

Immediately the rogues fell to pulling down the fine damask curtains in the windows, and other rich things; but one said to another with an oath, "Make the old dog tell us where the plate is hid." And another said, "If he won't tell you, cut his throat immediately.

The ancient gentleman, with signs of entreaty, as if begging for his life, and in a great fright, points to a door which being opened would let them into another parlour, which was the gaming room, and served as a drawing room to the first parlour, and by another door opened into the great saloon which looked into the gardens. They were some time forcing their way into that room, but when they came in, they were surprised to see the same old man, in the same dress and same chair, sitting at the upper end of the room, making the same gestures and silent entreaties as before.

They were not much concerned at first, but thought he had come in by another door, and began to swear at him for putting them to the trouble of breaking open the door when there was another way into the room. But another, wickeder than the first, said with a heavy curse: the old dog was got in by another door on purpose to convey away the plate and money; and bade knock his brains out. Upon which the first swore at him that if he did not immediately show them where it was he was a dead dog that moment.

Upon this furious usage he points to the doors which opened into the saloon, which, being a thin pair of folding doors, opened presently, and in they run into the great saloon; when looks at the further end of the room, there sat the ancient man again, in the same dress and posture as before.

Upon this sight, those that were foremost among them cried out aloud, "Why this old fellow deals with the Devil, sure! He's here afore us again."

But the case differed a little now, for when they came out of the first parlour, being eager for the plate and money and willing to find it all, the whole body of them run into the second parlour. But now, the ancient man pointing to the third room, they did not all immediately rush into the saloon, but four of them were left behind in the parlour or gaming room mentioned just now, not by order or design, but accidentally.

By this means they fell into the following confusion: for while some of them called out from the saloon that the old rogue was there before them again, others answered out of the parlour, "How the devil can that be? Why, he is here still in his chair, and all his rubbish."

With that, two of them run back into the first parlour, and there they saw him again sitting as before. Notwithstanding all this, far from guessing what the occasion should be, they fancied they were gamed, or suggested that they were but jested with, and that there were three several old men all dressed up in the same habits for the very same occasion, and to mock them, as if to let them know that the men above in the house were not afraid of them.

"Well," says one of the gang, "I'll dispatch one of the old rogues. I'll teach one of them how to make game at us." Upon which, raising his fusee as high as his arm would let him, he struck the ancient man, as he thought it was, with all his force. But behold! There was nothing in the chair, and his fusee flew into a thousand pieces, wounding his hand most grievously. And a piece of the barrel, striking him on the head, broke his face and knocked him down backward.

At the same time, one of those in the saloon running at the ancient man that sat there, swore he would tear his fine brocaded gown off, and then he would cut his throat. But when he went to take hold of him, there was nothing in the chair.

This happening in both rooms, they were all in most horrible confusion, and cried out in both rooms at the same moment, in a terrible manner.

As they were in the utmost amazement at the thing, so after the first clamor they stood looking upon one another for some time, without speaking a word more. But at length one said, "Let's go back into the first parlour and see if that's gone too."

And with that word, two or three that were on that side run into the room, and there sat the ancient figure as at first. Upon which they called to the company and told them they believed they were all bewitched, and it was certain they only fancied they saw a man in the other rooms, for there was the real old man sitting where he was at first.

Upon this they all ryn thither, saying they would see whether it was the devil or no. And one of them said, "Let me come. I'll speak to him. 'Tis not the first time I have talked with the devil."

"Nay," says another, "so will I." And then added with an oath: gentlemen that were upon such business as they were ought not to be afraid to speak to the devil.

A third (for now their courage began to rise again) calls aloud, "Let it be the devil, or the devil's grandmother. I'll parley with it. I am resolved I'll know what it is."

And with that he runs forward before the rest, and, crossing himself, says to the ancient man in the chair, "in the name of St. Francis, and St.—(and so reckoned up two or three saints' names that he depended were enough to fright the devil), what art thou?"

The figure never moved nor spoke. But looking at its face, they presently found that instead of his pitiful looks and seeming to beg for his life, as he did before, he was changed into the most horrible monster that ever was seen, and such as I cannot describe. And that instead of his hands held up to them to cry for mercy, there were two large fiery daggers, not flaming, but redhot and pointed with a livid bluish flame, and, in a word, the devil or something else in the most frightful shape that can be imagined. And it was my opinion, when I first read the story, the rogues were so frighted that their imagination afterwards formed a thing in their thoughts more terrible than the devil himself could appear in.

But be that as it will, his figure was such that when they came up to him not a man of them had courage to look inot his face, much less talk to him. And he that was so bold, and thus came armed with half a regiment of saints in his mouth, fell down flat on the ground, having fainted away, as they call it, with fright.

The steward and his three men were all this while above stairs, in the utmost concern at the danger they were in and expecting every moment the rogues would strive to force their way up, and cut their throats. They heard the confused noise that the fellows made below but could not imagine what it was, and much less the meaning of it. But while it lasted it came into the mind of one of the servants, that as it was certain the fellows were all in the parlour, and very busy there, whatever it was about, he might go up to the top of the house and throw one of their hand grenades down the chimney, and perhaps it might do some execution among them.

The steward approved of this design, only with his addition. "If we throw down but into one parlour, they will all fly into the gaming room, and so it will do no execution. But," says he, "take three, and put down one into each chimney, for the funnels go up all together, and then they will not know which way to run."

With these orders, two of the men who very well knew the place went up, and firing the fuses of the grenades, they put one shell into each of the funnels; and down they went roaring in the chimney with a terrible noise, and (which was more than all the rest) they came down into the parlour where almost all the rogues were, just at the moment that the fellow that spoke to the spectre was frightened into a swooning fit and fallen on the floor.

The whole gang was frighted beyond expression. Some run back into the gaming parlour whence they came, and some run to the other door which they came in at from the hall, but all at the same instant heard the devil, as they thought it was, coming down the chimney.

Had it been possible that the fuses of the grenades could have continued burning in the funnel of the chimneys, where the sound was a thousand times doubled by the hollow of the place, and where the soot burning fell down in flakes of fire, the rogues had been frighted out of their understandings; imagining, that as they had one dreadful devil just among them in the chair, so there were ten thousand more coming down the chimney to destroy them all, and perhaps to carry them all away.

But that could not be. So after they had been sufficiently scared with the noise, down came the shells into the rooms, all three together. It happened as luckily as if it had been contrived on purpose, that the shell which came down into the parlour where they all were, burst as soon as ever it came to the bottom, so that it did not give them time so much as to think what it might be, much less to know that it was really a hand grenade. But as it did great execution among them, so they as certainly believed it was the devil as the believed the spectre in the chair was the devil.

The noise of the bursting of the shell was so sudden and so unexpected that it confounded them, and the mischief was also terrible. The man that fainted and who lay on the ground was killed outright, and two more that stood just before the chimney. Five of them were desperately wounded, whereof one had both his legs broken, and was so desperate that when the people from the country came in, he shot himself through the head with his own pistol to prevent his being taken.

Had the rest of them fled out of the parlour into the two other rooms, it is probable they had been wounded by the other shells. But as they heard the noise in both the other rooms, and besides were under the surprise of its being not a hand grenade, but then devil, they had no power to stir. Nor if they had could they know which way to go to be safe. So they stood still till both the shells in the other rooms burst also. At which, being confounded, as well with the noise as with the smoke, and expecting more devils down the chimney where the stood, they run out all that way, and made to the door, helping their wounded men along as well as they could. Whereof one died in the fields after they were got away.

It must be observed, when they were thus alarmed with they knew not what coming down the chimney, they cried out that the devil in the chair had sent for more devils to destroy them. And it was supposed that had the shells never come down, they would all have run away. But certain it was that the artificial devil joining so critically as to time with the visionary devils, or whatever they were, completed their disorder and forced them to fly.

When they came to the door to the two men, they made signals for their comrades who were posted in the avenues to the house to come to their relief; who accordingly came up, and assisted to carry off their wounded men. But after hearing the relation of those that had been in the house and calling a short council a little away from the door (which, through dark as it was, the steward and his men could percieve from the window), they all resolved to make off.

There was another concurring accident which, though it does not relate to my subject, I must set down to complete the story: that two of these grenades by the fir of their fuses set the chimneys on fire. The third, being in a funnel that had no soot in it, the room having not been so much used, did not. This fire flaming out at the top, as is usual, was seen by somebody in the village, who run immediately and alarmed the priest or padre, and he again raised the whole town, believing there was some mischief fallen out and that the house was set on fire.

Had the rest of the gang not resolved to make off as is said above, they had certainly fallen into the hands of the townsmen, who ran immediately with what arms came next to hand, to the house. But the rogues were fled, leaving, as above, three of their company dead in the house, and one in the field.

Excerpt from *The History and Reality of Apparitions,* (1727)

What Was It? — A Mystery (1859)

Fitz James O'Brien

It is, I confess, with considerable diffidence that I approach the strange narrative which I am about to relate. The events which I purpose detailing are of so extraordinary and unheard-of a character that I am quite prepared to meet with an unusual amount of incredulity and scorn. I accept all such beforehand. I have, I trust, the literary courage to face unbelief. I have, after mature consideration, resolved to narrate, in as simple and straightforward a manner as I can compass, some facts that passed under my observation in the month of July last, and which, in the annals of the mysteries of physical science, are wholly unparalleled.

I live at No.— Twenty-sixth Street, in this city. The house is in some respects a curious one. It has enjoyed for the last two years the reputation of being haunted. It is a large and stately residence, surrounded by what was once a garden, but which is now only a green inclosure used for bleaching clothes. The dry basin of what has been a fountain, and a few fruit-trees, ragged and unpruned, indicate that this spot, in past days, was a pleasant, shady retreat, filled with fruits and flowers and the sweet murmur of waters.

The house is very spacious. A hall of noble size leads to a vast spiral staircase winding through its center, while the various apartments are of imposing dimensions. It was built some fifteen or twenty years since by Mr. A——, the well-known New York merchant, who five years ago threw the commercial world into convulsions by a stupendous bank fraud. Mr. A——, as every one knows, escaped to Europe, and died not long after of a broken heart. Almost immediately after the news of his decease reached this country, and was verified, the report spread in Twenty-sixth Street that No.— was haunted. Legal measures had dispossessed the widow of its former owner, and it was inhabited merely by a care taker and his wife, placed there by the house agent into whose hands it had passed for purposes of renting or sale. These people declared that they were troubled with unnatural noises. Doors were opened without any visible agency. The remnants of furniture scattered through the various rooms were, during the night, piled one upon the other by unknown hands. Invisible feet passed up and down the stairs in broad daylight, accompanied by the rustle of unseen silk dresses, and the gliding of viewless hands along the massive balusters. The care taker and his wife declared that they would live there no longer. The house agent laughed, dismissed them, and put others in their place. The noises and supernatural manifestations continued. The neighborhood caught up the story, and the house remained untenanted for three years. Several persons negotiated for it; but somehow, always before the bargain was closed, they heard the unpleasant rumors, and declined to treat any further.

It was in this state of things that my landlady—who at that time kept a boarding-house in Bleecker Street, and who wished to move farther up town—conceived the bold idea of renting No.— Twenty-sixth Street. Happening to have in her house rather a plucky and philosophical set of boarders, she laid down her scheme before us, stating candidly everything she had heard respecting the ghostly qualities of the establishment to which she wished to remove us. With the exception of two timid persons,—a sea captain and a returned Californian, who immediately gave notice that they would leave,—all of Mrs. Moffat's guests declared that they would accompany her in her chivalric incursion into the abode of spirits.

Our removal was effected in the month of May, and we were all charmed with our new residence. The portion of Twenty-sixth Street where our house is situated—between Seventh and Eighth Avenues—is one of the pleasantest localities in New York. The gardens back of the houses, running down nearly to the Hudson, form, in the summer time, a perfect avenue of verdure. The air is pure and invigorating, sweeping, as it does, straight across the river from the Weehawken heights, and even the ragged garden which surrounded the house on two sides, although displaying on washing days rather too much clothesline, still gave us a piece of greensward to look at, and a cool retreat in the summer evenings, where we smoked our cigars in the dusk, and watched the fireflies flashing their dark-lanterns in the long grass.

Of course we had no sooner established ourselves at No.— than we began to expect the ghosts. We absolutely awaited their advent with eagerness. Our dinner conversation was supernatural. One of the boarders, who had purchased Mrs. Crowe's "Night Side of Nature" for his own private delectation, was regarded as a public enemy by the entire household for not having bought twenty copies. The man led a life of supreme wretchedness while he was reading this volume. A system of espionage was established, of which he was the victim. If he incautiously laid the book down for an instant and left the room, it was immediately seized and read aloud in secret places to a select few. I found myself a person of immense importance, it having leaked out that I was tolerably well versed in the history of supernaturalism, and had once written a story, entitled "The Pot of Tulips," for Harper's Monthly, the foundation of which was a ghost. If a table or a wainscot panel happened to warp when we were assembled in the large drawing-room, there was an instant silence, and every one was prepared for an immediate clanking of chains and a spectral form.

After a month of psychological excitement, it was with the utmost dissatisfaction that we were forced to acknowledge that nothing in the remotest degree approaching the supernatural had manifested itself. Once the black butler asseverated that his candle had been blown out by some invisible agency while he was undressing himself for the night; but as I had more than once discovered this colored gentleman in a condition when one candle must have appeared to him like two, I thought it possible that, by going a step farther in his potations, he might have reversed his phenomenon, and seen no candle at all where he ought to have beheld one.

Things were in this state when an incident took place so awful and inexplicable in its character that my reason fairly reels at the bare memory of the occurrence. It was the tenth of July. After dinner was over I repaired with my friend, Dr. Hammond, to the garden to smoke my evening pipe. The Doctor and myself found ourselves in an unusually metaphysical mood. We lit our large meerschaums, filled with fine Turkish tobacco; we paced to and fro, conversing. A strange perversity dominated the currents of our thought. They would not flow through the sun-lit channels into which we strove to divert them. For some unaccountable reason they constantly diverged into dark and lonesome beds, where a continual gloom brooded. It was in vain that, after our old fashion, we flung ourselves on the shores of the East, and talked of its gay bazaars, of the splendors of the time of Haroun, of harems and golden palaces. Black afreets continually arose from the depths of our talk, and expanded, like the one the fisherman released from the copper vessel, until they blotted everything bright from our vision. Insensibly, we yielded to the occult force that swayed us, and indulged in gloomy speculation. We had talked some time upon the proneness of the human mind to mysticism, and the almost universal love of the Terrible, when Hammond suddenly said to me, "What do you consider to be the greatest element of Terror?"

The question, I own, puzzled me. That many things were terrible, I knew. Stumbling over a corpse in the dark; beholding, as I once did, a woman floating down a deep and rapid river, with wildly lifted arms, and awful, upturned face, uttering, as she sank, shrieks that rent one's heart, while we, the spectators, stood frozen at a window which overhung the river at a height of sixty feet, unable to make the slightest effort to save her, but dumbly watching her last supreme agony and her disappearance. A shattered wreck, with no life visible, encountered floating listlessly on the ocean, is a terrible object, for it suggests a huge terror, the proportions of which are veiled. But it now struck me for the first time that there must be one great and ruling embodiment of fear, a King of Terrors to which all others must succumb. What might it be? To what train of circumstances would it owe its existence?

"I confess, Hammond," I replied to my friend, "I never considered the subject before. That there must be one Something more terrible than any other thing, I feel. I cannot attempt, however, even the most vague definition."

"I am somewhat like you, Harry," he answered. "I feel my capacity to experience a terror greater than anything yet conceived by the human mind,—something combining in fearful and unnatural amalgamation hitherto supposed incompatible elements. The calling of the voices in Brockden Brown's novel of 'Wieland' is awful; so is the picture of the Dweller of the Threshold, in Bulwer's 'Zanoni';"but," he added, shaking his head gloomily, "there is something more horrible still than these."

"Look here, Hammond," I rejoined, "let us drop this kind of talk, for Heaven's sake!"

"I don't know what's the matter with me to-night," he replied, "but my brain is running upon all sorts of weird and awful thoughts. I feel as if I could write a story like Hoffman to night, if I were only master of a literary style."

"Well, if we are going to be Hoffmanesque in our talk, I'm off to bed. How sultry it is! Good night, Hammond."

"Good night, Harry. Pleasant dreams to you."

"To you, gloomy wretch, afreets, ghouls, and enchanters."

We parted, and each sought his respective chamber. I undressed quickly and got into bed, taking with me, according to my usual custom, a book, over which I generally read myself to sleep. I opened the volume as soon as I had laid my head upon the pillow, and instantly flung it to the other side of the room. It was Goudon's "History of Monsters"—a curious French work, which I had lately imported from Paris, but which, in the state of mind I had then reached, was anything but an agreeable companion. I resolved to go to sleep at once; so, turning down my gas until nothing but a little blue point of light glimmered on the top of the tube, I composed myself to rest.

The room was in total darkness. The atom of gas that still remained lighted did not illuminate a distance of three inches round the burner. I desperately drew my arm across my eyes, as if to shut out even the darkness, and tried to think of nothing. It was in vain. The confounded themes touched on by Hammond in the garden kept obtruding themselves on my brain. I battled against them. I erected ramparts of would-be blankness of intellect to keep them out. They still crowded upon me. While I was lying still as a corpse, hoping that by a perfect physical inaction I should hasten mental repose, an awful incident occurred. A Something dropped, as it seemed, from the ceiling, plumb upon my chest, and the next instant I felt two bony hands encircling my throat, endeavoring to choke me.

I am no coward, and am possessed of considerable physical strength. The suddenness of the attack, instead of stunning me, strung every nerve to its highest tension. My body acted from instinct, before my brain had time to realize the terrors of my position. In an instant I wound two muscular arms around the creature, and squeezed it, with all the strength of despair, against my chest. In a few seconds the bony hands that had fastened on my throat loosened their hold, and I was free to breathe once more. Then commenced a struggle of awful intensity. Immersed in the most profound darkness, totally ignorant of the nature of the Thing by which I was so suddenly attacked, finding my grasp slipping every moment, by reason, it seemed to me, of the entire nakedness of my assailant, bitten with sharp teeth in the shoulder, neck, and chest, having every moment to protect my throat against a pair of sinewy, agile hands, which my utmost efforts could not confine—these were a combination of circumstances to combat which required all the strength and skill and courage that I possessed.

At last, after a silent, deadly, exhausting struggle, I got my assailant under by a series of incredible efforts of strength. Once pinned, with my knee on what I made out to be its chest, I knew that I was victor. I rested for a moment to breathe. I heard the creature beneath me panting in the darkness, and felt the violent throbbing of a heart. It was apparently as exhausted as I was; that was one comfort. At this moment I remembered that I usually placed under my pillow, before going to bed, a large yellow silk pocket handkerchief, for use during the night. I felt for it instantly; it was there. In a few seconds more I had, after a fashion, pinioned the creature's arms.

I now felt tolerably secure. There was nothing more to be done but to turn on the gas, and, having first seen what my midnight assailant was like, arouse the household. I will confess to being actuated by a certain pride in not giving the alarm before; I wished to make the capture alone and unaided.

Never losing my hold for an instant, I slipped from the bed to the floor, dragging my captive with me. I had but a few steps to make to reach the gas-burner; these I made with the greatest caution, holding the creature in a grip like a vice. At last I got within arm's-length of the tiny speck of blue light which told me where the gas-burner lay. Quick as lightning I released my grasp with one hand and let on the full flood of light. Then I turned to look at my captive.

I cannot even attempt to give any definition of my sensations the instant after I turned on the gas. I suppose I must have shrieked with terror, for in less than a minute afterward my room was crowded with the inmates of the house. I shudder now as I think of that awful moment. I saw nothing! Yes; I had one arm firmly clasped round a breathing, panting, corporeal shape, my other hand gripped with all its strength a throat as warm, and apparently fleshly, as my own; and yet, with this living substance in my grasp, with its body pressed against my own, and all in the bright glare of a large jet of gas, I absolutely beheld nothing! Not even an outline,—a vapor!

I do not, even at this hour, realize the situation in which I found myself. I cannot recall the astounding incident thoroughly. Imagination in vain tries to compass the awful paradox.

It breathed. I felt its warm breath upon my cheek. It struggled fiercely. It had hands. They clutched me. Its skin was smooth, like my own. There it lay, pressed close up against me, solid as stone,—and yet utterly invisible!

I wonder that I did not faint or go mad on the instant. Some wonderful instinct must have sustained me; for, absolutely, in place of loosening my hold on the terrible Enigma, I seemed to gain an additional strength in my moment of horror, and tightened my grasp with such wonderful force that I felt the creature shivering with agony.

Just then Hammond entered my room at the head of the household. As soon as he beheld my face—which, I suppose, must have been an awful sight to look at—he hastened forward, crying, "Great heaven, Harry! what has happened?"

"Hammond! Hammond!" I cried, "come here. Oh! this is awful! I have been attacked in bed by something or other, which I have hold of; but I can't see it—I can't see it!"

Hammond, doubtless struck by the unfeigned horror expressed in my countenance, made one or two steps forward with an anxious yet puzzled expression. A very audible titter burst from the remainder of my visitors. This suppressed laughter made me furious. To laugh at a human being in my position! It was the worst species of cruelty. Now, I can understand why the appearance of a man struggling violently, as it would seem, with an airy nothing, and calling for assistance against a vision, should have appeared ludicrous. Then, so great was my rage against the mocking crowd that had I the power I would have stricken them dead where they stood.

"Hammond! Hammond!" I cried again, despairingly, "for God's sake come to me. I can hold the—the Thing but a short while longer. It is overpowering me. Help me! Help me!"

"Harry," whispered Hammond, approaching me, "you have been smoking too much."

"I swear to you, Hammond, that this is no vision," I answered, in the same low tone. "Don't you see how it shakes my whole frame with its struggles? If you don't believe me, convince yourself. Feel it,—touch it."

Hammond advanced and laid his hand on the spot I indicated. A wild cry of horror burst from him. He had felt it!

In a moment he had discovered somewhere in my room a long piece of cord, and was the next instant winding it and knotting it about the body of the unseen being that I clasped in my arms.

"Harry," he said, in a hoarse, agitated voice, for, though he preserved his presence of mind, he was deeply moved, "Harry, it's all safe now. You may let go, old fellow, if you're tired. The Thing can't move."

I was utterly exhausted, and I gladly loosed my hold.

Hammond stood holding the ends of the cord that bound the Invisible, twisted round his hand, while before him, self-supporting as it were, he beheld a rope laced and interlaced, and stretching tightly round a vacant space. I never saw a man look so thoroughly stricken with awe. Nevertheless his face expressed all the courage and determination which I knew him to possess. His lips, although white, were set firmly, and one could perceive at a glance that, although stricken with fear, he was not daunted.

The confusion that ensued among the guests of the house who were witnesses of this extraordinary scene between Hammond and myself,—who beheld the pantomime of binding this struggling Something,—who beheld me almost sinking from physical exhaustion when my task of jailer was over—the confusion and terror that took possession of the bystanders, when they saw all this, was beyond description.

The weaker ones fled from the apartment. The few who remained clustered near the door, and could not be induced to approach Hammond and his Charge. Still incredulity broke out through their terror. They had not the courage to satisfy themselves, and yet they doubted. It was in vain that I begged of some of the men to come near and convince themselves by touch of the existence in that room of a living being which was invisible. They were incredulous, but did not dare to undeceive themselves. How could a solid, living, breathing body be invisible, they asked. My reply was this. I gave a sign to Hammond, and both of us—conquering our fearful repugnance to touch the invisible creature—lifted it from the ground, manacled as it was, and took it to my bed. Its weight was about that of a boy of fourteen.

"Now, my friends," I said, as Hammond and myself held the creature suspended over the bed, "I can give you self-evident proof that here is a solid, ponderable body which, nevertheless, you cannot see. Be good enough to watch the surface of the bed attentively."

I was astonished at my own courage in treating this strange event so calmly; but I had recovered from my first terror, and felt a sort of scientific pride in the affair which dominated every other feeling.

The eyes of the bystanders were immediately fixed on my bed. At a given signal Hammond and I let the creature fall. There was the dull sound of a heavy body alighting on a soft mass. The timbers of the bed creaked. A deep impression marked itself distinctly on the pillow, and on the bed itself. The crowd who witnessed this gave a sort of low, universal cry, and rushed from the room. Hammond and I were left alone with our Mystery.

We remained silent for some time, listening to the low, irregular breathing of the creature on the bed, and watching the rustle of the bedclothes as it impotently struggled to free itself from confinement. Then Hammond spoke.

"Harry, this is awful."

"Aye, awful."

"But not unaccountable."

"Not unaccountable! What do you mean? Such a thing has never occurred since the birth of the world. I know not what to think, Hammond. God grant that I am not mad, and that this is not an insane fantasy!"

"Let us reason a little, Harry. Here is a solid body which we touch, but which we cannot see. The fact is so unusual that it strikes us with terror. Is there no parallel, though, for such a phenomenon? Take a piece of pure glass. It is tangible and transparent. A certain chemical coarseness is all that prevents its being so entirely transparent as to be totally invisible. It is not theoretically impossible, mind you, to make a glass which shall not reflect a single ray of light—a glass so pure and homogeneous in its atoms that the rays from the sun shall pass through it as they do through the air, refracted but not reflected. We do not see the air, and yet we feel it."

"That's all very well, Hammond, but these are inanimate substances. Glass does not breathe, air does not breathe. This thing has a heart that palpitates,—a will that moves it,— lungs that play, and inspire and respire."

"You forget the strange phenomena of which we have so often heard of late," answered the Doctor, gravely. "At the meetings called 'spirit circles,' invisible hands have been

thrust into the hands of those persons round the table—
warm, fleshly hands that seemed to pulsate with mortal life."

"What? Do you think, then, that this thing is—"

"I don't know what it is," was the solemn reply; "but please
the gods I will, with your assistance, thoroughly investigate
it."

We watched together, smoking many pipes, all night long,
by the bedside of the unearthly being that tossed and panted
until it was apparently wearied out. Then we learned by the
low, regular breathing that it slept.

The next morning the house was all astir. The boarders
congregated on the landing outside my room, and
Hammond and myself were lions. We had to answer a thousand questions as to the state of our extraordinary prisoner,
for as yet not one person in the house except ourselves could
be induced to set foot in the apartment.

The creature was awake. This was evidenced by the
convulsive manner in which the bedclothes were moved in
its efforts to escape. There was something truly terrible in
beholding, as it were, those second-hand indications of the
terrible writhings and agonized struggles for liberty which
themselves were invisible.

Hammond and myself had racked our brains during the
long night to discover some means by which we might realize the shape and general appearance of the Enigma. As well
as we could make out by passing our hands over the creature's form, its outlines and lineaments were human. There
was a mouth; a round, smooth head without hair; a nose,
which, however, was little elevated above the cheeks; and its
hands and feet felt like those of a boy. At first we thought of
placing the being on a smooth surface and tracing its outline

with chalk, as shoemakers trace the outline of the foot. This plan was given up as being of no value. Such an outline would give not the slightest idea of its conformation.

A happy thought struck me. We would take a cast of it in plaster of Paris. This would give us the solid figure, and satisfy all our wishes. But how to do it? The movements of the creature would disturb the setting of the plastic covering, and distort the mold. Another thought. Why not give it chloroform? It had respiratory organs—that was evident by its breathing. Once reduced to a state of insensibility, we could do with it what we would. Doctor X—— was sent for; and after the worthy physician had recovered from the first shock of amazement, he proceeded to administer the chloroform. In three minutes afterward we were enabled to remove the fetters from the creature's body, and a well-known modeler of this city was busily engaged in covering the invisible form with the moist clay. In five minutes more we had a mold, and before evening a rough fac simile of the mystery. It was shaped like a man,—distorted, uncouth, and horrible, but still a man. It was small, not over four feet and some inches in height, and its limbs revealed a muscular development that was unparalleled. Its face surpassed in hideousness anything I had ever seen. Gustave Dore, or Callot, or Tony Johannot, never conceived anything so horrible. There is a face in one of the latter's illustrations to "Un Voyage ou il vous plaira," which somewhat approaches the countenance of this creature, but does not equal it. It was the physiognomy of what I should have fancied a ghoul to be. It looked as if it was capable of feeding on human flesh.

Having satisfied our curiosity, and bound every one in the house to secrecy, it became a question what was to be done with our Enigma. It was impossible that we should keep such a horror in our house; it was equally impossible that such an awful being should be let loose upon the world. I confess that I would have gladly voted for the creature's destruction. But who would shoulder the responsibility? Who would undertake the execution of this horrible semblance of a human being? Day after day this question was deliberated gravely. The boarders all left the house. Mrs. Moffat was in despair, and threatened Hammond and myself with all sorts of legal penalties if we did not remove the Horror. Our answer was, "We will go if you like, but we decline taking this creature with us. Remove it yourself if you please. It appeared in your house. On you the responsibility rests." To this there was, of course, no answer. Mrs. Moffat could not obtain for love or money a person who would even approach the Mystery.

The most singular part of the transaction was that we were entirely ignorant of what the creature habitually fed on. Everything in the way of nutriment that we could think of was placed before it, but was never touched. It was awful to stand by, day after day, and see the clothes toss, and hear the hard breathing, and know that it was starving.

Ten, twelve days, a fortnight passed, and it still lived. The pulsations of the heart, however, were daily growing fainter, and had now nearly ceased altogether. It was evident that the creature was dying for want of sustenance. While this terrible life struggle was going on, I felt miserable. I could not sleep of nights. Horrible as the creature was, it was pitiful to think of the pangs it was suffering.

At last it died. Hammond and I found it cold and stiff one morning in the bed. The heart had ceased to beat, the lungs to inspire. We hastened to bury it in the garden. It was a strange funeral, the dropping of that viewless corpse into the damp hole. The cast of its form I gave to Dr. X——, who keeps it in his museum in Tenth Street.

As I am on the eve of a long journey from which I may not return, I have drawn up this narrative of an event the most singular that has ever come to my knowledge.

NOTE.—It was rumored that the proprietors of a well-known museum in this city had made arrangements with Dr. X—— to exhibit to the public the singular cast which Mr. Escott deposited with him. So extraordinary a history cannot fail to attract universal attention.

The Queen of the Bees (1876)

Emile Erckmann and Alexandre Chatrian

"As you go from Motiers-Navers to Boudry, on your way to Neufchatel," said the young professor of botany, "you follow a road between two walls of rocks of immense height; they reach a perpendicular elevation of five or six hundred feet, and are hung with wild plants, the mountain basil (thymus alpinus), ferus (polypodium), the whortleberry (vitis idoea), ground ivy, and other climbing plants producing a wonderful effect.

"The road winds along this defile; it rises, falls, turns, sometimes tolerably level, sometimes broken and abrupt, according to the thousand irregularities of the ground. Grey rocks almost meet in an arch overhead, others stand wide apart, leaving the distant blue visible, and discovering sombre and melancholy-looking depths, and rows of firs as far as the eye could reach.

"The Reuss flows along the bottom, sometimes leaping along in waterfalls, then creeping through thickets, or steaming, foaming, and thundering over precipices, while the echoes prolong the tumult and roar of its torrents in one immense endless hum. Since I left Tubingen the weather had continued fine; but when I reached the summit of this gigantic staircase, about two leagues distant from the little hamlet of Novisaigne, I suddenly noticed great grey clouds begin passing overhead, which soon filled up the defile entirely; this vapour was so dense that it soon penetrated my clothes as a heavy dew would have done.

"Although it was only two in the afternoon, the sky became clouded over as if darkness was coming on; and I foresaw a heavy storm was about to break over my head.

"I consequently began looking about for shelter, and I saw through one of those wide openings which afford you a perspective view of the Alps, about two or three hundred yards distant on the slope leading down to the lake, an ancient-looking grey châlet, moss-covered, with its small round windows and sloping roof loaded with large stones, its stairs outside the house, with a carved rail, and its basket-shaped balcony, on which the Swiss maidens generally hang their snowy linen and scarlet petticoats to dry.

"Precisely as I was looking down, a tall woman in a black cap was folding and collecting the linen which was blowing about in the wind.

"To the left of this building a very large apiary supported on beams, arranged like a balcony, formed a projection above the valley.

"You may easily believe that without the loss of a moment I set off bounding through the heather to seek for shelter from the coming storm, and well it was I lost no time, for I had hardly laid my hand on the handle of the door before the hurricane burst furiously overhead; every gust of wind seemed about to carry the cottage bodily away; but its foundations were strong, and the security of the good people within, by the warmth of their reception, completely reassured me about the probability of any accident.

"The cottage was inhabited by Walter Young, his wife Catherine, and little Raesel, their only daughter.

"I remained three days with them; for the wind, which went down about midnight, had so filled the valley of Neufchatel with mist, that the mountain where I had taken refuge was completely enveloped in it; it was impossible to walk twenty yards from the door without experiencing great difficulty in finding it again.

"Every morning these good people would say, when they saw me buckle on my knapsack—

"'What are you about, Mr. Hennetius? You cannot mean to go yet; you will never arrive anywhere. In the name of Heaven stay here a little longer!'

"And Young would open the door and exclaim—

"'Look there, sir; you must be tired of your life to risk it among these rocks. Why, the dove itself would be troubled to find the ark again in such a mist as this.'

"One glance at the mountain side was enough for me to make up my mind to put my stick back again in the corner.

"Walter Young was a man of the old times. He was nearly sixty; his grand head wore a calm and benevolent expression—a real Apostle's head. His wife, who always wore a black silk cap, pale and thoughtful, resembled him much in disposition. Their two profiles, as I looked at them defined sharply against the little panes of glass in the chalet's windows, recalled to my mind those drawings of Albert Durer the sight of which carried me back to the age of faith and the patriarchal manners of the fifteenth century. The long brown rafters of the ceiling, the deal table, the ashen chairs with the carved backs, the tin drinking-cups, the sideboard with its old-fashioned painted plates and dishes, the crucifix with the Saviour carved in box on an ebony cross, and the worm-eaten clock-case with its many weights and its porcelain dial, completed the illusion.

"But the face of their little daughter Raesel was still more touching. I think I can see her now, with her flat horsehair cap and watered black silk ribbons, her trim bodice and broad blue sash down to her knees, her little white hands crossed in the attitude of a dreamer, her long fair curls—all that was graceful, slender, and ethereal in nature. Yes, I can see Raesel now, sitting in a large leathern arm-chair, close to the blue curtain of the recess at the end of the room, smiling as she listened and meditated.

"Her sweet face had charmed me from the first moment I saw her and I was continually on the point of inquiring why she wore such an habitually melancholy air, why did she hold her pale face down so invariably, and why did she never raise her eyes when spoken to?

"Alas! the poor child had been blind from her birth.

"She had never seen the lake's vast expanse, nor its blue sheet blending so harmoniously with the sky, the fishermen's boats which ploughed its surface, the wooded heights which crowned it and cast their quivering reflection on its waters, the rocks covered with moss, the green Alpine plants in their vivid and brilliant colouring; nor had she ever watched the sun set behind the glaciers, nor the long shades of evening draw across the valleys, nor the golden broom, nor the endless heather—nothing. None of these things had she ever seen; nothing of what we saw every day from the windows of the chalet.

"'What an ironical commentary on the gifts of Fortune!' thought I, as I sat looking out of the window at the mist, in expectation of the sun's appearing once more, 'to be blind in this place! here in presence of Nature in its sublimest form, of such limitless grandeur! To be blind! Oh, Almighty God, who shall dare to dispute Thy impenetrable decrees, or who shall venture to murmur at the severity of Thy justice, even when its weight falls on an innocent child? But to be thus blind in the presence of Thy grandest creations, of creations which ceaselessly renew our enthusiasm, our love, and our adoration for Thy genius, Thy power, and Thy goodness; of what crime can this poor child have been guilty thus to deserve Thy chastisement?'

"And my reflections continually reverted to this topic.

"I asked myself, too, what compensation Divine pity could make its creature for the deprival of its greatest blessing, and, finding none, I began to doubt its power.

"'Man, in his presumption,' said the royal poet, 'dares to glorify himself in his knowledge, and judge the Eternal. But his wisdom is but folly, and his light darkness.'

"Oh that day one of Nature's great mysteries was revealed to me, doubtless with the purpose of humbling my vanity, and of teaching me that nothing is impossible to God, and that it is in His power only to multiply our senses, and by so doing gratify those who please Him."

Here the young professor took a pinch from his tortoise-shell snuff-box, raised his eyes to the ceiling with a contemplative air, and then, after a short pause, continued in these terms:—

"Does it not often happen to you, ladies, when you are in the country in fine weather in summer, especially after a brief storm, when the air is warm, and the exhalations from the ground filling it with the perfume of thousands of plants, and their sweet scent penetrates and warms you; when the foliage from the trees in the solitary avenues, as well as from the bushes, seems to lean over you as if it sought to take you in its arms and embrace you; when the minutest flowers, the humble daisy, the blue forget-me-not, the convolvulus in the hedgerows raise their heads and follow you with a longing look—does it not happen to you to experience an inexpressible sensation of languor, to sigh for no apparent reason, and even to feel inclined to shed tears, and to ask yourselves, 'Why does this feeling of love oppress me? why do my knees bend under me? whence these tears?'

"Whence indeed, ladies? Why from life, and the thousands of living things which surround you, lean to you, and call to you to stay with them, while they gently murmur, 'We love you; love us, and do not leave us.'

"You can easily imagine, then, the deep enthusiastic feeling and the religious sentiment of a person always in a similar state of ecstasy. Even if blind, abandoned by his friends, do you think there is nothing to envy in his lot? or that his destiny is not infinitely happier than our own? For my own part I have not the slightest doubt of it.

"But you will, doubtless, say such a condition is impossible—the mind of man would break down under such a load of happiness. And, moreover, whence could such happiness be derived? What organs could transmit, and where could it find, such a sensation of universal life?

"This, ladies, is a question to which I can give you no answer; but I ask you to listen and then judge.

"The very day I arrived at the chalet I had made a singular remark—the blind girl was especially uneasy about the bees.

"While the wind was roaring without Raesel sat with her head on her hands listening attentively.

"'Father,' said she, 'I think at the end of the apiary the third hive on the right is still open. Go and see. The wind blows from the north; all the bees are home; you can shut the hive.'

"And her father having gone out by a side door, when he returned he said—

"'It is all right, my child; I have closed the hive.'

"Half an hour afterwards the girl, rousing herself once more from her reverie, murmured—

"'There are no more bees about, but under the roof of the apiary there are some waiting; they are in the sixth hive near the door; please go and let them in, father.'

"The old man left the house at once. He was away more than a quarter of an hour; then he came back and told his daughter that everything was as she wished it—the bees had just gone into their hive.

"The child nodded, and replied—

"'Thank you, father.'

"Then she seemed to doze again.

"I was standing by the stove, lost in a labyrinth of reflections; how could that poor blind girl know that from such or such a hive there were still some bees absent, or that such a hive had been left open? This seemed inexplicable to me; but having been in the house hardly one hour, I did not feel justified in asking my hosts any questions with regard to their daughter, for it is sometimes painful to talk to people on subjects which interest them very nearly. I concluded that Young gave way to his daughter's fancies in order to induce her to believe she was of some service in the family, and that her forethought protected the bees from several accidents. That seemed the simplest explanation I could imagine, and I thought no more about it.

"About seven we supped on milk and cheese, and when it was time to retire Young led me into a goodsized room on the first floor, with a bed and a few chairs in it, panelled in fir, as is generally the case in the greater number of Swiss châlets. You are only separated from your neighbours by a deal partition, and you can hear every footstep and nearly every word.

"That night I was lulled to sleep by the whistling of the wind and the sound of the rain beating against the window-panes. The next day the wind had gone down and we were enveloped in mist. When I awoke I found my windows quite white, quite padded with mist. When I opened my window the valley looked like an immense stove; the tops of a few fir-trees alone showed their outlines against the sky; below, the clouds were in regular layers down to the surface of the lake; everything was calm, motionless, and silent.

"When I went down to the sitting-room I found my hosts seated at table, about to begin breakfast.

"'We have been waiting for you,' cried Young gaily.

"'You must excuse us,' said the mother; 'this is our regular breakfast hour.'

"'Of course, of course; I am obliged to you for not noticing my laziness.'

"Raesel was much more lively than the preceding evening; she had a fresh colour in her cheeks.

"'The wind has gone down,' said she; 'the storm has passed away without doing any harm.'

"'Shall I open the apiary?' asked Young.

"'No, not yet; the bees would lose themselves in this mist. Besides, everything is drenched with rain; the brambles and mosses are full of water; the least puff of wind would drown many of them. We must wait a little while. I know what is the matter: they feel dull, they want to work; they are tormented at the idea of devouring their honey instead of making it. But I cannot afford to lose them. Many of the hives are weak—they would starve in winter. We will see what the weather is like to-morrow.'

"The two old people sat and listened without making any observations.

"About nine the blind girl proposed to go and visit her bees; Young and Catherine followed her, and I did the same, from a very natural feeling of curiosity.

"We passed through the kitchen by a door which opened on to a terrace. Above us was the roof of the apiary; it was of thatch, and from its ledge honeysuckle and wild grapes hung in magnificent festoons. The hives were arranged on three shelves.

"Raesel went from one to the other, patting them, and murmuring—

"'Have a little patience; there is too much mist this morning. Ah! the greedy ones, how they grumble!'

"And we could hear a vague humming inside the hive, which increased in intensity until she had passed.

"That awoke all my curiosity once more. I felt there was some strange mystery which I could not fathom, but what was my surprise, when, as I went into the sitting-room, I heard the blind girl say in a melancholy tone of voice—

"'No, father, I would rather not see at all to-day than lose my eyes. I will sing, I will do something or other to pass the time, never mind what; but I will not let the bees out.'

"While she was speaking in this strange manner I looked at Walter Young, who glanced out of the window and then quietly replied—

"'You are right, child; I think you are right. Besides, there is nothing to see; the valley is quite white. It is not worth looking at.'

"And while I sat astounded at what I heard, the child continued—

"'What lovely weather we had the day before yesterday! Who would have thought that a storm on the lake would have caused all this mist? Now one must fold up its wings and crawl about like a wretched caterpillar.'

"Then again, after a few moments' silence—

"'How I enjoyed myself under the lofty pines on the Grinderwald! How the honey-dew dropped from the sky! It fell from every branch. What a harvest we made, and how sweet the air was on the shores of the lake, and in the rich Tannemath pastures—the green moss, and the sweet-smelling herbs! I sang, I laughed, and we filled our cells with wax and honey. How delightful to be everywhere, see everything, to fly humming about the woods, the mountains, and the valleys!'

"There was a fresh silence, while I sat, with mouth and eyes open, listening with the greatest attention, not knowing what to think or what to say.

"'And when the shower came,' she went on, 'how frightened we were! A great humble-bee, sheltered under the same fern as myself, shut his eyes at every flash; a grasshopper had sheltered itself under its great green branches, and some poor little crickets had scrambled up a poppy to save themselves from drowning. But what was most frightful was a nest of warblers quite close to us in a bush. The mother hovered round about us, and the little ones opened their beaks, yellow as far as their windpipes. How frightened we were! Good Lord, we were frightened indeed! Thanks be to Heaven, a puff of wind carried us off to the mountain side; and now the vintage is over we must not expect to get out again so soon.'

"On hearing these descriptions of Nature so true, at this worship of day and light, I could no longer entertain the least doubt on the subject.

"'The blind girl sees,' said I to myself; 'she sees through thousands of eyes; the apiary is her life, her soul. Every bee carries a part of her away into space, and then returns drawn to her by thousands of invisible threads. The blind girl penetrates the flowers and the mosses; she revels in their perfume; when the sun shines she is everywhere; in the mountain side, in the valleys, in the forests, as far as her sphere of attraction extends.'

"I sat confounded at this strange magnetic influence, and felt tempted to exclaim—

"'Honour, glory, honour to the power, the wisdom, and the infinite goodness of the Eternal God! For Him nothing is impossible. Every day, every instant of our lives reveals to us His magnificence.'

"While I was lost in these enthusiastic reflections, Raesel addressed me with a quiet smile.

"'Sir,' said she.

"'What, my child?'

"'You are very much surprised at me, and you are not the first person who has been so. The rector Hegel, of Neufchatel, and other travellers have been here on purpose to see me: they thought I was blind. You thought so too, did you not?'

"'I did indeed, my dear child, and I thank the Lord that I was mistaken.'

"'Yes,' said she, 'I know you are a good man—I can tell it by your voice. When the sun shines I shall open my eyes to look at you, and when you leave here I will accompany you to the foot of the mountain.'

"Then she began to laugh most artlessly.

"'Yes,' said she, 'you shall have music in your ears, and I will seat myself on your cheek; but you must take care—take care. You must not touch me, or I should sting you. You must promise not to be angry.'

"'I promise you, Raesel, I promise you I will not,' I said with tears in my eyes, 'and, moreover, I promise you never to kill a bee or any other insect except those which do harm.'

"'They are the eyes of the Lord,' she murmured. 'I can only see by my own poor bees, but He has every hive, every ant's nest, every leaf, every blade of grass. He lives, He feels, He loves, He suffers, He does good by means of all these. Oh, Monsieur Hennetius, you are right not to pain the Lord, who loves us so much!'

"Never in my life had I been so moved and affected, and it was a full minute before I could ask her—

"'So, my dear child, you see by your bees; will you explain to me how that is?'

"'I cannot tell, Monsieur Hennetius; it may be because I am so fond of them. When I was quite a little child they adopted me, and they have never once hurt me. At first I liked to sit for hours in the apiary all alone and listen to their humming for hours together. I could see nothing then, everything was dark to me; but insensibly light came upon me. At first I could see the sun a little, when it was very hot, then a little more, with the wild vine and the honeysuckle like a shade over me, then the full light of day. I began to emerge from myself; my spirit went forth with the bees. I could see the mountains, the rocks, the lake, the flowers and mosses, and in the evening, when quite alone, I reflected on these things. I thought how beautiful they were, and when people talked of this and that, of whortleberries, and mulberries, and heaths, I said to myself, "I know what all these things are like—they are black, or brown, or green." I could see them in my mind, and every day I became better acquainted with them, thanks to my dear bees; and therefore I love them dearly, Monsieur Hennetius. If you knew how it grieves me when the time comes for robbing them of their wax and their honey!'

"'I believe you, my child—I believe it does.'

"My delight at this wonderful discovery was boundless.

"Two days longer Raesel entertained me with a description of her impressions. She was acquainted with every flower, every Alpine plant, and gave me an account of a great number which have as yet received no botanical names, and which are probably only to be found in inaccessible situations.

"The poor girl was often much affected when she spoke of her dear friends, some little flowers.

"'Often and often,' said she, 'I have talked for hours with the golden broom or the tender blue-eyed forget-me-not, and shared in their troubles. They all wished to quit the earth and fly about; they all complained of their being condemned to dry up in the ground, and of being exposed to wait for days and weeks ere a drop of dew came to refresh them.'

"And so Raesel used to repeat to me endless conversations of this sort. It was marvellous! If you only heard her you would be capable of falling in love with a dogrose, or of feeling a lively sympathy and a profound sentiment of compassion for a violet, its misfortunes and its silent sufferings.

"What more can I tell you, ladies? It is painful to leave a subject where the soul has so many mysterious emanations; there is such a field for conjecture; but as everything in this world must have an end, so must even the pleasantest dreams.

"Early in the morning of the third day of my stay a gentle breeze began to roll away the mist from off the lake. I could see its folds become larger every second as the wind drove them along, leaving one blue corner in the sky, and then another; then the tower of a village church, some green pinnacles on the tops of the mountains, then a row of firs, a valley, all the time the immense mass of vapour slowly floated past us; by ten it had left us behind it, and the great cloud on the dry peaks of the Chasseron still wore a threatening aspect; but a last effort of the wind gave it a different direction, and it disappeared at last in the gorges of Saint-Croix.

"Then the mighty nature of the Alps seemed to me to have grown young again; the heather, the tall pines, the old chestnut-trees dripping with dew, shone with vigorous health; there was something in the view of them joyous, smiling, and serious all at once. One felt the hand of God was in it all—His eternity.

"I went downstairs lost in thought; Raesel was already in the apiary. Young opened the door and pointed her out to me sitting in the shade of the wild vine, with her forehead resting on her hands, as if in a doze.

"'Be careful,' said he to me, 'not to awake her; her mind is elsewhere; she sleeps; she is wandering about; she is happy.'

"The bees were swarming about by thousands, like a flood of gold over a precipice.

"I looked on at this wonderful sight for some seconds, praying the Lord would continue His love for the poor child.

"Then turning round—

"'Master Young,' said I, 'it is time to go.'

"He buckled my knapsack on for me himself, and put my stick into my hand.

"Mistress Catherine looked on kindly, and they both accompanied me to the threshold of the châlet.

"'Farewell!' said Walter, grasping my hand; 'a pleasant journey; and think of us sometimes!'

"'I can never forget you,' I replied, quite melancholy; 'may your bees flourish, and may Heaven grant you are as happy as you deserve to be!'

"'So be it, M. Hennetius,' said good Dame Catherine; 'amen; a happy journey, and good health to you.'

"I moved off.

"They remained on the terrace until I reached the road.

"Thrice I turned round and waved my cap, and they responded by waving their hands.

"Good people; why cannot we meet with such every day?'

"Little Raesel accompanied me to the foot of the mountain, as she had promised. For a long time her musical hum lightened the fatigue of my journey; I seemed to recognise her in every bee which came buzzing about my ears, and I fancied I could hear her say in a small shrill tone of voice—

"'Courage, M. Hennetius, courage; it is very hot, is it not? Come, let me give you a kiss; don't be afraid; you know we are very good friends.'

"It was only at the end of the valley that she took leave of me, when the sound of the lake drowned her gentle voice; but her idea followed me all through my journey, nor do I think it will ever leave me."

The Torture by Hope
(1883)

Villiers De L'isle Adam

M any years ago, as evening was closing in, the venerable Pedro Arbuez d'Espila, sixth prior of the Dominicans of Segovia, and third Grand Inquisitor of Spain, followed by a fra redemptor, and preceded by two familiars of the Holy Office, the latter carrying lanterns, made their way to a subterranean dungeon. The bolt of a massive door creaked, and they entered a mephitic in-pace, where the dim light revealed between rings fastened to the wall a bloodstained rack, a brazier, and a jug. On a pile of straw, loaded with fetters and his neck encircled by an iron carcan, sat a haggard man, of uncertain age, clothed in rags.

This prisoner was no other than Rabbi Aser Abarbanel, a Jew of Arragon, who—accused of usury and pitiless scorn for the poor—had been daily subjected to torture for more than a year. Yet "his blindness was as dense as his hide," and he had refused to abjure his faith.

Proud of a filiation dating back thousands of years, proud of his ancestors—for all Jews worthy of the name are vain of their blood—he descended Talmudically from Othoniel and consequently from Ipsiboa, the wife of the last judge of Israel, a circumstance which had sustained his courage amid incessant torture. With tears in his eyes at the thought of this resolute soul rejecting salvation, the venerable Pedro Arbuez d'Espila, approaching the shuddering rabbi, addressed him as follows:

"My son, rejoice: your trials here below are about to end. If in the presence of such obstinacy I was forced to permit, with deep regret, the use of great severity, my task of fraternal correction has its limits. You are the fig tree which, having failed so many times to bear fruit, at last withered, but God alone can judge your soul. Perhaps Infinite Mercy will shine upon you at the last moment! We must hope so. There are examples. So sleep in peace to-night. Tomorrow you will be included in the auto da fé: that is, you will be exposed to the quémadero, the symbolical flames of the Everlasting Fire: it burns, as you know, only at a distance, my son; and Death is at least two hours (often three) in coming, on account of the wet, iced bandages, with which we protect the heads and hearts of the condemned. There will be forty-three of you. Placed in the last row, you will have time to invoke God and offer to Him this baptism of fire, which is of the Holy Spirit. Hope in the Light, and rest."

With these words, having signed to his companions to unchain the prisoner, the prior tenderly embraced him. Then came the turn of the fra redemptor, who, in a low tone, entreated the Jew's forgiveness for what he had made him suffer for the purpose of redeeming him; then the two familiars silently kissed him. This ceremony over, the captive was left, solitary and bewildered, in the darkness.

* * *

Rabbi Aser Abarbanel, with parched lips and visage worn by suffering, at first gazed at the closed door with vacant eyes. Closed? The word unconsciously roused a vague fancy in his mind, the fancy that he had seen for an instant the light of the lanterns through a chink between the door and the wall. A morbid idea of hope, due to the weakness of his brain, stirred his whole being. He dragged himself toward the strange appearance. Then, very gently and cautiously, slipping one finger into the crevice, he drew the door toward him. Marvelous! By an extraordinary accident the familiar who closed it had turned the huge key an instant before it struck the stone casing, so that the rusty bolt not having entered the hole, the door again rolled on its hinges.

The rabbi ventured to glance outside. By the aid of a sort of luminous dusk he distinguished at first a semicircle of walls indented by winding stairs; and opposite to him, at the top of five or six stone steps, a sort of black portal, opening into an immense corridor, whose first arches only were visible from below.

Stretching himself flat he crept to the threshold. Yes, it was really a corridor, but endless in length. A wan light illumined it: lamps suspended from the vaulted ceiling lightened at intervals the dull hue of the atmosphere—the distance was veiled in shadow. Not a single door appeared in the whole extent! Only on one side, the left, heavily grated loopholes, sunk in the walls, admitted a light which must be that of evening, for crimson bars at intervals rested on the flags of the pavement. What a terrible silence! Yet, yonder, at the far end of that passage there might be a doorway of escape! The Jew's vacillating hope was tenacious, for it was the last.

Without hesitating, he ventured on the flags, keeping close under the loopholes, trying to make himself part of the blackness of the long walls. He advanced slowly, dragging himself along on his breast, forcing back the cry of pain when some raw wound sent a keen pang through his whole body.

Suddenly the sound of a sandaled foot approaching reached his ears. He trembled violently, fear stifled him, his sight grew dim. Well, it was over, no doubt. He pressed himself into a niche and, half lifeless with terror, waited.

It was a familiar hurrying along. He passed swiftly by, holding in his clenched hand an instrument of torture—a frightful figure—and vanished. The suspense which the rabbi had endured seemed to have suspended the functions of life, and he lay nearly an hour unable to move. Fearing an increase of tortures if he were captured, he thought of returning to his dungeon. But the old hope whispered in his soul that divine perhaps, which comforts us in our sorest trials. A miracle had happened. He could doubt no longer. He began to crawl toward the chance of escape. Exhausted by suffering and hunger, trembling with pain, he pressed onward. The sepulchral corridor seemed to lengthen myste-riously, while he, still advancing, gazed into the gloom where there must be some avenue of escape.

Oh! oh! He again heard footsteps, but this time they were slower, more heavy. The white and black forms of two inquisitors appeared, emerging from the obscurity beyond. They were conversing in low tones, and seemed to be discussing some important subject, for they were gesticulating vehemently.

At this spectacle Rabbi Aser Abarbanel closed his eyes: his heart beat so violently that it almost suffocated him; his rags were damp with the cold sweat of agony; he lay motionless by the wall, his mouth wide open, under the rays of a lamp, praying to the God of David.

Just opposite to him the two inquisitors paused under the light of the lamp—doubtless owing to some accident due to the course of their argument. One, while listening to his companion, gazed at the rabbi! And, beneath the look—whose absence of expression the hapless man did not at first notice—he fancied he again felt the burning pincers scorch his flesh, he was to be once more a living wound. Fainting, breathless, with fluttering eyelids, he shivered at the touch of the monk's floating robe. But—strange yet natural fact—the inquisitor's gaze was evidently that of a man deeply absorbed in his intended reply, engrossed by what he was hearing; his eyes were fixed—and seemed to look at the Jew without seeing him.

In fact, after the lapse of a few minutes, the two gloomy figures slowly pursued their way, still conversing in low tones, toward the place whence the prisoner had come; HE HAD NOT BEEN SEEN! Amid the horrible confusion of the rabbi's thoughts, the idea darted through his brain: "Can I be already dead that they did not see me?" A hideous impression roused him from his lethargy: in looking at the wall against which his face was pressed, he imagined he beheld two fierce eyes watching him! He flung his head back in a sudden frenzy of fright, his hair fairly bristling! Yet, no! No. His hand groped over the stones: it was the reflection of the inquisitor's eyes, still retained in his own, which had been refracted from two spots on the wall.

Forward! He must hasten toward that goal which he fancied (absurdly, no doubt) to be deliverance, toward the darkness from which he was now barely thirty paces distant. He pressed forward faster on his knees, his hands, at full length, dragging himself painfully along, and soon entered the dark portion of this terrible corridor.

Suddenly the poor wretch felt a gust of cold air on the hands resting upon the flags; it came from under the little door to which the two walls led.

Oh, Heaven, if that door should open outward. Every nerve in the miserable fugitive's body thrilled with hope. He examined it from top to bottom, though scarcely able to distinguish its outlines in the surrounding darkness. He passed his hand over it: no bolt, no lock! A latch! He started up, the latch yielded to the pressure of his thumb: the door silently swung open before him.

"HALLELUIA!" murmured the rabbi in a transport of gratitude as, standing on the threshold, he beheld the scene before him.

The door had opened into the gardens, above which arched a starlit sky, into spring, liberty, life! It revealed the neighboring fields, stretching toward the sierras, whose sinuous blue lines were relieved against the horizon. Yonder lay freedom! Oh, to escape! He would journey all night through the lemon groves, whose fragrance reached him. Once in the mountains and he was safe! He inhaled the delicious air; the breeze revived him, his lungs expanded! He felt in his swelling heart the Veni foràs of Lazarus! And to thank once more the God who had bestowed this mercy upon him, he extended his arms, raising his eyes toward Heaven. It was an ecstasy of joy!

Then he fancied he saw the shadow of his arms approach him—fancied that he felt these shadowy arms inclose, embrace him—and that he was pressed tenderly to some one's breast. A tall figure actually did stand directly before him. He lowered his eyes—and remained motionless, gasping for breath, dazed, with fixed eyes, fairly driveling with terror.

Horror! He was in the clasp of the Grand Inquisitor himself, the venerable Pedro Arbuez d'Espila, who gazed at him with tearful eyes, like a good shepherd who had found his stray lamb.

The dark-robed priest pressed the hapless Jew to his heart with so fervent an outburst of love, that the edges of the monochal haircloth rubbed the Dominican's breast. And while Aser Abarbanel with protruding eyes gasped in agony in the ascetic's embrace, vaguely comprehending that all the phases of this fatal evening were only a prearranged torture, that of HOPE, the Grand Inquisitor, with an accent of touching reproach and a look of consternation, murmured in his ear, his breath parched and burning from long fasting:

"What, my son! On the eve, perchance, of salvation—you wished to leave us?"

The Horla, or Modern Ghosts (1887)

Guy De Maupassant

May 8th. What a lovely day! I have spent all the morning lying in the grass in front of my house, under the enormous plantain tree which covers it, and shades and shelters the whole of it. I like this part of the country and I am fond of living here because I am attached to it by deep roots, profound and delicate roots which attach a man to the soil on which his ancestors were born and died, which attach him to what people think and what they eat, to the usages as well as to the food, local expressions, the peculiar language of the peasants, to the smell of the soil, of the villages and of the atmosphere itself.

I love my house in which I grew up. From my windows I can see the Seine which flows by the side of my garden, on the other side of the road, almost through my grounds, the great and wide Seine, which goes to Rouen and Havre, and which is covered with boats passing to and fro.

On the left, down yonder, lies Rouen, that large town with its blue roofs, under its pointed Gothic towers. They are innumerable, delicate or broad, dominated by the spire of the cathedral, and full of bells which sound through the blue air on fine mornings, sending their sweet and distant iron clang to me; their metallic sound which the breeze wafts in my direction, now stronger and now weaker, according as the wind is stronger or lighter.

What a delicious morning it was!

About eleven o'clock, a long line of boats drawn by a steam tug, as big as a fly, and which scarcely puffed while emitting its thick smoke, passed my gate.

After two English schooners, whose red flag fluttered toward the sky, there came a magnificent Brazilian three-master; it was perfectly white and wonderfully clean and shining. I saluted it, I hardly know why, except that the sight of the vessel gave me great pleasure.

May 12th. I have had a slight feverish attack for the last few days, and I feel ill, or rather I feel low-spirited.

Whence do these mysterious influences come, which change our happiness into discouragement, and our self-confidence into diffidence? One might almost say that the air, the invisible air is full of unknowable Forces, whose mysterious presence we have to endure. I wake up in the best spirits, with an inclination to sing in my throat. Why? I go down by the side of the water, and suddenly, after walking a short distance, I return home wretched, as if some misfortune were awaiting me there. Why? Is it a cold shiver which, passing over my skin, has upset my nerves and given me low spirits? Is it the form of the clouds, or the color of the sky, or the color of the surrounding objects which is so changeable, which have troubled my thoughts as they passed before my eyes? Who can tell? Everything that surrounds us, everything that we see without looking at it, everything that we touch without knowing it, everything that we handle without feeling it, all that we meet without clearly distinguishing it, has a rapid, surprising and inexplicable effect upon us and upon our organs, and through them on our ideas and on our heart itself.

How profound that mystery of the Invisible is! We cannot fathom it with our miserable senses, with our eyes which are unable to perceive what is either too small or too great, too near to, or too far from us; neither the inhabitants of a star nor of a drop of water ... with our ears that deceive us, for they transmit to us the vibrations of the air in sonorous notes. They are fairies who work the miracle of changing that movement into noise, and by that metamorphosis give birth to music, which makes the mute agitation of nature musical ... with our sense of smell which is smaller than that of a dog ... with our sense of taste which can scarcely distinguish the age of a wine!

Oh! If we only had other organs which would work other miracles in our favor, what a number of fresh things we might discover around us!

May 16th. I am ill, decidedly! I was so well last month! I am feverish, horribly feverish, or rather I am in a state of feverish enervation, which makes my mind suffer as much as my body. I have without ceasing that horrible sensation of some danger threatening me, that apprehension of some coming misfortune or of approaching death, that presentiment which is, no doubt, an attack of some illness which is still unknown, which germinates in the flesh and in the blood.

May 18th. I have just come from consulting my medical man, for I could no longer get any sleep. He found that my pulse was high, my eyes dilated, my nerves highly strung, but no alarming symptoms. I must have a course of shower-baths and of bromide of potassium.

May 25th. No change! My state is really very peculiar. As the evening comes on, an incomprehensible feeling of disquietude seizes me, just as if night concealed some terrible menace toward me. I dine quickly, and then try to read, but I do not understand the words, and can scarcely distinguish the letters. Then I walk up and down my drawing-room, oppressed by a feeling of confused and irresistible fear, the fear of sleep and fear of my bed.

About ten o'clock I go up to my room. As soon as I have got in I double lock, and bolt it: I am frightened—of what? Up till the present time I have been frightened of nothing—I open my cupboards, and look under my bed; I listen—I listen—to what? How strange it is that a simple feeling of discomfort, impeded or heightened circulation, perhaps the irritation of a nervous thread, a slight congestion, a small disturbance in the imperfect and delicate functions of our living machinery, can turn the most lighthearted of men into a melancholy one, and make a coward of the bravest! Then, I go to bed, and I wait for sleep as a man might wait for the executioner. I wait for its coming with dread, and my heart beats and my legs tremble, while my whole body shivers beneath the warmth of the bedclothes, until the moment when I suddenly fall asleep, as one would throw oneself into a pool of stagnant water in order to drown oneself. I do not feel coming over me, as I used to do formerly, this perfidious sleep which is close to me and watching me, which is going to seize me by the head, to close my eyes and annihilate me.

I sleep—a long time—two or three hours perhaps—then a dream—no—a nightmare lays hold on me. I feel that I am in bed and asleep—I feel it and I know it—and I feel also that somebody is coming close to me, is looking at me, touching me, is getting on to my bed, is kneeling on my chest, is taking my neck between his hands and squeezing it—squeezing it with all his might in order to strangle me.

I struggle, bound by that terrible powerlessness which paralyzes us in our dreams; I try to cry out—but I cannot; I want to move—I cannot; I try, with the most violent efforts and out of breath, to turn over and throw off this being which is crushing and suffocating me—I cannot!

And then, suddenly, I wake up, shaken and bathed in perspiration; I light a candle and find that I am alone, and after that crisis, which occurs every night, I at length fall asleep and slumber tranquilly till morning.

June 2d. My state has grown worse. What is the matter with me? The bromide does me no good, and the shower-baths have no effect whatever. Sometimes, in order to tire myself out, though I am fatigued enough already, I go for a walk in the forest of Roumare. I used to think at first that the fresh light and soft air, impregnated with the odor of herbs and leaves, would instill new blood into my veins and impart fresh energy to my heart. I turned into a broad ride in the wood, and then I turned toward La Bouille, through a narrow path, between two rows of exceedingly tall trees, which placed a thick, green, almost black roof between the sky and me.

A sudden shiver ran through me, not a cold shiver, but a shiver of agony, and so I hastened my steps, uneasy at being alone in the wood, frightened stupidly and without reason, at the profound solitude. Suddenly it seemed to me as if I were being followed, that somebody was walking at my heels, close, quite close to me, near enough to touch me.

I turned round suddenly, but I was alone. I saw nothing behind me except the straight, broad ride, empty and bordered by high trees, horribly empty; on the other side it also extended until it was lost in the distance, and looked just the same, terrible.

I closed my eyes. Why? And then I began to turn round on one heel very quickly, just like a top. I nearly fell down, and opened my eyes; the trees were dancing round me and the earth heaved; I was obliged to sit down. Then, ah! I no longer remembered how I had come! What a strange idea! What a strange, strange idea! I did not the least know. I started off to the right, and got back into the avenue which had led me into the middle of the forest.

June 3d. I have had a terrible night. I shall go away for a few weeks, for no doubt a journey will set me up again.

July 2d. I have come back, quite cured, and have had a most delightful trip into the bargain. I have been to Mont Saint-Michel, which I had not seen before.

What a sight, when one arrives as I did, at Avranches toward the end of the day! The town stands on a hill, and I was taken into the public garden at the extremity of the town. I uttered a cry of astonishment. An extraordinarily large bay lay extended before me, as far as my eyes could reach, between two hills which were lost to sight in the mist; and in the middle of this immense yellow bay, under a clear, golden sky, a peculiar hill rose up, somber and pointed in the midst of the sand. The sun had just disappeared, and under the still flaming sky the outline of that fantastic rock stood out, which bears on its summit a fantastic monument.

At daybreak I went to it. The tide was low as it had been the night before, and I saw that wonderful abbey rise up before me as I approached it. After several hours' walking, I reached the enormous mass of rocks which supports the little town, dominated by the great church. Having climbed the steep and narrow street, I entered the most wonderful Gothic building that has ever been built to God on earth, as large as a town, full of low rooms which seem buried beneath vaulted roofs, and lofty galleries supported by delicate columns.

I entered this gigantic granite jewel which is as light as a bit of lace, covered with towers, with slender belfries to which spiral staircases ascend, and which raise their strange heads that bristle with chimeras, with devils, with fantastic animals, with monstrous flowers, and which are joined together by finely carved arches, to the blue sky by day, and to the black sky by night.

When I had reached the summit, I said to the monk who accompanied me: "Father, how happy you must be here!" And he replied: "It is very windy, Monsieur;" and so we began to talk while watching the rising tide, which ran over the sand and covered it with a steel cuirass.

And then the monk told me stories, all the old stories belonging to the place, legends, nothing but legends.

One of them struck me forcibly. The country people, those belonging to the Mornet, declare that at night one can hear talking going on in the sand, and then that one hears two goats bleat, one with a strong, the other with a weak voice. Incredulous people declare that it is nothing but the cry of the sea birds, which occasionally resembles bleatings, and occasionally human lamentations; but belated fishermen swear that they have met an old shepherd, whose head, which is covered by his cloak, they can never see, wandering on the downs, between two tides, round the little town placed so far out of the world, and who is guiding and walking before them, a he-goat with a man's face, and a she-goat with a woman's face, and both of them with white hair; and talking incessantly, quarreling in a strange language, and then suddenly ceasing to talk in order to bleat with all their might.

"Do you believe it?" I asked the monk. "I scarcely know," he replied, and I continued: "If there are other beings besides ourselves on this earth, how comes it that we have not known it for so long a time, or why have you not seen them? How is it that I have not seen them?" He replied: "Do we see the hundred thousandth part of what exists? Look here; there is the wind, which is the strongest force in nature, which knocks down men, and blows down buildings, uproots trees, raises the sea into mountains of water, destroys cliffs and casts great ships onto the breakers; the wind which kills, which whistles, which sighs, which roars— have you ever seen it, and can you see it? It exists for all that, however."

I was silent before this simple reasoning. That man was a philosopher, or perhaps a fool; I could not say which exactly, so I held my tongue. What he had said, had often been in my own thoughts.

July 3d. I have slept badly; certainly there is some feverish influence here, for my coachman is suffering in the same way as I am. When I went back home yesterday, I noticed his singular paleness, and I asked him: "What is the matter with you, Jean?" "The matter is that I never get any rest, and my nights devour my days. Since your departure, monsieur, there has been a spell over me."

However, the other servants are all well, but I am very frightened of having another attack, myself.

July 4th. I am decidedly taken again; for my old nightmares have returned. Last night I felt somebody leaning on me who was sucking my life from between my lips with his mouth. Yes, he was sucking it out of my neck, like a leech would have done. Then he got up, satiated, and I woke up, so beaten, crushed and annihilated that I could not move. If this continues for a few days, I shall certainly go away again.

July 5th. Have I lost my reason? What has happened, what I saw last night, is so strange, that my head wanders when I think of it!

As I do now every evening, I had locked my door, and then, being thirsty, I drank half a glass of water, and I accidentally noticed that the water bottle was full up to the cut-glass stopper.

Then I went to bed and fell into one of my terrible sleeps, from which I was aroused in about two hours by a still more terrible shock.

Picture to yourself a sleeping man who is being murdered and who wakes up with a knife in his chest, and who is rattling in his throat, covered with blood, and who can no longer breathe, and is going to die, and does not understand anything at all about it—there it is.

Having recovered my senses, I was thirsty again, so I lit a candle and went to the table on which my water bottle was. I lifted it up and tilted it over my glass, but nothing came out.

It was empty! It was completely empty! At first I could not understand it at all, and then suddenly I was seized by such a terrible feeling that I had to sit down, or rather I fell into a chair! Then I sprang up with a bound to look about me, and then I sat down again, overcome by astonishment and fear, in front of the transparent crystal bottle! I looked at it with fixed eyes, trying to conjecture, and my hands trembled! Somebody had drunk the water, but who? I? I without any doubt. It could surely only be I? In that case I was a somnambulist. I lived, without knowing it, that double mysterious life which makes us doubt whether there are not two beings in us, or whether a strange, unknowable and invisible being does not at such moments, when our soul is in a state of torpor, animate our captive body which obeys this other being, as it does us ourselves, and more than it does ourselves.

Oh! Who will understand my horrible agony? Who will understand the emotion of a man who is sound in mind, wide awake, full of sound sense, and who looks in horror at the remains of a little water that has disappeared while he was asleep, through the glass of a water bottle? And I remained there until it was daylight, without venturing to go to bed again.

July 6th. I am going mad. Again all the contents of my water bottle have been drunk during the night—or rather, I have drunk it!

But is it I? Is it I? Who could it be? Who? Oh! God! Am I going mad? Who will save me?

July 10th. I have just been through some surprising ordeals. Decidedly I am mad! And yet!—

On July 6th, before going to bed, I put some wine, milk, water, bread and strawberries on my table. Somebody drank—I drank—all the water and a little of the milk, but neither the wine, bread nor the strawberries were touched.

On the seventh of July I renewed the same experiment, with the same results, and on July 8th, I left out the water and the milk and nothing was touched.

Lastly, on July 9th I put only water and milk on my table, taking care to wrap up the bottles in white muslin and to tie down the stoppers. Then I rubbed my lips, my beard and my hands with pencil lead, and went to bed.

Irresistible sleep seized me, which was soon followed by a terrible awakening. I had not moved, and my sheets were not marked. I rushed to the table. The muslin round the bottles remained intact; I undid the string, trembling with fear. All the water had been drunk, and so had the milk! Ah! Great God!—

I must start for Paris immediately.

July 12th. Paris. I must have lost my head during the last few days! I must be the plaything of my enervated imagination, unless I am really a somnambulist, or that I have been brought under the power of one of those influences which have been proved to exist, but which have hitherto been inexplicable, which are called suggestions. In any case, my mental state bordered on madness, and twenty-four hours of Paris sufficed to restore me to my equilibrium.

Yesterday after doing some business and paying some visits which instilled fresh and invigorating mental air into me, I wound up my evening at the Théâtre Français. A play by Alexandre Dumas the Younger was being acted, and his active and powerful mind completed my cure. Certainly solitude is dangerous for active minds. We require men who can think and can talk, around us. When we are alone for a long time we people space with phantoms.

I returned along the boulevards to my hotel in excellent spirits. Amid the jostling of the crowd I thought, not without irony, of my terrors and surmises of the previous week, because I believed, yes, I believed, that an invisible being lived beneath my roof. How weak our head is, and how quickly it is terrified and goes astray, as soon, as we are struck by a small, incomprehensible fact.

Instead of concluding with these simple words: "I do not understand because the cause escapes me," we immediately imagine terrible mysteries and supernatural powers.

July 14th. Fête of the Republic. I walked through the streets, and the crackers and flags amused me like a child. Still it is very foolish to be merry on a fixed date, by a Government decree. The populace is an imbecile flock of sheep, now steadily patient, and now in ferocious revolt. Say to it: "Amuse yourself," and it amuses itself. Say to it: "Go and fight with your neighbor," and it goes and fights. Say to it: "Vote for the Emperor," and it votes for the Emperor, and then say to it: "Vote for the Republic," and it votes for the Republic.

Those who direct it are also stupid; but instead of obeying men they obey principles, which can only be stupid, sterile, and false, for the very reason that they are principles, that is to say, ideas which are considered as certain and unchangeable, in this world where one is certain of nothing, since light is an illusion and noise is an illusion.

July 16th. I saw some things yesterday that troubled me very much.

I was dining at my cousin's Madame Sablé, whose husband is colonel of the 76th Chasseurs at Limoges. There were two young women there, one of whom had married a medical man, Dr. Parent, who devotes himself a great deal to nervous diseases and the extraordinary manifestations to which at this moment experiments in hypnotism and suggestion give rise.

He related to us at some length, the enormous results obtained by English scientists and the doctors of the medical school at Nancy, and the facts which he adduced appeared to me so strange, that I declared that I was altogether incredulous.

"We are," he declared, "on the point of discovering one of the most important secrets of nature, I mean to say, one of its most important secrets on this earth, for there are certainly some which are of a different kind of importance up in the stars, yonder. Ever since man has thought, since he has been able to express and write down his thoughts, he has felt himself close to a mystery which is impenetrable to his coarse and imperfect senses, and he endeavors to supplement the want of power of his organs by the efforts of his intellect. As long as that intellect still remained in its elementary stage, this intercourse with invisible spirits assumed forms which were commonplace though terrifying. Thence sprang the popular belief in the supernatural, the legends of wandering spirits, of fairies, of gnomes, ghosts, I might even say the legend of God, for our conceptions of the workman-creator, from whatever religion they may have come down to us, are certainly the most mediocre, the stupidest and the most unacceptable inventions that ever sprang from the frightened brain of any human creatures.

Nothing is truer than what Voltaire says: 'God made man in His own image, but man has certainly paid Him back again.'

"But for rather more than a century, men seem to have had a presentiment of something new. Mesmer and some others have put us on an unexpected track, and especially within the last two or three years, we have arrived at really surprising results."

My cousin, who is also very incredulous, smiled, and Dr. Parent said to her: "Would you like me to try and send you to sleep, Madame?" "Yes, certainly."

She sat down in an easy-chair, and he began to look at her fixedly, so as to fascinate her. I suddenly felt myself somewhat uncomfortable, with a beating heart and a choking feeling in my throat. I saw that Madame Sablé's eyes were growing heavy, her mouth twitched and her bosom heaved, and at the end of ten minutes she was asleep.

"Stand behind her," the doctor said to me, and so I took a seat behind her. He put a visiting card into her hands, and said to her: "This is a looking-glass; what do you see in it?" And she replied: "I see my cousin." "What is he doing?" "He is twisting his mustache." "And now?" "He is taking a photograph out of his pocket." "Whose photograph is it?" "His own."

That was true, and that photograph had been given me that same evening at the hotel.

"What is his attitude in this portrait?" "He is standing up with his hat in his hand."

So she saw on that card, on that piece of white pasteboard, as if she had seen it in a looking glass.

The young women were frightened, and exclaimed: "That is quite enough! Quite, quite enough!"

But the doctor said to her authoritatively: "You will get up at eight o'clock to-morrow morning; then you will go and call on your cousin at his hotel and ask him to lend you five thousand francs which your husband demands of you, and which he will ask for when he sets out on his coming journey."

Then he woke her up.

On returning to my hotel, I thought over this curious séance and I was assailed by doubts, not as to my cousin's absolute and undoubted good faith, for I had known her as well as if she had been my own sister ever since she was a child, but as to a possible trick on the doctor's part. Had not he, perhaps, kept a glass hidden in his hand, which he showed to the young woman in her sleep, at the same time as he did the card? Professional conjurers do things which are just as singular.

So I went home and to bed, and this morning, at about half-past eight, I was awakened by my footman, who said to me: "Madame Sablé has asked to see you immediately, Monsieur," so I dressed hastily and went to her.

She sat down in some agitation, with her eyes on the floor, and without raising her veil she said to me: "My dear cousin, I am going to ask a great favor of you." "What is it, cousin?" "I do not like to tell you, and yet I must. I am in absolute want of five thousand francs." "What, you?" "Yes, I, or rather my husband, who has asked me to procure them for him."

I was so stupefied that I stammered out my answers. I asked myself whether she had not really been making fun of me with Doctor Parent, if it were not merely a very well-acted farce which had been got up beforehand. On looking at her attentively, however, my doubts disappeared. She was trembling with grief, so painful was this step to her, and I was sure that her throat was full of sobs.

I knew that she was very rich and so I continued: "What! Has not your husband five thousand francs at his disposal! Come, think. Are you sure that he commissioned you to ask me for them?"

She hesitated for a few seconds, as if she were making a great effort to search her memory, and then she replied: "Yes ... yes, I am quite sure of it." "He has written to you?"

She hesitated again and reflected, and I guessed the torture of her thoughts. She did not know. She only knew that she was to borrow five thousand francs of me for her husband. So she told a lie. "Yes, he has written to me." "When, pray? You did not mention it to me yesterday." "I received his letter this morning." "Can you show it me?" "No; no ... no ... it contained private matters ... things too personal to ourselves.... I burnt it." "So your husband runs into debt?"

She hesitated again, and then murmured: "I do not know." Thereupon I said bluntly: "I have not five thousand francs at my disposal at this moment, my dear cousin."

She uttered a kind of cry as if she were in pain and said: "Oh! oh! I beseech you, I beseech you to get them for me...."

She got excited and clasped her hands as if she were praying to me! I heard her voice change its tone; she wept and stammered, harassed and dominated by the irresistible order that she had received.

"Oh! oh! I beg you to ... if you knew what I am suffering.... I want them to-day."

I had pity on her: "You shall have them by and by, I swear to you." "Oh! thank you! thank you! How kind you are!"

I continued: "Do you remember what took place at your house last night?" "Yes." "Do you remember that Doctor Parent sent you to sleep?" "Yes." "Oh! Very well then; he ordered you to come to me this morning to borrow five thousand francs, and at this moment you are obeying that suggestion."

She considered for a few moments, and then replied: "But as it is my husband who wants them...."

For a whole hour I tried to convince her, but could not succeed, and when she had gone I went to the doctor. He was just going out, and he listened to me with a smile, and said: "Do you believe now?" "Yes, I cannot help it." "Let us go to your cousin's."

She was already dozing on a couch, overcome with fatigue. The doctor felt her pulse, looked at her for some time with one hand raised toward her eyes which she closed by degrees under the irresistible power of this magnetic influence, and when she was asleep, he said:

"Your husband does not require the five thousand francs any longer! You must, therefore, forget that you asked your cousin to lend them to you, and, if he speaks to you about it, you will not understand him."

Then he woke her up, and I took out a pocketbook and said: "Here is what you asked me for this morning, my dear cousin." But she was so surprised that I did not venture to persist; nevertheless, I tried to recall the circumstance to her, but she denied it vigorously, thought that I was making fun of her, and in the end very nearly lost her temper.

There! I have just come back, and I have not been able to eat any lunch, for this experiment has altogether upset me.

July 19th. Many people to whom I have told the adventure have laughed at me. I no longer know what to think. The wise man says: Perhaps?

July 21st. I dined at Bougival, and then I spent the evening at a boatmen's ball. Decidedly everything depends on place and surroundings. It would be the height of folly to believe in the supernatural on the île de la Grenouillière[2] ... but on the top of Mont Saint-Michel? ... and in India? We are terribly under the influence of our surroundings. I shall return home next week.

July 30th. I came back to my own house yesterday. Everything is going on well.

August 2d. Nothing fresh; it is splendid weather, and I spend my days in watching the Seine flow past.

August 4th. Quarrels among my servants. They declare that the glasses are broken in the cupboards at night. The footman accuses the cook, who accuses the needlewoman, who accuses the other two. Who is the culprit? A clever person, to be able to tell.

August 6th. This time I am not mad. I have seen ... I have seen ... I have seen!... I can doubt no longer ... I have seen it!...

I was walking at two o'clock among my rose trees, in the full sunlight ... in the walk bordered by autumn roses which are beginning to fall. As I stopped to look at a Géant de Bataille, which had three splendid blooms, I distinctly saw the stalk of one of the roses bend, close to me, as if an invisible hand had bent it, and then break, as if that hand had picked it! Then the flower raised itself, following the curve which a hand would have described in carrying it toward a mouth, and it remained suspended in the transparent air, all alone and motionless, a terrible red spot, three yards from

my eyes. In desperation I rushed at it to take it! I found nothing; it had disappeared. Then I was seized with furious rage
against myself, for it is not allowable for a reasonable and
serious man to have such hallucinations.

But was it a hallucination? I turned round to look for the
stalk, and I found it immediately under the bush, freshly
broken, between two other roses which remained on the
branch, and I returned home then, with a much disturbed
mind; for I am certain now, as certain as I am of the alternation of day and night, that there exists close to me an invisible being that lives on milk and on water, which can touch
objects, take them and change their places; which is, consequently, endowed with a material nature, although it is
imperceptible to our senses, and which lives as I do, under
my roof....

August 7th. I slept tranquilly. He drank the water out of
my decanter, but did not disturb my sleep.

I ask myself whether I am mad. As I was walking just now
in the sun by the riverside, doubts as to my own sanity arose
in me; not vague doubts such as I have had hitherto, but
precise and absolute doubts. I have seen mad people, and I
have known some who have been quite intelligent, lucid,
even clear-sighted in every concern of life, except on one
point. They spoke clearly, readily, profoundly on everything, when suddenly their thoughts struck upon the breakers of their madness and broke to pieces there, and were
dispersed and foundered in that furious and terrible sea, full
of bounding waves, fogs and squalls, which is called
madness.

I certainly should think that I was mad, absolutely mad, if
I were not conscious, did not perfectly know my state, if I did

fathom it by analyzing it with the most complete lucidity. I should, in fact, be a reasonable man who was laboring under a hallucination. Some unknown disturbance must have been excited in my brain, one of those disturbances which physiologists of the present day try to note and to fix precisely, and that disturbance must have caused a profound gulf in my mind and in the order and logic of my ideas. Similar phenomena occur in the dreams which lead us through the most unlikely phantasmagoria, without causing us any surprise, because our verifying apparatus and our sense of control has gone to sleep, while our imaginative faculty wakes and works. Is it not possible that one of the imperceptible keys of the cerebral finger-board has been paralyzed in me? Some men lose the recollection of proper names, or of verbs or of numbers or merely of dates, in consequence of an accident. The localization of all the particles of thought has been proved nowadays; what then would there be surprising in the fact that my faculty of controlling the unreality of certain hallucinations should be destroyed for the time being!

I thought of all this as I walked by the side of the water. The sun was shining brightly on the river and made earth delightful, while it filled my looks with love for life, for the swallows, whose agility is always delightful in my eyes, for the plants by the riverside, whose rustling is a pleasure to my ears.

By degrees, however, an inexplicable feeling of discomfort seized me. It seemed to me as if some unknown force were numbing and stopping me, were preventing me from going farther and were calling me back. I felt that painful wish to return which oppresses you when you have left a beloved invalid at home, and when you are seized by a presentiment that he is worse.

I, therefore, returned in spite of myself, feeling certain that I should find some bad news awaiting me, a letter or a telegram. There was nothing, however, and I was more surprised and uneasy than if I had had another fantastic vision.

August 8th. I spent a terrible evening yesterday. He does not show himself any more, but I feel that he is near me, watching me, looking at me, penetrating me, dominating me and more redoubtable when he hides himself thus, than if he were to manifest his constant and invisible presence by supernatural phenomena. However, I slept.

August 9th. Nothing, but I am afraid.

August 10th. Nothing; what will happen to-morrow?

August 11th. Still nothing; I cannot stop at home with this fear hanging over me and these thoughts in my mind; I shall go away.

August 12th. Ten o'clock at night. All day long I have been trying to get away, and have not been able. I wished to accomplish this simple and easy act of liberty—go out—get into my carriage in order to go to Rouen—and I have not been able to do it. What is the reason?

August 13th. When one is attacked by certain maladies, all the springs of our physical being appear to be broken, all our energies destroyed, all our muscles relaxed, our bones to have become as soft as our flesh, and our blood as liquid as water. I am experiencing that in my moral being in a strange and distressing manner. I have no longer any strength, any courage, any self-control, nor even any power to set my own will in motion. I have no power left to will anything, but some one does it for me and I obey.

August 14th. I am lost! Somebody possesses my soul and governs it! Somebody orders all my acts, all my movements, all my thoughts. I am no longer anything in myself, nothing except an enslaved and terrified spectator of all the things which I do. I wish to go out; I cannot. He does not wish to, and so I remain, trembling and distracted in the armchair in which he keeps me sitting. I merely wish to get up and to rouse myself, so as to think that I am still master of myself: I cannot! I am riveted to my chair, and my chair adheres to the ground in such a manner that no force could move us.

Then suddenly, I must, I must go to the bottom of my garden to pick some strawberries and eat them, and I go there. I pick the strawberries and I eat them! Oh! my God! my God! Is there a God? If there be one, deliver me! save me! succor me! Pardon! Pity! Mercy! Save me! Oh! what sufferings! what torture! what horror!

August 15th. Certainly this is the way in which my poor cousin was possessed and swayed, when she came to borrow five thousand francs of me. She was under the power of a strange will which had entered into her, like another soul, like another parasitic and ruling soul. Is the world coming to an end?

But who is he, this invisible being that rules me? This unknowable being, this rover of a supernatural race?

Invisible beings exist, then! How is it then that since the beginning of the world they have never manifested themselves in such a manner precisely as they do to me? I have never read anything which resembles what goes on in my house. Oh! If I could only leave it, if I could only go away and flee, so as never to return, I should be saved; but I cannot.

August 16th. I managed to escape to-day for two hours, like a prisoner who finds the door of his dungeon accidentally open. I suddenly felt that I was free and that he was far away, and so I gave orders to put the horses in as quickly as possible, and I drove to Rouen. Oh! How delightful to be able to say to a man who obeyed you: "Go to Rouen!"

I made him pull up before the library, and I begged them to lend me Dr. Herrmann Herestauss's treatise on the unknown inhabitants of the ancient and modern world.

Then, as I was getting into my carriage, I intended to say: "To the railway station!" but instead of this I shouted—I did not say, but I shouted—in such a loud voice that all the passers-by turned round: "Home!" and I fell back onto the cushion of my carriage, overcome by mental agony. He had found me out and regained possession of me.

August 17th. Oh! What a night! what a night! And yet it seems to me that I ought to rejoice. I read until one o'clock in the morning! Herestauss, Doctor of Philosophy and Theogony, wrote the history and the manifestation of all those invisible beings which hover around man, or of whom he dreams. He describes their origin, their domains, their power; but none of them resembles the one which haunts me. One might say that man, ever since he has thought, has had a foreboding of, and feared a new being, stronger than himself, his successor in this world, and that, feeling him near, and not being able to foretell the nature of that master, he has, in his terror, created the whole race of hidden beings, of vague phantoms born of fear.

Having, therefore, read until one o'clock in the morning, I went and sat down at the open window, in order to cool my forehead and my thoughts, in the calm night air. It was very pleasant and warm! How I should have enjoyed such a night formerly!

There was no moon, but the stars darted out their rays in the dark heavens. Who inhabits those worlds? What forms, what living beings, what animals are there yonder? What do those who are thinkers in those distant worlds know more than we do? What can they do more than we can? What do they see which we do not know? Will not one of them, some day or other, traversing space, appear on our earth to conquer it, just as the Norsemen formerly crossed the sea in order to subjugate nations more feeble than themselves?

We are so weak, so unarmed, so ignorant, so small, we who live on this particle of mud which turns round in a drop of water.

I fell asleep, dreaming thus in the cool night air, and then, having slept for about three quarters of an hour, I opened my eyes without moving, awakened by I know not what confused and strange sensation. At first I saw nothing, and then suddenly it appeared to me as if a page of a book which had remained open on my table, turned over of its own accord. Not a breath of air had come in at my window, and I was surprised and waited. In about four minutes, I saw, I saw, yes I saw with my own eyes another page lift itself up and fall down on the others, as if a finger had turned it over. My armchair was empty, appeared empty, but I knew that he was there, he, and sitting in my place, and that he was reading. With a furious bound, the bound of an enraged wild beast that wishes to disembowel its tamer, I crossed my room to seize him, to strangle him, to kill him!... But before I could reach it, my chair fell over as if somebody had run away from me ... my table rocked, my lamp fell and went out, and my window closed as if some thief had been surprised and had fled out into the night, shutting it behind him.

So he had run away: he had been afraid; he, afraid of me!

So ... so ... to-morrow ... or later ... some day or other ... I should be able to hold him in my clutches and crush him against the ground! Do not dogs occasionally bite and strangle their masters?

August 18th. I have been thinking the whole day long. Oh! yes, I will obey him, follow his impulses, fulfill all his wishes, show myself humble, submissive, a coward. He is the stronger; but an hour will come....

August 19th. I know, ... I know ... I know all! I have just read the following in the Revue du Monde Scientifique: "A curious piece of news comes to us from Rio de Janeiro. Madness, an epidemic of madness, which may be compared to that contagious madness which attacked the people of Europe in the Middle Ages, is at this moment raging in the Province of San-Paulo. The frightened inhabitants are leaving their houses, deserting their villages, abandoning their land, saying that they are pursued, possessed, governed like human cattle by invisible, though tangible beings, a species of vampire, which feed on their life while they are asleep, and who, besides, drink water and milk without appearing to touch any other nourishment.

"Professor Dom Pedro Henriques, accompanied by several medical savants, has gone to the Province of San-Paulo, in order to study the origin and the manifestations of this surprising madness on the spot, and to propose such measures to the Emperor as may appear to him to be most fitted to restore the mad population to reason."

Ah! Ah! I remember now that fine Brazilian three-master which passed in front of my windows as it was going up the Seine, on the 8th of last May! I thought it looked so pretty, so white and bright! That Being was on board of her, coming from there, where its race sprang from. And it saw me! It saw my house which was also white, and it sprang from the ship onto the land. Oh! Good heavens!

Now I know, I can divine. The reign of man is over, and he has come. He whom disquieted priests exorcised, whom sorcerers evoked on dark nights, without yet seeing him appear, to whom the presentiments of the transient masters of the world lent all the monstrous or graceful forms of gnomes, spirits, genii, fairies, and familiar spirits. After the coarse conceptions of primitive fear, more clear-sighted men foresaw it more clearly. Mesmer divined him, and ten years ago physicians accurately discovered the nature of his power, even before he exercised it himself. They played with that weapon of their new Lord, the sway of a mysterious will over the human soul, which had become enslaved. They called it magnetism, hypnotism, suggestion ... what do I know? I have seen them amusing themselves like impudent children with this horrible power! Woe to us! Woe to man! He has come, the ... the ... what does he call himself ... the ... I fancy that he is shouting out his name to me and I do not hear him ... the ... yes ... he is shouting it out ... I am listening ... I cannot ... repeat ... it ... Horla ... I have heard ... the Horla ... it is he ... the Horla ... he has come!...

Ah! the vulture has eaten the pigeon, the wolf has eaten the lamb; the lion has devoured the buffalo with sharp horns;

man has killed the lion with an arrow, with a sword, with gunpowder; but the Horla will make of man what we have made of the horse and of the ox: his chattel, his slave and his food, by the mere power of his will. Woe to us!

But, nevertheless, the animal sometimes revolts and kills the man who has subjugated it.... I should also like ... I shall be able to ... but I must know him, touch him, see him! Learned men say that beasts' eyes, as they differ from ours, do not distinguish like ours do ... And my eye cannot distinguish this newcomer who is oppressing me.

Why? Oh! Now I remember the words of the monk at Mont Saint-Michel: "Can we see the hundred-thousandth part of what exists? Look here; there is the wind which is the strongest force in nature, which knocks men, and blows down buildings, uproots trees, raises the sea into mountains of water, destroys cliffs and casts great ships onto the breakers; the wind which kills, which whistles, which sighs, which roars—have you ever seen it, and can you see it? It exists for all that, however!"

And I went on thinking: my eyes are so weak, so imperfect, that they do not even distinguish hard bodies, if they are as transparent as glass!... If a glass without tinfoil behind it were to bar my way, I should run into it, just as a bird which has flown into a room breaks its head against the window panes. A thousand things, moreover, deceive him and lead him astray. How should it then be surprising that he cannot perceive a fresh body which is traversed by the light?

A new being! Why not? It was assuredly bound to come! Why should we be the last? We do not distinguish it, like all the others created before us. The reason is, that its nature is more perfect, its body finer and more finished than ours, that ours is so weak, so awkwardly conceived, encumbered with organs that are always tired, always on the strain like locks that are too complicated, which lives like a plant and like a beast, nourishing itself with difficulty on air, herbs and flesh, an animal machine which is a prey to maladies, to malformations, to decay; broken-winded, badly regulated, simple and eccentric, ingeniously badly made, a coarse and a delicate work, the outline of a being which might become intelligent and grand.

We are only a few, so few in this world, from the oyster up to man. Why should there not be one more, when once that period is accomplished which separates the successive apparitions from all the different species?

Why not one more? Why not, also, other trees with immense, splendid flowers, perfuming whole regions? Why not other elements besides fire, air, earth and water? There are four, only four, those nursing fathers of various beings! What a pity! Why are they not forty, four hundred, four thousand! How poor everything is, how mean and wretched! grudgingly given, dryly invented, clumsily made! Ah! the elephant and the hippopotamus, what grace! And the camel, what elegance!

But, the butterfly you will say, a flying flower! I dream of one that should be as large as a hundred worlds, with wings whose shape, beauty, colors, and motion I cannot even express. But I see it ... it flutters from star to star, refreshing them and perfuming them with the light and harmonious breath of its flight!... And the people up there look at it as it passes in an ecstasy of delight!...

What is the matter with me? It is he, the Horla who haunts me, and who makes me think of these foolish things! He is within me, he is becoming my soul; I shall kill him!

August 19th. I shall kill him. I have seen him! Yesterday I sat down at my table and pretended to write very assiduously. I knew quite well that he would come prowling round me, quite close to me, so close that I might perhaps be able to touch him, to seize him. And then!... then I should have the strength of desperation; I should have my hands, my knees, my chest, my forehead, my teeth to strangle him, to crush him, to bite him, to tear him to pieces. And I watched for him with all my overexcited organs.

I had lighted my two lamps and the eight wax candles on my mantelpiece, as if by this light I could have discovered him.

My bed, my old oak bed with its columns, was opposite to me; on my right was the fireplace; on my left the door which was carefully closed, after I had left it open for some time, in order to attract him; behind me was a very high wardrobe with a looking-glass in it, which served me to make my toilet every day, and in which I was in the habit of looking at myself from head to foot every time I passed it.

So I pretended to be writing in order to deceive him, for he also was watching me, and suddenly I felt, I was certain that he was reading over my shoulder, that he was there, almost touching my ear.

I got up so quickly, with my hands extended, that I almost fell. Eh! well?... It was as bright as at midday, but I did not see myself in the glass!... It was empty, clear, profound, full of light! But my figure was not reflected in it ... and I, I was opposite to it! I saw the large, clear glass from top to bottom, and I looked at it with unsteady eyes; and I did not dare to advance; I did not venture to make a movement, nevertheless, feeling perfectly that he was there, but that he would escape me again, he whose imperceptible body had absorbed my reflection.

How frightened I was! And then suddenly I began to see myself through a mist in the depths of the looking-glass, in a mist as it were through a sheet of water; and it seemed to me as if this water were flowing slowly from left to right, and making my figure clearer every moment. It was like the end of an eclipse. Whatever it was that hid me, did not appear to possess any clearly defined outlines, but a sort of opaque transparency, which gradually grew clearer.

At last I was able to distinguish myself completely, as I do every day when I look at myself.

I had seen it! And the horror of it remained with me and makes me shudder even now.

August 20th. How could I kill it, as I could not get hold of it? Poison? But it would see me mix it with the water; and then, would our poisons have any effect on its impalpable body? No ... no ... no doubt about the matter.... Then?... then?...

August 21st. I sent for a blacksmith from Rouen, and ordered iron shutters of him for my room, such as some private hotels in Paris have on the ground floor, for fear of thieves, and he is going to make me a similar door as well. I have made myself out as a coward, but I do not care about that!...

September 10th. Rouen, Hotel Continental. It is done; ... it is done ... but is he dead? My mind is thoroughly upset by what I have seen.

Well, then, yesterday the locksmith having put on the iron shutters and door, I left everything open until midnight, although it was getting cold.

Suddenly I felt that he was there, and joy, mad joy, took possession of me. I got up softly, and I walked to the right and left for some time, so that he might not guess anything; then I took off my boots and put on my slippers carelessly; then I fastened the iron shutters and going back to the door quickly I double-locked it with a padlock, putting the key into my pocket.

Suddenly I noticed that he was moving restlessly round me, that in his turn he was frightened and was ordering me to let him out. I nearly yielded, though I did not yet, but putting my back to the door I half opened it, just enough to allow me to go out backward, and as I am very tall, my head touched the lintel. I was sure that he had not been able to escape, and I shut him up quite alone, quite alone. What happiness! I had him fast. Then I ran downstairs; in the drawing-room, which was under my bedroom, I took the two lamps and I poured all the oil onto the carpet, the furniture, everywhere; then I set fire to it and made my escape, after having carefully double-locked the door.

I went and hid myself at the bottom of the garden in a clump of laurel bushes. How long it was! how long it was! Everything was dark, silent, motionless, not a breath of air and not a star, but heavy banks of clouds which one could not see, but which weighed, oh! so heavily on my soul.

I looked at my house and waited. How long it was! I already began to think that the fire had gone out of its own accord, or that he had extinguished it, when one of the lower windows gave way under the violence of the flames, and a long, soft, caressing sheet of red flame mounted up the white wall and kissed it as high as the roof. The light fell onto the trees, the branches, and the leaves, and a shiver of fear pervaded them also! The birds awoke; a dog began to howl, and it seemed to me as if the day were breaking! Almost immediately two other windows flew into fragments, and I saw that the whole of the lower part of my house was nothing but a terrible furnace. But a cry, a horrible, shrill, heartrending cry, a woman's cry, sounded through the night, and two garret windows were opened! I had forgotten the servants! I saw the terrorstruck faces, and their frantically waving arms!...

Then, overwhelmed with horror, I set off to run to the village, shouting: "Help! help! fire! fire!" I met some people who were already coming onto the scene, and I went back with them to see!

By this time the house was nothing but a horrible and magnificent funeral pile, a monstrous funeral pile which lit up the whole country, a funeral pile where men were burning, and where he was burning also, He, He, my prisoner, that new Being, the new master, the Horla!

Suddenly the whole roof fell in between the walls, and a volcano of flames darted up to the sky. Through all the windows which opened onto that furnace I saw the flames darting, and I thought that he was there, in that kiln, dead.

Dead? perhaps?... His body? Was not his body, which was transparent, indestructible by such means as would kill ours?

If he was not dead?... Perhaps time alone has power over that Invisible and Redoubtable Being. Why this transparent, unrecognizable body, this body belonging to a spirit, if it also had to fear ills, infirmities and premature destruction?

Premature destruction? All human terror springs from that! After man the Horla. After him who can die every day, at any hour, at any moment, by any accident, he came who was only to die at his own proper hour and minute, because he had touched the limits of his existence!

No ... no ... without any doubt ... he is not dead. Then ... then ... I suppose I must kill myself!

FOOTNOTE.—

This story is a tragic experience and prophecy. It was insanity that robbed the world of its most finished short story writer, the author of this tale; and even before his madness became overpowering, de Maupassant complained that he was haunted by his double—by a vision of another Self confronting and threatening him. He had run life at its top speed; this hallucination was the result.

Medical science defines in such cases "an image of memory which differs in intensity from the normal"—that is to say, a fixed idea so persistent and growing that to the thinker it seems utterly real.

—EDITOR.

The Yellow Wallpaper (1892)

Charlotte Perkins Gilman

It is very seldom that mere ordinary people like John and myself secure ancestral halls for the summer.

A colonial mansion, a hereditary estate, I would say a haunted house, and reach the height of romantic felicity—but that would be asking too much of fate!

Still I will proudly declare that there is something queer about it.

Else, why should it be let so cheaply? And why have stood so long untenanted?

John laughs at me, of course, but one expects that in marriage.

John is practical in the extreme. He has no patience with faith, an intense horror of superstition, and he scoffs openly at any talk of things not to be felt and seen and put down in figures.

John is a physician, and PERHAPS—(I would not say it to a living soul, of course, but this is dead paper and a great relief to my mind)—PERHAPS that is one reason I do not get well faster.

You see he does not believe I am sick!

And what can one do?

If a physician of high standing, and one's own husband, assures friends and relatives that there is really nothing the matter with one but temporary nervous depression—a slight hysterical tendency—what is one to do?

My brother is also a physician, and also of high standing, and he says the same thing.

So I take phosphates or phosphites—whichever it is, and tonics, and journeys, and air, and exercise, and am absolutely forbidden to "work" until I am well again.

Personally, I disagree with their ideas.

Personally, I believe that congenial work, with excitement and change, would do me good.

But what is one to do?

I did write for a while in spite of them; but it DOES exhaust me a good deal—having to be so sly about it, or else meet with heavy opposition.

I sometimes fancy that in my condition if I had less opposition and more society and stimulus—but John says the very worst thing I can do is to think about my condition, and I confess it always makes me feel bad.

So I will let it alone and talk about the house.

The most beautiful place! It is quite alone, standing well back from the road, quite three miles from the village. It makes me think of English places that you read about, for there are hedges and walls and gates that lock, and lots of separate little houses for the gardeners and people.

There is a DELICIOUS garden! I never saw such a garden—large and shady, full of box-bordered paths, and lined with long grape-covered arbors with seats under them.

There were greenhouses, too, but they are all broken now. There was some legal trouble, I believe, something about the heirs and coheirs; anyhow, the place has been empty for years.

That spoils my ghostliness, I am afraid, but I don't care—there is something strange about the house—I can feel it.

I even said so to John one moonlight evening, but he said what I felt was a DRAUGHT, and shut the window.

I get unreasonably angry with John sometimes. I'm sure I never used to be so sensitive. I think it is due to this nervous condition.

But John says if I feel so, I shall neglect proper self-control; so I take pains to control myself—before him, at least, and that makes me very tired.

I don't like our room a bit. I wanted one downstairs that opened on the piazza and had roses all over the window, and such pretty old-fashioned chintz hangings! but John would not hear of it.

He said there was only one window and not room for two beds, and no near room for him if he took another.

He is very careful and loving, and hardly lets me stir without special direction.

I have a schedule prescription for each hour in the day; he takes all care from me, and so I feel basely ungrateful not to value it more.

He said we came here solely on my account, that I was to have perfect rest and all the air I could get. "Your exercise depends on your strength, my dear," said he, "and your food somewhat on your appetite; but air you can absorb all the time." So we took the nursery at the top of the house.

It is a big, airy room, the whole floor nearly, with windows that look all ways, and air and sunshine galore. It was nursery first and then playroom and gymnasium, I should judge; for the windows are barred for little children, and there are rings and things in the walls.

The paint and paper look as if a boys' school had used it. It is stripped off—the paper—in great patches all around the head of my bed, about as far as I can reach, and in a great place on the other side of the room low down. I never saw a worse paper in my life.

One of those sprawling flamboyant patterns committing every artistic sin.

It is dull enough to confuse the eye in following, pronounced enough to constantly irritate and provoke study, and when you follow the lame uncertain curves for a little distance they suddenly commit suicide—plunge off at outrageous angles, destroy themselves in unheard of contradictions.

The color is repellent, almost revolting; a smouldering unclean yellow, strangely faded by the slow-turning sunlight.

It is a dull yet lurid orange in some places, a sickly sulphur tint in others.

No wonder the children hated it! I should hate it myself if I had to live in this room long.

There comes John, and I must put this away,—he hates to have me write a word.

We have been here two weeks, and I haven't felt like writing before, since that first day.

I am sitting by the window now, up in this atrocious nursery, and there is nothing to hinder my writing as much as I please, save lack of strength.

John is away all day, and even some nights when his cases are serious.

I am glad my case is not serious!

But these nervous troubles are dreadfully depressing.

John does not know how much I really suffer. He knows there is no REASON to suffer, and that satisfies him.

Of course it is only nervousness. It does weigh on me so not to do my duty in any way!

I meant to be such a help to John, such a real rest and comfort, and here I am a comparative burden already!

Nobody would believe what an effort it is to do what little I am able,—to dress and entertain, and order things.

It is fortunate Mary is so good with the baby. Such a dear baby!

And yet I CANNOT be with him, it makes me so nervous.

I suppose John never was nervous in his life. He laughs at me so about this wall-paper!

At first he meant to repaper the room, but afterwards he said that I was letting it get the better of me, and that nothing was worse for a nervous patient than to give way to such fancies.

He said that after the wall-paper was changed it would be the heavy bedstead, and then the barred windows, and then that gate at the head of the stairs, and so on.

"You know the place is doing you good," he said, "and really, dear, I don't care to renovate the house just for a three months' rental."

"Then do let us go downstairs," I said, "there are such pretty rooms there."

Then he took me in his arms and called me a blessed little goose, and said he would go down to the cellar, if I wished, and have it whitewashed into the bargain.

But he is right enough about the beds and windows and things.

It is an airy and comfortable room as any one need wish, and, of course, I would not be so silly as to make him uncomfortable just for a whim.

I'm really getting quite fond of the big room, all but that horrid paper.

Out of one window I can see the garden, those mysterious deepshaded arbors, the riotous old-fashioned flowers, and bushes and gnarly trees.

Out of another I get a lovely view of the bay and a little private wharf belonging to the estate. There is a beautiful shaded lane that runs down there from the house. I always fancy I see people walking in these numerous paths and arbors, but John has cautioned me not to give way to fancy in the least. He says that with my imaginative power and habit of story-making, a nervous weakness like mine is sure to lead to all manner of excited fancies, and that I ought to use my will and good sense to check the tendency. So I try.

I think sometimes that if I were only well enough to write a little it would relieve the press of ideas and rest me.

But I find I get pretty tired when I try.

It is so discouraging not to have any advice and companionship about my work. When I get really well, John says we will ask Cousin Henry and Julia down for a long visit; but he says he would as soon put fireworks in my pillow-case as to let me have those stimulating people about now.

I wish I could get well faster.

But I must not think about that. This paper looks to me as if it KNEW what a vicious influence it had!

There is a recurrent spot where the pattern lolls like a broken neck and two bulbous eyes stare at you upside down.

I get positively angry with the impertinence of it and the everlastingness. Up and down and sideways they crawl, and those absurd, unblinking eyes are everywhere. There is one place where two breadths didn't match, and the eyes go all up and down the line, one a little higher than the other.

I never saw so much expression in an inanimate thing before, and we all know how much expression they have! I used to lie awake as a child and get more entertainment and terror out of blank walls and plain furniture than most children could find in a toy store.

I remember what a kindly wink the knobs of our big, old bureau used to have, and there was one chair that always seemed like a strong friend.

I used to feel that if any of the other things looked too fierce I could always hop into that chair and be safe.

The furniture in this room is no worse than inharmonious, however, for we had to bring it all from downstairs. I suppose when this was used as a playroom they had to take the nursery things out, and no wonder! I never saw such ravages as the children have made here.

The wall-paper, as I said before, is torn off in spots, and it sticketh closer than a brother—they must have had perseverance as well as hatred.

Then the floor is scratched and gouged and splintered, the plaster itself is dug out here and there, and this great heavy bed which is all we found in the room, looks as if it had been through the wars.

But I don't mind it a bit—only the paper.

There comes John's sister. Such a dear girl as she is, and so careful of me! I must not let her find me writing.

She is a perfect and enthusiastic housekeeper, and hopes for no better profession. I verily believe she thinks it is the writing which made me sick!

But I can write when she is out, and see her a long way off from these windows.

There is one that commands the road, a lovely shaded winding road, and one that just looks off over the country. A lovely country, too, full of great elms and velvet meadows.

This wall-paper has a kind of sub-pattern in a different shade, a particularly irritating one, for you can only see it in certain lights, and not clearly then.

But in the places where it isn't faded and where the sun is just so—I can see a strange, provoking, formless sort of figure, that seems to skulk about behind that silly and conspicuous front design.

There's sister on the stairs!

Well, the Fourth of July is over! The people are gone and I am tired out. John thought it might do me good to see a little company, so we just had mother and Nellie and the children down for a week.

Of course I didn't do a thing. Jennie sees to everything now.

But it tired me all the same.

John says if I don't pick up faster he shall send me to Weir Mitchell in the fall.

But I don't want to go there at all. I had a friend who was in his hands once, and she says he is just like John and my brother, only more so!

Besides, it is such an undertaking to go so far.

I don't feel as if it was worth while to turn my hand over for anything, and I'm getting dreadfully fretful and querulous.

I cry at nothing, and cry most of the time.

Of course I don't when John is here, or anybody else, but when I am alone.

And I am alone a good deal just now. John is kept in town very often by serious cases, and Jennie is good and lets me alone when I want her to.

So I walk a little in the garden or down that lovely lane, sit on the porch under the roses, and lie down up here a good deal.

I'm getting really fond of the room in spite of the wall-paper. Perhaps BECAUSE of the wall-paper.

It dwells in my mind so!

I lie here on this great immovable bed—it is nailed down, I believe—and follow that pattern about by the hour. It is as good as gymnastics, I assure you. I start, we'll say, at the bottom, down in the corner over there where it has not been touched, and I determine for the thousandth time that I WILL follow that pointless pattern to some sort of a conclusion.

I know a little of the principle of design, and I know this thing was not arranged on any laws of radiation, or alternation, or repetition, or symmetry, or anything else that I ever heard of.

It is repeated, of course, by the breadths, but not otherwise.

Looked at in one way each breadth stands alone, the bloated curves and flourishes—a kind of "debased Romanesque" with delirium tremens—go waddling up and down in isolated columns of fatuity.

But, on the other hand, they connect diagonally, and the sprawling outlines run off in great slanting waves of optic horror, like a lot of wallowing seaweeds in full chase.

The whole thing goes horizontally, too, at least it seems so, and I exhaust myself in trying to distinguish the order of its going in that direction.

They have used a horizontal breadth for a frieze, and that adds wonderfully to the confusion.

There is one end of the room where it is almost intact, and there, when the crosslights fade and the low sun shines directly upon it, I can almost fancy radiation after all,—the interminable grotesques seem to form around a common centre and rush off in headlong plunges of equal distraction.

It makes me tired to follow it. I will take a nap I guess.

I don't know why I should write this.

I don't want to.

I don't feel able.

And I know John would think it absurd. But I MUST say what I feel and think in some way—it is such a relief!

But the effort is getting to be greater than the relief.

Half the time now I am awfully lazy, and lie down ever so much.

John says I musn't lose my strength, and has me take cod liver oil and lots of tonics and things, to say nothing of ale and wine and rare meat.

Dear John! He loves me very dearly, and hates to have me sick. I tried to have a real earnest reasonable talk with him the other day, and tell him how I wish he would let me go and make a visit to Cousin Henry and Julia.

But he said I wasn't able to go, nor able to stand it after I got there; and I did not make out a very good case for myself, for I was crying before I had finished.

It is getting to be a great effort for me to think straight. Just this nervous weakness I suppose.

And dear John gathered me up in his arms, and just carried me upstairs and laid me on the bed, and sat by me and read to me till it tired my head.

He said I was his darling and his comfort and all he had, and that I must take care of myself for his sake, and keep well.

He says no one but myself can help me out of it, that I must use my will and self-control and not let any silly fancies run away with me.

There's one comfort, the baby is well and happy, and does not have to occupy this nursery with the horrid wall-paper.

If we had not used it, that blessed child would have! What a fortunate escape! Why, I wouldn't have a child of mine, an impressionable little thing, live in such a room for worlds.

I never thought of it before, but it is lucky that John kept me here after all, I can stand it so much easier than a baby, you see.

Of course I never mention it to them any more—I am too wise,—but I keep watch of it all the same.

There are things in that paper that nobody knows but me, or ever will.

Behind that outside pattern the dim shapes get clearer every day.

It is always the same shape, only very numerous.

And it is like a woman stooping down and creeping about behind that pattern. I don't like it a bit. I wonder—I begin to think—I wish John would take me away from here!

It is so hard to talk with John about my case, because he is so wise, and because he loves me so.

But I tried it last night.

It was moonlight. The moon shines in all around just as the sun does.

I hate to see it sometimes, it creeps so slowly, and always comes in by one window or another.

John was asleep and I hated to waken him, so I kept still and watched the moonlight on that undulating wall-paper till I felt creepy.

The faint figure behind seemed to shake the pattern, just as if she wanted to get out.

I got up softly and went to feel and see if the paper DID move, and when I came back John was awake.

"What is it, little girl?" he said. "Don't go walking about like that—you'll get cold."

I though it was a good time to talk, so I told him that I really was not gaining here, and that I wished he would take me away.

"Why darling!" said he, "our lease will be up in three weeks, and I can't see how to leave before.

"The repairs are not done at home, and I cannot possibly leave town just now. Of course if you were in any danger, I could and would, but you really are better, dear, whether you can see it or not. I am a doctor, dear, and I know. You are gaining flesh and color, your appetite is better, I feel really much easier about you."

"I don't weigh a bit more," said I, "nor as much; and my appetite may be better in the evening when you are here, but it is worse in the morning when you are away!"

"Bless her little heart!" said he with a big hug, "she shall be as sick as she pleases! But now let's improve the shining hours by going to sleep, and talk about it in the morning!"

"And you won't go away?" I asked gloomily.

"Why, how can I, dear? It is only three weeks more and then we will take a nice little trip of a few days while Jennie is getting the house ready. Really dear you are better!"

"Better in body perhaps—" I began, and stopped short, for he sat up straight and looked at me with such a stern, reproachful look that I could not say another word.

"My darling," said he, "I beg of you, for my sake and for our child's sake, as well as for your own, that you will never for one instant let that idea enter your mind! There is nothing so dangerous, so fascinating, to a temperament like yours. It is a false and foolish fancy. Can you not trust me as a physician when I tell you so?"

So of course I said no more on that score, and we went to sleep before long. He thought I was asleep first, but I wasn't, and lay there for hours trying to decide whether that front pattern and the back pattern really did move together or separately.

On a pattern like this, by daylight, there is a lack of sequence, a defiance of law, that is a constant irritant to a normal mind.

The color is hideous enough, and unreliable enough, and infuriating enough, but the pattern is torturing.

You think you have mastered it, but just as you get well underway in following, it turns a back-somersault and there you are. It slaps you in the face, knocks you down, and tramples upon you. It is like a bad dream.

The outside pattern is a florid arabesque, reminding one of a fungus. If you can imagine a toadstool in joints, an interminable string of toadstools, budding and sprouting in endless convolutions—why, that is something like it.

That is, sometimes!

There is one marked peculiarity about this paper, a thing nobody seems to notice but myself, and that is that it changes as the light changes.

When the sun shoots in through the east window—I always watch for that first long, straight ray—it changes so quickly that I never can quite believe it.

That is why I watch it always.

By moonlight—the moon shines in all night when there is a moon—I wouldn't know it was the same paper.

At night in any kind of light, in twilight, candle light, lamplight, and worst of all by moonlight, it becomes bars! The outside pattern I mean, and the woman behind it is as plain as can be.

I didn't realize for a long time what the thing was that showed behind, that dim sub-pattern, but now I am quite sure it is a woman.

By daylight she is subdued, quiet. I fancy it is the pattern that keeps her so still. It is so puzzling. It keeps me quiet by the hour.

I lie down ever so much now. John says it is good for me, and to sleep all I can.

Indeed he started the habit by making me lie down for an hour after each meal.

It is a very bad habit I am convinced, for you see I don't sleep.

And that cultivates deceit, for I don't tell them I'm awake—O no!

The fact is I am getting a little afraid of John.

He seems very queer sometimes, and even Jennie has an inexplicable look.

It strikes me occasionally, just as a scientific hypothesis,— that perhaps it is the paper!

I have watched John when he did not know I was looking, and come into the room suddenly on the most innocent excuses, and I've caught him several times LOOKING AT THE PAPER! And Jennie too. I caught Jennie with her hand on it once.

She didn't know I was in the room, and when I asked her in a quiet, a very quiet voice, with the most restrained manner possible, what she was doing with the paper—she turned around as if she had been caught stealing, and looked quite angry—asked me why I should frighten her so!

Then she said that the paper stained everything it touched, that she had found yellow smooches on all my clothes and John's, and she wished we would be more careful!

Did not that sound innocent? But I know she was studying that pattern, and I am determined that nobody shall find it out but myself!

Life is very much more exciting now than it used to be. You see I have something more to expect, to look forward to, to watch. I really do eat better, and am more quiet than I was.

John is so pleased to see me improve! He laughed a little the other day, and said I seemed to be flourishing in spite of my wall-paper.

I turned it off with a laugh. I had no intention of telling him it was BECAUSE of the wall-paper—he would make fun of me. He might even want to take me away.

I don't want to leave now until I have found it out. There is a week more, and I think that will be enough.

I'm feeling ever so much better! I don't sleep much at night, for it is so interesting to watch developments; but I sleep a good deal in the daytime.

In the daytime it is tiresome and perplexing.

There are always new shoots on the fungus, and new shades of yellow all over it. I cannot keep count of them, though I have tried conscientiously.

It is the strangest yellow, that wall-paper! It makes me think of all the yellow things I ever saw—not beautiful ones like buttercups, but old foul, bad yellow things.

But there is something else about that paper—the smell! I noticed it the moment we came into the room, but with so much air and sun it was not bad. Now we have had a week of fog and rain, and whether the windows are open or not, the smell is here.

It creeps all over the house.

I find it hovering in the dining-room, skulking in the parlor, hiding in the hall, lying in wait for me on the stairs.

It gets into my hair.

Even when I go to ride, if I turn my head suddenly and surprise it—there is that smell!

Such a peculiar odor, too! I have spent hours in trying to analyze it, to find what it smelled like.

It is not bad—at first, and very gentle, but quite the subtlest, most enduring odor I ever met.

In this damp weather it is awful, I wake up in the night and find it hanging over me.

It used to disturb me at first. I thought seriously of burning the house—to reach the smell.

But now I am used to it. The only thing I can think of that it is like is the COLOR of the paper! A yellow smell.

There is a very funny mark on this wall, low down, near the mopboard. A streak that runs round the room. It goes behind every piece of furniture, except the bed, a long, straight, even SMOOCH, as if it had been rubbed over and over.

I wonder how it was done and who did it, and what they did it for. Round and round and round—round and round and round—it makes me dizzy!

I really have discovered something at last.

Through watching so much at night, when it changes so, I have finally found out.

The front pattern DOES move—and no wonder! The woman behind shakes it!

Sometimes I think there are a great many women behind, and sometimes only one, and she crawls around fast, and her crawling shakes it all over.

Then in the very bright spots she keeps still, and in the very shady spots she just takes hold of the bars and shakes them hard.

And she is all the time trying to climb through. But nobody could climb through that pattern—it strangles so; I think that is why it has so many heads.

They get through, and then the pattern strangles them off and turns them upside down, and makes their eyes white!

If those heads were covered or taken off it would not be half so bad.

I think that woman gets out in the daytime!

And I'll tell you why—privately—I've seen her!

I can see her out of every one of my windows!

It is the same woman, I know, for she is always creeping, and most women do not creep by daylight.

I see her on that long road under the trees, creeping along, and when a carriage comes she hides under the blackberry vines.

I don't blame her a bit. It must be very humiliating to be caught creeping by daylight!

I always lock the door when I creep by daylight. I can't do it at night, for I know John would suspect something at once.

And John is so queer now, that I don't want to irritate him. I wish he would take another room! Besides, I don't want anybody to get that woman out at night but myself.

I often wonder if I could see her out of all the windows at once.

But, turn as fast as I can, I can only see out of one at one time.

And though I always see her, she MAY be able to creep faster than I can turn!

I have watched her sometimes away off in the open country, creeping as fast as a cloud shadow in a high wind.

If only that top pattern could be gotten off from the under one! I mean to try it, little by little.

I have found out another funny thing, but I shan't tell it this time! It does not do to trust people too much.

There are only two more days to get this paper off, and I believe John is beginning to notice. I don't like the look in his eyes.

And I heard him ask Jennie a lot of professional questions about me. She had a very good report to give.

She said I slept a good deal in the daytime.

John knows I don't sleep very well at night, for all I'm so quiet!

He asked me all sorts of questions, too, and pretended to be very loving and kind.

As if I couldn't see through him!

Still, I don't wonder he acts so, sleeping under this paper for three months.

It only interests me, but I feel sure John and Jennie are secretly affected by it.

Hurrah! This is the last day, but it is enough. John is to stay in town over night, and won't be out until this evening.

Jennie wanted to sleep with me—the sly thing! but I told her I should undoubtedly rest better for a night all alone.

That was clever, for really I wasn't alone a bit! As soon as it was moonlight and that poor thing began to crawl and shake the pattern, I got up and ran to help her.

I pulled and she shook, I shook and she pulled, and before morning we had peeled off yards of that paper.

A strip about as high as my head and half around the room.

And then when the sun came and that awful pattern began to laugh at me, I declared I would finish it to-day!

We go away to-morrow, and they are moving all my furniture down again to leave things as they were before.

Jennie looked at the wall in amazement, but I told her merrily that I did it out of pure spite at the vicious thing.

She laughed and said she wouldn't mind doing it herself, but I must not get tired.

How she betrayed herself that time!

But I am here, and no person touches this paper but me— not ALIVE!

She tried to get me out of the room—it was too patent! But I said it was so quiet and empty and clean now that I believed I would lie down again and sleep all I could; and not to wake me even for dinner—I would call when I woke.

So now she is gone, and the servants are gone, and the things are gone, and there is nothing left but that great bedstead nailed down, with the canvas mattress we found on it.

We shall sleep downstairs to-night, and take the boat home to-morrow.

I quite enjoy the room, now it is bare again.

How those children did tear about here!

This bedstead is fairly gnawed!

But I must get to work.

I have locked the door and thrown the key down into the front path.

I don't want to go out, and I don't want to have anybody come in, till John comes.

I want to astonish him.

I've got a rope up here that even Jennie did not find. If that woman does get out, and tries to get away, I can tie her!

But I forgot I could not reach far without anything to stand on!

This bed will NOT move!

I tried to lift and push it until I was lame, and then I got so angry I bit off a little piece at one corner—but it hurt my teeth.

Then I peeled off all the paper I could reach standing on the floor. It sticks horribly and the pattern just enjoys it! All those strangled heads and bulbous eyes and waddling fungus growths just shriek with derision!

I am getting angry enough to do something desperate. To jump out of the window would be admirable exercise, but the bars are too strong even to try.

Besides I wouldn't do it. Of course not. I know well enough that a step like that is improper and might be misconstrued.

I don't like to LOOK out of the windows even—there are so many of those creeping women, and they creep so fast.

I wonder if they all come out of that wall-paper as I did?

But I am securely fastened now by my well-hidden rope—you don't get ME out in the road there!

I suppose I shall have to get back behind the pattern when it comes night, and that is hard!

It is so pleasant to be out in this great room and creep around as I please!

I don't want to go outside. I won't, even if Jennie asks me to.

For outside you have to creep on the ground, and everything is green instead of yellow.

But here I can creep smoothly on the floor, and my shoulder just fits in that long smooch around the wall, so I cannot lose my way.

Why there's John at the door!

It is no use, young man, you can't open it!

How he does call and pound!

Now he's crying for an axe.

It would be a shame to break down that beautiful door!

"John dear!" said I in the gentlest voice, "the key is down by the front steps, under a plantain leaf!"

That silenced him for a few moments.

Then he said—very quietly indeed, "Open the door, my darling!"

"I can't," said I. "The key is down by the front door under a plantain leaf!"

And then I said it again, several times, very gently and slowly, and said it so often that he had to go and see, and he got it of course, and came in. He stopped short by the door.

"What is the matter?" he cried. "For God's sake, what are you doing!"

I kept on creeping just the same, but I looked at him over my shoulder.

"I've got out at last," said I, "in spite of you and Jane. And I've pulled off most of the paper, so you can't put me back!"

Now why should that man have fainted? But he did, and right across my path by the wall, so that I had to creep over him every time!

Man-Size In Marble
(1893)

Edith Nesbit

Although every word of this story is as true as despair, I do not expect people to believe it. Nowadays a "rational explanation" is required before belief is possible. Let me then, at once, offer the "rational explanation" which finds most favour among those who have heard the tale of my life's tragedy. It is held that we were "under a delusion," Laura and I, on that 31st of October; and that this supposition places the whole matter on a satisfactory and believable basis. The reader can judge, when he, too, has heard my story, how far this is an "explanation," and in what sense it is "rational." There were three who took part in this: Laura and I and another man. The other man still lives, and can speak to the truth of the least credible part of my story.

* * *

I never in my life knew what it was to have as much money as I required to supply the most ordinary needs— good colours, books, and cab-fares—and when we were married we knew quite well that we should only be able to live at all by "strict punctuality and attention to business." I used to paint in those days, and Laura used to write, and we felt sure we could keep the pot at least simmering. Living in town was out of the question, so we went to look for a cottage in the country, which should be at once sanitary and picturesque. So rarely do these two qualities meet in one cottage that our search was for some time quite fruitless. We tried advertisements, but most of the desirable rural residences which we did look at proved to be lacking in both essentials, and when a cottage chanced to have drains it always had stucco as well and was shaped like a tea-caddy. And if we found a vine or rose-covered porch, corruption invariably lurked within. Our minds got so befogged by the eloquence of house-agents and the rival disadvantages of the fever-traps and outrages to beauty which we had seen and scorned, that I very much doubt whether either of us, on our wedding morning, knew the difference between a house and a haystack. But when we got away from friends and house-agents, on our honeymoon, our wits grew clear again, and we knew a pretty cottage when at last we saw one. It was at Brenzett—a little village set on a hill over against the southern marshes. We had gone there, from the seaside village where we were staying, to see the church, and two fields from the church we found this cottage. It stood quite by itself, about two miles from the village. It was a long, low building, with rooms sticking out in unexpected places. There was a bit of stone-work—ivy-covered and moss-grown, just two old rooms, all that was left of a big house that had once stood there—and round this stone-work the house had grown up. Stripped of its roses and jasmine it would have been hideous. As it stood it was charming, and after a brief examination we took it. It was absurdly cheap. The rest of our honeymoon we spent in grubbing about in second-hand shops in the county town, picking up bits of old oak and Chippendale chairs for our furnishing. We wound up with a run up to town and a visit to Liberty's, and soon the low oak-beamed lattice-windowed rooms began to be home. There was a jolly old-fashioned garden, with grass paths, and no end of hollyhocks and sunflowers, and big lilies. From the window you could see the marsh-pastures, and beyond them the blue, thin line of the sea. We were as happy as the summer was glorious, and settled down into work sooner than we ourselves expected. I was never tired of sketching the view and the wonderful cloud effects from the open lattice, and Laura would sit at the table and write verses about them, in which I mostly played the part of foreground.

We got a tall old peasant woman to do for us. Her face and figure were good, though her cooking was of the homeliest; but she understood all about gardening, and told us all the old names of the coppices and cornfields, and the stories of the smugglers and highwaymen, and, better still, of the "things that walked," and of the "sights" which met one in lonely glens of a starlight night. She was a great comfort to us, because Laura hated housekeeping as much as I loved folklore, and we soon came to leave all the domestic business to Mrs. Dorman, and to use her legends in little magazine stories which brought in the jingling guinea.

We had three months of married happiness, and did not have a single quarrel. One October evening I had been down to smoke a pipe with the doctor—our only neighbour—a pleasant young Irishman. Laura had stayed at home to finish a comic sketch of a village episode for the Monthly Marplot. I left her laughing over her own jokes, and came in to find her a crumpled heap of pale muslin weeping on the window seat.

"Good heavens, my darling, what's the matter?" I cried, taking her in my arms. She leaned her little dark head against my shoulder and went on crying. I had never seen her cry before—we had always been so happy, you see—and I felt sure some frightful misfortune had happened.

"What is the matter? Do speak."

"It's Mrs. Dorman," she sobbed.

"What has she done?" I inquired, immensely relieved.

"She says she must go before the end of the month, and she says her niece is ill; she's gone down to see her now, but I don't believe that's the reason, because her niece is always ill. I believe some one has been setting her against us. Her manner was so queer—"

"Never mind, Pussy," I said; "whatever you do, don't cry, or I shall have to cry too, to keep you in countenance, and then you'll never respect your man again!"

She dried her eyes obediently on my handkerchief, and even smiled faintly.

"But you see," she went on, "it is really serious, because these village people are so sheepy, and if one won't do a thing you may be quite sure none of the others will. And I shall have to cook the dinners, and wash up the hateful greasy plates; and you'll have to carry cans of water about, and clean the boots and knives—and we shall never have any time for work, or earn any money, or anything. We shall have to work all day, and only be able to rest when we are waiting for the kettle to boil!"

I represented to her that even if we had to perform these duties, the day would still present some margin for other toils and recreations. But she refused to see the matter in any but the greyest light. She was very unreasonable, my Laura, but I could not have loved her any more if she had been as reasonable as Whately.

"I'll speak to Mrs. Dorman when she comes back, and see if I can't come to terms with her," I said. "Perhaps she wants a rise in her screw. It will be all right. Let's walk up to the church."

The church was a large and lonely one, and we loved to go there, especially upon bright nights. The path skirted a wood, cut through it once, and ran along the crest of the hill through two meadows, and round the churchyard wall, over which the old yews loomed in black masses of shadow. This path, which was partly paved, was called "the bier-balk," for it had long been the way by which the corpses had been carried to burial. The churchyard was richly treed, and was shaded by great elms which stood just outside and stretched their majestic arms in benediction over the happy dead. A large, low porch let one into the building by a Norman doorway and a heavy oak door studded with iron. Inside, the arches rose into darkness, and between them the reticulated windows, which stood out white in the moonlight. In the chancel, the windows were of rich glass, which showed in faint light their noble colouring, and made the black oak of the choir pews hardly more solid than the shadows. But on each side of the altar lay a grey marble figure of a knight in full plate armour lying upon a low slab, with hands held up in everlasting prayer, and these figures, oddly enough, were always to be seen if there was any glimmer of light in the church. Their names were lost, but the peasants told of them that they had been fierce and wicked men, marauders by land and sea, who had been the scourge of their time, and had been guilty of deeds so foul that the house they had lived in—the big house, by the way, that had stood on the site of our cottage—had been stricken by lightning and the vengeance of Heaven. But for all that, the gold of their heirs had bought them a place in the church. Looking at the bad hard faces reproduced in the marble, this story was easily believed.

The church looked at its best and weirdest on that night, for the shadows of the yew trees fell through the windows upon the floor of the nave and touched the pillars with tattered shade. We sat down together without speaking, and watched the solemn beauty of the old church, with some of that awe which inspired its early builders. We walked to the chancel and looked at the sleeping warriors. Then we rested some time on the stone seat in the porch, looking out over the stretch of quiet moonlit meadows, feeling in every fibre of our being the peace of the night and of our happy love; and came away at last with a sense that even scrubbing and blackleading were but small troubles at their worst.

Mrs. Dorman had come back from the village, and I at once invited her to a tête-à-tête.

"Now, Mrs. Dorman," I said, when I had got her into my painting room, "what's all this about your not staying with us?"

"I should be glad to get away, sir, before the end of the month," she answered, with her usual placid dignity.

"Have you any fault to find, Mrs. Dorman?"

"None at all, sir; you and your lady have always been most kind, I'm sure—"

"Well, what is it? Are your wages not high enough?"

"No, sir, I gets quite enough."

"Then why not stay?"

"I'd rather not"—with some hesitation—"my niece is ill."

"But your niece has been ill ever since we came."

No answer. There was a long and awkward silence. I broke it.

"Can't you stay for another month?" I asked.

"No, sir. I'm bound to go by Thursday."

And this was Monday!

"Well, I must say, I think you might have let us know before. There's no time now to get any one else, and your mistress is not fit to do heavy housework. Can't you stay till next week?"

"I might be able to come back next week."

I was now convinced that all she wanted was a brief holiday, which we should have been willing enough to let her have, as soon as we could get a substitute.

"But why must you go this week?" I persisted. "Come, out with it."

Mrs. Dorman drew the little shawl, which she always wore, tightly across her bosom, as though she were cold. Then she said, with a sort of effort—

"They say, sir, as this was a big house in Catholic times, and there was a many deeds done here."

The nature of the "deeds" might be vaguely inferred from the inflection of Mrs. Dorman's voice—which was enough to make one's blood run cold. I was glad that Laura was not in the room. She was always nervous, as highly-strung natures are, and I felt that these tales about our house, told by this old peasant woman, with her impressive manner and contagious credulity, might have made our home less dear to my wife.

"Tell me all about it, Mrs. Dorman," I said; "you needn't mind about telling me. I'm not like the young people who make fun of such things."

Which was partly true.

"Well, sir"—she sank her voice—"you may have seen in the church, beside the altar, two shapes."

"You mean the effigies of the knights in armour," I said cheerfully.

"I mean them two bodies, drawed out man-size in marble," she returned, and I had to admit that her description was a thousand times more graphic than mine, to say nothing of a certain weird force and uncanniness about the phrase "drawed out man-size in marble."

"They do say, as on All Saints' Eve them two bodies sits up on their slabs, and gets off of them, and then walks down the aisle, in their marble"—(another good phrase, Mrs. Dorman)—"and as the church clock strikes eleven they walks out of the church door, and over the graves, and along the bier-balk, and if it's a wet night there's the marks of their feet in the morning."

"And where do they go?" I asked, rather fascinated.

"They comes back here to their home, sir, and if any one meets them—"

"Well, what then?" I asked.

But no—not another word could I get from her, save that her niece was ill and she must go. After what I had heard I scorned to discuss the niece, and tried to get from

Mrs. Dorman more details of the legend. I could get nothing but warnings.

"Whatever you do, sir, lock the door early on All Saints' Eve, and make the cross-sign over the doorstep and on the windows."

"But has any one ever seen these things?" I persisted.

"That's not for me to say. I know what I know, sir."

"Well, who was here last year?"

"No one, sir; the lady as owned the house only stayed here in summer, and she always went to London a full month afore the night. And I'm sorry to inconvenience you and your lady, but my niece is ill and I must go on Thursday."

I could have shaken her for her absurd reiteration of that obvious fiction, after she had told me her real reasons.

She was determined to go, nor could our united entreaties move her in the least.

I did not tell Laura the legend of the shapes that "walked in their marble," partly because a legend concerning our house might perhaps trouble my wife, and partly, I think, from some more occult reason. This was not quite the same to me as any other story, and I did not want to talk about it till the day was over. I had very soon ceased to think of the legend, however. I was painting a portrait of Laura, against the lattice window, and I could not think of much else. I had got a splendid background of yellow and grey sunset, and was working away with enthusiasm at her face. On Thursday Mrs. Dorman went. She relented, at parting, so far as to say—

"Don't you put yourself about too much, ma'am, and if there's any little thing I can do next week, I'm sure I shan't mind."

From which I inferred that she wished to come back to us after Halloween. Up to the last she adhered to the fiction of the niece with touching fidelity.

Thursday passed off pretty well. Laura showed marked ability in the matter of steak and potatoes, and I confess that my knives, and the plates, which I insisted upon washing, were better done than I had dared to expect.

Friday came. It is about what happened on that Friday that this is written. I wonder if I should have believed it, if any one had told it to me. I will write the story of it as quickly and plainly as I can. Everything that happened on that day is burnt into my brain. I shall not forget anything, nor leave anything out.

I got up early, I remember, and lighted the kitchen fire, and had just achieved a smoky success, when my little wife came running down, as sunny and sweet as the clear October morning itself. We prepared breakfast together, and found it very good fun. The housework was soon done, and when brushes and brooms and pails were quiet again, the house was still indeed. It is wonderful what a difference one makes in a house. We really missed Mrs. Dorman, quite apart from considerations concerning pots and pans. We spent the day in dusting our books and putting them straight, and dined gaily on cold steak and coffee. Laura was, if possible, brighter and gayer and sweeter than usual, and I began to think that a little domestic toil was really good for her. We had never been so merry since we were married, and the walk we had that afternoon was, I think, the happiest time of all my life. When we had watched the deep scarlet clouds slowly pale into leaden grey against a pale-green sky, and saw the white mists curl up along the hedgerows in the distant marsh, we came back to the house, silently, hand in hand.

"You are sad, my darling," I said, half-jestingly, as we sat down together in our little parlour. I expected a disclaimer, for my own silence had been the silence of complete happiness. To my surprise she said—

"Yes. I think I am sad, or rather I am uneasy. I don't think I'm very well. I have shivered three or four times since we came in, and it is not cold, is it?"

"No," I said, and hoped it was not a chill caught from the treacherous mists that roll up from the marshes in the dying light. No—she said, she did not think so. Then, after a silence, she spoke suddenly—

"Do you ever have presentiments of evil?"

"No," I said, smiling, "and I shouldn't believe in them if I had."

"I do," she went on; "the night my father died I knew it, though he was right away in the north of Scotland." I did not answer in words.

She sat looking at the fire for some time in silence, gently stroking my hand. At last she sprang up, came behind me, and, drawing my head back, kissed me.

"There, it's over now," she said. "What a baby I am! Come, light the candles, and we'll have some of these new Rubinstein duets."

And we spent a happy hour or two at the piano.

At about half-past ten I began to long for the good-night pipe, but Laura looked so white that I felt it would be brutal of me to fill our sitting-room with the fumes of strong cavendish.

"I'll take my pipe outside," I said.

"Let me come, too."

"No, sweetheart, not to-night; you're much too tired. I shan't be long. Get to bed, or I shall have an invalid to nurse to-morrow as well as the boots to clean."

I kissed her and was turning to go, when she flung her arms round my neck, and held me as if she would never let me go again. I stroked her hair.

"Come, Pussy, you're over-tired. The housework has been too much for you."

She loosened her clasp a little and drew a deep breath.

"No. We've been very happy to-day, Jack, haven't we? Don't stay out too long."

"I won't, my dearie."

I strolled out of the front door, leaving it unlatched. What a night it was! The jagged masses of heavy dark cloud were rolling at intervals from horizon to horizon, and thin white wreaths covered the stars. Through all the rush of the cloud river, the moon swam, breasting the waves and disappearing again in the darkness. When now and again her light reached the woodlands they seemed to be slowly and noiselessly waving in time to the swing of the clouds above them. There was a strange grey light over all the earth; the fields had that shadowy bloom over them which only comes from the marriage of dew and moonshine, or frost and starlight.

I walked up and down, drinking in the beauty of the quiet earth and the changing sky. The night was absolutely silent. Nothing seemed to be abroad. There was no skurrying of rabbits, or twitter of the half-asleep birds. And though the clouds went sailing across the sky, the wind that drove them never came low enough to rustle the dead leaves in the woodland paths. Across the meadows I could see the church tower standing out black and grey against the sky. I walked there thinking over our three months of happiness—and of my wife, her dear eyes, her loving ways. Oh, my little girl! my own little girl; what a vision came then of a long, glad life for you and me together!

I heard a bell-beat from the church. Eleven already! I turned to go in, but the night held me. I could not go back into our little warm rooms yet. I would go up to the church. I felt vaguely that it would be good to carry my love and thankfulness to the sanctuary whither so many loads of sorrow and gladness had been borne by the men and women of the dead years.

I looked in at the low window as I went by. Laura was half lying on her chair in front of the fire. I could not see her face, only her little head showed dark against the pale blue wall. She was quite still. Asleep, no doubt. My heart reached out to her, as I went on. There must be a God, I thought, and a God who was good. How otherwise could anything so sweet and dear as she have ever been imagined?

I walked slowly along the edge of the wood. A sound broke the stillness of the night, it was a rustling in the wood. I stopped and listened. The sound stopped too. I went on, and now distinctly heard another step than mine answer mine like an echo. It was a poacher or a wood-stealer, most likely, for these were not unknown in our Arcadian neighbourhood. But whoever it was, he was a fool not to step more lightly. I turned into the wood, and now the footstep seemed to come from the path I had just left. It must be an echo, I thought. The wood looked perfect in the moonlight. The large dying ferns and the brushwood showed where through thinning foliage the pale light came down. The tree trunks stood up like Gothic columns all around me. They reminded me of the church, and I turned into the bier-balk, and passed through the corpse-gate between the graves to the low porch. I paused for a moment on the stone seat where Laura and I had watched the fading landscape. Then I noticed that the door of the church was open, and I blamed myself for having left it unlatched the other night. We were the only people who ever cared to come to the church except on Sundays, and I was vexed to think that through our carelessness the damp autumn airs had had a chance of getting in and injuring the old fabric. I went in. It will seem strange, perhaps, that I should have gone half-way up the aisle before I remembered—with a sudden chill, followed by as sudden a rush of self-contempt—that this was the very day and hour when, according to tradition, the "shapes drawed out man-size in marble" began to walk.

Having thus remembered the legend, and remembered it with a shiver, of which I was ashamed, I could not do otherwise than walk up towards the altar, just to look at the figures—as I said to myself; really what I wanted was to assure myself, first, that I did not believe the legend, and, secondly, that it was not true. I was rather glad that I had come. I thought now I could tell Mrs. Dorman how vain her fancies were, and how peacefully the marble figures slept on through the ghastly hour. With my hands in my pockets I passed up the aisle. In the grey dim light the eastern end of the church looked larger than usual, and the arches above the two tombs looked larger too. The moon came out and showed me the reason. I stopped short, my heart gave a leap that nearly choked me, and then sank sickeningly.

The "bodies drawed out man-size" were gone, and their marble slabs lay wide and bare in the vague moonlight that slanted through the east window.

Were they really gone? or was I mad? Clenching my nerves, I stooped and passed my hand over the smooth slabs, and felt their flat unbroken surface. Had some one taken the things away? Was it some vile practical joke? I would make sure, anyway. In an instant I had made a torch of a newspaper, which happened to be in my pocket, and lighting it held it high above my head. Its yellow glare illumined the dark arches and those slabs. The figures were gone. And I was alone in the church; or was I alone?

And then a horror seized me, a horror indefinable and indescribable—an overwhelming certainty of supreme and accomplished calamity. I flung down the torch and tore along the aisle and out through the porch, biting my lips as I ran to keep myself from shrieking aloud. Oh, was I mad—or what was this that possessed me? I leaped the churchyard wall and took the straight cut across the fields, led by the light from our windows. Just as I got over the first stile, a dark figure seemed to spring out of the ground. Mad still with that certainty of misfortune, I made for the thing that stood in my path, shouting, "Get out of the way, can't you!"

But my push met with a more vigorous resistance than I had expected. My arms were caught just above the elbow and held as in a vice, and the raw-boned Irish doctor actually shook me.

"Would ye?" he cried, in his own unmistakable accents—" would ye, then?"

"Let me go, you fool," I gasped. "The marble figures have gone from the church; I tell you they've gone."

He broke into a ringing laugh. "I'll have to give ye a draught to-morrow, I see. Ye've bin smoking too much and listening to old wives' tales."

"I tell you, I've seen the bare slabs."

"Well, come back with me. I'm going up to old Palmer's—his daughter's ill; we'll look in at the church and let me see the bare slabs."

"You go, if you like," I said, a little less frantic for his laughter; "I'm going home to my wife."

"Rubbish, man," said he; "d'ye think I'll permit of that? Are ye to go saying all yer life that ye've seen solid marble endowed with vitality, and me to go all me life saying ye were a coward? No, sir—ye shan't do ut."

The night air—a human voice—and I think also the physical contact with this six feet of solid common sense, brought me back a little to my ordinary self, and the word "coward" was a mental shower-bath.

"Come on, then," I said sullenly; "perhaps you're right."

He still held my arm tightly. We got over the stile and back to the church. All was still as death. The place smelt very damp and earthy. We walked up the aisle. I am not ashamed to confess that I shut my eyes: I knew the figures would not be there. I heard Kelly strike a match.

"Here they are, ye see, right enough; ye've been dreaming or drinking, asking yer pardon for the imputation."

I opened my eyes. By Kelly's expiring vesta I saw two shapes lying "in their marble" on their slabs. I drew a deep breath, and caught his hand.

"I'm awfully indebted to you," I said. "It must have been some trick of light, or I have been working rather hard, perhaps that's it. Do you know, I was quite convinced they were gone."

"I'm aware of that," he answered rather grimly; "ye'll have to be careful of that brain of yours, my friend, I assure ye."

He was leaning over and looking at the right-hand figure, whose stony face was the most villainous and deadly in expression.

"By Jove," he said, "something has been afoot here—this hand is broken."

And so it was. I was certain that it had been perfect the last time Laura and I had been there.

"Perhaps some one has tried to remove them," said the young doctor.

"That won't account for my impression," I objected.

"Too much painting and tobacco will account for that, well enough."

"Come along," I said, "or my wife will be getting anxious. You'll come in and have a drop of whisky and drink confusion to ghosts and better sense to me."

"I ought to go up to Palmer's, but it's so late now I'd best leave it till the morning," he replied. "I was kept late at the Union, and I've had to see a lot of people since. All right, I'll come back with ye."

I think he fancied I needed him more than did Palmer's girl, so, discussing how such an illusion could have been possible, and deducing from this experience large generalities concerning ghostly apparitions, we walked up to our cottage. We saw, as we walked up the garden-path, that bright light streamed out of the front door, and presently saw that the parlour door was open too. Had she gone out?

"Come in," I said, and Dr. Kelly followed me into the parlour. It was all ablaze with candles, not only the wax ones, but at least a dozen guttering, glaring tallow dips, stuck in vases and ornaments in unlikely places. Light, I knew, was Laura's remedy for nervousness. Poor child! Why had I left her? Brute that I was.

We glanced round the room, and at first we did not see her. The window was open, and the draught set all the candles flaring one way. Her chair was empty and her handkerchief and book lay on the floor. I turned to the window. There, in the recess of the window, I saw her. Oh, my child, my love, had she gone to that window to watch for me? And what had come into the room behind her? To what had she turned with that look of frantic fear and horror? Oh, my little one, had she thought that it was I whose step she heard, and turned to meet—what?

She had fallen back across a table in the window, and her body lay half on it and half on the window-seat, and her head hung down over the table, the brown hair loosened and fallen to the carpet. Her lips were drawn back, and her eyes wide, wide open. They saw nothing now. What had they seen last?

The doctor moved towards her, but I pushed him aside and sprang to her; caught her in my arms and cried—

"It's all right, Laura! I've got you safe, wifie."

She fell into my arms in a heap. I clasped her and kissed her, and called her by all her pet names, but I think I knew all the time that she was dead. Her hands were tightly clenched. In one of them she held something fast. When I was quite sure that she was dead, and that nothing mattered at all any more, I let him open her hand to see what she held.

It was a grey marble finger.

The Mask (1895)

Robert W. Chambers

CAMILLA: You, sir, should unmask.

STRANGER: Indeed?

CASSILDA: Indeed it's time. We all have laid aside disguise but you.

STRANGER: I wear no mask.

CAMILLA: (Terrified, aside to Cassilda.) No mask? No mask!

– *The King in Yellow, Act I, Scene 2.*

I

Although I knew nothing of chemistry, I listened fascinated. He picked up an Easter lily which Geneviève had brought that morning from Notre Dame, and dropped it into the basin. Instantly the liquid lost its crystalline clearness. For a second the lily was enveloped in a milk-white foam, which disappeared, leaving the fluid opalescent. Changing tints of orange and crimson played over the surface, and then what seemed to be a ray of pure sunlight struck through from the bottom where the lily was resting. At the same instant he plunged his hand into the basin and drew out the flower. "There is no danger," he explained, "if you choose the right moment. That golden ray is the signal."

He held the lily toward me, and I took it in my hand. It had turned to stone, to the purest marble.

"You see," he said, "it is without a flaw. What sculptor could reproduce it?"

The marble was white as snow, but in its depths the veins of the lily were tinged with palest azure, and a faint flush lingered deep in its heart.

"Don't ask me the reason of that," he smiled, noticing my wonder. "I have no idea why the veins and heart are tinted, but they always are. Yesterday I tried one of Geneviève's gold-fish,—there it is."

The fish looked as if sculptured in marble. But if you held it to the light the stone was beautifully veined with a faint blue, and from somewhere within came a rosy light like the tint which slumbers in an opal. I looked into the basin. Once more it seemed filled with clearest crystal.

"If I should touch it now?" I demanded.

"I don't know," he replied, "but you had better not try."

"There is one thing I'm curious about," I said, "and that is where the ray of sunlight came from."

"It looked like a sunbeam true enough," he said. "I don't know, it always comes when I immerse any living thing. Perhaps," he continued, smiling, "perhaps it is the vital spark of the creature escaping to the source from whence it came."

I saw he was mocking, and threatened him with a mahl-stick, but he only laughed and changed the subject.

"Stay to lunch. Geneviève will be here directly."

"I saw her going to early mass," I said, "and she looked as fresh and sweet as that lily—before you destroyed it."

"Do you think I destroyed it?" said Boris gravely.

"Destroyed, preserved, how can we tell?"

We sat in the corner of a studio near his unfinished group of the "Fates." He leaned back on the sofa, twirling a sculptor's chisel and squinting at his work.

"By the way," he said, "I have finished pointing up that old academic Ariadne, and I suppose it will have to go to the Salon. It's all I have ready this year, but after the success the 'Madonna' brought me I feel ashamed to send a thing like that."

The "Madonna," an exquisite marble for which Geneviève had sat, had been the sensation of last year's Salon. I looked at the Ariadne. It was a magnificent piece of technical work, but I agreed with Boris that the world would expect something better of him than that. Still, it was impossible now to think of finishing in time for the Salon that splendid terrible group half shrouded in the marble behind me. The "Fates" would have to wait.

We were proud of Boris Yvain. We claimed him and he claimed us on the strength of his having been born in America, although his father was French and his mother was a Russian. Every one in the Beaux Arts called him Boris. And yet there were only two of us whom he addressed in the same familiar way—Jack Scott and myself.

Perhaps my being in love with Geneviève had something to do with his affection for me. Not that it had ever been acknowledged between us. But after all was settled, and she had told me with tears in her eyes that it was Boris whom she loved, I went over to his house and congratulated him. The perfect cordiality of that interview did not deceive either of us, I always believed, although to one at least it was a great comfort. I do not think he and Geneviève ever spoke of the matter together, but Boris knew.

Geneviève was lovely. The Madonna-like purity of her face might have been inspired by the Sanctus in Gounod's Mass. But I was always glad when she changed that mood for what we called her "April Manoeuvres." She was often as variable as an April day. In the morning grave, dignified and sweet, at noon laughing, capricious, at evening whatever one least expected. I preferred her so rather than in that Madonna-like tranquillity which stirred the depths of my heart. I was dreaming of Geneviève when he spoke again.

"What do you think of my discovery, Alec?"

"I think it wonderful."

"I shall make no use of it, you know, beyond satisfying my own curiosity so far as may be, and the secret will die with me."

"It would be rather a blow to sculpture, would it not? We painters lose more than we ever gain by photography."

Boris nodded, playing with the edge of the chisel.

"This new vicious discovery would corrupt the world of art. No, I shall never confide the secret to any one," he said slowly.

It would be hard to find any one less informed about such phenomena than myself; but of course I had heard of mineral springs so saturated with silica that the leaves and twigs which fell into them were turned to stone after a time. I dimly comprehended the process, how the silica replaced the vegetable matter, atom by atom, and the result was a duplicate of the object in stone. This, I confess, had never interested me greatly, and as for the ancient fossils thus produced, they disgusted me. Boris, it appeared, feeling curiosity instead of repugnance, had investigated the subject, and had accidentally stumbled on a solution which, attacking the immersed object with a ferocity unheard of, in a second did the work of years. This was all I could make out of the strange story he had just been telling me. He spoke again after a long silence.

"I am almost frightened when I think what I have found. Scientists would go mad over the discovery. It was so simple too; it discovered itself. When I think of that formula, and that new element precipitated in metallic scales—"

"What new element?"

"Oh, I haven't thought of naming it, and I don't believe I ever shall. There are enough precious metals now in the world to cut throats over."

I pricked up my ears. "Have you struck gold, Boris?"

"No, better;—but see here, Alec!" he laughed, starting up. "You and I have all we need in this world. Ah! how sinister and covetous you look already!" I laughed too, and told him I was devoured by the desire for gold, and we had better talk of something else; so when Geneviève came in shortly after, we had turned our backs on alchemy.

Geneviève was dressed in silvery grey from head to foot. The light glinted along the soft curves of her fair hair as she turned her cheek to Boris; then she saw me and returned my greeting. She had never before failed to blow me a kiss from the tips of her white fingers, and I promptly complained of the omission. She smiled and held out her hand, which dropped almost before it had touched mine; then she said, looking at Boris—

"You must ask Alec to stay for luncheon." This also was something new. She had always asked me herself until to-day.

"I did," said Boris shortly.

"And you said yes, I hope?" She turned to me with a charming conventional smile. I might have been an acquaintance of the day before yesterday. I made her a low bow. "J'avais bien l'honneur, madame," but refusing to take up our usual bantering tone, she murmured a hospitable common-place and disappeared. Boris and I looked at one another.

"I had better go home, don't you think?" I asked.

"Hanged if I know," he replied frankly.

While we were discussing the advisability of my departure Geneviève reappeared in the doorway without her bonnet. She was wonderfully beautiful, but her colour was too deep and her lovely eyes were too bright. She came straight up to me and took my arm.

"Luncheon is ready. Was I cross, Alec? I thought I had a headache, but I haven't. Come here, Boris;" and she slipped her other arm through his. "Alec knows that after you there is no one in the world whom I like as well as I like him, so if he sometimes feels snubbed it won't hurt him."

"À la bonheur!" I cried, "who says there are no thunder-storms in April?"

"Are you ready?" chanted Boris. "Aye ready;" and arm-in-arm we raced into the dining-room, scandalizing the servants. After all we were not so much to blame; Geneviève was eighteen, Boris was twenty-three, and I not quite twenty-one.

II

Some work that I was doing about this time on the decorations for Geneviève's boudoir kept me constantly at the quaint little hotel in the Rue Sainte-Cécile. Boris and I in those days laboured hard but as we pleased, which was fitfully, and we all three, with Jack Scott, idled a great deal together.

One quiet afternoon I had been wandering alone over the house examining curios, prying into odd corners, bringing out sweetmeats and cigars from strange hiding-places, and at last I stopped in the bathing-room. Boris, all over clay, stood there washing his hands.

The room was built of rose-coloured marble excepting the floor, which was tessellated in rose and grey. In the centre was a square pool sunken below the surface of the floor; steps led down into it, sculptured pillars supported a frescoed ceiling. A delicious marble Cupid appeared to have just alighted on his pedestal at the upper end of the room. The whole interior was Boris' work and mine. Boris, in his working-clothes of white canvas, scraped the traces of clay and red modelling wax from his handsome hands, and coquetted over his shoulder with the Cupid.

"I see you," he insisted, "don't try to look the other way and pretend not to see me. You know who made you, little humbug!"

It was always my rôle to interpret Cupid's sentiments in these conversations, and when my turn came I responded in such a manner, that Boris seized my arm and dragged me toward the pool, declaring he would duck me. Next instant he dropped my arm and turned pale. "Good God!" he said, "I forgot the pool is full of the solution!"

I shivered a little, and dryly advised him to remember better where he had stored the precious liquid.

"In Heaven's name, why do you keep a small lake of that gruesome stuff here of all places?" I asked.

"I want to experiment on something large," he replied.

"On me, for instance?"

"Ah! that came too close for jesting; but I do want to watch the action of that solution on a more highly organized living body; there is that big white rabbit," he said, following me into the studio.

Jack Scott, wearing a paint-stained jacket, came wandering in, appropriated all the Oriental sweetmeats he could lay his hands on, looted the cigarette case, and finally he and Boris disappeared together to visit the Luxembourg Gallery, where a new silver bronze by Rodin and a landscape of Monet's were claiming the exclusive attention of artistic France. I went back to the studio, and resumed my work. It was a Renaissance screen, which Boris wanted me to paint for Geneviève's boudoir. But the small boy who was unwillingly dawdling through a series of poses for it, to-day refused all bribes to be good. He never rested an instant in the same position, and inside of five minutes I had as many different outlines of the little beggar.

"Are you posing, or are you executing a song and dance, my friend?" I inquired.

"Whichever monsieur pleases," he replied, with an angelic smile.

Of course I dismissed him for the day, and of course I paid him for the full time, that being the way we spoil our models.

After the young imp had gone, I made a few perfunctory daubs at my work, but was so thoroughly out of humour, that it took me the rest of the afternoon to undo the damage I had done, so at last I scraped my palette, stuck my brushes in a bowl of black soap, and strolled into the smoking-room. I really believe that, excepting Geneviève's apartments, no room in the house was so free from the perfume of tobacco as this one. It was a queer chaos of odds and ends, hung with threadbare tapestry. A sweet-toned old spinet in good repair stood by the window. There were stands of weapons, some old and dull, others bright and modern, festoons of Indian and Turkish armour over the mantel, two or three good pictures, and a pipe-rack. It was here that we used to come for new sensations in smoking. I doubt if any type of pipe ever existed which was not represented in that rack. When we had selected one, we immediately carried it somewhere else and smoked it; for the place was, on the whole, more gloomy and less inviting than any in the house. But this afternoon, the twilight was very soothing, the rugs and skins on the floor looked brown and soft and drowsy; the big couch was piled with cushions—I found my pipe and curled up there for an unaccustomed smoke in the smoking-room. I had chosen one with a long flexible stem, and lighting it fell to dreaming. After a while it went out, but I did not stir. I dreamed on and presently fell asleep.

I awoke to the saddest music I had ever heard. The room was quite dark, I had no idea what time it was. A ray of moonlight silvered one edge of the old spinet, and the polished wood seemed to exhale the sounds as perfume floats above a box of sandalwood. Some one rose in the darkness, and came away weeping quietly, and I was fool enough to cry out "Geneviève!"

She dropped at my voice, and, I had time to curse myself while I made a light and tried to raise her from the floor. She shrank away with a murmur of pain. She was very quiet, and asked for Boris. I carried her to the divan, and went to look for him, but he was not in the house, and the servants were gone to bed. Perplexed and anxious, I hurried back to Geneviève. She lay where I had left her, looking very white.

"I can't find Boris nor any of the servants," I said.

"I know," she answered faintly, "Boris has gone to Ept with Mr. Scott. I did not remember when I sent you for him just now."

"But he can't get back in that case before to-morrow afternoon, and—are you hurt? Did I frighten you into falling? What an awful fool I am, but I was only half awake."

"Boris thought you had gone home before dinner. Do please excuse us for letting you stay here all this time."

"I have had a long nap," I laughed, "so sound that I did not know whether I was still asleep or not when I found myself staring at a figure that was moving toward me, and called out your name. Have you been trying the old spinet? You must have played very softly."

I would tell a thousand more lies worse than that one to see the look of relief that came into her face. She smiled adorably, and said in her natural voice: "Alec, I tripped on that wolf's head, and I think my ankle is sprained. Please call Marie, and then go home."

I did as she bade me, and left her there when the maid came in.

III

At noon next day when I called, I found Boris walking restlessly about his studio.

"Geneviève is asleep just now," he told me, "the sprain is nothing, but why should she have such a high fever? The doctor can't account for it; or else he will not," he muttered.

"Geneviève has a fever?" I asked.

"I should say so, and has actually been a little light-headed at intervals all night. The idea! gay little Geneviève, without a care in the world,—and she keeps saying her heart's broken, and she wants to die!"

My own heart stood still.

Boris leaned against the door of his studio, looking down, his hands in his pockets, his kind, keen eyes clouded, a new line of trouble drawn "over the mouth's good mark, that made the smile." The maid had orders to summon him the instant Geneviève opened her eyes. We waited and waited, and Boris, growing restless, wandered about, fussing with modelling wax and red clay. Suddenly he started for the next room. "Come and see my rose-coloured bath full of death!" he cried.

"Is it death?" I asked, to humour his mood.

"You are not prepared to call it life, I suppose," he answered. As he spoke he plucked a solitary goldfish squirming and twisting out of its globe. "We'll send this one after the other—wherever that is," he said. There was feverish excitement in his voice. A dull weight of fever lay on my limbs and on my brain as I followed him to the fair crystal pool with its pink-tinted sides; and he dropped the creature in. Falling, its scales flashed with a hot orange gleam in its angry twistings and contortions; the moment it struck the liquid it became rigid and sank heavily to the bottom. Then came the milky foam, the splendid hues radiating on the surface and then the shaft of pure serene light broke through from seemingly infinite depths. Boris plunged in his hand and drew out an exquisite marble thing, blue-veined, rose-tinted, and glistening with opalescent drops.

"Child's play," he muttered, and looked wearily, longingly at me,—as if I could answer such questions! But Jack Scott came in and entered into the "game," as he called it, with ardour. Nothing would do but to try the experiment on the white rabbit then and there. I was willing that Boris should find distraction from his cares, but I hated to see the life go out of a warm, living creature and I declined to be present. Picking up a book at random, I sat down in the studio to read. Alas! I had found *The King in Yellow*. After a few moments, which seemed ages, I was putting it away with a nervous shudder, when Boris and Jack came in bringing their marble rabbit. At the same time the bell rang above, and a cry came from the sick-room. Boris was gone like a flash, and the next moment he called, "Jack, run for the doctor; bring him back with you. Alec, come here."

I went and stood at her door. A frightened maid came out in haste and ran away to fetch some remedy. Geneviève, sitting bolt upright, with crimson cheeks and glittering eyes, babbled incessantly and resisted Boris' gentle restraint. He called me to help. At my first touch she sighed and sank back, closing her eyes, and then—then—as we still bent above her, she opened them again, looked straight into Boris' face—poor fever-crazed girl!—and told her secret. At the same instant our three lives turned into new channels; the bond that held us so long together snapped for ever and a new bond was forged in its place, for she had spoken my name, and as the fever tortured her, her heart poured out its load of hidden sorrow. Amazed and dumb I bowed my head, while my face burned like a live coal, and the blood surged in my ears, stupefying me with its clamour. Incapable of movement, incapable of speech, I listened to her feverish words in an agony of shame and sorrow. I could not silence her, I could not look at Boris. Then I felt an arm upon my shoulder, and Boris turned a bloodless face to mine.

"It is not your fault, Alec; don't grieve so if she loves you—" but he could not finish; and as the doctor stepped swiftly into the room, saying—"Ah, the fever!" I seized Jack Scott and hurried him to the street, saying, "Boris would rather be alone." We crossed the street to our own apartments, and that night, seeing I was going to be ill too, he went for the doctor again. The last thing I recollect with any distinctness was hearing Jack say, "For Heaven's sake, doctor, what ails him, to wear a face like that?" and I thought of *The King in Yellow* and the Pallid Mask.

I was very ill, for the strain of two years which I had endured since that fatal May morning when Geneviève murmured, "I love you, but I think I love Boris best," told on me at last. I had never imagined that it could become more than I could endure. Outwardly tranquil, I had deceived myself. Although the inward battle raged night after night, and I, lying alone in my room, cursed myself for rebellious thoughts unloyal to Boris and unworthy of Geneviève, the morning always brought relief, and I returned to Geneviève and to my dear Boris with a heart washed clean by the tempests of the night.

Never in word or deed or thought while with them had I betrayed my sorrow even to myself.

The mask of self-deception was no longer a mask for me, it was a part of me. Night lifted it, laying bare the stifled truth below; but there was no one to see except myself, and when the day broke the mask fell back again of its own accord. These thoughts passed through my troubled mind as I lay sick, but they were hopelessly entangled with visions of white creatures, heavy as stone, crawling about in Boris' basin,—of the wolf's head on the rug, foaming and snapping at Geneviève, who lay smiling beside it. I thought, too, of the King in Yellow wrapped in the fantastic colours of his tattered mantle, and that bitter cry of Cassilda, "Not upon us, oh King, not upon us!" Feverishly I struggled to put it from me, but I saw the lake of Hali, thin and blank, without a ripple or wind to stir it, and I saw the towers of Carcosa behind the moon. Aldebaran, the Hyades, Alar, Hastur, glided through the cloud-rifts which fluttered and flapped as they passed like the scolloped tatters of the King in Yellow. Among all these, one sane thought persisted. It never wavered, no matter what else was going on in my disordered mind, that my chief reason for existing was to meet some requirement of Boris and Geneviève. What this obligation was, its nature, was never clear; sometimes it seemed to be protection, sometimes support, through a great crisis. Whatever it seemed to be for the time, its weight rested only on me, and I was never so ill or so weak that I did not respond with my whole soul. There were always crowds of faces about me, mostly strange, but a few I recognized, Boris among them. Afterward they told me that this could not have been, but I know that once at least he bent over me. It was only a touch, a faint echo of his voice, then the clouds settled back on my senses, and I lost him, but he *did* stand there and bend over me *once* at least.

At last, one morning I awoke to find the sunlight falling across my bed, and Jack Scott reading beside me. I had not strength enough to speak aloud, neither could I think, much less remember, but I could smile feebly, as Jack's eye met mine, and when he jumped up and asked eagerly if I wanted anything, I could whisper, "Yes—Boris." Jack moved to the head of my bed, and leaned down to arrange my pillow: I did not see his face, but he answered heartily, "You must wait, Alec; you are too weak to see even Boris."

I waited and I grew strong; in a few days I was able to see whom I would, but meanwhile I had thought and remembered. From the moment when all the past grew clear again in my mind, I never doubted what I should do when the time came, and I felt sure that Boris would have resolved upon the same course so far as he was concerned; as for what pertained to me alone, I knew he would see that also as I did. I no longer asked for any one. I never inquired why no message came from them; why during the week I lay there, waiting and growing stronger, I never heard their name spoken. Preoccupied with my own searchings for the right way, and with my feeble but determined fight against despair, I simply acquiesced in Jack's reticence, taking for granted that he was afraid to speak of them, lest I should turn unruly and insist on seeing them. Meanwhile I said over and over to myself, how would it be when life began again for us all? We would take up our relations exactly as they were before Geneviève fell ill. Boris and I would look into each other's eyes, and there would be neither rancour nor cowardice nor mistrust in that glance. I would be with them again for a little while in the dear intimacy of their home, and then, without pretext or explanation, I would disappear from their lives for ever. Boris would know; Geneviève—the only comfort was that she would never know. It seemed, as I thought it over, that I had found the meaning of that sense of obligation which had persisted all through my delirium, and the only possible answer to it. So, when I was quite ready, I beckoned Jack to me one day, and said—

"Jack, I want Boris at once; and take my dearest greeting to Geneviève...."

When at last he made me understand that they were both dead, I fell into a wild rage that tore all my little convalescent strength to atoms. I raved and cursed myself into a relapse, from which I crawled forth some weeks afterward a boy of twenty-one who believed that his youth was gone for ever. I seemed to be past the capability of further suffering, and one day when Jack handed me a letter and the keys to Boris' house, I took them without a tremor and asked him to tell me all. It was cruel of me to ask him, but there was no help for it, and he leaned wearily on his thin hands, to reopen the wound which could never entirely heal. He began very quietly—

"Alec, unless you have a clue that I know nothing about, you will not be able to explain any more than I what has happened. I suspect that you would rather not hear these details, but you must learn them, else I would spare you the relation. God knows I wish I could be spared the telling. I shall use few words.

"That day when I left you in the doctor's care and came back to Boris, I found him working on the 'Fates.' Geneviève, he said, was sleeping under the influence of drugs. She had been quite out of her mind, he said. He kept on working, not talking any more, and I watched him. Before long, I saw that the third figure of the group—the one looking straight ahead, out over the world—bore his face; not as you ever saw it, but as it looked then and to the end. This is one thing for which I should like to find an explanation, but I never shall.

"Well, he worked and I watched him in silence, and we went on that way until nearly midnight. Then we heard the door open and shut sharply, and a swift rush in the next room. Boris sprang through the doorway and I followed; but we were too late. She lay at the bottom of the pool, her hands across her breast. Then Boris shot himself through the heart." Jack stopped speaking, drops of sweat stood under his eyes, and his thin cheeks twitched. "I carried Boris to his room. Then I went back and let that hellish fluid out of the pool, and turning on all the water, washed the marble clean of every drop. When at length I dared descend the steps, I found her lying there as white as snow. At last, when I had decided what was best to do, I went into the laboratory, and first emptied the solution in the basin into the waste-pipe; then I poured the contents of every jar and bottle after it. There was wood in the fire-place, so I built a fire, and breaking the locks of Boris' cabinet I burnt every paper, notebook and letter that I found there. With a mallet from the studio I smashed to pieces all the empty bottles, then loading them into a coal-scuttle, I carried them to the cellar and threw them over the red-hot bed of the furnace. Six times I made the journey, and at last, not a vestige remained of anything which might again aid in seeking for the formula which Boris had found. Then at last I dared call the doctor. He is a good man, and together we struggled to keep it from the public. Without him I never could have succeeded. At last we got the servants paid and sent away into the country, where old Rosier keeps them quiet with stones of Boris' and Geneviève's travels in distant lands, from whence they will not return for years. We buried Boris in the little cemetery of Sèvres. The doctor is a good creature, and knows when to pity a man who can bear no more. He gave his certificate of heart disease and asked no questions of me."

Then, lifting his head from his hands, he said, "Open the letter, Alec; it is for us both."

I tore it open. It was Boris' will dated a year before. He left everything to Geneviève, and in case of her dying childless, I was to take control of the house in the Rue Sainte-Cécile, and Jack Scott the management at Ept. On our deaths the property reverted to his mother's family in Russia, with the exception of the sculptured marbles executed by himself. These he left to me.

The page blurred under our eyes, and Jack got up and walked to the window. Presently he returned and sat down again. I dreaded to hear what he was going to say, but he spoke with the same simplicity and gentleness.

"Geneviève lies before the Madonna in the marble room. The Madonna bends tenderly above her, and Geneviève smiles back into that calm face that never would have been except for her."

His voice broke, but he grasped my hand, saying, "Courage, Alec." Next morning he left for Ept to fulfil his trust.

IV

The same evening I took the keys and went into the house I had known so well. Everything was in order, but the silence was terrible. Though I went twice to the door of the marble room, I could not force myself to enter. It was beyond my strength. I went into the smoking-room and sat down before the spinet. A small lace handkerchief lay on the keys, and I turned away, choking. It was plain I could not stay, so I locked every door, every window, and the three front and back gates, and went away. Next morning Alcide packed my valise, and leaving him in charge of my apartments I took the Orient express for Constantinople. During the two years that I wandered through the East, at first, in our letters, we never mentioned Geneviève and Boris, but gradually their names crept in. I recollect particularly a passage in one of Jack's letters replying to one of mine—

"What you tell me of seeing Boris bending over you while you lay ill, and feeling his touch on your face, and hearing his voice, of course troubles me. This that you describe must have happened a fortnight after he died. I say to myself that you were dreaming, that it was part of your delirium, but the explanation does not satisfy me, nor would it you."

Toward the end of the second year a letter came from Jack to me in India so unlike anything that I had ever known of him that I decided to return at once to Paris. He wrote: "I am well, and sell all my pictures as artists do who have no need of money. I have not a care of my own, but I am more restless than if I had. I am unable to shake off a strange anxiety about you. It is not apprehension, it is rather a breathless expectancy—of what, God knows! I can only say it is wearing me out.

Nights I dream always of you and Boris. I can never recall anything afterward, but I wake in the morning with my heart beating, and all day the excitement increases until I fall asleep at night to recall the same experience. I am quite exhausted by it, and have determined to break up this morbid condition. I must see you. Shall I go to Bombay, or will you come to Paris?"

I telegraphed him to expect me by the next steamer.

When we met I thought he had changed very little; I, he insisted, looked in splendid health. It was good to hear his voice again, and as we sat and chatted about what life still held for us, we felt that it was pleasant to be alive in the bright spring weather.

We stayed in Paris together a week, and then I went for a week to Ept with him, but first of all we went to the cemetery at Sèvres, where Boris lay.

"Shall we place the 'Fates' in the little grove above him?" Jack asked, and I answered—

"I think only the 'Madonna' should watch over Boris' grave." But Jack was none the better for my home-coming. The dreams of which he could not retain even the least definite outline continued, and he said that at times the sense of breathless expectancy was suffocating.

"You see I do you harm and not good," I said. "Try a change without me." So he started alone for a ramble among the Channel Islands, and I went back to Paris. I had not yet entered Boris' house, now mine, since my return, but I knew it must be done. It had been kept in order by Jack; there were servants there, so I gave up my own apartment and went there to live. Instead of the agitation I had feared, I found myself able to paint there tranquilly. I visited all the rooms—

all but one. I could not bring myself to enter the marble room where Geneviève lay, and yet I felt the longing growing daily to look upon her face, to kneel beside her.

One April afternoon, I lay dreaming in the smoking-room, just as I had lain two years before, and mechanically I looked among the tawny Eastern rugs for the wolf-skin. At last I distinguished the pointed ears and flat cruel head, and I thought of my dream where I saw Geneviève lying beside it. The helmets still hung against the threadbare tapestry, among them the old Spanish morion which I remembered Geneviève had once put on when we were amusing ourselves with the ancient bits of mail. I turned my eyes to the spinet; every yellow key seemed eloquent of her caress-ing hand, and I rose, drawn by the strength of my life's passion to the sealed door of the marble room. The heavy doors swung inward under my trembling hands. Sunlight poured through the window, tipping with gold the wings of Cupid, and lingered like a nimbus over the brows of the Madonna. Her tender face bent in compassion over a marble form so exquisitely pure that I knelt and signed myself. Geneviève lay in the shadow under the Madonna, and yet, through her white arms, I saw the pale azure vein, and beneath her softly clasped hands the folds of her dress were tinged with rose, as if from some faint warm light within her breast.

Bending, with a breaking heart, I touched the marble drapery with my lips, then crept back into the silent house.

A maid came and brought me a letter, and I sat down in the little conservatory to read it; but as I was about to break the seal, seeing the girl lingering, I asked her what she wanted.

She stammered something about a white rabbit that had been caught in the house, and asked what should be done with it I told her to let it loose in the walled garden behind the house, and opened my letter. It was from Jack, but so incoherent that I thought he must have lost his reason. It was nothing but a series of prayers to me not to leave the house until he could get back; he could not tell me why, there were the dreams, he said—he could explain nothing, but he was sure that I must not leave the house in the Rue Sainte-Cécile.

As I finished reading I raised my eyes and saw the same maid-servant standing in the doorway holding a glass dish in which two gold-fish were swimming: "Put them back into the tank and tell me what you mean by interrupting me," I said.

With a half-suppressed whimper she emptied water and fish into an aquarium at the end of the conservatory, and turning to me asked my permission to leave my service. She said people were playing tricks on her, evidently with a design of getting her into trouble; the marble rabbit had been stolen and a live one had been brought into the house; the two beautiful marble fish were gone, and she had just found those common live things flopping on the dining-room floor. I reassured her and sent her away, saying I would look about myself. I went into the studio; there was nothing there but my canvases and some casts, except the marble of the Easter lily. I saw it on a table across the room. Then I strode angrily over to it. But the flower I lifted from the table was fresh and fragile and filled the air with perfume.

Then suddenly I comprehended, and sprang through the hall-way to the marble room. The doors flew open, the sunlight streamed into my face, and through it, in a heavenly glory, the Madonna smiled, as Geneviève lifted her flushed face from her marble couch and opened her sleepy eyes.

A Thousand Deaths
(1899)

Jack London

I had been in the water about an hour, and cold, exhausted, with a terrible cramp in my right calf, it seemed as though my hour had come. Fruitlessly struggling against the strong ebb tide, I had beheld the maddening procession of the water-front lights slip by; but now I gave up attempting to breast the stream and contented myself with the bitter thoughts of a wasted career, now drawing to a close.

It had been my luck to come of good, English stock, but of parents whose account with the bankers far exceeded their knowledge of child-nature and the rearing of children. While born with a silver spoon in my mouth, the blessed atmosphere of the home circle was to me unknown. My father, a very learned man and a celebrated antiquarian, gave no thought to his family, being constantly lost in the abstractions of his study; while my mother, noted far more for her good looks than her good sense, sated herself with the adulation of the society in which she was perpetually plunged. I went through the regular school and college routine of a boy of the English bourgeois, and as the years brought me increasing strength and passions, my parents suddenly became aware that I was possessed of an immortal soul, and endeavored to draw the curb. But it was too late; I perpetrated the wildest and most audacious folly, and was disowned by my people, ostracized by the society I had so long outraged, and with the thousand pounds my father gave me, with the declaration that he would neither see me again nor give me more, I took a first-class passage to Australia.

Since then my life had been one long peregrination—from the Orient to the Occident, from the Arctic to the Antarctic—to find myself at last, an able seaman at thirty, in the full vigor of my manhood, drowning in San Francisco bay because of a disastrously successful attempt to desert my ship.

My right leg was drawn up by the cramp, and I was suffering the keenest agony. A slight breeze stirred up a choppy sea, which washed into my mouth and down my throat, nor could I prevent it. Though I still contrived to keep afloat, it was merely mechanical, for I was rapidly becoming unconscious. I have a dim recollection of drifting past the sea-wall, and of catching a glimpse of an up-river steamer's star-board light; then everything became a blank.

I heard the low hum of insect life, and felt the balmy air of a spring morning fanning my cheek. Gradually it assumed a rhythmic flow, to whose soft pulsations my body seemed to respond. I floated on the gentle bosom of a summer's sea, rising and falling with dreamy pleasure on each crooning wave. But the pulsations grew stronger; the humming, louder; the waves, larger, fiercer—I was dashed about on a stormy sea. A great agony fastened upon me. Brilliant, intermittent sparks of light flashed athwart my inner consciousness; in my ears there was the sound of many waters; then a sudden snapping of an intangible something, and I awoke.

The scene, of which I was protagonist, was a curious one. A glance sufficed to inform me that I lay on the cabin floor of some gentleman's yacht, in a most uncomfortable posture. On either side, grasping my arms and working them up and down like pump handles, were two peculiarly clad, dark-skinned creatures. Though conversant with most aboriginal types, I could not conjecture their nationality. Some attachment had been fastened about my head, which connected my respiratory organs with the machine I shall next describe. My nostrils, however, had been closed, forcing me to breathe through the mouth. Foreshortened by the obliquity of my line of vision, I beheld two tubes, similar to small hosing but of different composition, which emerged from my mouth and went off at an acute angle from each other. The first came to an abrupt termination and lay on the floor beside me; the second traversed the floor in numerous coils, connecting with the apparatus I have promised to describe.

In the days before my life had become tangential, I had dabbled not a little in science, and, conversant with the appurtenances and general paraphernalia of the laboratory, I appreciated the machine I now beheld. It was composed chiefly of glass, the construction being of that crude sort which is employed for experimentative purpose. A vessel of water was surrounded by an air chamber, to which was fixed a vertical tube, surmounted by a globe. In the center of this was a vacuum gauge. The water in the tube moved upward and downward, creating alternate inhalations and exhalations, which were in turn communicated to me through the hose. With this, and the aid of the men who pumped my arms so vigorously, had the process of breathing been artificially carried on, my chest rising and falling and my lungs expanding and contracting, till nature could be persuaded to again take up her wonted labor.

As I opened my eyes the appliance about my head, nostrils and mouth was removed. Draining a stiff three fingers of brandy, I staggered to my feet to thank my preserver, and confronted—my father. But long years of fellowship with danger had taught me self-control, and I waited to see if he would recognize me. Not so; he saw in me no more than a runaway sailor and treated me accordingly.

Leaving me to the care of the blackies, he fell to revising the notes he had made on my resuscitation. As I ate of the handsome fare served up to me, confusion began on deck, and from the chanteys of the sailors and the rattling of blocks and tackles I surmised that we were getting under way. What a lark! Off on a cruise with my recluse father into the wide Pacific! Little did I realize, as I laughed to myself, which side the joke was to be on. Aye, had I known, I would have plunged overboard and welcomed the dirty fo'c'sle from which I had just escaped.

I was not allowed on deck till we had sunk the Farallones and the last pilot boat. I appreciated this forethought on the part of my father and made it a point to thank him heartily, in my bluff seaman's manner. I could not suspect that he had his own ends in view, in thus keeping my presence secret to all save the crew. He told me briefly of my rescue by his sailors, assuring me that the obligation was on his side, as my appearance had been most opportune. He had constructed the apparatus for the vindication of a theory concerning certain biological phenomena, and had been waiting for an opportunity to use it.

"You have proved it beyond all doubt," he said; then added with a sigh, "but only in the small matter of drowning."

But, to take a reef in my yarn—he offered me an advance of two pounds on my previous wages to sail with him, and this I considered handsome, for he really did not need me. Contrary to my expectations, I did not join the sailors' mess, for'ard, being assigned to a comfortable stateroom and eating at the captain's table. He had perceived that I was no common sailor, and I resolved to take this chance for rein-stating myself in his good grates. I wove a fictitious past to account for my education and present position, and did my best to come in touch with him. I was not long in disclosing a predilection for scientific pursuits, nor he in appreciating my aptitude. I became his assistant, with a corresponding increase in wages, and before long, as he grew confidential and expounded his theories, I was as enthusiastic as himself.

The days flew quickly by, for I was deeply interested in my new studies, passing my waking hours in his well-stocked library, or listening to his plans and aiding him in his labora-tory work. But we were forced to forego many enticing experiments, a rolling ship not being exactly the proper place for delicate or intricate work. He promised me, however, many delightful hours in the magnificent labora-tory for which we were bound. He had taken possession of an uncharted South Sea island, as he said, and turned it into a scientific paradise.

We had not been on the island long, before I discovered the horrible mare's nest I had fallen into. But before I describe the strange things which came to pass, I must briefly outline the causes which culminated in as startling an experience as ever fell to the lot of man.

Late in life, my father had abandoned the musty charms of antiquity and succumbed to the more fascinating ones embraced under the general head of biology. Having been thoroughly grounded during his youth in the fundamentals, he rapidly explored all the higher branches as far as the scientific world had gone, and found himself on the no man's land of the unknowable. It was his intention to preempt some of this unclaimed territory, and it was at this stage of his investigations that we had been thrown together. Having a good brain, though I say it myself, I had mastered his speculations and methods of reasoning, becoming almost as mad as himself. But I should not say this. The marvelous results we afterward obtained can only go to prove his sanity. I can but say that he was the most abnormal specimen of cold-blooded cruelty I have ever seen.

After having penetrated the dual mysteries of physiology and psychology, his thought had led him to the verge of a great field, for which, the better to explore, he began studies in higher organic chemistry, pathology, toxicology and other sciences and sub-sciences rendered kindred as accessories to his speculative hypotheses. Starting from the proposition that the direct cause of the temporary and permanent arrest of vitality was due to the coagulation of certain elements and compounds in the protoplasm, he had isolated and subjected these various substances to innumerable experiments. Since the temporary arrest of vitality in an organism brought coma, and a permanent arrest death, he held that by artificial means this coagulation of the protoplasm could be retarded, prevented, and even overcome in the extreme states of solidification. Or, to do away with the technical nomenclature, he argued that death, when not violent and in which none of the organs had suffered injury, was merely suspended vitality; and that, in such instances, life could be induced to resume its functions by the use of proper methods. This, then, was his idea: To discover the method—and by practical experimentation prove the possibility—of renewing vitality in a structure from which life had seemingly fled. Of course, he recognized the futility of such endeavor after decomposition had set in; he must have organisms which but the moment, the hour, or the day before, had been quick with life. With me, in a crude way, he had proved this theory. I was really drowned, really dead, when picked from the water of San Francisco bay—but the vital spark had been renewed by means of his aerotherapeutical apparatus, as he called it.

Now to his dark purpose concerning me. He first showed me how completely I was in his power. He had sent the yacht away for a year, retaining only his two blackies, who were utterly devoted to him. He then made an exhaustive review of his theory and outlined the method of proof he had adopted, concluding with the startling announcement that I was to be his subject.

I had faced death and weighed my chances in many a desperate venture, but never in one of this nature. I can swear I am no coward, yet this proposition of journeying back and forth across the borderland of death put the yellow fear upon me. I asked for time, which he granted, at the same time assuring me that but one course was open—I must submit. Escape from the island was out of the question; escape by suicide was not to be entertained, though really preferable to what it seemed I must undergo; my only hope was to destroy my captors. But this latter was frustrated through the precautions taken by my father. I was subjected to a constant surveillance, even in my sleep being guarded by one or the other of the blacks.

Having pleaded in vain, I announced and proved that I was his son. It was my last card, and I had placed all my hopes upon it. But he was inexorable; he was not a father but a scientific machine. I wonder yet how it ever came to pass that he married my mother or begat me, for there was not the slightest grain of emotion in his make-up. Reason was all in all to him, nor could he understand such things as love or sympathy in others, except as petty weaknesses which should be overcome. So he informed me that in the beginning he had given me life, and who had better right to take it away than he? Such, he said, was not his desire, however; he merely wished to borrow it occasionally, promising to return it at the appointed time. Of course, there was a liability of mishaps, but I could do no more than take the chances, since the affairs of men were full of such.

The better to insure success, he wished me to be in the best possible condition, so I was dieted and trained like a great athlete before a decisive contest. What could I do? If I had to undergo the peril, it were best to be in good shape. In my intervals of relaxation he allowed me to assist in the arranging of the apparatus and in the various subsidiary experiments. The interest I took in all such operations can be imagined. I mastered the work as thoroughly as he, and often had the pleasure of seeing some of my suggestions or alterations put into effect. After such events I would smile grimly, conscious of officiating at my own funeral.

He began by inaugurating a series of experiments in toxicology. When all was ready, I was killed by a stiff dose of strychnine and allowed to lie dead for some twenty hours. During that period my body was dead, absolutely dead. All respiration and circulation ceased; but the frightful part of it was, that while the protoplasmic coagulation proceeded, I retained consciousness and was enabled to study it in all its ghastly details.

The apparatus to bring me back to life was an air-tight chamber, fitted to receive my body. The mechanism was simple—a few valves, a rotary shaft and crank, and an electric motor. When in operation, the interior atmosphere was alternately condensed and rarefied, thus communicating to my lungs an artificial respiration without the agency of the hosing previously used. Though my body was inert, and, for all I knew, in the first stages of decomposition, I was cognizant of everything that transpired. I knew when they placed me in the chamber, and though all my senses were quiescent, I was aware of hypodermic injections of a compound to react upon the coagulatory process. Then the chamber was closed and the machinery started. My anxiety was terrible; but the circulation became gradually restored, the different organs began to carry on their respective functions, and in an hour's time I was eating a hearty dinner.

It cannot be said that I participated in this series, nor in the subsequent ones, with much verve; but after two ineffectual attempts at escape, I began to take quite an interest. Besides, I was becoming accustomed. My father was beside himself at his success, and as the months rolled by his speculations took wilder and yet wilder flights. We ranged through the three great classes of poisons, the neurotics, the gaseous and the irritants, but carefully avoided some of the mineral irritants and passed the whole group of corrosives. During the poison régime I became quite accustomed to dying, and had but one mishap to shake my growing confidence. Scarifying a number of lesser blood vessels in my arm. he introduced a minute quantity of that most frightful of poisons, the arrow poison, or curare. I lost consciousness at the start, quickly followed by the cessation of respiration and circulation, and so far had the solidification of the protoplasm advanced, that he gave up all hope. But at the last moment he applied a discovery he had been working upon, receiving such encouragement as to redouble his efforts.

In a glass vacuum, similar but not exactly like a Crookes' tube, was placed a magnetic field. When penetrated by polarized light it gave no phenomena of phosphorescence nor of rectilinear projection of atoms, but emitted non-luminous rays, similar to the X ray. While the X ray could reveal opaque objects hidden in dense mediums, this was possessed of far subtler penetrations. By this he photographed my body, and found on the negative an infinite number of blurred shadows, due to the chemical and electric motions still going on. This was an infallible proof that the rigor mortis in which I lay was not genuine; that is, those mysterious forces, those delicate bonds which held my soul to my body, were still in action. The resultants of all other poisons were unapparent, save those of mercurial compounds, which usually left me languid for several days.

Another series of delightful experiments was with electricity. We verified Testa's assertion that high currents were utterly harmless by passing 100,000 volts through my body. As this did not affect me, the current was reduced to 2,500, and I was quickly electrocuted. This time he ventured so far as to allow me to remain dead, or in a state of suspended vitality, for three days. It took four hours to bring me back.

Once, he superinduced lockjaw; but the agony of dying was so great that I positively refused to undergo similar experiments. The easiest deaths were by asphyxiation, such as drowning, strangling, and suffocation by gas; while those by morphine, opium, cocaine and chloroform, were not at all hard.

Another time, after being suffocated, he kept me in cold storage for three months, not permitting me to freeze or decay. This was without my knowledge, and I was in a great fright on discovering the lapse of time. I became afraid of what he might do with me when I lay dead, my alarm being increased by the predilection he was beginning to betray toward vivisection. The last time I was resurrected, I discovered that he had been tampering with my breast. Though he had carefully dressed and sewed the incisions up, they were so severe that I had to take to my bed for some time. It was during this convalescence that I evolved the plan by which I ultimately escaped.

While feigning unbounded enthusiasm in the work, I asked and received a vacation for my moribund occupation. During this period I devoted myself to laboratory work, while he was too deep in the vivisection of the many animals captured by the blacks to take notice of my work.

It was on these two propositions that I constructed my theory: First, electrolysis, or the decomposition of water into its constituent gases by means of electricity; and, second, by the hypothetical existence of a force, the converse of gravitation, which Astor has named "apergy." Terrestrial attraction, for instance, merely draws objects together but does not combine them; hence, apergy is merely repulsion. Now, atomic or molecular attraction not only draws objects together but integrates them; and it was the converse of this, or a disintegrative force, which I wished to not only discover and produce, but to direct at will. Thus the molecules of hydrogen and oxygen reacting on each other, separate and create new molecules, containing both elements and forming water. Electrolysis causes these molecules to split up and resume their original condition, producing the two gases separately. The force I wished to find must not only do this with two, but with all elements, no matter in what compounds they exist. If I could then entice my father within its radius, he would be instantly disintegrated and sent flying to the four quarters, a mass of isolated elements.

It must not be understood that this force, which I finally came to control, annihilated matter; it merely annihilated form. Nor, as I soon discovered, had it any effect on inorganic structure; but to all organic form it was absolutely fatal. This partiality puzzled me at first, though had I stopped to think deeper I would have seen through it. Since the number of atoms in organic molecules is far greater than in the most complex mineral molecules, organic compounds are characterized by their instability and the ease with which they are split up by physical forces and chemical reagents.

By two powerful batteries, connected with magnets constructed specially for this purpose, two tremendous forces were projected. Considered apart from each other, they were perfectly harmless; but they accomplished their purpose by focusing at an invisible point in mid-air. After practically demonstrating its success, besides narrowly escaping being blown into nothingness, I laid my trap. Concealing the magnets, so that their force made the whole space of my chamber doorway a field of death, and placing by my couch a button by which I could throw on the current from the storage batteries, I climbed into bed.

The blackies still guarded my sleeping quarters, one relieving the other at midnight. I turned on the current as soon as the first man arrived. Hardly had I begun to doze, when I was aroused by a sharp, metallic tinkle. There, on the mid-threshold, lay the collar of Dan, my father's St. Bernard. My keeper ran to pick it up. He disappeared like a gust of wind, his clothes falling to the floor in a heap. There was a slight whiff of ozone in the air, but since the principal gaseous components of his body were hydrogen, oxygen and nitrogen, which are equally colorless and odorless, there was no other manifestation of his departure. Yet when I shut off the current and removed the garments, I found a deposit of carbon in the form of animal charcoal; also other powders, the isolated, solid elements of his organism, such as sulphur, potassium and iron. Resetting the trap, I crawled back to bed. At midnight I got up and removed the remains of the second blacky, and then slept peacefully till morning.

I was awakened by the strident voice of my father, who was calling to me from across the laboratory. I laughed to myself. There had been no one to call him and he had overslept. I could hear him as he approached my room with the intention of rousing me, and so I sat up in bed, the better to observe his translation—perhaps apotheosis were a better term. He paused a moment at the threshold, then took the fatal step. Puff! It was like the wind sighing among the pines.

He was gone. His clothes fell in a fantastic heap on the floor. Besides ozone, I noticed the faint, garlic-like odor of phosphorous. A little pile of elementary solids lay among his garments. That was all. The wide world lay before me. My captors were not.

Luella Miller (1903)

Mary Wilkins-Freeman

Close to the village street stood the one-story house in which Luella Miller, who had an evil name in the village, had dwelt. She had been dead for years, yet there were those in the village who, in spite of the clearer light which comes on a vantage-point from a long-past danger, half believed in the tale which they had heard from their childhood. In their hearts, although they scarcely would have owned it, was a survival of the wild horror and frenzied fear of their ancestors who had dwelt in the same age with Luella Miller. Young people even would stare with a shudder at the old house as they passed, and children never played around it as was their wont around an untenanted building. Not a window in the old Miller house was broken: the panes reflected the morning sunlight in patches of emerald and blue, and the latch of the sagging front door was never lifted, although no bolt secured it. Since Luella Miller had been carried out of it, the house had had no tenant except one friendless old soul who had no choice between that and the far-off shelter of the open sky. This old woman, who had survived her kindred and friends, lived in the house one week, then one morning no smoke came out of the chimney, and a body of neighbours, a score strong, entered and found her dead in her bed. There were dark whispers as to the cause of her death, and there were those who testified to an expression of fear so exalted that it showed forth the state of the departing soul upon the dead face. The old woman had been hale and hearty when she entered the house, and in seven days she was dead; it seemed that she had fallen a victim to some uncanny power. The minister talked in the pulpit with covert severity against the sin of superstition; still the belief prevailed. Not a soul in the village but would have chosen the almshouse rather than that dwelling. No vagrant, if he heard the tale, would seek shelter beneath that old roof, unhallowed by nearly half a century of superstitious fear.

There was only one person in the village who had actually known Luella Miller. That person was a woman well over eighty, but a marvel of vitality and unextinct youth. Straight as an arrow, with the spring of one recently let loose from the bow of life, she moved about the streets, and she always went to church, rain or shine. She had never married, and had lived alone for years in a house across the road from Luella Miller's.

This woman had none of the garrulousness of age, but never in all her life had she ever held her tongue for any will save her own, and she never spared the truth when she essayed to present it. She it was who bore testimony to the life, evil, though possibly wittingly or designedly so, of Luella Miller, and to her personal appearance. When this old woman spoke—and she had the gift of description, although her thoughts were clothed in the rude vernacular of her native village—one could seem to see Luella Miller as she had really looked. According to this woman, Lydia Anderson by name, Luella Miller had been a beauty of a type rather unusual in New England. She had been a slight, pliant sort of creature, as ready with a strong yielding to fate and as unbreakable as a willow. She had glimmering lengths of straight, fair hair, which she wore softly looped round a long, lovely face. She had blue eyes full of soft pleading, little slender, clinging hands, and a wonderful grace of motion and attitude.

"Luella Miller used to sit in a way nobody else could if they sat up and studied a week of Sundays," said Lydia Anderson, "and it was a sight to see her walk. If one of them willows over there on the edge of the brook could start up and get its roots free of the ground, and move off, it would go just the way Luella Miller used to. She had a green shot silk she used to wear, too, and a hat with green ribbon streamers, and a lace veil blowing across her face and out sideways, and a green ribbon flyin' from her waist. That was what she came out bride in when she married Erastus Miller. Her name before she was married was Hill. There was always a sight of"l's" in her name, married or single. Erastus Miller was good lookin', too, better lookin' than Luella. Sometimes I used to think that Luella wa'n't so handsome after all. Erastus just about worshiped her. I used to know him pretty well. He lived next door to me, and we went to school together. Folks used to say he was waitin' on me, but he wa'n't. I never thought he was except once or twice when he said things that some girls might have suspected meant somethin'. That was before Luella came here to teach the district school. It was funny how she came to get it, for folks said she hadn't any education, and that one of the big girls, Lottie Henderson, used to do all the teachin' for her, while she sat back and did embroidery work on a cambric pocket-handkerchief. Lottie Henderson was a real smart girl, a splendid scholar, and she just set her eyes by Luella, as all the girls did. Lottie would have made a real smart woman, but she died when Luella had been here about a year—just faded away and died: nobody knew what ailed her. She dragged herself to that schoolhouse and helped Luella teach till the very last minute. The committee all knew how Luella didn't do much of the work herself, but they winked at it. It wa'n't long after Lottie died that Erastus married her. I always thought he hurried it up because she wa'n't fit to teach. One of the big boys used to help her after Lottie died, but he hadn't much government, and the school didn't do very well, and Luella might have had to give it up, for the committee couldn't have shut their eyes to things much longer. The boy that helped her was a real honest, innocent sort of fellow, and he was a good scholar, too. Folks said he overstudied, and that was the reason he was took crazy the year after Luella married, but I don't know. And I don't know what made Erastus Miller go into consumption of the blood the year after he was married: consumption wa'n't in his family. He just grew weaker and weaker, and went almost bent double when he tried to wait on Luella, and he spoke feeble, like an old man. He worked terrible hard till the last trying to save up a little to leave Luella. I've seen him out in the worst storms on a wood-sled—he used to cut and sell wood—and he was hunched up on top lookin' more dead than alive. Once I couldn't stand it: I went over and helped him pitch some wood on the cart—I was always strong in my arms. I wouldn't stop for all he told me to, and I guess he was glad enough for the help. That was only a week before he died. He fell on the kitchen floor while he was gettin' breakfast. He always got the breakfast and let Luella lay abed. He did all the sweepin' and the washin' and the ironin' and most of the cookin'. He couldn't bear to have Luella lift her finger, and she let him do for her. She lived like a queen for all the work she did. She didn't even do her sewin'. She said it made her shoulder ache to sew, and poor Erastus's sister Lily used to do all her sewin'. She wa'n't able to, either; she was never strong in her back, but she did it beautifully. She had to, to suit Luella, she was so dreadful particular. I never saw anythin' like the fagottin' and hemstitchin' that Lily Miller did for Luella. She made all Luella's weddin' outfit, and that green silk dress, after Maria Babbit cut it. Maria she cut it for nothin', and she did a lot more cuttin' and fittin' for nothin' for Luella, too. Lily Miller went to live with Luella after Erastus died. She gave up her home, though she was real attached to it and wa'n't a mite afraid to stay alone. She rented it and she went to live with Luella right away after the funeral."

Then this old woman, Lydia Anderson, who remembered Luella Miller, would go on to relate the story of Lily Miller. It seemed that on the removal of Lily Miller to the house of her dead brother, to live with his widow, the village people first began to talk. This Lily Miller had been hardly past her first youth, and a most robust and blooming woman, rosy-cheeked, with curls of strong, black hair overshadowing round, candid temples and bright dark eyes. It was not six months after she had taken up her residence with her sister-in-law that her rosy colour faded and her pretty curves became wan hollows. White shadows began to show in the black rings of her hair, and the light died out of her eyes, her features sharpened, and there were pathetic lines at her mouth, which yet wore always an expression of utter sweetness and even happiness. She was devoted to her sister; there was no doubt that she loved her with her whole heart, and was perfectly content in her service. It was her sole anxiety lest she should die and leave her alone.

"The way Lily Miller used to talk about Luella was enough to make you mad and enough to make you cry," said Lydia Anderson. "I've been in there sometimes toward the last when she was too feeble to cook and carried her some blancmange or custard—somethin' I thought she might relish, and she'd thank me, and when I asked her how she was, say she felt better than she did yesterday, and asked me if I didn't think she looked better, dreadful pitiful, and say poor Luella had an awful time takin' care of her and doin' the work—she wa'n't strong enough to do anythin'—when all the time Luella wa'n't liftin' her finger and poor Lily didn't get any care except what the neighbours gave her, and Luella eat up everythin' that was carried in for Lily. I had it real straight that she did. Luella used to just sit and cry and do nothin'. She did act real fond of Lily, and she pined away considerable, too. There was those that thought she'd go into a decline herself. But after Lily died, her Aunt Abby Mixter came, and then Luella picked up and grew as fat and rosy as ever. But poor Aunt Abby begun to droop just the way Lily had, and I guess somebody wrote to her married daughter, Mrs. Sam Abbot, who lived in Barre, for she wrote her mother that she must leave right away and come and make her a visit, but Aunt Abby wouldn't go. I can see her now. She was a real good-lookin' woman, tall and large, with a big, square face and a high forehead that looked of itself kind of benevolent and good. She just tended out on Luella as if she had been a baby, and when her married daughter sent for her she wouldn't stir one inch. She'd always thought a lot of her daughter, too, but she said Luella needed her and her married daughter didn't. Her daughter kept writin' and writin', but it didn't do any good. Finally she came, and when she saw how bad her mother looked, she broke down and cried and all but went on her knees to have her come away. She spoke her mind out to Luella, too. She told her that she'd killed her husband and everybody that had anythin' to do with her, and she'd thank her to leave her mother alone. Luella went into hysterics, and Aunt Abby was so frightened that she called me after her daughter went. Mrs. Sam Abbot she went away fairly cryin' out loud in the buggy, the neighbours heard her, and well she might, for she never saw her mother again alive. I went in that night when Aunt Abby called for me, standin' in the door with her little green-checked shawl over her head. I can see her now. 'Do come over here, Miss Anderson,' she sung out, kind of gasping for breath. I didn't stop for anythin'. I put over as fast as I could, and when I got there, there was Luella laughin' and cryin' all together, and Aunt Abby trying to hush her, and all the time she herself was white as a sheet and shakin' so she could hardly stand. 'For the land sakes, Mrs. Mixter,' says I, 'you look worse than she does. You ain't fit to be up out of your bed.'

"'Oh, there ain't anythin' the matter with me,' says she. Then she went on talkin' to Luella. 'There, there, don't, don't, poor little lamb,' says she. 'Aunt Abby is here. She ain't goin' away and leave you. Don't, poor little lamb.'

"'Do leave her with me, Mrs. Mixter, and you get back to bed,' says I, for Aunt Abby had been layin' down considerable lately, though somehow she contrived to do the work.

"'I'm well enough,' says she. 'Don't you think she had better have the doctor, Miss Anderson?'

"'The doctor,' says I, 'I think YOU had better have the doctor. I think you need him much worse than some folks I could mention.' And I looked right straight at Luella Miller laughin' and cryin' and goin' on as if she was the centre of all creation. All the time she was actin' so—seemed as if she was too sick to sense anythin'—she was keepin' a sharp lookout as to how we took it out of the corner of one eye. I see her. You could never cheat me about Luella Miller. Finally I got real mad and I run home and I got a bottle of valerian I had, and I poured some boilin' hot water on a handful of catnip, and I mixed up that catnip tea with most half a wineglass of valerian, and I went with it over to Luella's. I marched right up to Luella, a-holdin' out of that cup, all smokin'. 'Now,' says I, 'Luella Miller, 'YOU SWALLER THIS!'

"'What is—what is it, oh, what is it?' she sort of screeches out. Then she goes off a-laughin' enough to kill.

"'Poor lamb, poor little lamb,' says Aunt Abby, standin' over her, all kind of tottery, and tryin' to bathe her head with camphor.

"'YOU SWALLER THIS RIGHT DOWN,' says I. And I didn't waste any ceremony. I just took hold of Luella Miller's chin and I tipped her head back, and I caught her mouth open with laughin', and I clapped that cup to her lips, and I fairly hollered at her: 'Swaller, swaller, swaller!' and she gulped it right down. She had to, and I guess it did her good. Anyhow, she stopped cryin' and laughin' and let me put her to bed, and she went to sleep like a baby inside of half an hour. That was more than poor Aunt Abby did. She lay awake all that night and I stayed with her, though she tried not to have me; said she wa'n't sick enough for watchers. But I stayed, and I made some good cornmeal gruel and I fed her a teaspoon every little while all night long. It seemed to me as if she was jest dyin' from bein' all wore out. In the mornin' as soon as it was light I run over to the Bisbees and sent Johnny Bisbee for the doctor. I told him to tell the doctor to hurry, and he come pretty quick. Poor Aunt Abby didn't seem to know much of anythin' when he got there. You couldn't hardly tell she breathed, she was so used up. When the doctor had gone, Luella came into the room lookin' like a baby in her ruffled nightgown. I can see her now. Her eyes were as blue and her face all pink and white like a blossom, and she looked at Aunt Abby in the bed sort of innocent and surprised. 'Why,' says she, 'Aunt Abby ain't got up yet?'

"'No, she ain't,' says I, pretty short.

"'I thought I didn't smell the coffee,' says Luella.

"'Coffee,' says I. 'I guess if you have coffee this mornin' you'll make it yourself.'

"'I never made the coffee in all my life,' says she, dreadful astonished. 'Erastus always made the coffee as long as he lived, and then Lily she made it, and then Aunt Abby made it. I don't believe I CAN make the coffee, Miss Anderson.'

"'You can make it or go without, jest as you please,' says I.

"'Ain't Aunt Abby goin' to get up?' says she.

"'I guess she won't get up,' says I, 'sick as she is.' I was gettin' madder and madder. There was somethin' about that little pink-and-white thing standin' there and talkin' about coffee, when she had killed so many better folks than she was, and had jest killed another, that made me feel 'most as if I wished somebody would up and kill her before she had a chance to do any more harm.

"'Is Aunt Abby sick?' says Luella, as if she was sort of aggrieved and injured.

"'Yes,' says I, 'she's sick, and she's goin' to die, and then you'll be left alone, and you'll have to do for yourself and wait on yourself, or do without things.' I don't know but I was sort of hard, but it was the truth, and if I was any harder than Luella Miller had been I'll give up. I ain't never been sorry that I said it. Well, Luella, she up and had hysterics again at that, and I jest let her have 'em. All I did was to bundle her into the room on the other side of the entry where Aunt Abby couldn't hear her, if she wa'n't past it—I don't know but she was—and set her down hard in a chair and told her not to come back into the other room, and she minded. She had her hysterics in there till she got tired. When she found out that nobody was comin' to coddle her and do for her she stopped. At least I suppose she did. I had all I could do with poor Aunt Abby tryin' to keep the breath of life in her. The doctor had told me that she was dreadful low, and give me some very strong medicine to give to her in drops real often, and told me real particular about the nourishment. Well, I did as he told me real faithful till she wa'n't able to swaller any longer. Then I had her daughter sent for. I had begun to realize that she wouldn't last any time at all. I hadn't realized it before, though I spoke to Luella the way I did. The doctor he came, and Mrs. Sam Abbot, but when she got there it was too late; her mother was dead. Aunt

Abby's daughter just give one look at her mother layin' there, then she turned sort of sharp and sudden and looked at me.

"'Where is she?' says she, and I knew she meant Luella.

"'She's out in the kitchen,' says I. 'She's too nervous to see folks die. She's afraid it will make her sick.'

"The Doctor he speaks up then. He was a young man. Old Doctor Park had died the year before, and this was a young fellow just out of college. 'Mrs. Miller is not strong,' says he, kind of severe, 'and she is quite right in not agitating herself.'

"'You are another, young man; she's got her pretty claw on you,' thinks I, but I didn't say anythin' to him. I just said over to Mrs. Sam Abbot that Luella was in the kitchen, and Mrs. Sam Abbot she went out there, and I went, too, and I never heard anythin' like the way she talked to Luella Miller. I felt pretty hard to Luella myself, but this was more than I ever would have dared to say. Luella she was too scared to go into hysterics. She jest flopped. She seemed to jest shrink away to nothin' in that kitchen chair, with Mrs. Sam Abbot standin' over her and talkin' and tellin' her the truth. I guess the truth was most too much for her and no mistake, because Luella presently actually did faint away, and there wa'n't any sham about it, the way I always suspected there was about them hysterics. She fainted dead away and we had to lay her flat on the floor, and the Doctor he came runnin' out and he said somethin' about a weak heart dreadful fierce to Mrs. Sam Abbot, but she wa'n't a mite scared. She faced him jest as white as even Luella was layin' there lookin' like death and the Doctor feelin' of her pulse.

"'Weak heart,' says she, 'weak heart; weak fiddlesticks! There ain't nothin' weak about that woman. She's got strength enough to hang onto other folks till she kills 'em.

Weak? It was my poor mother that was weak: this woman killed her as sure as if she had taken a knife to her.'

"But the Doctor he didn't pay much attention. He was bendin' over Luella layin' there with her yellow hair all streamin' and her pretty pink-and-white face all pale, and her blue eyes like stars gone out, and he was holdin' onto her hand and smoothin' her forehead, and tellin' me to get the brandy in Aunt Abby's room, and I was sure as I wanted to be that Luella had got somebody else to hang onto, now Aunt Abby was gone, and I thought of poor Erastus Miller, and I sort of pitied the poor young Doctor, led away by a pretty face, and I made up my mind I'd see what I could do.

"I waited till Aunt Abby had been dead and buried about a month, and the Doctor was goin' to see Luella steady and folks were beginnin' to talk; then one evenin', when I knew the Doctor had been called out of town and wouldn't be round, I went over to Luella's. I found her all dressed up in a blue muslin with white polka dots on it, and her hair curled jest as pretty, and there wa'n't a young girl in the place could compare with her. There was somethin' about Luella Miller seemed to draw the heart right out of you, but she didn't draw it out of ME. She was settin' rocking in the chair by her sittin'-room window, and Maria Brown had gone home. Maria Brown had been in to help her, or rather to do the work, for Luella wa'n't helped when she didn't do anythin'. Maria Brown was real capable and she didn't have any ties; she wa'n't married, and lived alone, so she'd offered. I couldn't see why she should do the work any more than Luella; she wa'n't any too strong; but she seemed to think she could and Luella seemed to think so, too, so she went over and did all the work—washed, and ironed, and baked, while

Luella sat and rocked. Maria didn't live long afterward. She began to fade away just the same fashion the others had. Well, she was warned, but she acted real mad when folks said anythin': said Luella was a poor, abused woman, too delicate to help herself, and they'd ought to be ashamed, and if she died helpin' them that couldn't help themselves she would—and she did.

"'I s'pose Maria has gone home,' says I to Luella, when I had gone in and sat down opposite her.

"'Yes, Maria went half an hour ago, after she had got supper and washed the dishes,' says Luella, in her pretty way.

"'I suppose she has got a lot of work to do in her own house to-night,' says I, kind of bitter, but that was all thrown away on Luella Miller. It seemed to her right that other folks that wa'n't any better able than she was herself should wait on her, and she couldn't get it through her head that anybody should think it WA'N'T right.

"'Yes,' says Luella, real sweet and pretty, 'yes, she said she had to do her washin' to-night. She has let it go for a fortnight along of comin' over here.'

"'Why don't she stay home and do her washin' instead of comin' over here and doin' YOUR work, when you are just as well able, and enough sight more so, than she is to do it?' says I.

"Then Luella she looked at me like a baby who has a rattle shook at it. She sort of laughed as innocent as you please. 'Oh, I can't do the work myself, Miss Anderson,' says she. 'I never did. Maria HAS to do it.'

"Then I spoke out: 'Has to do it!' says I. 'Has to do it!' She don't have to do it, either. Maria Brown has her own home and enough to live on. She ain't beholden to you to come over here and slave for you and kill herself.'

"Luella she jest set and stared at me for all the world like a doll-baby that was so abused that it was comin' to life.

"'Yes,' says I, 'she's killin' herself. She's goin' to die just the way Erastus did, and Lily, and your Aunt Abby. You're killin' her jest as you did them. I don't know what there is about you, but you seem to bring a curse,' says I. 'You kill everybody that is fool enough to care anythin' about you and do for you.'

"She stared at me and she was pretty pale.

"'And Maria ain't the only one you're goin' to kill,' says I. 'You're goin' to kill Doctor Malcom before you're done with him.'

"Then a red colour came flamin' all over her face. 'I ain't goin' to kill him, either,' says she, and she begun to cry.

"'Yes, you BE!' says I. Then I spoke as I had never spoke before. You see, I felt it on account of Erastus. I told her that she hadn't any business to think of another man after she'd been married to one that had died for her: that she was a dreadful woman; and she was, that's true enough, but some-times I have wondered lately if she knew it—if she wa'n't like a baby with scissors in its hand cuttin' everybody without knowin' what it was doin'.

"Luella she kept gettin' paler and paler, and she never took her eyes off my face. There was somethin' awful about the way she looked at me and never spoke one word. After awhile I quit talkin' and I went home. I watched that night, but her lamp went out before nine o'clock, and when Doctor Malcom came drivin' past and sort of slowed up he see there wa'n't any light and he drove along. I saw her sort of shy out of meetin' the next Sunday, too, so he shouldn't go home with her, and I begun to think mebbe she did have some conscience after all. It was only a week after that that Maria Brown died—sort of sudden at the last, though everybody had seen it was comin'. Well, then there was a good deal of feelin' and pretty dark whispers. Folks said the days of witchcraft had come again, and they were pretty shy of Luella. She acted sort of offish to the Doctor and he didn't go there, and there wa'n't anybody to do anythin' for her. I don't know how she DID get along. I wouldn't go in there and offer to help her—not because I was afraid of dyin' like the rest, but I thought she was just as well able to do her own work as I was to do it for her, and I thought it was about time that she did it and stopped killin' other folks. But it wa'n't very long before folks began to say that Luella herself was goin' into a decline jest the way her husband, and Lily, and Aunt Abby and the others had, and I saw myself that she looked pretty bad. I used to see her goin' past from the store with a bundle as if she could hardly crawl, but I remembered how Erastus used to wait and 'tend when he couldn't hardly put one foot before the other, and I didn't go out to help her.

"But at last one afternoon I saw the Doctor come drivin' up like mad with his medicine chest, and Mrs. Babbit came in after supper and said that Luella was real sick.

"'I'd offer to go in and nurse her,' says she, 'but I've got my children to consider, and mebbe it ain't true what they say, but it's queer how many folks that have done for her have died.'

"I didn't say anythin', but I considered how she had been Erastus's wife and how he had set his eyes by her, and I made up my mind to go in the next mornin', unless she was better, and see what I could do; but the next mornin' I see her at the window, and pretty soon she came steppin' out as spry as you please, and a little while afterward Mrs. Babbit came in and told me that the Doctor had got a girl from out of town, a Sarah Jones, to come there, and she said she was pretty sure that the Doctor was goin' to marry Luella.

"I saw him kiss her in the door that night myself, and I knew it was true. The woman came that afternoon, and the way she flew around was a caution. I don't believe Luella had swept since Maria died. She swept and dusted, and washed and ironed; wet clothes and dusters and carpets were flyin' over there all day, and every time Luella set her foot out when the Doctor wa'n't there there was that Sarah Jones helpin' of her up and down the steps, as if she hadn't learned to walk.

"Well, everybody knew that Luella and the Doctor were goin' to be married, but it wa'n't long before they began to talk about his lookin' so poorly, jest as they had about the others; and they talked about Sarah Jones, too.

"Well, the Doctor did die, and he wanted to be married first, so as to leave what little he had to Luella, but he died before the minister could get there, and Sarah Jones died a week afterward.

"Well, that wound up everything for Luella Miller. Not another soul in the whole town would lift a finger for her. There got to be a sort of panic. Then she began to droop in good earnest. She used to have to go to the store herself, for Mrs. Babbit was afraid to let Tommy go for her, and I've seen her goin' past and stoppin' every two or three steps to rest. Well, I stood it as long as I could, but one day I see her comin' with her arms full and stoppin' to lean against the Babbit fence, and I run out and took her bundles and carried them to her house. Then I went home and never spoke one word to her though she called after me dreadful kind of pitiful. Well, that night I was taken sick with a chill, and I was sick as I wanted to be for two weeks. Mrs. Babbit had seen me run out to help Luella and she came in and told me I was goin' to die on account of it. I didn't know whether I was or not, but I considered I had done right by Erastus's wife.

"That last two weeks Luella she had a dreadful hard time, I guess. She was pretty sick, and as near as I could make out nobody dared go near her. I don't know as she was really needin' anythin' very much, for there was enough to eat in her house and it was warm weather, and she made out to cook a little flour gruel every day, I know, but I guess she had a hard time, she that had been so petted and done for all her life.

"When I got so I could go out, I went over there one morning. Mrs. Babbit had just come in to say she hadn't seen any smoke and she didn't know but it was somebody's duty to go in, but she couldn't help thinkin' of her children, and I got right up, though I hadn't been out of the house for two weeks, and I went in there, and Luella she was layin' on the bed, and she was dyin'.

"She lasted all that day and into the night. But I sat there after the new doctor had gone away. Nobody else dared to go there. It was about midnight that I left her for a minute to run home and get some medicine I had been takin', for I begun to feel rather bad.

"It was a full moon that night, and just as I started out of my door to cross the street back to Luella's, I stopped short, for I saw something."

Lydia Anderson at this juncture always said with a certain defiance that she did not expect to be believed, and then proceeded in a hushed voice:

"I saw what I saw, and I know I saw it, and I will swear on my death bed that I saw it. I saw Luella Miller and Erastus Miller, and Lily, and Aunt Abby, and Maria, and the Doctor, and Sarah, all goin' out of her door, and all but Luella shone white in the moonlight, and they were all helpin' her along till she seemed to fairly fly in the midst of them. Then it all disappeared. I stood a minute with my heart poundin', then I went over there. I thought of goin' for Mrs. Babbit, but I thought she'd be afraid. So I went alone, though I knew what had happened. Luella was layin' real peaceful, dead on her bed."

This was the story that the old woman, Lydia Anderson, told, but the sequel was told by the people who survived her, and this is the tale which has become folklore in the village.

Lydia Anderson died when she was eighty-seven. She had continued wonderfully hale and hearty for one of her years until about two weeks before her death.

One bright moonlight evening she was sitting beside a window in her parlour when she made a sudden exclamation, and was out of the house and across the street before the neighbour who was taking care of her could stop her. She followed as fast as possible and found Lydia Anderson stretched on the ground before the door of Luella Miller's deserted house, and she was quite dead.

The next night there was a red gleam of fire athwart the moonlight and the old house of Luella Miller was burned to the ground. Nothing is now left of it except a few old cellar stones and a lilac bush, and in summer a helpless trail of morning glories among the weeds, which might be considered emblematic of Luella herself.

Oh, Whistle, and I'll Come to You, My Lad (1904)

M. R. James

'I suppose you will be getting away pretty soon, now Full term is over, Professor,' said a person not in the story to the Professor of Ontography, soon after they had sat down next to each other at a feast in the hospitable hall of St. James's College.

The Professor was young, neat, and precise in speech.

'Yes,' he said; 'my friends have been making me take up golf this term, and I mean to go to the East Coast—in point of fact to Burnstow—(I dare say you know it) for a week or ten days, to improve my game. I hope to get off to-morrow.'

'Oh, Parkins,' said his neighbour on the other side, 'if you are going to Burnstow, I wish you would look at the site of the Templars' preceptory, and let me know if you think it would be any good to have a dig there in the summer.'

It was, as you might suppose, a person of antiquarian pursuits who said this, but, since he merely appears in this prologue, there is no need to give his entitlements.

'Certainly,' said Parkins, the Professor: 'if you will describe to me whereabouts the site is, I will do my best to give you an idea of the lie of the land when I get back; or I could write to you about it, if you would tell me where you are likely to be.'

'Don't trouble to do that, thanks. It's only that I'm thinking of taking my family in that direction in the Long, and it occurred to me that, as very few of the English preceptories have ever been properly planned, I might have an opportunity of doing something useful on off-days.'

The Professor rather sniffed at the idea that planning out a preceptory could be described as useful. His neighbour continued:

'The site—I doubt if there is anything showing above ground—must be down quite close to the beach now. The sea has encroached tremendously, as you know, all along that bit of coast. I should think, from the map, that it must be about three-quarters of a mile from the Globe Inn, at the north end of the town. Where are you going to stay?'

'Well, at the Globe Inn, as a matter of fact,' said Parkins; 'I have engaged a room there. I couldn't get in anywhere else; most of the lodging-houses are shut up in winter, it seems; and, as it is, they tell me that the only room of any size I can have is really a double-bedded one, and that they haven't a corner in which to store the other bed, and so on. But I must have a fairly large room, for I am taking some books down, and mean to do a bit of work; and though I don't quite fancy having an empty bed—not to speak of two—in what I may call for the time being my study, I suppose I can manage to rough it for the short time I shall be there.'

'Do you call having an extra bed in your room roughing it, Parkins?' said a bluff person opposite. 'Look here, I shall come down and occupy it for a bit; it'll be company for you.'

The Professor quivered, but managed to laugh in a courteous manner.

'By all means, Rogers; there's nothing I should like better. But I'm afraid you would find it rather dull; you don't play golf, do you?'

'No, thank Heaven!' said rude Mr. Rogers.

'Well, you see, when I'm not writing I shall most likely be out on the links, and that, as I say, would be rather dull for you, I'm afraid.'

'Oh, I don't know! There's certain to be somebody I know in the place; but, of course, if you don't want me, speak the word, Parkins; I shan't be offended. Truth, as you always tell us, is never offensive.'

Parkins was, indeed, scrupulously polite and strictly truthful. It is to be feared that Mr. Rogers sometimes practised upon his knowledge of these characteristics. In Parkins's breast there was a conflict now raging, which for a moment or two did not allow him to answer. That interval being over, he said:

'Well, if you want the exact truth, Rogers, I was considering whether the room I speak of would really be large enough to accommodate us both comfortably; and also whether (mind, I shouldn't have said this if you hadn't pressed me) you would not constitute something in the nature of a hindrance to my work.'

Rogers laughed loudly.

'Well done, Parkins!' he said. 'It's all right. I promise not to interrupt your work; don't you disturb yourself about that.

No, I won't come if you don't want me; but I thought I should do so nicely to keep the ghosts off.' Here he might have been seen to wink and to nudge his next neighbour. Parkins might also have been seen to become pink. 'I beg pardon, Parkins,' Rogers continued; 'I oughtn't to have said that. I forgot you didn't like levity on these topics.'

'Well,' Parkins said, 'as you have mentioned the matter, I freely own that I do not like careless talk about what you call ghosts. A man in my position,' he went on, raising his voice a little, 'cannot, I find, be too careful about appearing to sanction the current beliefs on such subjects. As you know, Rogers, or as you ought to know; for I think I have never concealed my views—'

'No, you certainly have not, old man,' put in Rogers sotto voce.

'—I hold that any semblance, any appearance of concession to the view that such things might exist is to me a renunciation of all that I hold most sacred. But I'm afraid I have not succeeded in securing your attention.'

'Your undivided attention, was what Dr. Blimber actually said[^ Mr. Rogers was wrong, vide 'Dombey and Son,' chapter xii.],' Rogers interrupted, with every appearance of an earnest desire for accuracy. 'But I beg your pardon, Parkins: I'm stopping you.'

'No, not at all,' said Parkins. 'I don't remember Blimber; perhaps he was before my time. But I needn't go on. I'm sure you know what I mean.'

'Yes, yes,' said Rogers, rather hastily—'just so. We'll go into it fully at Burnstow, or somewhere.'

In repeating the above dialogue I have tried to give the impression which it made on me, that Parkins was something of an old woman—rather henlike, perhaps, in his little ways; totally destitute, alas! of the sense of humour, but at the same time dauntless and sincere in his convictions, and a man deserving of the greatest respect. Whether or not the reader has gathered so much, that was the character which Parkins had.

On the following day Parkins did, as he had hoped, succeed in getting away from his college, and in arriving at Burnstow. He was made welcome at the Globe Inn, was safely installed in the large double-bedded room of which we have heard, and was able before retiring to rest to arrange his materials for work in apple-pie order upon a commodious table which occupied the outer end of the room, and was surrounded on three sides by windows looking out seaward; that is to say, the central window looked straight out to sea, and those on the left and right commanded prospects along the shore to the north and south respectively. On the south you saw the village of Burnstow. On the north no houses were to be seen, but only the beach and the low cliff backing it. Immediately in front was a strip—not considerable—of rough grass, dotted with old anchors, capstans, and so forth; then a broad path; then the beach. Whatever may have been the original distance between the Globe Inn and the sea, not more than sixty yards now separated them.

The rest of the population of the inn was, of course, a golfing one, and included few elements that call for a special description. The most conspicuous figure was, perhaps, that of an ancien militaire, secretary of a London club, and possessed of a voice of incredible strength, and of views of a pronouncedly Protestant type. These were apt to find utterance after his attendance upon the ministrations of the Vicar, an estimable man with inclinations towards a picturesque ritual, which he gallantly kept down as far as he could out of deference to East Anglian tradition.

Professor Parkins, one of whose principal characteristics was pluck, spent the greater part of the day following his arrival at Burnstow in what he had called improving his game, in company with this Colonel Wilson: and during the afternoon—whether the process of improvement were to blame or not, I am not sure—the Colonel's demeanour assumed a colouring so lurid that even Parkins jibbed at the thought of walking home with him from the links. He determined, after a short and furtive look at that bristling moustache and those incarnadined features, that it would be wiser to allow the influences of tea and tobacco to do what they could with the Colonel before the dinner-hour should render a meeting inevitable.

'I might walk home to-night along the beach,' he reflected—'yes, and take a look—there will be light enough for that—at the ruins of which Disney was talking. I don't exactly know where they are, by the way; but I expect I can hardly help stumbling on them.'

This he accomplished, I may say, in the most literal sense, for in picking his way from the links to the shingle beach his foot caught, partly in a gorse-root and partly in a biggish stone, and over he went. When he got up and surveyed his surroundings, he found himself in a patch of somewhat broken ground covered with small depressions and mounds. These latter, when he came to examine them, proved to be simply masses of flints embedded in mortar and grown over with turf. He must, he quite rightly concluded, be on the site of the preceptory he had promised to look at. It seemed not unlikely to reward the spade of the explorer; enough of the foundations was probably left at no great depth to throw a good deal of light on the general plan. He remembered vaguely that the Templars, to whom this site had belonged, were in the habit of building round churches, and he thought a particular series of the humps or mounds near him did appear to be arranged in something of a circular form. Few people can resist the temptation to try a little amateur research in a department quite outside their own, if only for the satisfaction of showing how successful they would have been had they only taken it up seriously. Our Professor, however, if he felt something of this mean desire, was also truly anxious to oblige Mr. Disney. So he paced with care the circular area he had noticed, and wrote down its rough dimensions in his pocket-book. Then he proceeded to examine an oblong eminence which lay east of the centre of the circle, and seemed to his thinking likely to be the base of a platform or altar. At one end of it, the northern, a patch of the turf was gone—removed by some boy or other creature ferae naturae. It might, he thought, be as well to probe the soil here for evidences of masonry, and he took out his knife and began scraping away the earth. And now followed another little discovery: a portion of soil fell inward as he scraped, and disclosed a small cavity. He lighted one match after another to help him to see of what nature the hole was, but the wind was too strong for them all. By tapping and scratching the sides with his knife, however, he was able to make out that it must be an artificial hole in masonry. It was rectangular, and the sides, top, and bottom, if not actually plastered, were smooth and regular. Of course it was empty. No! As he withdrew the knife he heard a metallic clink, and when he introduced his hand it met with a cylindrical object lying on the floor of the hole. Naturally enough, he picked it up, and when he brought it into the light, now fast fading, he could see that it, too, was of man's making—a metal tube about four inches long, and evidently of some considerable age.

By the time Parkins had made sure that there was nothing else in this odd receptacle, it was too late and too dark for him to think of undertaking any further search. What he had done had proved so unexpectedly interesting that he determined to sacrifice a little more of the daylight on the morrow to archæology. The object which he now had safe in his pocket was bound to be of some slight value at least, he felt sure.

Bleak and solemn was the view on which he took a last look before starting homeward. A faint yellow light in the west showed the links, on which a few figures moving towards the club-house were still visible, the squat martello tower, the lights of Aldsey village, the pale ribbon of sands intersected at intervals by black wooden groynings, the dim and murmuring sea. The wind was bitter from the north, but was at his back when he set out for the Globe. He quickly rattled and clashed through the shingle and gained the sand, upon which, but for the groynings which had to be got over every few yards, the going was both good and quiet. One last look behind, to measure the distance he had made since leaving the ruined Templars' church, showed him a prospect of company on his walk, in the shape of a rather indistinct personage in the distance, who seemed to be making great efforts to catch up with him, but made little, if any, progress. I mean that there was an appearance of running about his movements, but that the distance between him and Parkins did not seem materially to lessen. So, at least, Parkins thought, and decided that he almost certainly did not know him, and that it would be absurd to wait until he came up. For all that, company, he began to think, would really be very welcome on that lonely shore, if only you could choose your companion. In his unenlightened days he had read of meetings in such places which even now would hardly bear thinking of. He went on thinking of them, however, until he reached home, and particularly of one which catches most people's fancy at some time of their childhood. 'Now I saw in my dream that Christian had gone but a very little way when he saw a foul fiend coming over the field to meet him.' 'What should I do now,' he thought, 'if I looked back and caught sight of a black figure sharply defined against the yellow sky, and saw that it had horns and wings? I wonder whether I should stand or run for it. Luckily, the gentleman behind is not of that kind, and he seems to be about as far off now as when I saw him first. Well, at this rate he won't get his dinner as soon as I shall; and, dear me! it's within a quarter of an hour of the time now. I must run!'

Parkins had, in fact, very little time for dressing. When he met the Colonel at dinner, Peace—or as much of her as that gentleman could manage—reigned once more in the military bosom; nor was she put to flight in the hours of bridge that followed dinner, for Parkins was a more than respectable player. When, therefore, he retired towards twelve o'clock, he felt that he had spent his evening in quite a satisfactory way, and that, even for so long as a fortnight or three weeks, life at the Globe would be supportable under similar conditions—'especially,' thought he, 'if I go on improving my game.'

As he went along the passages he met the boots of the Globe, who stopped and said:

'Beg your pardon, sir, but as I was a-brushing your coat just now there was somethink fell out of the pocket. I put it on your chest of drawers, sir, in your room, sir—a piece of a pipe or somethink of that, sir. Thank you, sir. You'll find it on your chest of drawers, sir—yes, sir. Good-night, sir.'

The speech served to remind Parkins of his little discovery of that afternoon. It was with some considerable curiosity that he turned it over by the light of his candles. It was of bronze, he now saw, and was shaped very much after the manner of the modern dog-whistle; in fact it was—yes, certainly it was—actually no more nor less than a whistle. He put it to his lips, but it was quite full of a fine, caked-up sand or earth, which would not yield to knocking, but must be loosened with a knife. Tidy as ever in his habits, Parkins cleared out the earth on to a piece of paper, and took the latter to the window to empty it out. The night was clear and bright, as he saw when he had opened the casement, and he stopped for an instant to look at the sea and note a belated wanderer stationed on the shore in front of the inn. Then he shut the window, a little surprised at the late hours people kept at Burnstow, and took his whistle to the light again. Why, surely there were marks on it, and not merely marks, but letters! A very little rubbing rendered the deeply-cut inscription quite legible, but the Professor had to confess, after some earnest thought, that the meaning of it was as obscure to him as the writing on the wall to Belshazzar.

There were legends both on the front and on the back of the whistle. The one read thus:

The other:

'I ought to be able to make it out,' he thought; 'but I suppose I am a little rusty in my Latin. When I come to think of it, I don't believe I even know the word for a whistle. The long one does seem simple enough. It ought to mean, "Who is this who is coming?" Well, the best way to find out is evidently to whistle for him.'

He blew tentatively and stopped suddenly, startled and yet pleased at the note he had elicited. It had a quality of infinite distance in it, and, soft as it was, he somehow felt it must be audible for miles round. It was a sound, too, that seemed to have the power (which many scents possess) of forming pictures in the brain. He saw quite clearly for a moment a vision of a wide, dark expanse at night, with a fresh wind blowing, and in the midst a lonely figure—how employed, he could not tell. Perhaps he would have seen more had not the picture been broken by the sudden surge of a gust of wind against his casement, so sudden that it made him look up, just in time to see the white glint of a sea-bird's wing somewhere outside the dark panes.

The sound of the whistle had so fascinated him that he could not help trying it once more, this time more boldly. The note was little, if at all, louder than before, and repetition broke the illusion—no picture followed, as he had half hoped it might. 'But what is this? Goodness! what force the wind can get up in a few minutes! What a tremendous gust! There! I knew that window-fastening was no use! Ah! I thought so—both candles out. It is enough to tear the room to pieces.'

The first thing was to get the window shut. While you might count twenty Parkins was struggling with the small casement, and felt almost as if he were pushing back a sturdy burglar, so strong was the pressure. It slackened all at once, and the window banged to and latched itself. Now to relight the candles and see what damage, if any, had been done. No, nothing seemed amiss; no glass even was broken in the casement. But the noise had evidently roused at least one member of the household: the Colonel was to be heard stumping in his stockinged feet on the floor above, and growling.

Quickly as it had risen, the wind did not fall at once. On it went, moaning and rushing past the house, at times rising to a cry so desolate that, as Parkins disinterestedly said, it might have made fanciful people feel quite uncomfortable; even the unimaginative, he thought after a quarter of an hour, might be happier without it.

Whether it was the wind, or the excitement of golf, or of the researches in the preceptory that kept Parkins awake, he was not sure. Awake he remained, in any case, long enough to fancy (as I am afraid I often do myself under such conditions) that he was the victim of all manner of fatal disorders: he would lie counting the beats of his heart, convinced that it was going to stop work every moment, and would entertain grave suspicions of his lungs, brain, liver, etc.—suspicions which he was sure would be dispelled by the return of daylight, but which until then refused to be put aside. He found a little vicarious comfort in the idea that someone else was in the same boat. A near neighbour (in the darkness it was not easy to tell his direction) was tossing and rustling in his bed, too.

The next stage was that Parkins shut his eyes and determined to give sleep every chance. Here again over-excitement asserted itself in another form—that of making pictures. Experto crede, pictures do come to the closed eyes of one trying to sleep, and often his pictures are so little to his taste that he must open his eyes and disperse the images.

Parkins's experience on this occasion was a very distressing one. He found that the picture which presented itself to him was continuous. When he opened his eyes, of course, it went; but when he shut them once more it framed itself afresh, and acted itself out again, neither quicker nor slower than before. What he saw was this:

A long stretch of shore—shingle edged by sand, and intersected at short intervals with black groynes running down to the water—a scene, in fact, so like that of his afternoon's walk that, in the absence of any landmark, it could not be distinguished therefrom. The light was obscure, conveying an impression of gathering storm, late winter evening, and slight cold rain. On this bleak stage at first no actor was visible. Then, in the distance, a bobbing black object appeared; a moment more, and it was a man running, jumping, clambering over the groynes, and every few seconds looking eagerly back. The nearer he came the more obvious it was that he was not only anxious, but even terribly frightened, though his face was not to be distinguished. He was, moreover, almost at the end of his strength. On he came; each successive obstacle seemed to cause him more difficulty than the last. 'Will he get over this next one?' thought Parkins; 'it seems a little higher than the others.' Yes; half climbing, half throwing himself, he did get over, and fell all in a heap on the other side (the side nearest to the spectator). There, as if really unable to get up again, he remained crouching under the groyne, looking up in an attitude of painful anxiety.

So far no cause whatever for the fear of the runner had been shown; but now there began to be seen, far up the shore, a little flicker of something light-coloured moving to and fro with great swiftness and irregularity. Rapidly growing larger, it, too, declared itself as a figure in pale, fluttering draperies, ill-defined. There was something about its motion which made Parkins very unwilling to see it at close quarters. It would stop, raise arms, bow itself toward the sand, then run stooping across the beach to the water-edge and back again; and then, rising upright, once more continue its course forward at a speed that was startling and terrifying. The moment came when the pursuer was hovering about from left to right only a few yards beyond the groyne where the runner lay in hiding. After two or three ineffectual castings hither and thither it came to a stop, stood upright, with arms raised high, and then darted straight forward towards the groyne.

It was at this point that Parkins always failed in his resolution to keep his eyes shut. With many misgivings as to incipient failure of eyesight, overworked brain, excessive smoking, and so on, he finally resigned himself to light his candle, get out a book, and pass the night waking, rather than be tormented by this persistent panorama, which he saw clearly enough could only be a morbid reflection of his walk and his thoughts on that very day.

The scraping of match on box and the glare of light must have startled some creatures of the night—rats or what not—which he heard scurry across the floor from the side of his bed with much rustling. Dear, dear! the match is out! Fool that it is! But the second one burnt better, and a candle and book were duly procured, over which Parkins pored till sleep of a wholesome kind came upon him, and that in no long space. For about the first time in his orderly and prudent life he forgot to blow out the candle, and when he was called next morning at eight there was still a flicker in the socket and a sad mess of guttered grease on the top of the little table.

After breakfast he was in his room, putting the finishing touches to his golfing costume—fortune had again allotted the Colonel to him for a partner—when one of the maids came in.

'Oh, if you please,' she said, 'would you like any extra blankets on your bed, sir?'

'Ah! thank you,' said Parkins. 'Yes, I think I should like one. It seems likely to turn rather colder.'

In a very short time the maid was back with the blanket.

'Which bed should I put it on, sir?' she asked.

'What? Why, that one—the one I slept in last night,' he said, pointing to it.

'Oh yes! I beg your pardon, sir, but you seemed to have tried both of 'em; leastways, we had to make 'em both up this morning.'

'Really? How very absurd!' said Parkins. 'I certainly never touched the other, except to lay some things on it. Did it actually seem to have been slept in?'

'Oh yes, sir!' said the maid. 'Why, all the things was crumpled and throwed about all ways, if you'll excuse me, sir—quite as if anyone 'adn't passed but a very poor night, sir.'

'Dear me,' said Parkins. 'Well, I may have disordered it more than I thought when I unpacked my things. I'm very sorry to have given you the extra trouble, I'm sure. I expect a friend of mine soon, by the way—a gentleman from Cambridge—to come and occupy it for a night or two. That will be all right, I suppose, won't it?'

'Oh yes, to be sure, sir. Thank you, sir. It's no trouble, I'm sure,' said the maid, and departed to giggle with her colleagues.

Parkins set forth, with a stern determination to improve his game.

I am glad to be able to report that he succeeded so far in this enterprise that the Colonel, who had been rather repining at the prospect of a second day's play in his company, became quite chatty as the morning advanced; and his voice boomed out over the flats, as certain also of our own minor poets have said, 'like some great bourdon in a minster tower.'

'Extraordinary wind, that, we had last night,' he said. 'In my old home we should have said someone had been whistling for it.'

'Should you, indeed!' said Parkins. 'Is there a superstition of that kind still current in your part of the country?'

'I don't know about superstition,' said the Colonel. 'They believe in it all over Denmark and Norway, as well as on the Yorkshire coast; and my experience is, mind you, that there's generally something at the bottom of what these country-folk hold to, and have held to for generations. But it's your drive' (or whatever it might have been: the golfing reader will have to imagine appropriate digressions at the proper intervals).

When conversation was resumed, Parkins said, with a slight hesitancy:

'Apropos of what you were saying just now, Colonel, I think I ought to tell you that my own views on such subjects are very strong. I am, in fact, a convinced disbeliever in what is called the "supernatural."'

'What!' said the Colonel, 'do you mean to tell me you don't believe in second-sight, or ghosts, or anything of that kind?'

'In nothing whatever of that kind,' returned Parkins firmly.

'Well,' said the Colonel, 'but it appears to me at that rate, sir, that you must be little better than a Sadducee.'

Parkins was on the point of answering that, in his opinion, the Sadducees were the most sensible persons he had ever read of in the Old Testament; but, feeling some doubt as to whether much mention of them was to be found in that work, he preferred to laugh the accusation off.

'Perhaps I am,' he said; 'but—Here, give me my cleek, boy! —Excuse me one moment, Colonel.' A short interval. 'Now, as to whistling for the wind, let me give you my theory about it. The laws which govern winds are really not at all perfectly known—to fisher-folk and such, of course, not known at all. A man or woman of eccentric habits, perhaps, or a stranger, is seen repeatedly on the beach at some unusual hour, and is heard whistling. Soon afterwards a violent wind rises; a man who could read the sky perfectly or who possessed a barometer could have foretold that it would. The simple people of a fishing-village have no barometers, and only a few rough rules for prophesying weather. What more natural than that the eccentric person-age I postulated should be regarded as having raised the wind, or that he or she should clutch eagerly at the reputa-tion of being able to do so? Now, take last night's wind: as it happens, I myself was whistling. I blew a whistle twice, and the wind seemed to come absolutely in answer to my call. If anyone had seen me—'

The audience had been a little restive under this harangue, and Parkins had, I fear, fallen somewhat into the tone of a lecturer; but at the last sentence the Colonel stopped.

'Whistling, were you?' he said. 'And what sort of whistle did you use? Play this stroke first.' Interval.

'About that whistle you were asking, Colonel. It's rather a curious one. I have it in my— No; I see I've left it in my room. As a matter of fact, I found it yesterday.'

And then Parkins narrated the manner of his discovery of the whistle, upon hearing which the Colonel grunted, and opined that, in Parkins's place, he should himself be careful about using a thing that had belonged to a set of Papists, of whom, speaking generally, it might be affirmed that you never knew what they might not have been up to. From this topic he diverged to the enormities of the Vicar, who had given notice on the previous Sunday that Friday would be the Feast of St. Thomas the Apostle, and that there would be service at eleven o'clock in the church. This and other similar proceedings constituted in the Colonel's view a strong presumption that the Vicar was a concealed Papist, if not a Jesuit; and Parkins, who could not very readily follow the Colonel in this region, did not disagree with him. In fact, they got on so well together in the morning that there was no talk on either side of their separating after lunch.

Both continued to play well during the afternoon, or, at least, well enough to make them forget everything else until the light began to fail them. Not until then did Parkins remember that he had meant to do some more investigating at the preceptory; but it was of no great importance, he reflected. One day was as good as another; he might as well go home with the Colonel.

As they turned the corner of the house, the Colonel was almost knocked down by a boy who rushed into him at the very top of his speed, and then, instead of running away, remained hanging on to him and panting. The first words of the warrior were naturally those of reproof and objurgation, but he very quickly discerned that the boy was almost speechless with fright. Inquiries were useless at first. When the boy got his breath he began to howl, and still clung to the Colonel's legs. He was at last detached, but continued to howl.

'What in the world is the matter with you? What have you been up to? What have you seen?' said the two men.

'Ow, I seen it wive at me out of the winder,' wailed the boy, 'and I don't like it.'

'What window?' said the irritated Colonel. 'Come, pull yourself together, my boy.'

'The front winder it was, at the 'otel,' said the boy.

At this point Parkins was in favour of sending the boy home, but the Colonel refused; he wanted to get to the bottom of it, he said; it was most dangerous to give a boy such a fright as this one had had, and if it turned out that people had been playing jokes, they should suffer for it in some way. And by a series of questions he made out this story: The boy had been playing about on the grass in front of the Globe with some others; then they had gone home to their teas, and he was just going, when he happened to look up at the front winder and see it a-wiving at him. It seemed to be a figure of some sort, in white as far as he knew—couldn't see its face;

but it wived at him, and it warn't a right thing—not to say not a right person. Was there a light in the room? No, he didn't think to look if there was a light. Which was the window? Was it the top one or the second one? The seckind one it was—the big winder what got two little uns at the sides.

'Very well, my boy,' said the Colonel, after a few more questions. 'You run away home now. I expect it was some person trying to give you a start. Another time, like a brave English boy, you just throw a stone—well, no, not that exactly, but you go and speak to the waiter, or to Mr. Simpson, the landlord, and—yes—and say that I advised you to do so.'

The boy's face expressed some of the doubt he felt as to the likelihood of Mr. Simpson's lending a favourable ear to his complaint, but the Colonel did not appear to perceive this, and went on:

'And here's a sixpence—no, I see it's a shilling—and you be off home, and don't think any more about it.'

The youth hurried off with agitated thanks, and the Colonel and Parkins went round to the front of the Globe and reconnoitred. There was only one window answering to the description they had been hearing.

'Well, that's curious,' said Parkins; 'it's evidently my window the lad was talking about. Will you come up for a moment, Colonel Wilson? We ought to be able to see if anyone has been taking liberties in my room.'

They were soon in the passage, and Parkins made as if to open the door. Then he stopped and felt in his pockets.

'This is more serious than I thought,' was his next remark. 'I remember now that before I started this morning I locked the door. It is locked now, and, what is more, here is the key.'

And he held it up. 'Now,' he went on, 'if the servants are in the habit of going into one's room during the day when one is away, I can only say that—well, that I don't approve of it at all.' Conscious of a somewhat weak climax, he busied himself in opening the door (which was indeed locked) and in lighting candles. 'No,' he said, 'nothing seems disturbed.'

'Except your bed,' put in the Colonel.

'Excuse me, that isn't my bed,' said Parkins. 'I don't use that one. But it does look as if someone had been playing tricks with it.'

It certainly did: the clothes were bundled up and twisted together in a most tortuous confusion. Parkins pondered.

'That must be it,' he said at last: 'I disordered the clothes last night in unpacking, and they haven't made it since. Perhaps they came in to make it, and that boy saw them through the window; and then they were called away and locked the door after them. Yes, I think that must be it.'

'Well, ring and ask,' said the Colonel, and this appealed to Parkins as practical.

The maid appeared, and, to make a long story short, deposed that she had made the bed in the morning when the gentleman was in the room, and hadn't been there since. No, she hadn't no other key. Mr. Simpson he kep' the keys; he'd be able to tell the gentleman if anyone had been up.

This was a puzzle. Investigation showed that nothing of value had been taken, and Parkins remembered the disposition of the small objects on tables and so forth well enough to be pretty sure that no pranks had been played with them. Mr. and Mrs. Simpson furthermore agreed that neither of them had given the duplicate key of the room to any person whatever during the day. Nor could Parkins, fair-minded man as he was, detect anything in the demeanour of master, mistress, or maid that indicated guilt. He was much more inclined to think that the boy had been imposing on the Colonel.

The latter was unwontedly silent and pensive at dinner and throughout the evening. When he bade good-night to Parkins, he murmured in a gruff undertone:

'You know where I am if you want me during the night.'

'Why, yes, thank you, Colonel Wilson, I think I do; but there isn't much prospect of my disturbing you, I hope. By the way,' he added, 'did I show you that old whistle I spoke of? I think not. Well, here it is.'

The Colonel turned it over gingerly in the light of the candle.

'Can you make anything of the inscription?' asked Parkins, as he took it back.

'No, not in this light. What do you mean to do with it?'

'Oh, well, when I get back to Cambridge I shall submit it to some of the archæologists there, and see what they think of it; and very likely, if they consider it worth having, I may present it to one of the museums.'

''M!' said the Colonel. 'Well, you may be right. All I know is that, if it were mine, I should chuck it straight into the sea. It's no use talking, I'm well aware, but I expect that with you it's a case of live and learn. I hope so, I'm sure, and I wish you a good-night.'

He turned away, leaving Parkins in act to speak at the bottom of the stair, and soon each was in his own bedroom.

By some unfortunate accident, there were neither blinds nor curtains to the windows of the Professor's room. The previous night he had thought little of this, but to-night there seemed every prospect of a bright moon rising to shine directly on his bed, and probably wake him later on. When he noticed this he was a good deal annoyed, but, with an ingenuity which I can only envy, he succeeded in rigging up, with the help of a railway-rug, some safety-pins, and a stick and umbrella, a screen which, if it only held together, would completely keep the moonlight off his bed. And shortly afterwards he was comfortably in that bed. When he had read a somewhat solid work long enough to produce a decided wish for sleep, he cast a drowsy glance round the room, blew out the candle, and fell back upon the pillow.

He must have slept soundly for an hour or more, when a sudden clatter shook him up in a most unwelcome manner. In a moment he realized what had happened: his carefully-constructed screen had given way, and a very bright frosty moon was shining directly on his face. This was highly annoying. Could he possibly get up and reconstruct the screen? or could he manage to sleep if he did not?

For some minutes he lay and pondered over the possibilities; then he turned over sharply, and with all his eyes open lay breathlessly listening. There had been a movement, he was sure, in the empty bed on the opposite side of the room. To-morrow he would have it moved, for there must be rats or something playing about in it. It was quiet now. No! the commotion began again. There was a rustling and shaking: surely more than any rat could cause

I can figure to myself something of the Professor's bewilderment and horror, for I have in a dream thirty years back seen the same thing happen; but the reader will hardly, perhaps, imagine how dreadful it was to him to see a figure suddenly sit up in what he had known was an empty bed.

He was out of his own bed in one bound, and made a dash towards the window, where lay his only weapon, the stick with which he had propped his screen. This was, as it turned out, the worst thing he could have done, because the personage in the empty bed, with a sudden smooth motion, slipped from the bed and took up a position, with outspread arms, between the two beds, and in front of the door. Parkins watched it in a horrid perplexity. Somehow, the idea of getting past it and escaping through the door was intolerable to him; he could not have borne—he didn't know why—to touch it; and as for its touching him, he would sooner dash himself through the window than have that happen. It stood for the moment in a band of dark shadow, and he had not seen what its face was like. Now it began to move, in a stooping posture, and all at once the spectator realized, with some horror and some relief, that it must be blind, for it seemed to feel about it with its muffled arms in a groping and random fashion. Turning half away from him, it became suddenly conscious of the bed he had just left, and darted towards it, and bent and felt over the pillows in a way which made Parkins shudder as he had never in his life thought it possible. In a very few moments it seemed to know that the bed was empty, and then, moving forward into the area of light and facing the window, it showed for the first time what manner of thing it was.

Parkins, who very much dislikes being questioned about it, did once describe something of it in my hearing, and I gathered that what he chiefly remembers about it is a horrible, an intensely horrible, face of crumpled linen. What expression he read upon it he could not or would not tell, but that the fear of it went nigh to maddening him is certain.

But he was not at leisure to watch it for long. With formidable quickness it moved into the middle of the room, and, as it groped and waved, one corner of its draperies swept across Parkins's face. He could not, though he knew how perilous a sound was—he could not keep back a cry of disgust, and this gave the searcher an instant clue. It leapt towards him upon the instant, and the next moment he was halfway through the window backwards, uttering cry upon cry at the utmost pitch of his voice, and the linen face was thrust close into his own. At this, almost the last possible second, deliverance came, as you will have guessed: the Colonel burst the door open, and was just in time to see the dreadful group at the window. When he reached the figures only one was left. Parkins sank forward into the room in a faint, and before him on the floor lay a tumbled heap of bed-clothes.

Colonel Wilson asked no questions, but busied himself keeping everyone else out of the room and in getting Parkins back to his bed; and himself, wrapped in a rug, occupied the other bed, for the rest of the night. Early on the next day Rogers arrived, more welcome than he would have been a day before, and the three of them held a very long consultation in the Professor's room. At the end of it the Colonel left the hotel door carrying a small object between his finger and thumb, which he cast as far into the sea as a very brawny arm could send it. Later on the smoke of a burning ascended from the back premises of the Globe.

Exactly what explanation was patched up for the staff and visitors at the hotel I must confess I do not recollect. The Professor was somehow cleared of the ready suspicion of delirium tremens, and the hotel of the reputation of a troubled house.

There is not much question as to what would have happened to Parkins if the Colonel had not intervened when he did. He would either have fallen out of the window or else lost his wits. But it is not so evident what more the creature that came in answer to the whistle could have done than frighten. There seemed to be absolutely nothing material about it save the bed-clothes of which it had made itself a body. The Colonel, who remembered a not very dissimilar occurrence in India, was of opinion that if Parkins had closed with it it could really have done very little, and that its one power was that of frightening. The whole thing, he said, served to confirm his opinion of the Church of Rome.

There is really nothing more to tell, but, as you may imagine, the Professor's views on certain points are less clear cut than they used to be. His nerves, too, have suffered: he cannot even now see a surplice hanging on a door quite unmoved, and the spectacle of a scarecrow in a field late on a winter afternoon has cost him more than one sleepless night.

August Heat (1910)

William Fryer Harvey

PHENISTONE ROAD, CLAPHAM.
August 20th, 190--.

I have had what I believe to be the most remarkable day in my life, and while the events are still fresh in my mind, I wish to put them down on paper as clearly as possible.

Let me say at the outset that my name is James Clarence Withencroft.

I am forty years old, in perfect health, never having known a day's illness.

By profession I am an artist, not a very successful one, but I earn enough money by my black-and-white work to satisfy my necessary wants.

My only near relative, a sister, died five years ago, so that I am independent. I breakfasted this morning at nine, and after glancing through the morning paper I lighted my pipe and proceeded to let my mind wander in the hope that I might chance upon some subject for my pencil.

The room, though door and windows were open, was oppressively hot, and I had just made up my mind that the coolest and most comfortable place in the neighbourhood would be the deep end of the public swimming bath, when the idea came.

I began to draw. So intent was I on my work that I left my lunch untouched, only stopping work when the clock of St. Jude's struck four.

The final result, for a hurried sketch, was, I felt sure, the best thing I had done. It showed a criminal in the dock immediately after the judge had pronounced sentence. The man was fat—enormously fat. The flesh hung in rolls about his chin; it creased his huge, stumpy neck. He was clean shaven (perhaps I should say a few days before he must have been clean shaven) and almost bald. He stood in the dock, his short, clumsy fingers clasping the rail, looking straight in front of him. The feeling that his expression conveyed was not so much one of horror as of utter, absolute collapse.

There seemed nothing in the man strong enough to sustain that mountain of flesh.

I rolled up the sketch, and without quite knowing why, placed it in my pocket. Then with the rare sense of happiness which the knowledge of a good thing well done gives, I left the house.

I believe that I set out with the idea of calling upon Trenton, for I remember walking along Lytton Street and turning to the right along Gilchrist Road at the bottom of the hill where the men were at work on the new tram lines.

From there onwards I have only the vaguest recollection of where I went. The one thing of which I was fully conscious was the awful heat, that came up from the dusty asphalt pavement as an almost palpable wave. I longed for the thunder promised by the great banks of copper-coloured cloud that hung low over the western sky.

I must have walked five or six miles, when a small boy roused me from my reverie by asking the time.

It was twenty minutes to seven.

When he left me I began to take stock of my bearings. I found myself standing before a gate that led into a yard bordered by a strip of thirsty earth, where there were flowers, purple stock and scarlet geranium. Above the entrance was a board with the inscription—

CHS. ATKINSON. MONUMENTAL MASON.
WORKER IN ENGLISH AND ITALIAN MARBLES

From the yard itself came a cheery whistle, the noise of hammer blows, and the cold sound of steel meeting stone.

A sudden impulse made me enter.

A man was sitting with his back towards me, busy at work on a slab of curiously veined marble. He turned round as he heard my steps and I stopped short.

It was the man I had been drawing, whose portrait lay in my pocket.

He sat there, huge and elephantine, the sweat pouring from his scalp, which he wiped with a red silk handkerchief. But though the face was the same, the expression was absolutely different.

He greeted me smiling, as if we were old friends, and shook my hand.

I apologised for my intrusion.

"Everything is hot and glary outside," I said. "This seems an oasis in the wilderness."

"I don't know about the oasis," he replied, "but it certainly is hot, as hot as hell. Take a seat, sir!"

He pointed to the end of the gravestone on which he was at work, and I sat down.

"That's a beautiful piece of stone you've got hold of," I said.

He shook his head. "In a way it is," he answered; "the surface here is as fine as anything you could wish, but there's a big flaw at the back, though I don't expect you'd ever notice it. I could never make really a good job of a bit of marble like that. It would be all right in the summer like this; it wouldn't mind the blasted heat. But wait till the winter comes. There's nothing quite like frost to find out the weak points in stone."

"Then what's it for?" I asked.

The man burst out laughing.

"You'd hardly believe me if I was to tell you it's for an exhibition, but it's the truth. Artists have exhibitions: so do grocers and butchers; we have them too. All the latest little things in headstones, you know."

He went on to talk of marbles, which sort best withstood wind and rain, and which were easiest to work; then of his garden and a new sort of carnation he had bought. At the end of every other minute he would drop his tools, wipe his shining head, and curse the heat.

I said little, for I felt uneasy. There was something unnatural, uncanny, in meeting this man.

I tried at first to persuade myself that I had seen him before, that his face, unknown to me, had found a place in some out-of-the-way corner of my memory, but I knew that

I was practising little more than a plausible piece of self-deception.

Mr. Atkinson finished his work, spat on the ground, and got up with a sigh of relief.

"There! what do you think of that?" he said, with an air of evident pride. The inscription which I read for the first time was this—

SACRED TO THE MEMORY
OF
JAMES CLARENCE WITHENCROFT.
BORN JAN. 18TH, 1860.
HE PASSED AWAY VERY SUDDENLY
ON AUGUST 20TH, 190--

"In the midst of life we are in death."

For some time I sat in silence. Then a cold shudder ran down my spine. I asked him where he had seen the name.

"Oh, I didn't see it anywhere," replied Mr. Atkinson. "I wanted some name, and I put down the first that came into my head. Why do you want to know?"

"It's a strange coincidence, but it happens to be mine." He gave a long, low whistle.

"And the dates?"

"I can only answer for one of them, and that's correct."

"It's a rum go!" he said.

But he knew less than I did. I told him of my morning's work. I took the sketch from my pocket and showed it to him. As he looked, the expression of his face altered until it became more and more like that of the man I had drawn.

"And it was only the day before yesterday," he said, "that I told Maria there were no such things as ghosts!"

Neither of us had seen a ghost, but I knew what he meant. "You probably heard my name," I said.

"And you must have seen me somewhere and have forgotten it! Were you at Clacton-on-Sea last July?"

I had never been to Clacton in my life. We were silent for some time. We were both looking at the same thing, the two dates on the gravestone, and one was right.

"Come inside and have some supper," said Mr. Atkinson.

His wife was a cheerful little woman, with the flaky red cheeks of the country-bred. Her husband introduced me as a friend of his who was an artist. The result was unfortunate, for after the sardines and watercress had been removed, she brought out a Doré Bible, and I had to sit and express my admiration for nearly half an hour.

I went outside, and found Atkinson sitting on the gravestone smoking.

We resumed the conversation at the point we had left off. "You must excuse my asking," I said, "but do you know of anything you've done for which you could be put on trial?"

He shook his head. "I'm not a bankrupt, the business is prosperous enough. Three years ago I gave turkeys to some of the guardians at Christmas, but that's all I can think of. And they were small ones, too," he added as an afterthought.

He got up, fetched a can from the porch, and began to water the flowers. "Twice a day regular in the hot weather," he said, "and then the heat sometimes gets the better of the delicate ones. And ferns, good Lord! they could never stand it. Where do you live?"

I told him my address. It would take an hour's quick walk to get back home.

"It's like this," he said. "We'll look at the matter straight. If you go back home to-night, you take your chance of accidents. A cart may run over you, and there's always banana skins and orange peel, to say nothing of fallen ladders."

He spoke of the improbable with an intense seriousness that would have been laughable six hours before. But I did not laugh.

"The best thing we can do," he continued, "is for you to stay here till twelve o'clock. We'll go upstairs and smoke, it may be cooler inside."

To my surprise I agreed.

* * *

We are sitting now in a long, low room beneath the eaves. Atkinson has sent his wife to bed. He himself is busy sharpening some tools at a little oilstone, smoking one of my cigars the while.

The air seems charged with thunder. I am writing this at a shaky table before the open window.

The leg is cracked, and Atkinson, who seems a handy man with his tools, is going to mend it as soon as he has finished putting an edge on his chisel.

It is after eleven now. I shall be gone in less than an hour.

But the heat is stifling.

It is enough to send a man mad.

The Spider (1908)

Hans Heinz Ewers

When the student of medicine, Richard Bracque-mont, decided to move into room #7 of the small Hotel Stevens, Rue Alfred Stevens (Paris 6), three persons had already hanged themselves from the cross-bar of the window in that room on three successive Fridays.

The first was a Swiss traveling salesman. They found his corpse on Saturday evening. The doctor determined that the death must have occurred between five and six o'clock on Friday afternoon. The corpse hung on a strong hook that had been driven into the window's cross-bar to serve as a hanger for articles of clothing. The window was closed, and the dead man had used the curtain cord as a noose. Since the window was very low, he hung with his knees practically touching the floor—a sign of the great discipline the suicide must have exercised in carrying out his design. Later, it was learned that he was a married man, a father. He had been a man of a continually happy disposition; a man who had achieved a secure place in life. There was not one written word to be found that would have shed light on his suicide...not even a will.

Furthermore, none of his acquaintances could recall hearing anything at all from him that would have permitted anyone to predict his end.

The second case was not much different. The artist, Karl Krause, a high wire cyclist in the nearby Medrano Circus, moved into room ^{1}7 two days later. When he did not show up at Friday's performance, the director sent an employee to the hotel. There, he found Krause in the unlocked room hanging from the window cross-bar in circumstances exactly like those of the previous suicide. This death was as perplexing as the first. Krause was popular. He earned a very high salary, and had appeared to enjoy life at its fullest. Once again, there was no suicide note; no sinister hints. Krause's sole survivor was his mother to whom the son had regularly sent 300 marks on the first of the month.

For Madame Dubonnet, the owner of the small, cheap guesthouse whose clientele was composed almost completely of employees in a nearby Montmartre vaudeville theater, this second curious death in the same room had very unpleasant consequences. Already several of her guests had moved out, and other regular clients had not come back. She appealed for help to her personal friend, the inspector of police of the ninth precinct, who assured her that he would do everything in his power to help her. He pushed zealously ahead not only with the investigation into the grounds for the suicides of the two guests, but he also placed an officer in the mysterious room.

This man, Charles-Maria Chaumié, actually volunteered for the task. Chaumié was an old "Marsouin," a marine sergeant with eleven years of service, who had lain so many nights at posts in Tonkin and Annam, and had greeted so many stealthily creeping river pirates with a shot from his rifle that he seemed ideally suited to encounter the "ghost" that everyone on Rue Alfred Stevens was talking about.

From then on, each morning and each evening, Chaumié paid a brief visit to the police station to make his report, which, for the first few days, consisted only of his statement that he had not noticed anything unusual. On Wednesday evening, however, he hinted that he had found a clue.

Pressed to say more, he asked to be allowed more time before making any comment, since he was not sure that what he had discovered had any relationship to the two deaths, and he was afraid he might say something that would make him look foolish.

On Thursday, his behavior seemed a bit uncertain, but his mood was noticeably more serious. Still, he had nothing to report. On Friday morning, he came in very excited and spoke, half humorously, half seriously, of the strangely attractive power that his window had. He would not elaborate this notion and said that, in any case, it had nothing to do with the suicides; and that it would be ridiculous of him to say any more. When, on that same Friday, he failed to make his regular evening report, someone went to his room and found him hanging from the cross-bar of the window.

All the circumstances, down to the minutest detail, were the same here as in the previous cases. Chaumié's legs dragged along the ground. The curtain cord had been used for a noose. The window was closed, the door to the room had not been locked and death had occurred at six o'clock. The dead man's mouth was wide open, and his tongue protruded from it.

Chaumié's death, the third in as many weeks in room #7, had the following consequences: all the guests, with the exception of a German high-school teacher in room #16, moved out. The teacher took advantage of the occasion to have his rent reduced by a third. The next day, Mary Garden, the famous Opéra Comique singer, drove up to the Hotel Stevens and paid two hundred francs for the red curtain cord, saying it would bring her luck. The story, small consolation for Madame Dubonnet, got into the papers.

If these events had occurred in summer, in July or August, Madame Dubonnet would have secured three times that price for her cord, but as it was in the middle of a troubled year, with elections, disorders in the Balkans, bank crashes in New York, the visit of the King and Queen of England, the result was that the affaire Rue Alfred Stevens was talked of less than it deserved to be. As for the newspaper accounts, they were brief, being essentially the police reports word for word.

These reports were all that Richard Bracquemont, the medical student, knew of the matter.

There was one detail about which he knew nothing because neither the police inspector nor any of the eyewitnesses had mentioned it to the press. It was only later, after what happened to the medical student, that anyone remembered that when the police removed Sergeant Charles-Maria Chaumié's body from the window cross-bar a large black spider crawled from the dead man's open mouth. A hotel porter flicked it away, exclaiming, "Ugh, another of those damned creatures."

When in later investigations which concerned themselves mostly with Bracquemont the servant was interrogated, he said that he had seen a similar spider crawling on the Swiss traveling salesman's shoulder when his body was removed from the window cross-bar. But Richard Bracquemont knew nothing of all this.

It was more than two weeks after the last suicide that Bracquemont moved into the room. It was a Sunday. Bracquemont conscientiously recorded everything that happened to him in his journal. That journal now follows.

Monday, February 28 I moved in yesterday evening. I unpacked my two wicker suitcases and straightened the room a little. Then I went to bed. I slept so soundly that it was nine o'clock the next morning before a knock at my door woke me. It was my hostess, bringing me breakfast herself. One could read her concern for me in the eggs, the bacon and the superb café au lait she brought me. I washed and dressed, then smoked a pipe as I watched the servant make up the room.

So, here I am. I know well that the situation may prove dangerous, but I think I may just be the one to solve the problem. If, once upon a time, Paris was worth a mass (conquest comes at a dearer rate these days), it is well worth risking my life pour un si bel enjeu. I have at least one chance to win, and I mean to risk it. As it is, I'm not the only one who has had this notion. Twenty-seven people have tried for access to the room. Some went to the police, some went directly to the hotel owner. There were even three women among the candidates. There was plenty of competition. No doubt the others are poor devils like me.

And yet, it was I who was chosen. Why? Because I was the only one who hinted that I had some plan—or the semblance of a plan. Naturally, I was bluffing.

These journal entries are intended for the police. I must say that it amuses me to tell those gentlemen how neatly I fooled them. If the Inspector has any sense, he'll say, "Hm. This Bracquemont is just the man we need." In any case, it doesn't matter what he'll say. The point is I'm here now, and I take it as a good sign that I've begun my task by bamboozling the police.

I had gone first to Madame Dubonnet, and it was she who sent me to the police. They put me off for a whole week—as they put off my rivals as well. Most of them gave up in disgust, having something better to do than hang around the musty squad room. The Inspector was beginning to get irritated at my tenacity. At last, he told me I was wasting my time. That the police had no use for bungling amateurs. "Ah, if only you had a plan. Then..."

On the spot, I announced that I had such a plan, though naturally I had no such thing. Still, I hinted that my plan was brilliant, but dangerous, that it might lead to the same end as that which had overtaken the police officer, Chaumié. Still, I promised to describe it to him if he would give me his word that he would personally put it into effect. He made excuses, claiming he was too busy but when he asked me to give him at least a hint of my plan, I saw that I had picqued his interest.

I rattled off some nonsense made up of whole cloth. God alone knows where it all came from.

I told him that six o'clock of a Friday is an occult hour. It is the last hour of the Jewish week; the hour when Christ disappeared from his tomb and descended into hell. That he would do well to remember that the three suicides had taken place at approximately that hour. That was all I could tell him just then, I said, but I pointed him to The Revelations of St. John.

The Inspector assumed the look of a man who understood all that I had been saying, then he asked me to come back that evening.

I returned, precisely on time, and noted a copy of the New Testament on the Inspector's desk. I had, in the meantime, been at the Revelations myself without however having understood a syllable. Perhaps the Inspector was cleverer than I. Very politely—nay—deferentially, he let me know that, despite my extremely vague intimations, he believed he grasped my line of thought and was ready to expedite my plan in every way.

And here, I must acknowledge that he has indeed been tremendously helpful. It was he who made the arrangement with the owner that I was to have anything I needed so long as I stayed in the room. The Inspector gave me a pistol and a police whistle, and he ordered the officers on the beat to pass through the Rue Alfred Stevens as often as possible, and to watch my window for any signal. Most important of all, he had a desk telephone installed which connects directly with the police station. Since the station is only four minutes away, I see no reason to be afraid.

Wednesday, March 1 Nothing has happened. Not yesterday. Not today.

Madame Dubonnet brought a new curtain cord from another room—the rooms are mostly empty, of course. Madame Dubonnet takes every opportunity to visit me, and each time she brings something with her. I have asked her to tell me again everything that happened here, but I have learned nothing new. She has her own opinion of the suicides. Her view is that the music hall artist, Krause, killed himself because of an unhappy love affair. During the last year that Krause lived in the hotel, a young woman had made frequent visits to him. These visits had stopped, just before his death. As for the Swiss gentleman, Madame Dubonnet confessed herself baffled. On the other hand, the death of the policeman was easy to explain. He had killed himself just to annoy her.

These are sad enough explanations, to be sure, but I let her babble on to take the edge off my boredom.

Thursday, March 3 Still nothing. The Inspector calls twice a day. Each time, I tell him that all is well. Apparently, these words do not reassure him.

I have taken out my medical books and I study, so that my self-imposed confinement will have some purpose.

Friday. March 4 I ate uncommonly well at noon. The landlady brought me half a bottle of champagne. It seemed a meal for a condemned man. Madame Dubonnet looked at me as if I were already three-quarters dead. As she was leaving, she begged me tearfully to come with her, fearing no doubt that I would hang myself 'just to annoy her.'

I studied the curtain cord once again. Would I hang myself with it? Certainly, I felt little desire to do so. The cord is stiff and rough—not the sort of cord one makes a noose of. One would need to be truly determined before one could imitate the others.

I am seated now at my table. At my left, the telephone. At my right, the revolver. I'm not frightened; but I am curious.

Six o'clock, the same evening Nothing has happened. I was about to add, "Unfortunately." The fatal hour has come—and has gone, like any six o'clock on any evening. I won't hide the fact that I occasionally felt a certain impulse to go to the window, but for a quite different reason than one might imagine.

The Inspector called me at least ten times between five and six o'clock. He was as impatient as I was. Madame Dubonnet, on the other hand, is happy. A week has passed without someone in #7 hanging himself. Marvelous.

Monday, March 7 I have a growing conviction that I will learn nothing; that the previous suicides are related to the circumstances surrounding the lives of the three men. I have asked the Inspector to investigate the cases further, convinced that someone will find their motivations. As for me, I hope to stay here as long as possible. I may not conquer Paris here, but I live very well and I'm fattening up nicely. I'm also studying hard, and I am making real progress. There is another reason, too, that keeps me here.

Wednesday, March 9 So! I have taken one step more. Clarimonda.

I haven't yet said anything about Clarimonda. It is she who is my "third" reason for staying here. She is also the reason I was tempted to go to the window during the "fateful" hour last Friday. But of course, not to hang myself.

Clarimonda. Why do I call her that? I have no idea what her name is, but it ought to be Clarimonda. When finally I ask her name, I'm sure it will turn out to be Clarimonda.

I noticed her almost at once...in the very first days. She lives across the narrow street; and her window looks right into mine. She sits there, behind her curtains.

I ought to say that she noticed me before I saw her; and that she was obviously interested in me. And no wonder.

The whole neighborhood knows I am here, and why. Madame Dubonnet has seen to that.

I am not of a particularly amorous disposition. In fact, my relations with women have been rather meager. When one comes from Verdun to Paris to study medicine, and has hardly money enough for three meals a day, one has something else to think about besides love. I am then not very experienced with women, and I may have begun my adventure with her stupidly. Never mind. It's exciting just the same.

At first, the idea of establishing some relationship with her simply did not occur to me. It was only that, since I was here to make observations, and, since there was nothing in the room to observe, I thought I might as well observe my neighbor—openly, professionally. Anyhow, one can't sit all day long just reading.

Clarimonda, I have concluded, lives alone in the small flat across the way. The flat has three windows, but she sits only before the window that looks into mine. She sits there, spinning on an old-fashioned spindle, such as my grandmother inherited from a great aunt. I had no idea anyone still used such spindles. Clarimonda's spindle is a lovely object. It appears to be made of ivory; and the thread she spins is of an exceptional fineness. She works all day behind her curtains, and stops spinning only as the sun goes down. Since darkness comes abruptly here in this narrow street and in this season of fogs, Clarimonda disappears from her place at five o'clock each evening.

I have never seen a light in her flat.

What does Clarimonda look like? I'm not quite sure. Her hair is black and wavy; her face pale.

Her nose is short and finely shaped with delicate nostrils that seem to quiver. Her lips, too, are pale: and when she smiles, it seems that her small teeth are as keen as those of some beast of prey.

Her eyelashes are long and dark; and her huge dark eyes have an intense glow. I guess all these details more than I know them. It is hard to see clearly through the curtains.

Something else: she always wears a black dress embroidered with a lilac motif; and black gloves, no doubt to protect her hands from the effects of her work. It is a curious sight: her delicate hands moving perpetually, swiftly grasping the thread, pulling it, releasing it, taking it up again; as if one were watching the indefatigable motions of an insect.

Our relationship? For the moment, still very superficial, though it feels deeper. It began with a sudden exchange of glances in which each of us noted the other. I must have pleased her, because one day she studied me a while longer, then smiled tentatively. Naturally, I smiled back. In this fashion, two days went by, each of us smiling more frequently with the passage of time. Yet something kept me from greeting her directly.

Until today. This afternoon, I did it. And Clarimonda returned my greeting. It was done subtly enough, to be sure, but I saw her nod.

Thursday, March 10 Yesterday, I sat for a long time over my books, though I can't truthfully say that I studied much. I built castles in the air and dreamed of Clarimonda.

I slept fitfully.

This morning, when I approached my window, Clarimonda was already in her place. I waved, and she nodded back. She laughed and studied me for a long time.

I tried to read, but I felt much too uneasy. Instead, I sat down at my window and gazed at Clarimonda. She too had laid her work aside. Her hands were folded in her lap. I drew my curtain wider with the window cord, so that I might see better. At the same moment, Clarimonda did the same with the curtains at her window. We exchanged smiles.

We must have spent a full hour gazing at each other.

Finally, she took up her spinning.

Saturday, March 12 The days pass. I eat and drink. I sit at the desk. I light my pipe; I look down at my book but I don't read a word, though I try again and again. Then I go to the window where I wave to Clarimonda. She nods. We smile. We stare at each other for hours.

Yesterday afternoon, at six o'clock, I grew anxious. The twilight came early, bringing with it something like anguish. I sat at my desk. I waited until I was invaded by an irresistible need to go to the window—not to hang myself; but just to see Clarimonda. I sprang up and stood beside the curtain where it seemed to me I had never been able to see so clearly, though it was already dark.

Clarimonda was spinning, but her eyes looked into mine. I felt myself strangely contented even as I experienced a light sensation of fear.

The telephone rang. It was the Inspector tearing me out of my trance with his idiotic questions.

I was furious.

This morning, the Inspector and Madame Dubonnet visited me. She is enchanted with how things are going. I have now lived for two weeks in room #7. The Inspector, however, does not feel he is getting results. I hinted mysteriously that I was on the trail of something most unusual.

The jackass took me at my word and fulfilled my dearest wish. I've been allowed to stay in the room for another week. God knows it isn't Madame Dubonnet's cooking or wine-cellar that keeps me here. How quickly one can be sated with such things. No. I want to stay because of the window Madame Dubonnet fears and hates. That beloved window that shows me Clarimonda.

I have stared out of my window, trying to discover whether she ever leaves her room, but I've never seen her set foot on the street.

As for me, I have a large, comfortable armchair and a green shade over the lamp whose glow envelopes me in warmth. The Inspector has left me with a huge packet of fine tobacco—and yet I cannot work. I read two or three pages only to discover that I haven't understood a word. My eyes see the letters, but my brain refuses to make any sense of them. Absurd. As if my brain were posted: 'No Trespassing.' It is as if there were no room in my head for any other thought than the one: Clarimonda. I push my books away; I lean back deeply into my chair. I dream.

Sunday, March 13 This morning I watched a tiny drama while the servant was tidying my room. I was strolling in the corridor when I paused before a small window in which a large garden spider had her web.

Madame Dubonnet will not have it removed because she believes spiders bring luck, and she's had enough misfortunes in her house lately. Today, I saw a much smaller spider, a male, moving across the strong threads towards the middle of the web, but when his movements alerted the female, he drew back shyly to the edge of the web from which he made a second attempt to cross it. Finally, the female in the middle appeared attentive to his wooing, and stopped moving. The male tugged at a strand gently, then more strongly till the whole web shook. The female stayed motionless. The male moved quickly forward and the female received him quietly, calmly, giving herself over completely to his embraces. For a long minute, they hung together motionless at the center of the huge web.

Then I saw the male slowly extricating himself, one leg over the other. It was as if he wanted tactfully to leave his companion alone in the dream of love, but as he started away, the female, overwhelmed by a wild life, was after him, hunting him ruthlessly. The male let himself drop from a thread; the female followed, and for a while the lovers hung there, imitating a piece of art. Then they fell to the window-sill where the male, summoning all his strength, tried again to escape. Too late. The female already had him in her powerful grip, and was carrying him back to the center of the web. There, the place that had just served as the couch for their lascivious embraces took on quite another aspect. The lover wriggled, trying to escape from the female's wild embrace, but she was too much for him. It was not long before she had wrapped him completely in her thread, and he was helpless. Then she dug her sharp pincers into his body, and sucked full draughts of her young lover's blood. Finally, she detached herself from the pitiful and unrecognizable shell of his body and threw it out of her web.

So that is what love is like among these creatures. Well for me that I am not a spider.

Monday, March 14 I don't look at my books any longer. I spend my days at the window. When it is dark, Clarimonda is no longer there, but if I close my eyes, I continue to see her.

This journal has become something other than I intended. I've spoken about Madame Dubonnet, about the Inspector; about spiders and about Clarimonda. But I've said nothing about the discoveries I undertook to make. It can't be helped.

Tuesday, March 15 We have invented a strange game, Clarimonda and I. We play it all day long. I greet her; then she greets me. Then I tap my fingers on the windowpanes. The moment she sees me doing that, she too begins tapping. I wave to her; she waves back. I move my lips as if speaking to her; she does the same. I run my hand through my sleep-disheveled hair and instantly her hand is at her forehead. It is a child's game, and we both laugh over it. Actually, she doesn't laugh. She only smiles a gently contained smile. And I smile back in the same way.

The game is not as trivial as it seems. It's not as if we were grossly imitating each other—that would weary us both. Rather, we are communicating with each other. Sometimes, telepathically, it would seem, since Clarimonda follows my movements instantaneously almost before she has had time to see them. I find myself inventing new movements, or new combinations of movements, but each time she repeats them with disconcerting speed. Sometimes. I change the order of the movements to surprise her, making whole series of gestures as rapidly as possible; or I leave out some motions and weave in others, the way children play "Simon Says." What is amazing is that Clarimonda never once makes a mistake, no matter how quickly I change gestures.

That's how I spend my days...hut never for a moment do I feel that I'm killing time. It seems, on the contrary, that never in my life have I been better occupied.

Wednesday. March 16 Isn't it strange that it hasn't occurred to me to put my relationship with Clarimonda on a more serious basis than these endless games. Last night, I thought about this...I can, of course, put on my hat and coat, walk down two flights of stairs, take five steps across the street and mount two flights to her door which is marked with a small sign that says "Clarimonda." Clarimonda what? I don't know. Something. Then I can knock and...

Up to this point I imagine everything very clearly, but I cannot see what should happen next. I know that the door opens. But then I stand before it, looking into a dark void. Clarimonda doesn't come. Nothing comes. Nothing is there, only the black, impenetrable dark.

Sometimes, it seems to me that there can be no other Clarimonda but the one I see in the window; the one who plays gesture-games with me. I cannot imagine a Clarimonda wearing a hat, or a dress other than her black dress with the lilac motif. Nor can I imagine a Clarimonda without black gloves. The very notion that I might encounter Clarimonda somewhere in the streets or in a restaurant eating, drinking or chatting is so improbable that it makes me laugh.

Sometimes I ask myself whether I love her. It's impossible to say, since I have never loved before. However, if the feeling that I have for Clarimonda is really—love, then love is something entirely different from anything I have seen among my friends or read about in novels.

It is hard for me to be sure of my feelings and harder still to think of anything that doesn't relate to Clarimonda or, what is more important, to our game. Undeniably, it is our game that concerns me. Nothing else—and this is what I understand least of all.

There is no doubt that I am drawn to Clarimonda, but with this attraction there is mingled another feeling, fear. No. That's not it either. Say rather a vague apprehension in the presence of the unknown. And this anxiety has a strangely voluptuous quality so that I am at the same time drawn to her even as I am repelled by her. It is as if I were moving in giant circles around her, sometimes coming close, sometimes retreating...back and forth, back and forth.

Once, I am sure of it, it will happen, and I will join her.

Clarimonda sits at her window and spins her slender, eternally fine thread, making a strange cloth whose purpose I do not understand. I am amazed that she is able to keep from tangling her delicate thread. Hers is surely a remarkable design, containing mythical beasts and strange masks.

Thursday, March 17 I am curiously excited. I don't talk to people any more. I barely say "hello" to Madame Dubonnet or to the servant. I hardly give myself time to eat. All I can do is sit at the window and play the game with Clarimonda. It is an enthralling game. Overwhelming.

I have the feeling something will happen tomorrow.

Friday, March 18 Yes. Yes. Something will happen today. I tell myself—as loudly as I can—that that's why I am here. And yet, horribly enough, I am afraid. And in the fear that the same thing is going to happen to me as happened to my predecessors, there is strangely mingled another fear: a terror of Clarimonda. And I cannot separate the two fears.

I am frightened. I want to scream.

Six o'clock, evening I have my hat and coat on. Just a couple of words.

At five o'clock, I was at the end of my strength. I'm perfectly aware now that there is a relationship between my despair and the "sixth hour" that was so significant in the previous weeks. I no longer laugh at the trick I played the Inspector.

I was sitting at the window, trying with all my might to stay in my chair, but the window kept drawing me. I had to resume the game with Clarimonda. And yet, the window horrified me. I saw the others hanging there: the Swiss traveling salesman, fat, with a thick neck and a grey stubbly beard; the thin artist; and the powerful police sergeant. I saw them, one after the other, hanging from the same hook, their mouths open, their tongues sticking out. And then, I saw myself among them.

Oh, this unspeakable fear. It was clear to me that it was provoked as much by Clarimonda as by the cross-bar and the horrible hook. May she pardon me...but it is the truth. In my terror, I keep seeing the three men hanging there, their legs dragging on the floor.

And yet, the fact is I had not felt the slightest desire to hang myself; nor was I afraid that I would want to do so. No, it was the window I feared; and Clarimonda. I was sure that something horrid was going to happen. Then I was overwhelmed by the need to go to the window—to stand before it. I had to...

The telephone rang. I picked up the receiver and before I could hear a word, I screamed, "Come. Come at once."

It was as if my shrill cry had in that instant dissipated the shadows from my soul. I grew calm.

I wiped the sweat from my forehead. I drank a glass of water. Then I considered what I should say to the Inspector when he arrived. Finally, I went to the window. I waved and smiled. And Clarimonda too waved and smiled.

Five minutes later, the Inspector was here. I told him that I was getting to the bottom of the matter, but I begged him not to question me just then. That very soon I would be in a position to make important revelations. Strangely enough, though I was lying to him. I myself had the feeling that I was telling the truth. Even now, against my will, I have that same conviction.

The Inspector could not help noticing my agitated state of mind, especially since I apologized for my anguished cry over the telephone. Naturally, I tried to explain it to him, and yet I could not find a single reason to give for it. He said affectionately that there was no need ever to apologize to him; that he was always at my disposal; that that was his duty. It was better that he should come a dozen times to no effect rather than fail to be here when he was needed. He invited me to go out with him for the evening. It would be a distraction for me. It would do me good not to be alone for a while. I accepted the invitation though I was very reluctant to leave the room.

Saturday, March 19 We went to the Gaieté Roche-chouart, La Cigale, and La Lune Rousse. The Inspector was right: It was good for me to get out and breathe the fresh air. At first, I had an uncomfortable feeling, as if I were doing something wrong; as if I were a deserter who had turned his back on the flag. But that soon went away. We drank a lot, laughed and chatted. This morning, when I went to my window, Clarimonda gave me what I thought was a look of reproach, though I may only have imagined it. How could she have known that I had gone out last night? In any case, the look lasted only for an instant, then she smiled again.

We played the game all day long.

Sunday, March 20 Only one thing to record: we played the game.

Monday, March 21 We played the game—all day long.

Tuesday, March 22 Yes, the game. We played it again. And nothing else. Nothing at all.

Sometimes I wonder what is happening to me? What is it I want? Where is all this leading? I know the answer: there is nothing else I want except what is happening. It is what I want...what I long for. This only.

Clarimonda and I have spoken with each other in the course of the last few days, but very briefly; scarcely a word. Sometimes we moved our lips, but more often we just looked at each other with deep understanding.

I was right about Clarimonda's reproachful look because I went out with the Inspector last Friday. I asked her to forgive me. I said it was stupid of me, and spiteful to have gone. She forgave me, and I promised never to leave the window again. We kissed, pressing our lips against each of our windowpanes.

Wednesday, March 23 I know now that I love Clarimonda. That she has entered into the very fiber of my being. It may be that the loves of other men are different. But does there exist one head, one ear, one hand that is exactly like hundreds of millions of others? There are always differences, and it must be so with love. My love is strange, I know that, but is it any the less lovely because of that? Besides, my love makes me happy.

If only I were not so frightened. Sometimes my terror slumbers and I forget it for a few moments, then it wakes and does not leave me. The fear is like a poor mouse trying to escape the grip of a powerful serpent. Just wait a bit, poor sad terror. Very soon, the serpent love will devour you.

Thursday, March 24 I have made a discovery: I don't play with Clarimonda. She plays with me.

Last night, thinking as always about our game, I wrote down five new and intricate gesture patterns with which I intended to surprise Clarimonda today. I gave each gesture a number. Then I practiced the series, so I could do the motions as quickly as possible, forwards or backwards. Or sometimes only the even-numbered ones, sometimes the odd. Or the first and the last of the five patterns. It was tiring work, but it made me happy and seemed to bring Clarimonda closer to me. I practiced for hours until I got all the motions down pat, like clockwork.

This morning, I went to the window. Clarimonda and I greeted each other, then our game began. Back and forth! It was incredible how quickly she understood what was to be done; how she kept pace with me.

There was a knock at the door. It was the servant bringing me my shoes. I took them. On my way back to the window, my eye chanced to fall on the slip of paper on which I had noted my gesture patterns. It was then that I understood: in the game just finished, I had not made use of a single one of my patterns.

I reeled back and had to hold on to the chair to keep from falling. It was unbelievable. I read the paper again—and again. It was still true: I had gone through a long series of gestures at the window, and not one of the patterns had been mine.

I had the feeling, once more, that I was standing before Clarimonda's wide open door, through which, though I stared. I could see nothing but a dark void. I knew, too, that if I chose to turn from that door now. I might be saved; and that I still had the power to leave. And yet, I did not leave—because I felt myself at the very edge of the mystery: as if I were holding the secret in my hands.

"Paris! You will conquer Paris," I thought. And in that instant, Paris was more powerful than Clarimonda.

I don't think about that any more. Now, I feel only love. Love, and a delicious terror.

Still, the moment itself endowed me with strength. I read my notes again, engraving the gestures on my mind. Then I went back to the window only to become aware that there was not one of my patterns that I wanted to use. Standing there, it occurred to me to rub the side of my nose; instead I found myself pressing my lips to the windowpane. I tried to drum with my fingers on the window sill; instead, I brushed my fingers through my hair. And so I understood that it was not that Clarimonda did what I did. Rather, my gestures followed her lead and with such lightning rapidity that we seemed to be moving simultaneously. I, who had been so proud because I thought I had been influencing her, I was in fact being influenced by her. Her influence...so gentle...so delightful.

I have tried another experiment. I clenched my hands and put them in my pockets firmly intending not to move them one bit. Clarimonda raised her hand and, smiling at me, made a scolding gesture with her finger. I did not budge, and yet I could feel how my right hand wished to leave my pocket. I shoved my fingers against the lining, but against my will, my hand left the pocket; my arm rose into the air. In my turn, I made a scolding gesture with my finger and smiled.

It seemed to me that it was not I who was doing all this. It was a stranger whom I was watching.

But, of course, I was mistaken. It was I making the gesture, and the person watching me was the stranger; that very same stranger who, not long ago, was so sure that he was on the edge of a great discovery. In any case, it was not I.

Of what use to me is this discovery? I am here to do Clarimonda's will. Clarimonda, whom I love with an anguished heart.

Friday, March 25 I have cut the telephone cord. I have no wish to be continually disturbed by the idiotic inspector just as the mysterious hour arrives.

God. Why did I write that? Not a word of it is true. It is as if someone else were directing my pen.

But I want to...want to...to write the truth here...though it is costing me great effort. But I want to...once more...do what I want.

I have cut the telephone cord...ah...

Because I had to...there it is. Had to...

We stood at our windows this morning and played the game, which is now different from what it was yesterday. Clarimonda makes a movement and I resist it for as long as I can. Then I give in and do what she wants without further struggle. I can hardly express what a joy it is to be so conquered; to surrender entirely to her will.

We played. All at once, she stood up and walked back into her room, where I could not see her; she was so engulfed by the dark. Then she came back with a desk telephone, like mine, in her hands. She smiled and set the telephone on the window sill, after which she took a knife and cut the cord. Then I carried my telephone to the window where I cut the cord. After that, I returned my phone to its place.

That's how it happened...

I sit at my desk where I have been drinking tea the servant brought me. He has come for the empty teapot, and I ask him for the time, since my watch isn't running properly. He says it is five fifteen. Five fifteen...

I know that if I look out of my window, Clarimonda will be there making a gesture that I will have to imitate. I will look just the same. Clarimonda is there, smiling. If only I could turn my eyes away from hers.

Now she parts the curtain. She takes the cord. It is red, just like the cord in my window. She ties a noose and hangs the cord on the hook in the window cross-bar.

She sits down and smiles.

No. Fear is no longer what I feel. Rather, it is a sort of oppressive terror which I would not want to avoid for anything in the world. Its grip is irresistible, profoundly cruel, and voluptuous in its attraction.

I could go to the window, and do what she wants me to do, but I wait. I struggle. I resist though I feel a mounting fascination that becomes more intense each minute.

Here I am once more. Rashly, I went to the window where I did what Clarimonda wanted. I took the cord, tied a noose, and hung it on the hook...

Now, I want to see nothing else—except to stare at this paper. Because if I look. I know what she will do...now...at

the sixth hour of the last day of the week. If I see her, I will
have to do what she wants. Have to...

I won't see her...

I laugh. Loudly. No. I'm not laughing. Something is
laughing in me, and I know why. It is because of my...I
won't...

I won't, and yet I know very well that I have to...have to
look at her. I must...must...and then...all that follows.

If I still wait, it is only to prolong this exquisite torture.
Yes, that's it. This breathless anguish is my supreme delight.
I write quickly, quickly...just so I can continue to sit here; so
I can attenuate these seconds of pain.

Again, terror. Again. I know that I will look toward her.
That I will stand up. That I will hang myself.

That doesn't frighten me. That is beautiful...even
precious.

There is something else. What will happen afterwards? I
don't know, but since my torment is so delicious. I feel...feel
that something horrible must follow.

Think...think...Write something. Anything at all...to keep
from looking toward her...

My name...Richard Bracquemont. Richard Bracquemon-
t...Richard Bracquemont...

Richard...

I can't...go on. I must...no...no...must look at her...Richard
Bracquemont...no . .

. no more...Richard...Richard Bracque—...

The inspector of the ninth precinct, after repeated and
vain efforts to telephone Richard, arrived at the Hotel
Stevens at 6:05. He found the body of the student Richard
Bracquemont hanging from the cross-bar of the window in

room #7, in the same position as each of his three predecessors.

The expression on the student's face, however, was different, reflecting an appalling fear.

Bracquemont's eyes were wide open and bulging from their sockets. His lips were drawn into a rictus, and his jaws were clamped together. A huge black spider whose body was dotted with purple spots lay crushed and nearly bitten in two between his teeth.

On the table, there lay the student's journal. The inspector read it and went immediately to investigate the house across the street. What he learned was that the second floor of that building had not been lived in for many months.

The Monster Maker
(1887)

W. C. Morrow

A young man of refined appearance, but evidently suffering great mental distress, presented himself one morning at the residence of a singular old man, who was known as a surgeon of remarkable skill. The house was a queer and primitive brick affair, entirely out of date, and tolerable only in the decayed part of the city in which it stood. It was large, gloomy, and dark, and had long corridors and dismal rooms; and it was absurdly large for the small family—man and wife—that occupied it. The house described, the man is portrayed—but not the woman. He could be agreeable on occasion, but, for all that, he was but animated mystery. His wife was weak, wan, reticent, evidently miserable, and possibly living a life of dread or horror—perhaps witness of repulsive things, subject of anxieties, and victim of fear and tyranny; but there is a great deal of guessing in these assumptions. He was about sixty-five years of age and she about forty. He was lean, tall, and bald, with thin, smooth-shaven face, and very keen eyes; kept always at home, and was slovenly. The man was strong, the woman weak; he dominated, she suffered.

Although he was a surgeon of rare skill, his practice was almost nothing, for it was a rare occurrence that the few who knew of his great ability were brave enough to penetrate the gloom of his house, and when they did so it was with deaf ear turned to sundry ghoulish stories that were whispered concerning him. These were, in great part, but exaggerations of his experiments in vivisection; he was devoted to the science of surgery.

The young man who presented himself on the morning just mentioned was a handsome fellow, yet of evident weak character and unhealthy temperament—sensitive, and easily exalted or depressed. A single glance convinced the surgeon that his visitor was seriously affected in mind, for there was never bolder skull-grin of melancholia, fixed and irremediable.

A stranger would not have suspected any occupancy of the house The street door—old, warped, and blistered by the sun—was locked, and the small, faded-green window-blinds were closed. The young man rapped at the door. No answer. He rapped again. Still no sign. He examined a slip of paper, glanced at the number of the house, and then, with the impatience of a child, he furiously kicked the door. There were signs of numerous other such kicks. A response came in the shape of a shuffling footstep in the hail, a turning of the rusty key, and a sharp face that peered through a cautious opening in the door.

"Are you the doctor?" asked the young man.

"Yes, yes! Come in," briskly replied the master of the house.

The young man entered. The old surgeon closed the door and carefully locked it. "This way."

he said, advancing to a rickety flight of stairs. The young man followed. The surgeon led the way up the stairs, turned into a narrow, musty-smelling corridor at the left, traversed it, rattling the loose boards under his feet, at the farther end opened a door at the right, and beckoned his visitor to enter. The young man found himself in a pleasant room, furnished in antique fashion and with hard simplicity.

"Sit down," said the old man, placing a chair so that its occupant should face a window that looked out upon a dead wall about six feet from the house. He threw open the blind, and a pale light entered. He then seated himself near his visitor and directly facing him, and with a searching look, that had all the power of a microscope, he proceeded to diagnosticate the case.

"Well?" he presently asked..The young man shifted uneasily in his seat.

"I—I have come to see you," he finally stammered, "because I'm in trouble."

"Ah!"

"Yes; you see, I—that is—I have given it up."

"Ah!" There was pity added to sympathy in the ejaculation.

"That's it. Given it up," added the visitor. He took from his pocket a role of banknotes, and with the utmost deliberation he counted them out upon his knee. "Five thousand dollars," he calmly remarked. "That is for you. It's all I have; but I presume—I imagine—no; that is not the word—assume—yes; that's the word—assume that five thousand—is it really that much? Let me count." He counted again. "That five thousand dollars is a sufficient fee for what I want you to do."

The surgeon's lips curled pityingly—perhaps disdainfully also. "What do you want me to do?" he carelessly inquired.

The young man rose, looked around with a mysterious air, approached the surgeon, and laid the money across his knee. Then he stopped and whispered two words in the surgeon's ear.

These words produced an electric effect. The old man started violently; then, springing to his feet, he caught his visitor angrily, and transfixed him with a look that was as sharp as a knife. His eyes flashed, and he opened his mouth to give utterance to some harsh imprecation, when he suddenly checked himself. The anger left his face, and only pity remained. He relinquished his grasp, picked up the scattered notes, and, offering them to the visitor, slowly said:

"I do not want your money. You are simply foolish. You think you are in trouble. Well, you do not know what trouble is. Your only trouble is that you have not a trace of manhood in your nature. You are merely insane—I shall not say pusillanimous. You should surrender yourself to the authorities, and be sent to a lunatic asylum for proper treatment."

The young man keenly felt the intended insult, and his eyes flashed dangerously.

"You old dog—you insult me thus!" he cried. "Grand airs, these, you give yourself! Virtuously indignant, old murderer, you! Don't want my money, eh? When a man comes to you himself and wants it done, you may fly into a passion and spurn his money; but let an enemy of his come and pay you, and you are only too willing. How many such jobs have you done in this miserable old hole? It is a good thing for you that the police have not run you down, and brought spade and shovel with them. Do you know what is said of you? Do you think you have kept your windows so closely shut that no sound has ever penetrated beyond them? Where do you keep your infernal implements?"

He had worked himself into a high passion. His voice was hoarse, loud, and rasping. His eyes, bloodshot, started from their sockets. His whole frame twitched, and his fingers writhed. But he was in the presence of a man infinitely his superior. Two eyes, like those of a snake, burned two holes through him. An overmastering, inflexible presence confronted one weak and passionate.

The result came.

"Sit down," commanded the stem voice of the surgeon.

It was the voice of father to child, of master to slave. The fury left the visitor, who, weak and overcome, fell upon a chair.

Meanwhile, a peculiar light had appeared in the old surgeon's face, the dawn of a strange idea; a gloomy ray, strayed from the fires of the bottomless pit; the baleful light that illumines the way of the enthusiast. The old man remained a moment in profound abstraction, gleams of eager intelligence bursting momentarily through the cloud of sombre meditation that covered his face.

Then broke the broad light of a deep, impenetrable determination. There was something sinister in it, suggesting the sacrifice of something held sacred. After a struggle, mind had vanquished conscience.

Taking a piece of paper and a pencil, the surgeon carefully wrote answers to questions which he peremptorily addressed to his visitor, such as his name, age, place of residence, occupation, and the like, and the same inquiries concerning his parents, together with other particular matters.

"Does anyone know you came to this house?" he asked.

"No."

"You swear it?"

"Yes."

"But your prolonged absence will cause alarm and lead to search."

"I have provided against that."

"How?"

"By depositing a note in the post, as I came along, announcing my intention to drown myself."

"The river will be dragged."

"What then?" asked the young man, shrugging his shoulders with careless indifference. "Rapid undercurrent, you know. A good many are never found."

There was a pause.

"Are you ready?" finally asked the surgeon.

"Perfectly." The answer was cool and determined.

The manner of the surgeon, however, showed much perturbation. The pallor that had come into his face at the moment his decision was formed became intense. A nervous tremulousness overcame his frame. Above it shone the light of enthusiasm.

"Have you a choice in the method?" he asked.

"Yes; extreme anaesthesia."

"With what agent?"

"The surest and quickest."

"Do you desire any—any subsequent disposition?"

"No; only nullification; simply a blowing out, as of a candle in the wind; a puff—then darkness, without a trace. A sense of your own safety may suggest the method. I leave it to you."

"No delivery to your friends?"

"None whatever."

Another pause.

"Did you say you are quite ready?" asked the surgeon.

"Quite ready."

"And perfectly willing?"

"Anxious."

"Then wait a moment."

With this request the old surgeon rose to his feet and stretched himself. Then with the stealthiness of a cat he opened the door and peered into the hall, listening intently. There was no sound. He softly closed the door and locked it. Then he closed the window-blinds and locked them. This done, he opened a door leading into an adjoining room, which, though it had no window, was lighted by means of a small skylight. The young man watched closely. A strange change had come over him. While his determination had not one whit lessened, a look of great relief came into his face, displacing the haggard, despairing look of a half-hour before.

Melancholic then, he was ecstatic now..The opening of a second door disclosed a curious sight. In the centre of the room, directly under the skylight, was an operating-table, such as is used by demonstrators of anatomy. A glass case against the wall held surgical instruments of every kind. Hanging in another case were human skeletons of various sizes. In sealed jars, arranged on shelves, were monstrosities of divers kinds preserved in alcohol. There were also, among innumerable other articles scattered about the room, a manikin, a stuffed cat, a desiccated human heart, plaster casts of various parts of the body, numerous charts, and a large assortment of drugs and chemicals. There was also a lounge, which could be opened to form a couch. The surgeon opened it and moved the operating-table aside, giving its place to the lounge.

"Come in," he called to his visitor.

The young man obeyed without the least hesitation.

"Take off your coat."

He complied.

"Lie down on that lounge."

In a moment the young man was stretched at full length, eyeing the surgeon. The latter undoubtedly was suffering under great excitement, but he did not waver; his movements were sure and quick. Selecting a bottle containing a liquid, he carefully measured out a certain quantity. While doing this he asked:

"Have you ever had any irregularity of the heart?"

"No."

The answer was prompt, but it was immediately followed by a quizzical look in the speaker's face.

"I presume," he added, "you mean by your question that it might be dangerous to give me a certain drug. Under the circumstances, however, I fail to see any relevancy in your question."

This took the surgeon aback; but he hastened to explain that he did not wish to inflict unnecessary pain, and hence his question.

He placed the glass on a stand, approached his visitor, and carefully examined his pulse.

"Wonderful!" he exclaimed.

"Why?"

"It is perfectly normal."

"Because I am wholly resigned. Indeed, it has been long since I knew such happiness. It is not active, but infinitely sweet."

"You have no lingering desire to retract?"

"None whatever."

The surgeon went to the stand and returned with the draught.

"Take this." he said kindly.

The young man partially raised himself and took the glass in his hand. He did not show the vibration of a single nerve. He drank the liquid, draining the last drop. Then he returned the glass with a smile.

"Thank you," he said; "you are the noblest man that lives. May you always prosper and be happy! You are my benefactor, my liberator. Bless you, bless you! You reach down from your seat with the gods and lift me up into glorious peace and rest. I love you—I love you with all my heart!"

These words, spoken earnestly, in a musical, low voice, and accompanied with a smile of ineffable tenderness, pierced the old man's heart. A suppressed convulsion swept over him; fintense anguish wrung his vitals; perspiration trickled down his face. The young man continued to smile.

"Ah, it does me good!" said he.

The surgeon, with a strong effort to control himself, sat down upon the edge of the lounge and took his visitor's wrist, counting the pulse "How long will it take?" the young man asked.

"Ten minutes. Two have passed." The voice was hoarse.

"Ah, only eight minutes more!...Delicious, delicious! I feel it coming...What was that? Ah, I understand. Music...Beautiful!...Coming, coming...Is that—that—water?. . .Trickling? Dripping? Doctor!"

"Well?"

"Thank you...thank you...Noble man,...my savior,...my bene...bene...factor.....trickling,...trickling...Dripping, dripping.. . Doctor!"

"Well?"

"Doctor!"

"Past hearing," muttered the surgeon.

"Doctor!"

"And blind."

Response was made by a firm grasp of the hand.

"Doctor!"

"And numb."

"Doctor!"

The old man watched and waited.

"Dripping,...dripping."

The last drop had run. There was a sigh, and nothing more.

The surgeon laid down the hand.

"The first step," he groaned, rising to his feet; then his whole frame dilated. "The first step is the most difficult, yet the simplest. A providential delivery into my hands of that for which I have hungered for forty years. No withdrawal now! It is possible, because scientific; rational, but perilous. If I succeed—if? I shall succeed. I will succeed... And after success—what?...Yes, what? Publish the plan and the result? The gallows...So long as it shall exist...and I exist, the gallows. That much... But how account for its presence? Ah, that pinches hard! I must trust to the future."

He tore himself from the revery and started.

"I wonder if she heard or saw anything."

With that reflection he cast a glance upon the form on the lounge, and then left the room, locked the door, locked also the door of the outer room, walked down two or three corridors, penetrated to a remote part of the house, and rapped at a door. It was opened by his wife. He, by this time, had regained complete mastery over himself.

"I thought I heard some one in the house just now," he said, "but I can find no one."

"I heard nothing."

He was greatly relieved.

"I did hear some one knock at the door less than an hour ago," she resumed, "and heard you speak, I think. Did he come in?"

"No."

The woman glanced at his feet and seemed perplexed..."I am almost certain," she said, "that I heard foot-falls in the house, and yet I see that you are wearing slippers."

"Oh, I had on my shoes then!"

"That explains it," said the woman, satisfied; "I think the sound you heard must have been caused by rats."

"Ah, that was it!" exclaimed the surgeon. Leaving, he closed the door, reopened it, and said, "I do not wish to be disturbed to-day." He said to himself, as he went down the hall, "All is clear there."

He returned to the room in which his visitor lay, and made a careful examination.

"Splendid specimen!" he softly exclaimed; "every organ sound; every function perfect; fine, large frame; well-shaped muscles, strong and sinewy; capable of wonderful development—if given opportunity...I have no doubt it can be done. Already I have succeeded with a dog—a task less difficult than this, for in a man the cerebrum overlaps the cerebellum, which is not the case with a dog. This gives a wide range for accident, with but one opportunity in a lifetime! In the cerebrum, the intellect and the affections; in the cerebellum, the senses and the motor forces; in the medulla oblongata, control of the diaphragm. In these two latter lie all the essentials of simple existence. The cerebrum is merely an adornment; that is to say, reason and the affections are almost purely ornamental. I have already proved it. My dog, with its cerebrum removed, was idiotic, but it retained its physical senses to a certain degree."

While thus ruminating he made careful preparations. He moved the couch, replaced the operating-table under the skylight, selected a number of surgical instruments, prepared certain drug mixtures, and arranged water, towels, and all the accessories of a tedious surgical operation.

Suddenly he burst into laughter.

"Poor fool!" he exclaimed. "Paid me five thousand dollars to kill him! Didn't have the courage to snuff his own candle! Singular, singular, the queer freaks these madmen have! You thought you were dying, poor idiot! Allow me to inform you, sir, that you are as much alive at this moment as ever you were in your life. But it will be all the same to you. You shall never be more conscious than you are now; and for all practical purposes, so far as they concern you, you are dead henceforth, though you shall live. By the way, how should you feel without a head? Ha, ha, ha... But that's a sorry joke."

He lifted the unconscious form from the lounge and laid it upon the operating table.

* * *

About three years afterwards the following conversation was held between a captain of police and a detective:

"She may be insane," suggested the captain.

"I think she is."

"And yet you credit her story!"

"I do."

"Singular!"

"Not at all. I myself have learned something."

"What!"

"Much, in one sense; little, in another. You have heard those queer stories of her husband. Well, they are all nonsensical—probably with one exception. He is generally a harmless old fellow, but peculiar. He has performed some wonderful surgical operations. The people in his neighborhood are ignorant, and they fear him and wish to be rid of him; hence they tell a great many lies about him, and they come to believe their own stories. The one important thing that I have learned is that he is almost insanely enthusiastic on the subject of surgery—especially experimental surgery; and with an enthusiast there is hardly such a thing as a scruple. It is this that gives me confidence in the woman's story."

"You say she appeared to be frightened?"

"Doubly so—first, she feared that her husband would learn of her betrayal of him; second, the discovery itself had terrified her."

"But her report of this discovery is very vague," argued the captain. "He conceals everything from her. She is merely guessing."

"In part—yes; in other part—no. She heard the sounds distinctly, though she did not see clearly. Horror closed her eyes. What she thinks she saw is, I admit, preposterous; but she undoubtedly saw something extremely frightful. There are many peculiar little circumstances. He has eaten with her but few times during the last three years, and nearly always carries his food to his private rooms. She says that he either consumes an enormous quantity, throws much away, or is feeding something that eats prodigiously. He explains this to her by saying that he has animals with which he experiments. This is not true. Again, he always keeps the door to these rooms carefully locked; and not only that, but he has had the doors doubled and otherwise strengthened, and has heavily barred a window that looks from one of the rooms upon a dead wall a few feet distant."

"What does it mean?" asked the captain.

"A prison."

"For animals, perhaps."

"Certainly not."

"Why!"

"Because, in the first place, cages would have been better; in the second place, the security that he has provided is infinitely greater than that required for the confinement of ordinary animals."

"All this is easily explained: he has a violent lunatic under treatment."

"I had thought of that, but such is not the fact."

"How do you know?"

"By reasoning thus: He has always refused to treat cases of lunacy; he confines himself to surgery: the walls are not padded, for the woman has heard sharp blows upon them; no human strength, however morbid, could possibly require such resisting strength as has been provided; he would not be likely to conceal a lunatic's confinement from the woman; no lunatic could consume all the food that he provides; so extremely violent mania as these precautions indicate could not continue three years; if there is a lunatic in the case it is very probable that there should have been communication with some one outside concerning the patient, and there has been none; the woman has listened at the keyhole and has heard no human voice within: and last, we have heard the woman's vague description of what she saw."

"You have destroyed every possible theory," said the captain, deeply interested, "and have suggested nothing new."

"Unfortunately, I cannot; but the truth may be very simple, after all. The old surgeon is so peculiar that I am prepared to discover something remarkable."

"Have you suspicions?"

"I have."

"Of what?" "A crime. The woman suspects it."

"And betrays it?"

"Certainly, because it is so horrible that her humanity revolts; so terrible that her whole nature demands of her that she hand over the criminal to the law; so frightful that she is in mortal terror; so awful that it has shaken her mind."

"What do you propose to do?" asked the captain.

"Secure evidence. I may need help."

"You shall have all the men you require. Go ahead, but be careful. You are on dangerous ground. You would be a mere plaything in the hands of that man."

Two days afterwards the detective again sought the captain.

"I have a queer document," he said, exhibiting torn fragments of paper, on which there was writing. "The woman stole it and brought it to me. She snatched a handful out of a book, getting only a part of each of a few leaves."

These fragments, which the men arranged as best they could, were (the detective explained) torn by the surgeon's wife from the first volume of a number of manuscript books which her husband had written on one subject,—-the very one that was the cause of her excitement. "About the time that he began a certain experiment three years ago," continued the detective, "he removed everything from the suite of two rooms containing his study and his operating-room. In one of the bookcases that he removed to a room across the passage was a drawer, which he kept locked, but which he opened from time to time. As is quite common with such pieces of furniture, the lock of the drawer is a very poor one; and so the woman, while making a thorough search yesterday, found a key on her bunch that fitted this lock. She opened the drawer, drew out the bottom book of a pile (so that its mutilation would more likely escape discovery), saw that it might contain a clew, and tore out a handful of the leaves. She had barely replaced the book, locked the drawer, and made her escape when her husband appeared. He hardly ever allows her to be out of his sight when she is in that part of the house."

The fragments read as follows: "...the motory nerves. I had hardly dared to hope for such a result, although inductive reasoning had convinced me of its possibility, my only doubt having been on the score of my lack of skill. Their operation has been only slightly impaired, and even this would not have been the case had the operation been performed in infancy, before the intellect had sought and obtained recognition as an essential part of the whole. Therefore I state, as a proved fact, that the cells of the motory nerves have inherent forces sufficient to the purposes of those nerves. But hardly so with the sensory nerves. These latter are, in fact, an offshoot of the former, evolved from them by natural (though not essential) heterogeneity, and to a certain extent are dependent on the evolution and expansion of a contemporaneous tendency, that developed into mentality, or mental function. Both of these latter tendencies, these evolvements, are merely refinements of the motory system, and not independent entities; that is to say, they are blossoms of a plant that propagates from its roots. The motory system is the first.

". . nor am I surprised that such prodigious muscular energy is developing. It promises yet to surpass the wildest dreams of human strength. I account for it thus: the powers of assimilation had reached their full development. They had formed the habit of doing a certain amount of work. They sent their product to all parts of the system. As a result of my operation the consumption of these products was reduced fully one-half; that is to say, about one-half of the demand for them was withdrawn. But force of habit required the production to proceed. This production was strength, vitality, energy. Thus double the usual quantity of this strength, this energy, was stored in the remaining...developed a tendency that did surprise me. Nature, no longer suffering the distraction of extraneous interferences, and at the same time being cut in two (as it were), with reference to this case, did not fully adjust herself to the new situation, as does a magnet, which, when divided at the point of equilibrium, renews itself in its two fragments by investing each with opposite poles; but, on the contrary, being severed from laws that theretofore had controlled her, and possessing still that mysterious tendency to develop into something more potential and complex, she blindly (having lost her lantern) pushed her demands for material that would secure this development, and as blindly used it when it was given her. Hence this marvellous voracity, this insatiable hunger, this wonderful ravenousness; and hence also (there being nothing but the physical part to receive this vast storing of energy) this strength that is becoming almost hourly Herculean, almost daily appalling. It is becoming a serious...narrow escape today. By some means, while I was absent, it unscrewed the stopper of the silver feeding-pipe (which I have already herein termed 'the artificial mouth'), and in one of its curious antics, allowed all the chyle to escape from its stomach through the tube. Its hunger then became intense—I may say furious. I placed my hands upon it to push it into a chair, when, feeling my touch, it caught me, clasped me around the neck, and would have crushed me to death instantly had I not slipped from its powerful grasp. Thus I always had to be on my guard. I have provided the screw stopper with a spring catch, and usually docile when not hungry; slow and heavy in its movements, which are, of course, purely unconscious: any apparent excitement in movement being due to local irregularities in the blood-supply of the cerebellum, which, if I did not have it enclosed in a silver case that is immovable, I should expose and—"

The captain looked at the detective with a puzzled air.

"I don't understand it all," said he.

"Nor I," agreed the detective. "What do you propose to do?"

"Make a raid."

"Do you want a man?"

"Three. The strongest men in your district."

"Why, the surgeon is old and weak!"

"Nevertheless, I want three strong men; and for that matter, prudence really advises me to take twenty."

* * *

At one o'clock the next morning a cautious, scratching sound might have been heard in the ceiling of the surgeon's operating-room. Shortly afterwards the skylight sash was carefully raised and laid aside. A man peered into the opening. Nothing could be heard.

"That is singular," thought the detective.

He cautiously lowered himself to the floor by a rope, and then stood for some moments listening intently. There was a dead silence. He shot the slide of a dark-lantern, and rapidly swept the room with the light. It was bare, with the exception of a strong iron staple and ring, screwed to the floor in the centre of the room, with a heavy chain attached.

The detective then turned his attention to the outer room; it was perfectly bare. He was deeply perplexed. Returning to the inner room, he called softly to the men to descend. While they were thus occupied he re-entered the outer room and examined the door. A glance sufficed. It was kept closed by a spring attachment, and was locked with a strong spring-lock that could be drawn from the inside.

"The bird has just flown," mused the detective. "A singular accident! The discovery and proper use of this thumb-bolt might not have happened once in fifty years, if my theory is correct.".By this time the men were behind him. He noise-lessly drew the spring-bolt, opened the door, and looked out into the hall. He heard a peculiar sound. It was as though a gigantic lobster was floundering and scrambling in some distant part of the old house. Accompanying this sound was a loud, whistling breathing, and frequent rasping gasps.

These sounds were heard by still an other person, the surgeon's wife; for they originated very near her rooms, which were a considerable distance from her husband's. She had been sleeping lightly, tortured by fear and harassed by frightful dreams. The conspiracy into which she had recently entered, for the destruction of her husband, was a source of great anxiety. She constantly suffered from the most gloomy forebodings, and lived in an atmosphere of terror. Added to the natural horror of her situation were those countless sources of fear which a fright-shaken mind creates and then magnifies. She was, indeed, in a pitiable suite, having been driven first by terror to desperation, and then to madness.

Startled thus out of fitful slumber by the noise at her door, she sprang from her bed to the floor, every terror that lurked

in her acutely tense in mind and diseased imagination starting up and almost overwhelming her. The idea of flight—
one of the strongest of all instincts—seized upon her, and she
ran to the door, beyond all control of reason. She drew the
bolt and flung the door wide open, and then fled wildly
down the passage, the appalling hissing and rasping gurgle
ringing in her ears apparently with a thousandfold intensity.
But the passage was in absolute darkness, and she had not
taken a half-dozen steps when she tripped upon an unseen
object on the floor. She fell headlong upon it, encountering
in it a large, soft, warm substance that writhed and
squirmed, and from which came the sounds that had awakened her. Instantly realizing her situation, she uttered a
shriek such as only an unnamable terror can inspire. But
hardly had her cry started the echoes in the empty corridor
when it was suddenly stifled. Two prodigious arms had
closed upon her and crushed the life out of her.

The cry performed the office of directing the detective and
his assistants, and it also aroused the old surgeon, who occupied rooms between the officers and the objects of their
search. The cry of agony pierced him to the marrow, and a
realization of the cause of it burst upon him with frightful
force.

"It has come at last!" he gasped, springing from his bed.

Snatching from a table a dimly-burning lamp and a long
knife which he had kept at hand for three years, he dashed
into the corridor. The four officers had already started
forward, but when they saw him emerge they halted in
silence. In that moment of stillness the surgeon paused to
listen. He heard the hissing sound and the clumsy floundering of a bulky, living object in the direction of his wife's

apartments. It evidently was advancing towards him. A turn in the corridor shut out the view. He turned up the light, which revealed a ghastly pallor in his face.

"Wife!" he called.

There was no response. He hurriedly advanced, the four men following quietly. He turned the angle of the corridor, and ran so rapidly that by the time the officers had come in sight of him again he was twenty steps away. He ran past a huge, shapeless object, sprawling, crawling, and floundering along, and arrived at the body of his wife.

He gave one horrified glance at her face, and staggered away. Then a fury seized him.

Clutching the knife firmly, and holding the lamp aloft, he sprang toward the ungainly object in the corridor. It was then that the officers, still advancing cautiously, saw a little more clearly, though still indistinctly, the object of the surgeon's fury, and the cause of the look of unutterable anguish in his face. The hideous sight caused them to pause. They saw what appeared to be a man, yet evidently was not a man; huge, awkward, shapeless; a squirming, lurching, stumbling mass, completely naked. It raised its broad shoulders. It had no head, but instead of it a small metallic ball surmounting its massive neck.

"Devil!" exclaimed the surgeon, raising the knife.

"Hold, there!" commanded a stern voice.

The surgeon quickly raised his eyes and saw the four officers, and for a moment fear paralyzed his arm.

"The police!" he gasped.

Then, with a look of redoubled fury, he sent the knife to the hilt into the squirming mass before him. The wounded monster sprang to its feet and wildly threw its arms about, meanwhile emitting fearful sounds from a silver tube through which it breathed. The surgeon aimed another blow, but never gave it. In his blind fury he lost his caution, and was caught in an iron grasp. The struggling threw the lamp some feet toward the officers, and it fell to the floor, shattered to pieces. Simultaneously with the crash the oil took fire, and the corridor was filled with flame.

The officers could not approach. Before them was the spreading blaze, and secure behind it were two forms struggling in a fearful embrace. They heard cries and gasps, and saw the gleaming of a knife.

The wood in the house was old and dry. It took fire at once, and the flames spread with great rapidity. The four officers turned and fled, barely escaping with their lives. In an hour nothing remained of the mysterious old house and its inmates but a blackened ruin.

The Sumach (1919)

Ulric Daubeny

"How red that Sumach is!"

Irene Barton murmured something commonplace, for to her the tree brought painful recollections. Her visitor, unconscious of this fact, proceeded to elaborate.

"Do you know, Irene, that tree gives me the creeps! I can't explain, except that it is not a nice tree, not a good tree. For instance, why should its leaves be red in August, when they are not supposed to turn until October?"

"What queer ideas you have, May! The tree is right enough, although its significance to me is sad. Poor Spot, you know; we buried him beneath it two days ago. Come, and see his grave."

The two women left the terrace, where this conversation had been taking place, and leisurely strolled across the lawn, at the end of which, in almost startling isolation, grew the Sumach. At least, Mrs. Watcombe, who evinced so great an interest in the tree, questioned whether it actually was a Sumach, for the foliage was unusual, and the branches gnarled and twisted beyond recognition. Just now, the leaves were stained with splashes of dull crimson, but rather than droop, they had a bloated appearance, as if the luxuriance of the growth were not altogether healthy.

For several moments they stood regarding the pathetic little grave, and the silence was only broken when Mrs. Watcombe darted beneath the tree, and came back with something in her hand.

"Irene, look at this dead thrush. Poor little thing! Such splendid plumage, yet it hardly weighs a sugar plum!"

Mrs. Barton regarded it with wrinkled brows.

"I cannot understand what happens to the birds, May—unless someone lays poison. We continually find them dead about the garden, and usually beneath, or very near, this tree."

It is doubtful whether Mrs. Watcombe listened. Her attention seemed to wander that morning, and she was studying the twisted branches of the Sumach with a thoughtful scrutiny.

"Curious that the leaves should turn at this time of year," she murmured. "It brings to mind poor Geraldine's illness. This tree had an extraordinary fascination for her, you know. It was quite scarlet then, yet that was only June, and it had barely finished shooting."

"My dear May! You have red leaves on the brain this morning!" Irene retorted, uncertain whether to be irritated or amused. "I can't think why you are so concerned about the colour. It is only the result of two days' excessive heat, for scarcely a leaf was touched, when I buried poor old Spot."

The conversation seemed absurdly trivial, yet, Mrs. Watcombe gone, Irene could not keep her mind from dwelling on her cousin's fatal illness. The news had reached them with the shock of the absolutely unexpected. Poor

Geraldine, who had always been so strong, to have fallen victim to acute anæmia! It was almost unbelievable, that heart failure should have put an end to her sweet young life, after a few days' ailing. Of course, the sad event had wrought a wonderful change for Irene and her husband, giving them, in place of a cramped suburban villa, this beautiful country home, Cleeve Grange.

Everything for her was filled with the delight of novelty, for she had ruled as mistress over the charmed abode for only one short week. Hilary, her husband, was yet a stranger to the more intimate of its attractions, being detained in London by the winding-up of business affairs.

Several days elapsed, for the most part given solely to the keen pleasure of arranging and re-arranging the new home. As time went by, the crimson splashes on the Sumach faded, the leaves becoming green again, though drooping as if from want of moisture. Irene noticed this when she paid her daily visits to the pathetic little dog grave, trying to induce flowers to take root upon it, but do what she might, they invariably faded. Nothing, not even grass, would grow beneath the Sumach. Only death seemed to thrive there, she mused in a fleeting moment of depression, as she searched around for more dead birds. But none had fallen since the thrush, picked up by Mrs. Watcombe.

One evening, the heat inside the house becoming insupportable, Irene wandered into the garden, her steps mechanically leading her to the little grave beneath the Sumach. In the uncertain moonlight, the twisted trunk and branches of the old tree were suggestive of a rustic seat, and feeling tired, she lifted herself into the natural bower, and lolled back, joyously inhaling the cool night air. Presently she dropped asleep, and in a curiously vivid manner, dreamt of Hilary; that he had completed his business in London, and was coming home. They met at evening, near the garden gate, and Hilary spread wide his arms, and eagerly folded them about her. Swiftly the dream began to change, assuming the characteristics of a nightmare. The sky grew strangely dark, the arms fiercely masterful, while the face which bent to kiss her neck was not that of her young husband: it was leering, wicked, gnarled like the trunk of some weather-beaten tree. Chilled with horror, Irene fought long and desperately against the vision, to be at last awakened by her own frightened whimpering. Yet returning consciousness did not immediately dissipate the nightmare. In imagination she was still held rigid by brutal arms, and it was only after a blind, half waking struggle that she freed herself, and went speeding across the lawn, towards the lighted doorway.

Next morning Mrs. Watcombe called, and subjected her to a puzzled scrutiny.

"How pale you look Irene. Do you feel ill?"

"Ill? No, only a little languid. I find this hot weather very trying."

Mrs. Watcombe studied her with care, for the pallor of Irene's face was very marked. In contrast, a vivid spot of red showed on the slender neck, an inch or so below the ear. Intuitively a hand went up, as Irene turned to her friend in explanation.

"It feels so sore. I think I must have grazed the skin, last night, while sitting in the Sumach."

"Sitting in the Sumach!" echoed Mrs. Watcombe in surprise. "How curious you should do that. Poor Geraldine used to do the same, just before she was taken ill, and yet at the last she was seized with a perfect horror of the tree. Goodness, but it is quite red again, this morning!"

Irene swung round in the direction of the tree filled with a vague repugnance. Sure enough, the leaves no longer drooped, nor were they green. They had become flecked once more with crimson, and the growth had quite regained its former vigour.

"Eugh!" she breathed, hurriedly turning to the house. "It reminds me of a horrid nightmare. I have rather a head this morning: let's go in, and talk of something else!"

As the day advanced, the heat grew more oppressive and night brought with it a curious stillness, the stillness which so often presages a heavy thunderstorm. No bird had offered up its evening hymn, no breeze came sufficient to stir a single leaf: everything was pervaded by the silence of expectancy.

The interval between dinner and bedtime is always a dreary one for those accustomed to companionship, and left all alone, Irene's restlessness momentarily increased. First the ceiling, then the very atmosphere seemed to weigh heavy upon her head. Although windows and doors were all flung wide, the airlessness of the house grew less and less endurable, until from sheer desperation she made her escape into the garden, where a sudden illumination of the horizon gave warning of the approaching storm. Feeling somewhat at a loss, she roamed aimlessly awhile, pausing sometimes to catch the echoes of distant thunder, until at last she found herself standing over Spot's desolate little grave. The sight struck her with a sense of utter loneliness, and the tears sprang to her eyes, in poignant longing for the companionship of her faithful pet.

Moved by she knew not what, Irene swung herself into the comfortable branches of the old Sumach, and soothed by the reposeful attitude, her head soon began to nod in slumber. Afterwards it was a doubtful memory whether she actually did sleep, or whether the whole experience was not a kind of waking nightmare. Something of the previous evening's dream returned to her, but this time with added horror, for it commenced with no pleasurable vision of her husband. Instead, relentless, stick-like arms immediately closed in upon her, their vice-like grip so tight that she could scarcely breathe. Down darted the awful head, rugged and lined by every sin, darting at the fair, white neck as a wild beast on its prey. The foul lips began to eat into her skin... She struggled desperately, madly, for to her swooning senses, the very branches of the tree became endowed with active life, coiling unmercifully around her, tenaciously clinging to her limbs, and tugging at her dress. Pain at last spurred her to an heroic effort, the pain of something—perhaps a twig—digging deep into her unprotected neck. With a choking cry she freed herself, and nerved by a sudden burst thunder, ran tottering towards the shelter of the house.

Having gained the cosy lounge-hall, Irene sank into an armchair, gasping hysterically for breath. Gusts of refreshing wind came through the open windows, but although the atmosphere rapidly grew less stagnant, an hour passed before she could make sufficient effort to crawl upstairs to bed. In her room, a further shock awaited her. The bloodless, drawn face reflected in the mirror was scarcely recognisable. The eyes lacked lustre, the lips were white, the skin hung flabby on the shrunken flesh, giving it a look of premature old age. A tiny trickle of dry blood, the solitary smudge of colour, stained the chalky pallor of her neck. Taking up a hand-glass, she examined this with momentary concern. It was the old wound re-opened, an angry looking sore, almost like the bite of some small, or very sharp-toothed animal. It smarted painfully...

Mrs. Watcombe, bursting into the breakfast room next morning, with suggestions of an expedition to the neighbouring town, was shocked at Irene's looks, and insisted on going at once to fetch the doctor. Mrs. Watcombe fussed continually throughout the interview, and insisted on an examination of the scar upon Irene's neck. Patient and doctor had regarded this as a negligible detail, but finally the latter subjected it to a slightly puzzled scrutiny, advising that it should be kept bandaged. He suggested that Irene was suffering from anaemia, and would do well to keep as quiet as possible, building up her strength with food, open windows, and a generous selection of pills and tonics. But despite these comforting arrangements, no one was entirely satisfied. The doctor lacked something in assurance, Irene was certain that she could not really be anæmic, while Mrs. Watcombe was obsessed by inward misgivings, perfectly indefinable, yet none the less disturbing. She left the house as a woman bent under a load of care. Passing up the lane, her glance lighted on the old Sumach, more crimson now, more flourishing in its growth than she had seen it since the time of Geraldine's fatal illness.

"I loathe that horrid old tree!" she murmured, then added, struck by a nameless premonition, "Her husband ought to know. I shall wire to him at once."

Irene, womanlike, put to use her enforced idleness by instituting a rearrangement of the box-room, the only part of her new home which yet remained unexplored. Among the odds and ends of rubbish to be thrown away, there was a little note book, apparently unused. In idle curiosity, Irene picked it up, and was surprised to learn, from an inscription, that her cousin Geraldine had intended to use it as a diary. A date appeared—only a few days prior to the poor girl's death—but no entries had been made, though the first two pages of the book had certainly been removed. As Irene put it down, there fluttered to the ground a torn scrap of writing. She stooped, and continued stooping, breathlessly staring at the words that had been written by her cousin's hand— Sumach fascinates m—

In some unaccountable manner this applied to her. It was obvious what tree was meant, the old Sumach at the end of the lawn; and it fascinated her, Irene, though not until that moment had she openly recognised the fact. Searching hurriedly through the note book, she discovered, near the end, a heap of torn paper, evidently the first two pages of a diary. She turned the pieces in eager haste. Most of them bore no more than one short word, or portions of a longer one, but a few bigger fragments proved more enlightening, and filled with nervous apprehension, she carried the book to her escritoire, and spent the remainder of the afternoon trying to piece together the torn-up pages.

Meanwhile, Mrs. Watcombe was worrying and fretting over Irene's unexpected illness. Her pallor, her listlessness, even the curious mark upon her neck gave cause for positive alarm, so exactly did they correspond with symptoms exhibited by her cousin Geraldine, during the few days prior to her death. She wished that the village doctor, who had attended the earlier case, would return soon from his holiday, as his locum tenens seemed sadly wanting in that authoritative decision which is so consoling to patients, relatives, and friends. Feeling, as an old friend, responsible for the welfare of Irene, she wired to Hilary, telling him of the sudden illness, and advising him to return without delay.

The urgency of the telegram alarmed him, so much so that he left London by the next train, arriving at Cleeve Grange shortly after dark.

"Where is your mistress?" was his first enquiry, as the maid met him in the hall.

"Upstairs, Sir. She complained of feeling tired, and said she would go to bed."

He hurried to her room, only to find it empty. He called, he rang for the servants; in a moment the whole house was astir, yet nowhere was Irene to be found. Deeming it possible that she might have gone to see Mrs. Watcombe, Hilary was about to follow, when that lady herself was ushered in.

"I saw the lights of your cab—" she commenced, cutting short the sentence, as she met his questioning glance.

"Where is Irene?"

"Irene? My dear Hilary, is she not here?"

"No. We can't find her anywhere. I thought she might have been with you."

For the space of half a second, Mrs. Watcombe's face presented a picture of astonishment; then the expression changed to one of dismayed concern.

"She is in that tree! I'm certain of it! Hilary, we must fetch her in at once!"

Completely at a loss to understand, he followed the excited woman into the garden, stumbling blindly in her wake across the lawn. The darkness was intense, and a terrific wind beat them back as if with living hands. Irene's white dress at length became discernible, dimly thrown up against the pitchy background, and obscured in places by the twists and coils of the old Sumach. Between them they grasped the sleeping body, but the branches were swung wildly in the gale, and to Hilary's confused imagination it was as if they had literally to tear it from the tree's embrace. At last they regained the shelter of the house, and laid their inanimate burden upon the sofa. She was quite unconscious, pale as death, and her face painfully contorted, as if with fear. The old wound on the neck, now bereft of bandages, had been re-opened, and was wet with blood.

Hilary rushed off to fetch the doctor, while Mrs. Watcombe and the servants carried Irene to her room. Several hours passed before she recovered consciousness, and during that time Hilary was gently but firmly excluded from the sick room. Bewildered and disconsolate, he wandered restlessly about the house, until his attention was arrested by the unusual array of torn-up bits of paper on Irene's desk. He saw that she had been sorting out the pieces, and sticking them together as the sentences became complete. The work was barely half finished, yet what there was to read, struck him as exceedingly strange:

> The seat in the old Sumach fascinates me. I find myself going back to it unconsciously, nay, even against my will. Oh, but the nightmare visions it always brings me! In them I seem to plumb the very depths of terror. Their memory preys upon my mind, and every day my strength grows less. Dr. H. speaks of anæmia...

That was as far as Irene had proceeded. Hardly knowing why he did so, Hilary resolved to complete the task, but the chill of early morning was in the air before it was finished. Cramped and stiff, he was pushing back his chair when a footstep sounded in the doorway, and Mrs. Watcombe entered.

"Irene is better," she volunteered immediately. "She is sleeping naturally, and Doctor Thomson says there is no longer any immediate danger. The poor child is terribly weak and bloodless."

"May—tell me—what is the meaning of all this? Why has Irene suddenly become so ill? I can't understand it!"

Mrs. Watcombe's face was preternaturally grave.

"Even the doctor admits that he is puzzled," she answered very quietly. "The symptoms all point to a sudden and excessive loss of blood, though in cases of acute anæmia—"

"God! But—not like Geraldine? I can't believe it!"

"Neither can I. Oh, Hilary, you may think me mad, but I can't help feeling that there is some unknown, some awful influence at work. Irene was perfectly well three days ago, and it was the same with Geraldine before she was taken ill. The cases are so exactly similar... Irene was trying to tell me something about a diary, but the poor girl was too exhausted to make herself properly understood."

"Diary? Geraldine's diary, do you think? She must mean that. I have just finished piecing it together, but frankly, I can't make head or tail of it!"

Mrs. Watcombe rapidly scanned the writing, then studied it again with greater care. Finally she read the second part aloud.

"Listen, Hilary! This seems to me important.

"Dr. H. speaks of anæmia. Pray heaven, he may be correct, for my thoughts sometimes move in a direction which foreshadows nothing short of lunacy—or so people would tell me, if I could bring myself to confide these things. I must fight alone, clinging to the knowledge that it is usual for anæmic persons to be obsessed by unhealthy fancies. If only I had not read those horribly suggestive words in Barrett..."

"Barrett? What can she mean, May?"

"Wait a moment. Barrett? Barrett's Traditions of the County, perhaps. I have noticed a copy in the library. Let us go there; it may give the clue!"

The book was quickly found, and a marker indicated the passage to which Geraldine apparently referred.

"At Cleeve, I was reminded of another of those traditions, so rapidly disappearing before the spread of education. It concerned the old belief in vampires, spirits of the evil dead, who, by night, could assume a human form, and scour the countryside in search of victims. Suspected vampires, if caught, were buried with the mouth stuffed full of garlic, and a stake plunged through the heart, whereby they were rendered harmless, or, at least, confined to that one particular locality.

"Some thirty years ago, an old man pointed out a tree which was said to have grown from such a stake. So far as I can recollect, it was an unusual variety of Sumach, and had been enclosed during a recent extension to the garden of the old Grange..."

"Come outside," said Mrs. Watcombe, breaking a
   long and solemn silence. "I want you to see that tree."

The sky was suffused with the blush of early dawn and the shrubs, the flowers, even the dew upon the grass caught and reflected something of the pink effulgence. The Sumach alone stood out, dark and menacing. During the night its leaves had become a hideous, mottled purple; its growth was oily, bloated, unnaturally vigorous, like that of some rank and poisonous weed.

Mrs. Watcombe, looking from afar, spoke in frightened, husky tones.

"See, Hilary! It was exactly like that when—when Geraldine died!"

* * *

When evening fell, the end of the lawn was strangely bare. In place of the old tree, there lay an enormous heap of smouldering embers,—enormous, because the Sumach had been too sodden with dark and sticky sap, to burn without the assistance of large quantities of other timber.

Many weeks elapsed before Irene was sufficiently recovered to walk as far as Spot's little grave. She was surprised to find it almost hidden in a bed of garlic.

Hilary explained, that it was the only plant they could induce to grow there.

Beyond the Door (1923)

Paul Suter

"You haven't told me yet how it happened," I said to Mrs. Malkin.

She set her lips and eyed me, sharply.

"Didn't you talk with the coroner, sir?"

"Yes, of course," I admitted; "but as I understand you found my uncle, I thought—"

"Well, I wouldn't care to say anything about it," she interrupted, with decision.

This housekeeper of my uncle's was somewhat taller than I, and much heavier—two physical preponderance which afford any woman possessing them an advantage over the inferior male. She appeared a subject for diplomacy rather than argument.

Noting her ample jaw, her breadth of cheek, the unsentimental glint of her eye, I decided on conciliation. I placed a chair for her, there in my Uncle Godfrey's study, and dropped into another, myself.

"At least, before we go over the other parts of the house, suppose we rest a little," I suggested, in my most unctuous manner. "The place rather gets on one's nerves—don't you think so?"

It was sheer luck—I claim no credit for it. My chance reflection found the weak spot in her fortifications. She replied to it with an undoubted smack of satisfaction:

"It's more than seven years that I've been doing for Mr. Sarston, sir: Bringing him his meals regular as clockwork, keeping the house clean—as clean as he'd let me—and sleeping at my own home, o'nights; and in all that time, I've said, over and over, there ain't a house in New York the equal of this for queerness."

"Nor anywhere else," I encouraged her, with a laugh; and her confidence opened another notch:

"You're likely right in that, too sir. As I've said to poor Mr. Sarston, many a time, 'It's all well enough,' says I, 'to have bugs for a hobby. You can afford it; and being a bachelor and by yourself, you don't have to consider other people's likes and dislikes. And it's all well enough if you want to,' says I, 'to keep thousands and thousands o'them in cabinets, all over the place, the way you do. But when it comes to pinnin' them on the walls in regular armies,' I say, 'and on the ceiling of your own study; and even on different parts of the furniture, so that a body don't know what awful thing she's agoin' to find under her hand of a sudden when she does the dusting; why, then,' I says to him, 'it's drivin' a decent woman too far.'"

"And did he never try to reform his ways when you told him that?" I asked, smiling.

"To be frank with you, Mr. Robinson, when I talked like that to him, he generally raised my pay. And what was a body to do then?"

"I can't see how Lucy Lawton stood the place as long as she did," I observed, watching Mrs. Malkin's red face very closely.

She swallowed the bait, and leaned forward, hands on knees.

"Poor girl, it got on her nerves. But she was the quiet kind. You never saw her, sir?"

I shook my head.

"One of them slim, faded girls, with light hair, and hardly a word to say for herself. I don't believe she got to know the next-door neighbor in the whole year she lived with your uncle. She was an orphan, wasn't she, sir?"

"Yes," I said. "Godfrey Sarston and I were her only living relatives. That was why she came from Australia to stay with him, after her father's death."

Mrs. Malkin nodded. I was hoping that, by putting a check on my eagerness, I could lead her on to a number of things I greatly desired to know. Up to the time I had induced the housekeeper to show me through this strange house of my Uncle Godfrey's, the whole affair had been a mystery of lips which closed and faces which were averted at my approach. Even the coroner seemed unwilling to tell me just how my uncle had died."

"Did you understand she was going to live with him, sir?" asked Mrs. Malkin, looking hard at me.

I confined myself to a nod.

"Well, so did I. Yet, after a year, back she went."

"She went suddenly?" I suggested.

"So suddenly that I never knew a thing about it till after she was gone. I came to do my chores one day, and she was here. I came the next, and she had started back to Australia. That's how sudden she went."

"They must have had a falling-out," I conjectured. "I suppose it was because of the house."

"Maybe it was and maybe it wasn't."

"You know of other reasons?"

"I have eyes in my head," she said. "But I'm not going to talk about it. Shall we be getting on now, sir?"

I tried another lead:

"I hadn't seen my uncle in five years, you know. He seemed terribly changed. He was not an old man, by any means, yet when I saw him at the funeral—" I paused, expectantly.

To my relief, she responded readily:

"He looked that way for the last few months, especially the last week. I spoke to him about it, two days before—before it happened, sir—and told him he'd do well to see the doctor again. But he cut me off short. My sister took sick the same day, and I was called out of town. The next time I saw him, he was—"

She paused, and then went on, sobbing:

"To think of him lyin' there in that awful place, and callin' and callin' for me, as I know he must, and me not around to hear him!"

As she stopped again, suddenly, and threw a suspicious glance at me, I hastened to insert a matter-of-fact question:

"Did he appear ill on that last day?"

"Not so much ill, as—"

"Yes?" I prompted.

She was silent a long time, while I waited, afraid that some word of mine had brought back her former attitude of hostility. Then she seemed to make up her mind.

"I oughtn't to say another word. I've said too much, already. But you've been liberal with me, sir, and I know somethin' you've a right to be told, which I'm thinkin' no one else is agoin' to tell you. Look at the bottom of his study door a minute, sir."

I followed her direction. What I saw led me to drop to my hands and knees, the better to examine it.

"Why should he put a rubber strip on the bottom of his door?" I asked, getting up.

She replied with another enigmatical suggestion:

"Look at these, if you will, sir. You'll remember that he slept in this study. That was his bed, over there in the alcove."

"Bolts!" I exclaimed. And I reinforced sight with touch by shooting one of them back and forth a few times. "Double bolts on the inside of his bedroom door! An upstairs room, at that. What was the idea?"

Mrs. Malkin portentously shook her head and sighed, as one unburdening her mind.

"Only this can I say, sir: He was afraid of something—terribly afraid, sir. Something that came in the night."

"What was it?" I demanded.

"I don't know, sir."

"It was in the night that—it happened?" I asked.

She nodded; then, as if the prologue were over, as if she had prepared my mind sufficiently, she produced something from under her apron. She must have been holding it there all the time.

"It's his diary, sir. It was lying here on the floor. I saved it for you, before the police could get their hands on it."

I opened the little book. One of the sheets near the back was crumpled, and I glanced at it, idly. What I read there impelled me to slap the covers shut again.

"Did you read this?" I demanded.

She met my gaze, frankly.

"I looked into it, sir, just as you did—only just looked into it. Not for worlds would I do even that again!"

"I noticed some reference here to a slab in the cellar. What slab is that?"

"It covers an old, dried-up well, sir."

"Will you show it to me?"

"You can find it for yourself, sir. if you wish. I'm not goin' down there," she said, decidedly.

"Ah, well, I've seen enough for today," I told her. "I'll take the diary back to my hotel and read it."

I did not return to my hotel, however. In my one brief glance into the little book, I had seen something which had bitten into my soul; only a few words, but they had brought me very near to that queer, solitary man who had been my uncle.

I dismissed Mrs. Malkin, and remained in the study. There was the fitting place to read the diary he had left behind him.

His personality lingered like a vapor in that study. I settled into his deep morris chair, and turned it to catch the light from the single, narrow window—the light, doubtless, by which he had written much of his work on entomology.

That same struggling illumination played shadowy tricks with hosts of wall-crucified insects, which seemed engaged in a united effort to crawl upward in sinuous lines. Some of their number, impaled to the ceiling itself, peered quiveringly down on the aspiring multitude. The whole house, with its crisp dead, rustling in any vagrant breeze, brought back to my mind the hand that had pinned them, one by one, on wall and ceiling and furniture. A kindly hand, I reflected, though eccentric; one not to be turned aside from it's single hobby.

When quiet, peering Uncle Godfrey went, there passed out another of those scientific enthusiasts, whose passion for exact truth in some one direction has extended the bounds of human knowledge. Could not his unquestioned merits have been balanced against his sin? Was it necessary to even-handed justice that he die face-to-face with Horror, struggling with the thing he most feared? I ponder the question still, though his body—strangely bruised—has been long at rest.

The entries in the little book began with the fifteenth of June. Everything before that date had been torn out. There, in the room where it had been written, I read my Uncle Godfrey's diary.

> "It is done. I am trembling so that the words will hardly form under my pen, my mind is collected. My course was for the best. Suppose I had married her? She would have been unwilling to live in this house. At the outset, her wishes would have come between me and my work, and that would have been only the beginning.

"As a married man, I could not have concentrated properly, I could not have surrounded myself with the atmosphere indispensable to the writing of my book. My scientific message would never have been delivered. As it is, though my heart is sore, I shall stifle these memories in work.

"I wish I had been more gentle with her, eqpecially when she sank to her knees before me, tonight. She kissed my hand. I should not have repulsed her so roughly. In particular, my words could have been better chosen. I said to her bitterly: 'Get up, and don't nuzzle my hand like a dog.' She rose, without a word, and left me. How was I to know that, within an hour—

"I am largely to blame. Yet, had I taken any other course afterward than the one I did, the authorities would have misunderstood."

Again there followed a space from which the sheets had been torn; but from the sixteenth of July, all the pages were intact. Something had come over the writing, too. It was still precise and clear—my Uncle Godfrey's characteristic hand—but the letters were less firm. As the entries approached the end, this difference became still more marked. Here follows, then, the whole of his story; or as much of it as will ever be known. I shall let his words speak for him, without further interruption:

"My nerves are becoming more seriously affected. If certain annoyances do not shortly cease, I shall be obliged to procure medical advice. To be more specific, I find myself, at times, obsessed by an almost uncontrollable desire to descend to the oeilar and lift the slab over the old well.

"I never have yielded to the impulse, but it has persisted for minutes together with such intensity that I have had to put work aside, and literally hold myself down in my chair. This insane desire comes only in the dead of night, when its disquieting effect is heightened by the various noises peculiar to the house.

"For instance, there often is a draft of air along the hallways, which causes a rustling among the specimens impaled on the walls. Lately, too, there have been other nocturnal sounds, strongly suggestive of the clamor of rats and mice. This calls for investigation. I have been at considerable expense to make the house proof against rodents, which might destroy some of my best specimens, some structural defect has opened a way for them, the situation must be corrected at once."

"July 17th. The foundations and cellar were examined today by a workman. He states positively that there is no place of ingress for rodents. He contented himself with looking at the slab over the old well, without lifting it."

"July 19th. While I was sitting in this chair late last night, writing, the impulse to descend to the cellar suddenly came upon me with tremendous insistence. I yielded-which, perhaps, was as well. For at least I satisfied myself that the disquiet which possesses me has no external cause.

"The long journey through the hallways was difficult. Several times, I was keenly awere of the same sounds (perhaps I should say, the same IMPRESSIONS of sounds) that I had erroneously laid to rats. I am convinced now that they are mere symptoms of my nervous condition. Further indications of this came in the fact that, as I opened the cellar door, the small noises abrupthy ceased. There wae no final scamper of tiny footfalls to suggest rats disturbed at their occupations.

"Indeed, I wes conscious of a certain impression of expectant silence—as if the thing behind the noises, whatever it was, had paused to watch me enter its domain. Throughout my time in the cellar, I seemed surrounded by this same atmosphere. Sheer 'nerves,' of course.

"In the main, I held myself well under control. As I was about to leave the cellar, however, I unguardedly glanced back over my shoulder at the stone slab covering the old well. At that, a violent tremor came over me, and, losing all command, I rushed back up the cellar stairs, thence to this study. My nerves are playing me sorry tricks."

"July 30th. For more than a week, all has been well. The tone of my nerves seems distinctly better. Mrs. Malkin, who has remarked several times lately upon my paleness, expressed conviction this afternoon that I am nearly my old self again. This is encouraging. I was beginning to fear that the severe strain of the past few months had left an indelible mark upon me. With continued health, I shall be able to finish my book by spring."

"July 31st. Mrs. Malkin remained rather late tonight in connection with some item of housework, and it was quite dark when I returned to my study from bolting the street door after her. The blackness of the upper hall, which the former owner of the house inexplicably failed to wire for electricity, was profound. As I came to the top of the second flight of stairs, something clutched at my foot, and, for an instant, almost pulled me back. I freed myself and ran to the study."

"August 3rd. Again the awful insistence. I sit here, with this diary upon my knee, and it seems that fingers of iron are tearing at me. I WILL NOT go! My nerves may be utterly unstrung again (I fear they are), but I am still their master."

"August 4th. I did not yield, last night. After a bitter struggle, which must have lasted nearly an hour, the desire to go to the cellar suddenly departed. I must not give in at any time."

"August 5th. Tonight, the rat noises (I shall call them that for want of & more appropriate term) are very noticable. I went to the length of unbolting my door and stepping into the hallway to listen. After a few minutes, I seemed to be aware of something large and gray watching me from the darkness at the end of the passage. This is a bizarre statement, of course, but it exactly describes my impression. I withdrew hastily into the study, and bolted the door."Now that nervous condition is so palpably affecting the optic nerve, I must not much longer delay seeing a specialist. But—how much shall I tell him?"

"August 8th. Several times, tonight, while sitting here at my work, I have seem to hear soft footsteps in the passage. 'Nerves' again of course or some new trick of the wind among the specimens on the walls."

"August 9th. By my watch it is four o'clock in the morning. My mind is made up to record the experience I have passed through. Calmness may come that way.

"Feeling rather fatigued last night, from the strain of a weary day of research, I retired early. My sleep was more refreshing than usual, as it is likely to be when one is genuinely tired I awakened, however (it must have been about an hour ago), with a start of tremendous violence.

"There was moonlight in the room. My nerves were 'on edge', but, for a moment, I saw nothing unusual. Then, glancing toward the door, I perceived what appeared to be thin, white fingers, thrust under it—exactly as if someone outside the door were trying to attract my attention in that manner. I rose and turned on the light, but the fingers were gone.

"Needless to say, I did not open the door. I write the ocurrence down, just as it took place, or as it seemed; but I can not trust myself to comment upon it."

"August 10th. Have fastened heavy rubber strips on the bottom of my bedroom door."

"August 15th. All quiet, for several nights. I am hoping that the rubber strips, being something definite and tangible, have had a salutary effect upon my nerves. Perhaps I shall not need to see a doctor."

"August 17th. Once more, I have been aroused from sleep. The interruptions seem to come always at the same hour—about three o'clock in the morning. I had been dreaming of the well in the cellar—the same dream, over and over—everything black except the slab, and a figure with bowed head and averted face sitting there. Also, I had vague dreams about a dog. Can it be that my last words to her have impressed that on my mind? I must pull myself together. In particular I must not under any pressure, yield and visit the cellar after nightfall."

"August 18th. Am feeling much more hopeful. Mrs. Malkin remarked on it, while serving dinner. This improvement is due largely to a consultation I have had with Dr. Sartwell, the distinguished specialist in nervous diseases. I went into full details with him, excepting certain reservations. He scouted the idea that my experiences could be other than purely mental.

"When he recommended a change of scene (which I had been expecting) I told him positively that it was out of the question. He said then that, with the aid of a tonic and an occasional sleeping draft, I am likely to progress well enongh at home. This is distinctly encouraging. I erred in not going to him at the start. Without doubt, most, if not all, of my hallucinations could have been averted.

"I have been suffering a needless penalty from my nerves for an action I took solely in the interests of science. I have no disposition to tolerate it further. From today, I shall report regularly to Dr. Sartwell."

"August 19th. Used the sleeping draft last night, with gratifying results. The doctor says I must repeat the dose for several nights, until my nerves are well under control again."

"August 21st. All well. It seems I have found the way out—a very simple and prosaic way. I might have avoided much needless annoyance by seeking expert advice at the beginning. Before retiring, last night, I unbolted my study door and took a turn up and down the passage. I felt no trepidation. The place was as it used to be, before these fancies assailed me. A visit to the cellar after nightfall will be the test for my complete recovery, but I am not yet quite ready for that. Patience!"

"August 22nd. I have just read yesterday's entry, thinking to steady myself. It is cheerful—almost gay; and there are other entries like it in preceding pages. I am a mouse, in the grip of a cat. Let me have freedom for ever so short a time, and I begin to rejoice at my escape. Then the paw descends again.

"It is four in the morning—the usual hour. I retired rather late, last night, after administering the draft. Instead of the dreamless sleep, which heretofore has followed the use of the drug, the slumber into which I fell was punctuated by recurrent visions of the slab, with the bowed figure upon it. Also, had one poignant dream in which the dog was involved.

"At length, I awakened, and reached mechanically for the light switch beside my bed. When my hand encountered nothing, I suddenty realised the truth. I was standing in my study, with my other hand upon the doorknob. It required only a moment, of course, to find the light and switch it on. I saw then that the bolt had been drawn back.

"The door was quite unlocked. My awakening must have interrupted me in the very act of opening it. I could hear something restlessly in the passage outside the door."

"August 23rd. I must beware of sleeping at night. Without confiding the fact to Dr. Sartwell, I have begun to take the drug in the daytime. at first, Mrs. Malkin's views on the subject were pronounced, but my explanation of 'doctor's orders' has silenced her. I am awake for breakfast and supper, and sleep in the hourse between. She is leaving me, each evening, a cold lunch to be eaten at midnight."

"August 26th. Several times, I have caught myself nodding in my chair. The last time, I am sure that, on arousing, I perceived the rubber strip under the door bend inward, as if something were pushing it from the other side. I must not, under any circumstances, permit myself to fall asleep."

"September 2nd. Mrs. Malkin is to be away. because of her sister's illness. I can not help dreading her absence. Though she is here only in the daytime, even that companionship is very welcome."

"September 3rd. Let me put this into writing. The mere labor of composition has a soothing influence upon me. God knows, I need such an influence now, as never before!

"In spite of all my watchfulness, I fell asleep, tonight—across my bed. I must have been utterly exhausted. The dream I had was the one about the dog. I was patting the creature's head, over and over.

"I awoke, at last, to find myself in darkness, and in a standing position. There was a suggestion of chill and earthiness in the air. While I was drowsily trying to get my bearings, I became aware that something was nuzzling my hand, as a dog might do.

"Still saturated with my dream, I was not greatly astonished. I extended my hand, to pat the dog's head. That brought me to my senses. I was standing in the cellar.

"THE THING BEFORE ME WAS NOT A DOG!

"I can not tell how I fled back up the cellar stairs. I know, however, that, as I turned, the slab was visible, in spite of the darkness, with something sitting upon it. All the way up the stairs, hands snatched at my feet."

This entry seemed to finish the diary, for blank pages followed it; but I remembered the crumpled sheet, near the back of the book. It was partly torn out, as if a hand had clutched it, convulsively. The writing on it, too, was markedly in contrast to the precise, albeit nervous penmanship of even the last entry I had perused. I was forced to hold the scrawl up to the light to decipher it. This is what I read:

"My hand keeps on writing, in spite of myself. What is this? I do not wish to write, but it compels me. Yes, yes, I will tell the truth, I will tell the truth."

A heavy blot followed, partly covering the writing. With difficulty, I made it out:

The guilt is mine—mine, only. I loved her too well, yet I was unwilling to marry. though she entreated me on her knees—though she kissed my hand. I told her my scientific work came first. She did it, herself. I was not expecting that—I swear I was not expecting it. But I was afraid the authorities would misunderstand. So I took what seemed the best course. She had no friends here who would inquire.

"It is waiting outside my door. I FEEL it. It compels me through my thoughts. My hand keeps on writing. I must not fall asleep. I must think only of what I am writing. I must—"

Then came the words I had seen when Mrs. Malkin had handed me the book. They were written very large. In places, the pen had dug through the paper. Though they were scrawled, I read them at a glance:

"Not that! Oh, my God, anything but that! Anything—"

By what strange compulsion was the hand forced to write down what was in the brain; even to the ultimate thoughts; even to those final words?

The gray light from outside, slanting down through two dull little windows, sank into the sodden hole near the inner wall. The coroner and I stood in the cellar, but not too near the hole.

A small, demonstrative, dark man—the chief of detectives—stood a little apart from us, his eyes intent, his natural animation suppressed. We were watching the stooped shoulders of a police constable, who was angling in the well.

"See anything, Walters?" inquired the detective, raspingly.

The policeman shook his head.

The little man turned his questioning to me.

"You're quite sure?" he demanded.

"Ask the coroner. He saw the diary," I told him.

"I'm afraid there can be no doubt," the coroner confirmed, in his heavy, tired voice.

He was an old man, with lacklustre eyes. It had seemed best to me, on the whole, that he should read my uncle's diary. His position entitled him to all the available facts. What we were seeking in the well might especially concern him.

He looked at me opaquely now, while the policeman bent double again. Then he spoke—like one who reluctantly and at last does his duty. He nodded toward the slab of gray stone, which lay in the shadow to the left of the well.

"It doesn't seem very heavy, does it?" he suggested, in an undertone.

I shook my head. "Still, it's stone," I demurred. "A man would have to be rather strong to lift it."

"To lift it—yes." He glanced about the cellar. "Ah, I forgot," he said, abruptly. "It is in my office, as part of the evidence." He went on, half to himself: "A man—even though not very strong—could take a stick—for instance, the stick that is now in my office—and prop up the slab. If he wished to look into the well," he whispered.

The policeman interrupted, straightening again with a groan, and laying his electric torch beside the well.

"It's breaking my back," he complained. "There's dirt down there. It seems loose, but I can't get through it. Somebody'll have to go down."

The detective cut in: "I'm lighter than you, Walters."

"I'm not afraid, sir."

"I didn't say you were," the little man snapped. "There's nothing down there, anyway—though we'll have to prove that, I suppose." He glanced truculently at me, but went on talking to the constable: "Rig the rope around me, and don't bungle the knot. I've no intention of falling into the place."

"There is something there," whispered the coroner, slowly, to me. His eyes left the little detective and the policeman, carefully tying and testing knots, and turned again to the square slab of stone.

"Suppose—while a man was looking into that hole—with the stone propped up—he should accidentally knock the prop away?" He was still whispering.

"A stone so light that he could prop it up wouldn't be heavy enough to kill him." I objected.

"No." He laid a hand on my shoulder. "Not to kill him—to paralyze him—if it struck the spine in a certain way. To render him helpless, but not unconscious. The post mortem would disclose that, through the bruises on the body."

The policeman and the detective had adjusted the knots to their satisfaction. They were bickering now as to the details of the descent.

"Would that cause death?" I whispered.

"You must remember that the housekeeper was absent for two days. In two days, even that pressure—" He stared at me hard, to make sure that I understood—"with the head down—"

Again the policeman interrupted:

"I'll stand at the well, if you gentlemen will grab the rope behind me. It won't be much of a pull. I'll take the brunt of it."

We let the little man down, with the electric torch strapped to his waist, and some sort of implement—a trowel or a small spade—in his hand. It seemed a long time before his voice, curiously hollow, directed us to stop. The hole must have been deep.

We braced ourselves. I was second, the coroner, last. The policeman relieved his strain somewhat by snagging the rope against the edge of the well, but I marveled, nevertheless, at the ease with which he held the weight. Very little of it came to me.

A noise like muffled scratching reached us from below. Occasionally, the rope shook and shifted slightly at the edge of the hole. At last, the detective's hollow voice spoke.

"What does he say?" the coroner demanded.

The policeman turned his square, dogged face toward us.

"I think he's found something," he explained.

The rope jerked and shifted again. Some sort of struggle seemed to be going on below. The weight suddenly increased, and as suddenly lessened, as if something had been grasped. then had managed to elude the grasp and slip away. I could catch the detective's rapid breathing now; also the sound of inarticulate speech in his hollow voice.

The next words I caught came more clearly. They were a command to pull up. At the same moment, the weight on the rope grew heavier, and remained so.

The policeman's big shoulders began straining, rhythmically.

"All together," he directed. "Take it easy. Pull when I do."

Slowly, the rope passed through our hands. With each fresh grip that we took, a small section of it dropped to the floor behind us. I began to feel the strain. I could tell from the coroner's labored breathing that he felt it more, being an old man. The policeman, however, seemed untiring.

The rope tightened, suddenly, and there was an ejaculation from below—just below. Still holding fast, the policeman contrived to stoop over and look. He translated the ejaculation for us.

"Let down a little. He's stuck with it against the side."

We slackened the rope, until the detective's voice gave us the word again.

The rhythmic tugging continued. Something dark appeared, quite abruptly, at the top of the hole. My nerves leapt in spite of me. but it was merely the top of the detective's head—his dark hair. Something white came next—his pale face, with staring eyes. Then his shoulders, bowed forward, the better to support what was in his arms. Then—

I looked away; but, as he laid his burden down at the side of the well, the detective whispered to us:

"He had her covered up with dirt—covered up. . . . ."

He began to laugh—a little, high cackle. like a child's—until the coroner took him by the shoulders and deliberately shook him. Then the policeman led him out of the cellar.

It was not then, but afterward, that I put my question to the coroner.

"Tell me," I demanded. "People pass there at all hours. Why didn't my uncle call for help?"

"I have thought of that." he replied. "I believe he did call. I think, probably, he screamed. But his head was down, and he couldn't raise it. His screams must have been swallowed up in the well."

"You are sure he didn't murder her?" He had given me that assurance before, but I wished it again.

"Almost sure," he declared. "Though it was on his account, undoubtedly, that she killed herself. Few of us are punished as accurately for our sins as he was."

One should be thankful, even for crumbs of comfort. I am thankful.

But there are times when my uncle's face rises before me. After all, we were the same blood; our sympathies had much in common; under any given circumstances, our thoughts and feelings must have been largely the same. I seem to see him in that final death march along the unlighted passageway—obeying an imperative summons—going on, step by step—down the stairway to the first floor, down the cellar stairs—at last, lifting the slab.

I try not to think of the final expiation. Yet was it final? I wonder. Did the last Door of all, when it opened, find him willing to pass through? Or was Something waiting beyond that Door?

Lamp Light

RADIO PLAY

LampLight Radio Play

Inspired by the radio of the past, but built for modern ears, LampLight Radio Plays are audio adaptations of stories from LampLight Magazine. Expect great performances, naturalistic sound design, and immersive stories to unsettle and entertain.

lamplightmagazine.com/radioplay

LampLight

Volume One
Edited by Jacob Haddon

LampLight Volume 1

lamplightmagazine.com/volume-1

This 450 page anthology of the first year of LampLight Magazine collects four amazing issues from September 2012 - June 2013.

Features the complete serial novella "And I Watered It With Tears" by Kevin Lucia. Fiction and interviews with Robert Ford, Kelli Owen, Ronald Malfi, and Elizabeth Massie.

J.F. Gonzalez takes us through the history of the genre with his Shadows in the Attic articles. LampLight classics bring you some of those past voices to experience again.

Fiction by William Meikle, Nathan Yocum, Rahul Kanakia, Ian Creasey, Mandy DeGeit, D.J. Cockburn, Christopher Fryer, Christopher Kelly, Tim Lieder, Jamie Lackey, Matthew Warner, Sheri White, Dinos Kellis, S. R. Mastrantone, Mjke Wood, Delbert R. Gardner, Michele Mixell, Sarah Rhett, Armel Dagorn, E. Catherine Tobler

LampLight

Volume Two
Edited by Jacob Haddon

LampLight Volume 2

lamplightmagazine.com/volume-2

This second annual anthology from LampLight Magazine collects the four great issues from September 2013 to June 2014

Includes the complete novella, The Devoted, featuring Jonathan Crowley, by James A Moore.

Fiction and interviews from our featured writers: Norman Prentiss, Kealan Patrick Burke, Mary SanGiovanni and Holly Newstein.

J.F. Gonzalez continues his history of the genre in his Shadows in the Attic series. LampLight Classics brings you some great classic stories.

Fiction by: Michael Knost, Christopher Bleakley, Emma Whitehall, David Tallerman, M. R. Jordan, Lauren Forry, Dave Thomas, Arinn Dembo, Bracken MacLeod, doungjai gam, Tim W Boiteau, Alethea Eason, Lucy A Snyder, Colleen Jurkiewicz, Curtis James McConnell, Victor Cypert, Catherine Grant

Printed by BoD™in Norderstedt, Germany